OWEN'S DAUGHTER

Finding Casey
Solomon's Oak
The Owl & Moon Café
The Wilder Sisters
Loving Chloe
Shadow Ranch
Blue Rodeo
Hank & Chloe
Fault Line (stories)

The Bad Girl Creek trilogy:
Bad Girl Creek
Along Came Mary
Goodbye, Earl

OWEN'S DAUGHTER

A Novel

Jo-Ann Mapson

B L O O M S B U R Y

NEW YORK · LONDON · NEW DELHI · SYDNEY

Published by Bloomsbury USA, New York
Bloomsbury is a trademark of Bloomsbury Publishing Plc

All papers used by Bloomsbury USA are natural, recyclable
products made from wood grown in well-managed
forests. The manufacturing processes conform to the
environmental regulations of the country of origin.

LIBRARY OF CONGRESS CATALOGING-
IN-PUBLICATION DATA

Mapson, Jo-Ann.
Owen's daughter : a novel / Jo-Ann Mapson. — First U.S. edition.
pages cm
Hardcover ISBN 978-1-62040-147-7
Trade paperback ISBN 978-1-62040-973-2
1. Fathers and daughters—Fiction. I. Title.
PS3563.A62O85 2014
813'.54—dc23
2014003627

First U.S. edition 2014

1 3 5 7 9 10 8 6 4 2

Typeset by Hewer Text UK Ltd, Edinburgh
Printed and bound in the U.S.A. by Thomson-
Shore Inc, Dexter, Michigan

Bloomsbury books may be purchased for business or promotional use.
For information on bulk purchases please contact Macmillan Corporate
and Premium Sales Department at specialmarkets@macmillan.com.

To
Judi Hendricks,
Lois Gilbert,
&
to my son, Jack,
who inspired the first book, this book,
and no doubt what will come after.
Thank you for listening.

You must find grace within the calamity—
that's where all the beauty lives.
—ALICE ANDERSON
"The Birds"
The Watermark

DOLORES

JUST AS POLLEN becomes a passenger riding the wind's coattails, a spirit, too, can travel great distances. One day you may find me at 103 Ave de Colibri, a place I'm quite fond of because I lived there, once, and in that way, I always will. I've watched people come and go, tearing down the stables where beloved horses lived, the Appaloosa mare, her chestnut foal, as well as the chocolate-eyed bay stallion.

I see everything.

I watch the new owners whitewash the walls in the traditional way, using lime and water. Later, a traveler shows a man how to make glue so that he can apply wallpaper. Wallpaper inside an adobe house? Don't forget the turpentine, he warns, turpentine is an insecticide. The fumes are terrible, and anyone who sleeps in that room is plagued with bad dreams.

Time is fluid, flowing both ways.

Some years later the wallpaper comes down, and others paint the rooms sky blue. Still others think red walls are a good idea, but not for long, and they argue about color, but actually they are arguing about something much deeper than paint, and come apart, sell the house, and then move. The latest is diamond plaster, a mixture of white clay, ocher pigment, and crushed mother-of-pearl. When the sun shines in the kitchen window, the walls wink as if they are holding back the stars.

But next door, at 105, there are worse secrets.

One summer an Englishwoman stands outside, wishing on a star. The famous Santa Fe wind blows restlessly through the trees. Left alone by her trader husband, who travels for business, she feels lost and alone. No babies have arrived. Her Spanish isn't good. Her Navajo is nonexistent. Using sign language, her maid shows her how to keep a house, how to use beeswax to keep the furniture from drying out in the high desert climate. One morning, she stands alongside the maid and learns to make tortillas on the *comal*, a smooth clay griddle. The trick is to remember that lard itself is an ingredient, and as such is dependent on the condition of the animal from whence it came. One must adjust the amount of masa, sprinkling it slowly, dripping in the water, and use both hands to mix. She is quiet while the dough rests under a flour sack dish towel, hoping her new skills will please the husband, who comes home from his travels unhappy, and drinks, and sometimes, though she tells no one, he hits her. The maid rubs salve on the bruises but says nothing.

She wished on that star every night.

Wishing is the business of children.

Once the woman was in love, with a farm boy who worked her father's land. She and her lover couldn't keep their hands off each other. Her father forbade the union and arranged a proper marriage to a man who would elevate his family's status. The newlyweds took a boat all the way from England, over that rolling sea, and then a train through the dust, only to arrive here to what the woman called a mud hut. She cried. This so-called town was overrun with gamblers and drunks, Spanish men fond of harassing women, Native men who looked so frighteningly different that the farthest she ventured was the *estable*, or the stable, where the horses were kept. Her family shipped her grandmother's English sideboard to her, across that ocean, believing familiar things would help her settle in. Waiting for it to arrive, the woman imagined where to place it and how it might look when it was filled with her blue-and-white china that had come all the way from the Orient, her husband's gift to her when they married. The hired men struggled bringing the sideboard in the front door. Her trader husband, cheated out of money from a deal he'd been working on all week, returned home. There stood his formerly unhappy wife, smiling as she pressed coins into the hands of the hired men. She was taking coins out of his purse, his hard-earned money, to pay men who couldn't speak English. He slapped the purse onto the floor, demanding to know how much she had paid them. Take the money out of the grocery budget, she said. How much? With his hands around her neck, she confessed. Three dollars. At dinner, she was not allowed to eat. That night he hit her again. When she woke on the floor in front of her beloved sideboard, she realized beauty meant nothing in the face of sorrow. The next time her husband went on a trading trip, she decided to sell the sideboard. It would bring enough money that she could return to London or head west, to California. All she needed was a buyer. A chance to arrange her travel.

But no one wanted to buy from a woman. They had no rights.

One night, her drunken husband threatened to push it over. Bust it into pieces. Burn it for firewood. Burn everything she had. Her horses, her linens, the pearl necklace of her grandmother's. He lunged forward, and she did her best to stop him, rushing to save at least her dishes. He hit her with a piece of firewood and sent her to the afterlife. He took a drink of snake-bite—whiskey—before he dragged her body to the barn. He placed her in the stall of the horse she loved best, the sweet-natured mare. He finished his drink before going in search of the sheriff and the doctor. The sheriff declared it an accident. Horse must have got spooked, kicked her to the ground. What a shame, the doctor said. She was such a pretty woman. Pretty but stupid, the husband said. They hauled her body away in a horse-drawn wagon. He shot the mare and had her carcass dragged away.

Only the maid suspected what the husband had done. She didn't show up for work the next day, but she came a few days later and continued to cook and clean the way she always had. Actually, she cooked a little differently, because quite soon the husband went a little mad, and then he became ill, bedridden. Her recipes came from her ancestors. Foxglove salad. Delphinium tea. The cherry laurel made into a jam. Yew berries.

A lingering punishment, accompanied by suffering. Only then, the peace of death.

The sideboard stayed with the house whenever it sold. Too heavy to move, it fit the room just right. Generations of families used it to store their treasures, and there it stands still. In the year 1966, a young couple painted it sky blue. Imagine the history! they said to anyone who visited. What stories it could tell, said the next owners, and finally, the old woman who owned it last hired a furniture maker to restore it to its original state, a walnut stain. Now her niece uses it to hold woven baskets, books, and toys for the child she sometimes babysits.

History is trapped in every object, no matter how small. Story lurks in empty spaces.

Over generations, I've watched women burn meals here, and cry. Bake cookies to decorate, to prove to the grandchildren that holidays are sweet times, exempt from whippings. Women smiling while their hearts are breaking over their husbands' secret lovers. Planning a Christmas meal that takes three days to prepare. They believe that a sumptuous feast, with everyone gathered around the table, will make everything better. They run themselves ragged, then slump at the table, too tired to enjoy the meal. Unhappy that the children are fighting, or the men are drunk, again, or that one of her sons, she is positive, has stolen her mother's sterling silver Chantilly spoons and sold them to purchase drugs.

A wall's purpose is to separate and to hold things in, so why should it surprise you that rooms contain secrets? In these various rooms, people make love, give birth, miscarry, weep silently, rage inwardly, consider leaving, break the law, commit adultery, force unwanted sex upon each other, contemplate suicide, murder, and eventually die. Some of them go so off course in life, it makes sense that people are mortal.

I was once that sort of person. Earthly. Salt water and flesh.

With my limited abilities, I remind people of the reasons to stay. They are the main characters in this never-ending play. Don't they know they can change the ending? I pop open the cupboard latches. Blow out the candles. I press hard enough to make the beams groan. I turn the bathroom tap so it will drip. On certain days, when the conditions are just so, when it is essential, I may appear, but not for long. It's exhausting to project a corporeal form, to get the features in the right places. Another day, in another home, I peer over the shoulder of a writer in his office on Upper Canyon Road. When he falters, I whisper in his ear, *Don't stop now. I want to hear more.*

Other days I feel too confined indoors and ride the wind to Navajo Lake, to get away from these messy, stupid people, and I swim with the fish. I pluck the bait from a fisherman's hook. Farther north, I perch atop Shiprock and commune with *those ones*—what the Navajo call their dead—who unfortunately don't speak English or Spanish. Their Navajo is so formal, I often don't understand. I never stay long. We all have our work to do. Today, it's up to me to whisper into this young mother's ear as she writes to her long-lost father. She's so angry that the room she is in cowers around her. Anger has its time and place, but stay there too long and it will chain you to a stake in the ground, like a mistreated dog.

Dogs, by the way, can see me just fine.

December 2009, 32 degrees

Dear Daddy,

Part of the program at Cottonwoods Rehab is to work the Twelve Steps, and that's what I'm doing writing this letter to you. I hate all the Steps, but Step Five particularly sucks. By comparison, Step Four is Yay! We're having cherry pie for dessert, but not until you eat the liver and spinach. Step Five is Sorry, we're having textured vegetable protein loaf from now on, and don't expect ketchup, just clean your plate. Duncan, my group leader, and FBI (Full Blooded Indian, Navajo), says working the Steps is the only way to get out of this hellhole so I don't have a choice. Just so you know, I've written dozens of letters to you, but this one I'm actually going to mail.

The problem is, I have no idea where to send it, so I'm going with the last address you gave to Mama, that P.O. box in Blue Dog, New Mexico. Sounds like made-up Hollywood movie towns with dirt roads, dust devils, fake Indians war-whooping all over the place, and one bar that never closes. Duncan says that it doesn't matter if the letter never reaches you. He says the reason to write you letters is to forgive you and to clean my own house.

As if I had a house to clean! Or even a pot to pee in.

I do forgive you, Daddy, when it comes to you bailing out on Mama. I understand why you left. But the part I have trouble forgiving is that you left *me*, too. Mama's no easier to put up with these days. When Howie, the real estate baron with the blond toupee, fled Colorado, Mama bought a plane ticket to Phoenix, pounded a "For Sale" sign into the lawn, left me ten thousand dollars, the keys to the Mercedes, and a note that said, "This ought to get you through school. Try not to get pregnant."

She headed for the airport, and adios, childhood.

Which is my way of telling you that you're a grandpa, and that Mama made up all those updates about me being in college because she never could face the truth. My daughter Gracie is nearly four years old now. I haven't seen her for some time. I'm going to miss her birthday. No family visits are allowed at Cottonwoods, plus Rocky (her dad) is on the pro rodeo circuit, so he's always traveling. All my life I was good at things. I broke barrel racing records in my age division. I got an A in chemistry. My science teachers all told me I should go to medical school. I chose early acceptance to Stanford. I could have been a large animal vet.

But I had hormones, and those eggs that drop like a lottery ball every month. I got pregnant.

Rocky and I did the "right" thing and got married. I tried to make dinners with the four food groups, and learn to clean house and be a good mom. Life in a doublewide just wasn't for me. At first it was pain pills for my broken elbow. Then it was a glass of vodka for me, because that makes a colicky baby totally tolerable. Rocky drank all the time, so why shouldn't I?

Then it was a countdown to five P.M. before I hauled out the vodka, mixed with Gracie's grape juice, not a bad taste, really. From time to time I worked a waitress job. All that free alcohol made me a better waitress. Fifty-dollar-bill tips, and once I got a free ski weekend, even. Other times my tips were a handful of oxy, which from the start made me feel like a better version of me. Like I could do figure eights on ice cubes. Pretty soon I was snorting it three times a day and powering down the drinks. Rocky loved me partying with him. When we weren't partying, though, marriage wasn't much of anything. I moved out and took Gracie with me. Everything seemed manageable, and we'd even started sharing custody. Then I got in a wreck with Gracie in the car. She was fine, but I got arrested for DWI and a bunch of other stuff, old news in New Mexico. The judge was up for reappointment and wanted to make an example out of me. He said he'd drop the felony child endangerment if I went to rehab. Otherwise, it was straight to jail, but that wasn't the worst thing.

He gave Rocky full custody. No matter what I said, he wouldn't budge.

Getting sober is way harder than I imagined. Not even three months in, this cook who had a crush on me smuggled in a twelve-ounce bottle of Mexican vanilla extract filled with Jack Daniel's. I chugged the whole thing and ended up in the hospital with alcohol poisoning, where I had a seizure and had to be put on dialysis. I was afraid I'd get kicked out of rehab. Never occurred to me *I could've died* until I was back in the world. Are you sober, Daddy? Living under some freeway overpass? Down in Florida working on a fishing boat? I haven't seen or heard from you in ten years, but I feel closer to you than ever, now that we have common ground beyond our love for horses, namely drinking. Speaking of Lightning, he is fourteen. Sometimes I think I should sell him, but what if he missed me as much as I'd miss him? Every night here I shut my eyes and see him so clear. I smell alfalfa, hear his deep, whispery nicker. I feel his warm breath against my neck and tears run down my face like one of those chains that make music just from rain and I want to be out of this place so bad.

You I can't picture at all.

They're big on religion here. I ask questions nobody can answer. If God created humans in his image, why are humans such fuck-ups? Does that mean God is also a drunk, a bad parent, and an idiot?

When I think about Step Five, admitting to our wrongdoings, et cetera, I wonder about you, Daddy. Maybe you're the one who needs to work that step. I was a spoiled rotten child, and I used that to my advantage, playing you and Mama against each other because it helped me get my way, whether it meant overpriced movie theater candy or an electric guitar I played twice and then abandoned. But I was a *child*. Things got worse after you left, and I'm positive that's where I started going downhill. I am working hard on changing my life. It's taking *a while*. Duncan says that every day is just one day to get through, and worrying how long it'll take is "stinkin' thinkin'." Yeah, but when you're a hundred miles from a Walgreens and sitting in group therapy with people you wouldn't otherwise give the time of day, it's hard not to dwell on the past. Daddy, I apologize for using passive-aggressive behavior on you. Maybe I learned it from Mama, but I'm the one who did it. I guess I thought getting whatever I wanted would make up for all the fighting you two did. I was mad at Mama for kicking you out.

But I was furious at you leaving *me*.

You could be in Timbuktu for all I know. Maybe you have another family, with better kids. Life goes on. But even when I was hammered drunk or high on the pill *du jour*, not one day went by I didn't think of you. And miss you. I don't care why you disappeared on me. I love you anyway. Wherever you are, I hope you are doing all right, staying sober, and won't think too poorly of me for turning out like this. I hope you got that sheep ranch you always talked about, and that you are flush with friends. Out riding fences at sunrise, your favorite time of day. I hope that sometimes you think about me. Even all messed up I am still your little girl. Remember me sitting in front of you on your horse? You reciting cowboy poetry? I loved those times.

The future's up for grabs, but nothing will ever change the past.

Love,

Sara Kay

P.S. I go by Skye now.

P.P.S. I still love you, Daddy.

P.P.P.S. Gracie is adorable.

Chapter 1

Thursday, April 1, 2010
Seven A.M., 59 degrees

PEOPLE SAY THERE is nothing more romantic than a
New Mexico sunset. Clearly those people have never
witnessed a New Mexico sunrise. The sky starts out purple and
then is streaked with gold and pink before blue starts to sneak in.
The colors of the sky thread through tent rocks, fairy chimneys,
and hoodoos. The rock formations could only be the work of a
drunken, celestial hand. Skye will never forget them rising out of
the desert floor. Or the lake-blue sky overhead with the cottony
clouds lined up like soldiers. When she's back in the world, gain-
fully employed and reunited with Gracie, this place will haunt
her dreams.

For the last nine months as she tried to get sober, the rocks
were the first things she saw every morning. In high school her
science teacher taught that the rocks near the Four Corners were
made up of volcanic ash, earthquakes, and time. Some, like
Shiprock, which is miles away from Cottonwoods Rehab but
visible in all kinds of weather, loom taller than skyscrapers.
Minerals and weather can't explain everything. Over and over

she listened to Duncan tell her the story of how his people—the
Anasazi/Navajo/Diné—came to earth:

A long time ago, Anasazi people lived here, growing the three
sisters: beans, corn, and squash. They collected their water
from the rivers and plucked piñon nuts from trees by the thousands. Life was good for the People. They prospered. But there
came a day when enemies arrived, and surrounded the Anasazi.
Having no understanding of war, and no weapons, the People
prayed to the gods for safety. And they prayed so intensely that
the gods pushed Shiprock up out of the earth, and the women
and children, the old men, too, were safe on top of the seven-
thousand-foot tall mountain. *Ah-sheh-heh'!* Thank you! The
enemies, seeing they'd angered the gods, fled.

But once a war has begun, there is no going back to peace.

Life on the mountain returned to normal. Every day the
young men of the tribe climbed down a rocky path to tend
crops and fetch water. One day, *aieee! Ne-ol,* a storm came.
Lightning struck the dry piñon trees below. One cannot eat
fruit from a lightning-struck tree without getting sick. The
lightning caught a tree on fire. The fire spread to the crops,
aieee! And lightning struck again, destroying the path the men
climbed up and down every day. The men were down below,
watching as lightning sheared off the hoodoo, trapping the
women, children, and elders atop the peak. *Ah-ho-tai,* they
said. This is how it is. There was no time to be sad. *Be-ke-a-ti,*
the men talked it over. Only a shaman is allowed to touch rock
struck by lightning. The men, *ta-bilh,* began the arduous
process of creating another path. Cutting rock takes time, so
long that *those ones,* the women, children, and elders waiting

atop, starved to death. The People were heartbroken. They forbade anyone to climb the mountain for fear of disturbing the *ch'iid.i*, ghosts.

All Skye had to do was catch sight of Shiprock and the story went right through her heart. Maybe it's a fable. Maybe like all of Duncan's stories he was speaking figuratively, but she feels a kinship with the Anasazi on the morning she's leaving Cottonwoods for the larger world. For months her known path has been cut off deliberately, but if she stays here, she's locking herself away from everything. Isn't that a kind of starvation?

A month ago, March, with snow still on the ground, Duncan told her, "It's time. Go out into the world now."

Skye shook her head, no. She was sure he was wrong.

"You have to try someday," Duncan said.

Today might not be the best day, either, but she has to try.

Since dawn, she's stood in the shade of the porch waiting on her ride, arranged three weeks ago via text messages and e-mails. Rocky Elliot, her soon-to-be ex-husband, also the father of her daughter, Gracie, isn't due until ten A.M., but she can't go back inside Cottonwoods because what if she decides she can't leave after all? So she's waiting here on the *portal*, which is what folks call patios here. She's slathered on sunscreen and is wearing her Ed Hardy hoodie with the *Love Kills* tattoo design on the front that doesn't seem funny anymore. Yesterday in her last group, Duncan said, "Skye, this is the beginning of the story that you get to write."

"Yeah, right," she said. "Once upon a time there was this twenty-two-year-old alcoholic, pill-popping mother who turned into a sober, princess-perfect mother and lived the greatest life ever without alcohol or drugs. Then, one day, relief arrived like a bus that got her through the roughest day: six OxyContin and a greyhound, vodka and grapefruit juice on the rocks."

Duncan, the dark skin over his Indian cheekbones, the white teeth in the wide, generous mouth, smiled. "A story can start in the ugliest place on earth. Where it goes from there is up to you."

The world is a sharp-edged place filled with temptation. Without drinking or pills, there's nothing between her tender skin and the world.

Skye was delivered to Cottonwoods with a blood alcohol level of 0.29, which is a hair from unconscious. At the time it felt like the only way she could cross that boundary from the world she knew to what had to be. Today she's walking out purely under the power of her plain self, with the help of her so-called Higher Power. She will not drink. She will not take so much as an aspirin.

So *One Day at a Time* says.

Skye had this idea that rehab would restore her to the girl she was at seventeen, but that person was *vamanos*, gone, as out of reach as Shiprock. After the morning hike one day, she started walking toward Shiprock, just to see the mountain closer up, but the path was like running in a dream. No number of steps seemed to close the distance between that mountain and her. Once upon a time, she was Sara Kay Sampson, the smartest girl in the class. While the rest of the kids went to parties, got drunk, and hooked up, Skye took the long view—veterinary school—and earned all A's, maintaining perfect attendance. Other than riding horses, she didn't mingle or make friends. There would be plenty of time for partying after college.

On her application essay to Stanford, she listed all her hard-earned accomplishments: 4.5 GPA. Captain of the debate team. Add in her 13.8-second barrel race win in girls twelve and under, Miss Colorado Rodeo Queen, junior counselor at YWCA horse camp. They couldn't say no. They said yes.

Right before her seventeenth birthday, she met Rocky.

Pre-Rocky, Sara loved only her leopard Appaloosa gelding, Lightning, the spotted horse she had trained from a colt. Maybe Lightning was her first addiction, when her dad left. The intoxicating smell of horse sweat, learning to trick ride—moves like spin-the-horn and the hippodrome—breaking records fearlessly. She couldn't get enough of the thrill. As a child her heart was big enough to hold only two men, her gelding and her dad. For a while after Dad bailed, the horse filled the void. Then Mama began marrying whatever man could keep her in style. The first one was the nicest, Klaus Krieger. He loved how smart Sara was and gave her a hundred-dollar bill for every A she brought home. He was stunned at his luck marrying Mama. When he died it hurt so much that Sara took one of the painkillers Lightning needed when he came up lame, just to see if it might erase the heartache. She was amazed at how well bute canceled the pain. Funny jokes became fall-down hilarious. Getting bucked off was nothing. Sara figured that was the moment she turned into a substance abuser, when that numbing blur became the goal.

After that she started drinking six-packs with Francisco, the barn manager. One day she passed clean out and woke up in an empty stall. Whether or not Francisco took advantage was a fuzzy area she tried not to think about. Instead she took two of Mama's

Vicodin and drank a half bottle of sparkling wine, fell asleep in the bathtub, and woke up in cold water, the room dark, nobody home. It was never just aspirin for a headache; she'd send in the bazookas.

At the rodeo where she was elected queen, Rocky showed up, blond and tall and dressed in chaps studded with Swarovski crystals. He was a champion bull rider who everyone said had ridden Dillinger to get his Professional Bull Riders ring of honor. People said he could ride a Maytag washing machine on the spin cycle. He was an Oklahoma boy, passing through Denver on his way to the next rodeo.

Sara was stunned by his flash and charmed by his sweet talk. Between two trailers, she threw herself at him.

"How old are you?" he asked between kisses.

"Seventeen," she said, lying by a couple of months.

He pushed her away. "Y'all're too young for me right now," he said, "but you won't be in a year," and winked. "You wait for me, and I'll see you then," he said, and tipped his hat.

That gave her enough material for a year's worth of dreams.

Stepdad Klaus Krieger had left Mama a wealthy widow. She drank hard for a couple of years and went on spending sprees. Skye lost track of how many times she dragged her boozy, weeping mother to bed. "Pour me another tequila, Sheila," replaced "Mother."

Then Mama married husband number three, Howard Young, that real estate baron. He bought Sara a canopy bed she was too old for and insisted on adopting her. They went to court and everything, declaring her father had abandoned her. Mama insisted she'd tried to find him, but Skye had always wondered if she'd tried her hardest. Four years later, after making a record

number of bad real estate loans, old Howie hightailed it to Texas
to lie low for a while. On a plane to Arizona, Mama read an
article in the *Delta Skymiles* magazine on this plastic surgeon
voted number one in the entire Southwest. First came the lipo.
Then the face lift. Then the fat suctioned out of her knees and
injected into the backs of her hands, a sign that her mother had
truly gone off the deep end. When Sara told her that she'd been
accepted to Stanford early admittance, her reply was, "Oh, honey,
no. California sun is the worst! You'll end up with more spots on
your face than a Toll House cookie."

It turned out Sara wouldn't need the sun block. She graduated
high school at the top of her class, with a baby bump under her
graduation robe courtesy of Rocky Elliot, the pro rodeo bull
rider from Weatherford, Oklahoma, who remembered her on his
next pass through Denver. He was a tall, blond farm boy equipped
with nothing but muscle in his cranium. One minute Sara was in
love with a star, drinking cinnamon schnapps, dancing the two-
step in whatever town the rodeo was in that month. The next she
was on her knees puking her guts up into the toilet in a motel so
cheap, she saw daylight through the floorboards.

Stanford was out the window. A *child* was growing inside her!
She saw what she wanted to see—that Disney fairy tale of marrying an all-American, bona fide cowboy. Rocky promised her the
kind of life she'd always dreamed of—a family all her own where
the parents *stayed* married.

They did the deed in Vegas, a western-themed affair that cost
six hundred and fifty dollars. Rocky talked her into pawning the
diamond tennis bracelet poor old dead Klaus had given her for
her thirteenth birthday. At the chapel, they were given the choice
of a cowboy minister or a crazy miner minister. They opted for

the crazy miner. Rocky's mom, Rita, chain-smoked the entire time, jingling her plastic cup full of quarters, eager to get back to the slots. Sara's mom was on her honeymoon with the plastic surgeon, husband number four.

When Sara gave birth to a daughter, she was determined her little girl would in no way end up like her. Gracie would go to the best preschool, attend church every Sunday wearing a straw hat with a yellow ribbon and, on her feet, white patent-leather shoes. She'd play only with high-class kids, and she'd take ballet lessons and learn to ride English. Skye still wanted that for her. But not long after Gracie was born, Rocky started disappearing for weeks at a time. When he was home, he'd drink sunup to sundown, take pills, or worse. After their marriage was over and Sara had the car accident, she'd called her mother and left a message: "Mama, I'm in trouble here, and I could use a hand. Rocky might get custody, but we both know he can't manage it. If you take Gracie, I could do inpatient rehab. It's either that or jail. Please, Mama. I'll never ask you for anything again, I promise."

Mama didn't reply.

Getting sober meant she had to leave Gracie with someone. But nobody else would step up. Which meant anytime there was a rodeo, Rocky would leave Gracie with his mother, Rita, a compulsively gambling, boxed-wine-drinking, cafeteria Christian who could spend twelve hours straight in the casinos and smoked two packs a day. Her views on child raising? Kool-Aid built bones as well as cow's milk. It was acceptable to feed Gracie Trix cereal three times a day because she liked it. And television, that great mother's little helper, never hurt a flea, let alone a nearly-four-year-old taken from her mother.

So much could happen in nine months.

"Little Gee," as Skye called her, was tomboy tough, talked early, and nothing held her back except for asthma. Rita promised she'd remember to refill Gracie's inhaler prescription, and Rocky said he'd get home every weekend so she wouldn't forget him.

So she left her little blond pumpkin there in Albuquerque at the Trailer Ranch. Grace Eleanor Elliot, who smiled like an angel and dressed up her plastic horses, brushing their tails until the hair fell out.

Any second now Rocky would pull up in his Ford 350 dually. Built Ford Tough rodeo sponsors gave him a new ride every couple of years. Even if he was wearing those cigarette leg Wranglers, another shiny belt buckle, and his Old Gringo Rockrazz boots, Skye was determined she wouldn't sleep with him again. If she did, the divorce would take even longer. Plus, she'd be back to drinking and using within twenty-four hours.

You are not that person anymore, she told herself.

After a week at Cottonwoods, all this starting over gave her an idea, and she changed her name from Sara to Skye. Sara Kay sounded like the name of a twelve-year-old who pitched fits in order to get whatever she wanted. Skye was wide open. The new name marked her rebirth. Even Duncan approved.

That first week, she wondered how a woman of twenty-two could feel so worn out. One lesson she learned at Cottonwoods is that the truth is a trailer you drag behind you wherever you go. In every meeting they made you tell your story, out loud and over and over: *Hello, my name is Skye, and I am an alcoholic and an addict. I am someone not even a three-year-old can count on to fix her Cheerios every morning.* Shame was a powerful motivator. Gracie deserved better. Skye wanted her back permanently, and the only way was to get and stay sober.

Nights were the hardest time at Cottonwoods, and not just because there was no Ambien allowed. As she lay there sober, in the dark, lights out, all her mistakes reared up to haunt her. If it hadn't been for "Tesuque," the Hollywood director who paid for rehab, Gracie could have ended up standing at a gravestone reading the short version of her mother's life:

SARA KAY ELLIOT

DIED AGE TWENTY-TWO

FORMER RODEO QUEEN, ALCOHOLIC,

POPPER OF PILLS

But that wasn't the worst of it. This was: A mother who chose getting high over her child.

The day Tesuque had his chauffeur drop her off, she'd been high for days, partly because of losing Gracie. The other part was, why not go out loaded? She knew what it cost to go to rehab, to stay long enough for it to work. It was more than she could possibly earn in two years if she didn't spend a dime, whereas drinking was cheaper. "Tesuque" was a regular at her restaurant, the Guadalupe BBQ. He always made sure to sit in her area, and he always ordered a black and brown—bourbon and blackberry syrup—that he left untouched. After a while, she started drinking it for him. Why let all that alcohol go to waste? What with customers buying her shots, some nights she'd have five or six drinks at work. One night, when her shift ended, Tesuque was waiting for her. He stood out on Guadalupe Street and told her, "You're too smart to be working as a waitress, and you're ruining your good looks with alcohol. Go to rehab."

"Even if I did have a problem, which I don't," she said, "I can't afford it."

To which he said, "What if I can? Would you go then?"

"Look. You could buy me a solid gold grand freaking piano and I still wouldn't sleep with you," she said, and turned to walk away.

But he caught her arm. "I've seen this disease chew up folks and spit them out unrecognizable. I lost my career and two wives before I stopped."

"Then why do you order a black and brown every night?"

"To prove to myself I can let it sit there. But I've noticed you can't."

She wanted to laugh it off, walk away, a dozen different things. But she stood there and listened.

"It's too late for me to make repairs, but not for you. With my income, I can afford to be generous. And I think you're worth the investment."

"There's no way I can pay you back without winning the lottery."

"What if I said I don't want to be paid back?"

Skye laughed. "When a man says something like that, he either wants sex or he's a control freak who wants you to wear a dog collar."

"I'm betting your life has been filled with men who let you down."

"So what if it has?"

"So I've seen you with your little girl. You don't want to lose her, do you?"

"I happen to be a great mother."

"I'm sure you are," he said. "I'm a great father. I love my kids with all my heart. But drinking took them away from me, and eventually, I guarantee, that will happen to you. It's already started, hasn't it?"

How did he know she was scheduled for court in a couple of days? Everybody else in New Mexico could rack up the DWIs, but the judge she was assigned was reportedly hard-core.

"Listen to me, Sara. Not all of us men are bad guys. You have to learn to trust one sometime so you can recognize the others of our species. I'm harmless. So you might as well start with me, or I guarantee you'll end up with nothing."

The truth was, she couldn't see Rocky springing for a grave marker. She'd spent three months in rehab before she understood that Rocky, in addition to his addiction, was probably brain-damaged from falling off bulls. He always was kind of ADHD. He couldn't do anything that took longer than a minute. While that was good for riding rodeo bulls, it was hell on birth control. The whole nine months of pregnancy, Skye lived in a state of equal parts terror and nausea. There was no drinking because she couldn't keep anything down. Once Gracie arrived, it was hard to imagine life without those pink cheeks and big eyes, but somehow the using sneaked back in.

And then Tesuque offered her a way out.

It's high noon. The temperature is a solid, airless 80 degrees. And it will get hotter. Here comes Nola, her psycho roommate, with a bologna sandwich and a cup of vanilla pudding. Skye hated Nola the second they met. She wasn't there for alcohol or drug addiction—no, her weakness was laxative pills and her larger issue was eating, or the lack of it. Her simpering vegetarian diet was about twenty-five calories daily—couldn't she just start eating normally? She could throw the laxatives in the same trash can as Skye's OxyContin pills and avoid the mirror. But Nola had been hospitalized twice since Skye had been at Cottonwoods, while Skye had only her one slip with the vanilla Jack Daniel's.

Everything inside her wanted to say *No, thanks* to the sandwich, but her belly knew that breakfast was a long time ago. "Thanks," she said, and after Nola left, she ate the bologna and threw the sandwich bread to a brown rez dog that was always hanging around. The pudding, she wolfed down. The sugar rush helped for about fifteen minutes but turned into a king-size headache.

Cottonwoods' menu is carb-heavy, which is why her street clothes are so tight. The tank top that once hung on her now shows back fat. Her skinny jeans cut painfully at the crotch. She ties her sweatshirt around her hips so she can leave the top button of her jeans undone. When a person stops drinking and dropping Oxy like Pez, what's left? Sex and carbohydrates. The Cottonwoods program made everyone sign a paper promising you wouldn't have sex with the therapists, your fellow inmates, or the adorable chef no matter how often he winked and gave you extra fries. It's simple math: Subtract drugs, booze, and sex. What's left? Cookies. Peanut butter right off the spoon. Mashed potatoes. Her world did a complete 180. She could be thrown out on the street for an orgasm, but not for scarfing down a twelve-ounce bag of chocolate chips she stole from the kitchen.

Now it's one P.M. The temperature is 86, 88, 90. The sun is blinding. All those formerly pretty rocks look like needles stabbing the sky. Rocky should have been here by now. He'd promised he'd pick her up before noon. Did she get the day wrong? Did he have a car accident? Is he in a different time zone? The plan was for them to drive to his mother's trailer park in Albuquerque, where she'd pick up Gracie, then to the body shop in Santa Fe to pick up the Mercedes her mother had given her years ago, which had endured moves from Denver to Santa Fe without any problems. Her twin mechanics—Lobo and Lalo— had been kind enough to store the car until she got out. She would drive Gracie to Santa Fe to Mama's vacation home on Canyon Road. *You can stay there on a temporary basis, but don't you dare mess up my pied-à-terre,* she'd text-messaged Skye. Pied-à-terre, Skye thinks, seriously? From there on, the plan is admittedly vague, but how hard can it be to find employment with tourist season just around the corner? Who knows, maybe her community service hours will lead to a decent job.

In the Cottonwoods program, they have a saying: You're only as sick as your secrets. Hers is: Rocky had agreed to return Gracie to her, and in return she would pay him five hundred dollars a month to forget about what the judge said, which was that in his opinion, Skye shouldn't even be allowed to have a pet goldfish. Five hundred dollars a month seems easier than finishing her community service, hiring a lawyer, and scheduling a hearing with Judge Assmuncher. Waiting for the court to pronounce her worthy enough to share custody could take months.

Rocky said he could sure use the five hundred, and while he enjoyed the *idea* of being a father, it was the day-to-day thing he couldn't quite hack. He wanted to be quit of Skye as much as she did him. He promised the divorce would be a cinch. Sign papers, shake hands, get back her mother's car, and *Adios, señora, hola, muchacha.*

"Hey," she asks the UPS driver who shows up with packages at two thirty. The temperature has climbed to 92. "If you're headed south, can I hitch a ride with you?"

"Wish I could, hon," he says, grinning behind his sunglasses. "Against company rules." He rushes in to deliver the package, his muscular calves a thing of hirsute beauty, and then he's gone, a cartoonish trail of dust around his tires. The world goes quiet except for the mechanical waterfall on the other side of the portal and the hum of the air conditioner's motor. It's Africa hot now. Her armpits are damp and her headache traveled from her temples to her jaw before taking up residence in her eye sockets. Skye is all teeth and bad mood. Leaving a place you hate shouldn't be this difficult. She thinks about walking down to the highway and sticking her thumb out, but after nine months of watching *48 Hours* on TV, she is convinced the world is full of perverts and sociopaths. And given her luck, most of them are driving through the Four Corners today.

Luck, and her lack of it, makes her think about casinos. Just north of Santa Fe are the Camel Rock, Pojoaque, and Buffalo Thunder casinos, open all night. She could get a job at one of them. She's good at math and card tricks, and lying comes naturally. The atmosphere of booze is a worry, but she'll do what she has to for Gracie.

The clock ticks on and still no Rocky. Three thirty arrives, what Duncan calls "the arsenic hour," when the recovering

inmates get the itchies and the shakes, and the urge to use pops
its ugly head up, screaming, *Feed me!*

She recites the Serenity Prayer to herself, determined not to
lose her nine months of sobriety.

High desert sunlight is brutal, burning the blue right out of
your eyes. It takes more than just the color with it. She's seen the
gaze of long-termers who will never leave Cottonwoods, like
Nola. Everyone talks about his or her Higher Power every ding-
dang minute. The first time Skye heard Duncan say "the Steps,"
she pictured one of those staircases in an M. C. Escher print that
lead nowhere. She doesn't want to leave Cottonwoods only to
end up bagging Snickers bars at the Farmington CVS or running
credit cards through the scanner machine at the last gas station
before the Indian tipi motel in Gallup. That path leads to welfare,
strip joints, and homeless shelters where they make you leave the
second the sun comes up.

She fixes in her mind the image of her blond-headed little girl,
dragging a currycomb around with both hands. Skye's watched
her hug the legs of draft horses and brush out their feathers, the
fluffy hair that grows from the horse's hock like fleece on Ugg
boots. Since the day she was born, Gracie has had no fear. Skye
takes her baby picture out of her wallet and rubs her thumb over
the wrinkled paper. Skye screamed her way through labor, but
when Gracie was born all she did was look around the room as if
she were thinking about ordering new wallpaper. Her newborn
head reminded Skye of a peony, a bloom too heavy for its stem,
yet right away she could tell Gracie was trying to lift hers up, to
take the world right in and make it her own.

Skye doesn't plan on repeating the experience anytime soon, but her mind goes there sometimes. How it felt to push Gracie out of her body—ripping pain one second and a rush not unlike OxyContin the next. Could she rewrite Gracie's birth, she would have a better version—one with her mother there in the delivery room, and outside, doling out bubblegum cigars, Daddy. Rocky wouldn't have to be there at all. Having done his part, Rocky would, as a praying mantis has the sense to do, die after mating.

It's so hot that she surrenders and heads into the building for a bottle of water.

Nobody is sitting in reception. She guesses the phone that rings over and over is getting the answering machine. That's too bad. Because once the urge to commit to rehab strikes, you have to go right that second. The first ring, you think, Yes, this is the way. The second ring, you think, Maybe all it takes is me saying no to what's offered. By the third ring, you talk yourself into believing everyone drinks this way and you hang up.

The Cottonwoods lobby features a huge gray sectional couch, tall, indoor cacti with the needles clipped off, old *Better Homes and Gardens* magazines and *New Yorker* issues with the addresses snipped out. Against one wall a fake waterfall spills over rough slate into a semicircular pond filled with plastic plants and a few elderly goldfish. On the other wall is the R. C. Gorman print *Navajo Chiles*. In the picture, one of his trademark plus-size Navajo women sits on the ground next to a basket of spilled chiles. Because of the way the sun blasts through the floor-to-ceiling windows in the lobby, what should be red chiles are peach colored. Chiles *lite*. It's the perfect shade for Cottonwoods, where in order to get and keep you sober, they suck the life out of everything and replace it with a paler version. And as with everyone at Cottonwoods, there is a story behind the painting you could have gone your whole life without knowing.

The good part: R. C. Gorman's father was a Navajo-code talker who helped win the Second World War. R.C. grew up tending sheep in Canyon de Chelly, where he often got in trouble for painting on the rocks. He ran the first successful Native American–owned art gallery in the state of New Mexico. If you went into his gallery and he was there working, he'd sign your print.

The bad part: In 1997, the FBI began assembling a child molestation case against Gorman. Before anything could be proven, the statute of limitations ran out, and Gorman died, at age seventy-four. The cloud of suspicion will never lift. Every time Skye looks at the woman in the print, all she can think is, Take that damn thing down and replace it with a landscape. Gorman's gone, and no one will ever know the truth, but it hurts her to wonder about any child going through that kind of abuse. It makes her think of Gracie, and how easily she would be able to kill anyone who touched her in the wrong way. And yet, she understands how it's easy to malign famous people. That's why "Tesuque," the retired Hollywood director-benefactor who paid for her rehab, said his one condition was that she would never reveal his real name. "The last thing I need is something like this to bite me in the ass," he said. "My exes will be at their attorneys' offices in ten minutes, asking for more alimony."

The first three months she was here, Skye waited every day for things to blow up, for the bill to go unpaid, for the news that she was eighty-sixed and owed a ton of money besides. Just because you can't see the spark doesn't mean the fuse isn't burning. Tesuque didn't write to ask how she was doing. He didn't call to check on her. But he paid the bill, and after the vanilla Jack Daniel's episode, she got sober.

Which was when the real work began. Making her list of amends, she realized how broken she must have appeared to Tesuque, how immature to the judge. But what especially hurt, what cut her to the marrow, was realizing that no matter how clever she thought she was, she couldn't hide her drunkenness from a three-year-old. Gracie would pat her mouth and Skye would open it, thinking this was some kind of game, but it wasn't. Her daughter had been checking for the smell of alcohol. The day she figured that out was the day she began in earnest to try to stay sober. "My soul is as dry as tinder in an old-growth forest," she said in group, where of course everyone was chain-smoking cigarettes. But damn it all, it hurts to be *sober!* Every minute of every day here she'd felt jumpy, as if her nerves were growing back twice as sensitive. Duncan said that was normal. With her first paycheck she planned to purchase a decent pair of sunglasses. Hopefully Ray-Bans. Anything to soften the glare.

Outside again. On the portal of Cottonwoods, where things have cooled down at least 10 degrees. That's the high desert for you. When night arrives, you better have a jacket. There is so much red dirt all around this part of New Mexico, it could be mistaken for a crime scene. Every day in rehab she went for the morning mountain hike and the dirt got everywhere. She'd blow her nose, out it came. The dust got into her pores. Left marks on her bedsheets. She loved monsoon season because it kept the red dirt pinned to the earth long enough to fill the dead-looking arroyos, making the riverbeds come to life. Water hurries every-thing into blossom.

Sun's going down. No doubt about it, that beautiful New Mexico sunset is on its way. It occurs to her that today is April Fool's Day and she sighs. She heads indoors.

Skye uses the reception phone to call Rocky's cell again. "This message box is full," is all she gets, which is more than she expected. Usually it's no bars of connectivity. The coverage is spotty in the places he travels. If only she'd kept the card with Tesuque's phone number, she could call him. But the day she left for rehab, she wasn't big on organization—she was higher than the proverbial kite.

Checking to make sure no one's watching, she picks up the phone and dials her mother's cell. It goes straight to voice mail. "Mama," she whispers, trying to keep the emotion out of her voice, "I'm supposed to be released today. I'm sober through and through. But Rocky never showed. Would there be any chance at all you could come for me? Or could you send someone? I'm sorry to ask for help. If there was another way . . ." Her voice trails off and she hangs up the phone.

Mama doesn't call back, and Skye didn't really expect her to.

It's no use calling anyone else. Either they will see "Cottonwoods Rehab" on caller ID and not pick up, or like hers, their phones have been disconnected from not paying the bill.

She flops back on the lobby sectional, her nerves shot and her throat dry. Where is Rocky? The stack of color brochures falls to the floor. She picks them up, stacking them into piles. They're like an advertisement for the most fun camp ever. Hikes, crafts, movie nights, choir groups who sing "Kumbaya" and stay friends for life.

Duncan said Cottonwoods was deliberately built on leased Navajo land because of its remoteness. The whole of the county was dry. Not much of it was developed. To buy Tampax, a person had to drive an hour to a CVS. The only place to eat is the Chat 'n Chew, which passes off canned chili as homemade. Across the empty prairie there is nothing but footprints and tire tracks and weeds. The same land as in old black-and-white spaghetti westerns, where the Indians galloped bravely into war on second-rate ponies, only to get picked off by soldiers with rifles.

Being stood up by your soon-to-be ex-husband, having your hard-earned sobriety come to nothing, and not so much as a Tylenol for the pain of it? This is as real as it gets, she supposes. Fresh tears burn her eyes. She hears the bell for dinner, and she's so hungry that it hurts, but she cannot will her body to move.

The landscape goes purple. Gone from view are the sharp-edged rocks and the dry, spiky cacti. Soon coyotes will start howling to one another. Skye's pretty sure she can live without alcohol, but life without OxyContin will take some getting used to. "How," she'd asked Duncan, "will I make it when my heart is breaking twenty-four hours a day?"

"You'll gut it out," he'd said. "Down below the breastbone, the sternum, lies the xiphoid process, an actual joint. Yours hurting means you're healing." Duncan had told her to "picture your heart glowing, getting stronger."

"You mean, like heartburn?" Skye had asked. Both times in detox, her heart had felt singed, bitter to have to let go of those nice, predictable drugs. Rapid heartbeat, nausea, the headache from hell. Seizures she doesn't remember, but Duncan said he took video of it, in case she wants to see herself pee uncontrol-lably or vomit or any of the ugly stuff.

She never wants to go through detox again.

Here they come. The fellow inmates skulk by on their way to dinner. A few of them smirk as though they'd expected Rocky wouldn't show. For a moment, Skye thinks when Rocky arrives she'll leap into the air and wrap her legs around his waist just to show the nonbelievers that she still has what it takes to snare a man on looks alone. And the next moment, she imagines a funnel in her mouth, pouring down a bottle of whiskey. Or licking Oxy dots off a strip of paper like that candy Gracie begs for.

Lord, it hurts to be sober.

She skips dinner.

Rocky swears he'll kick drugs, yet come rodeo season, all bets are off. If only he could get rid of that addiction thing—that thing he encouraged in her—he might be a decent dad. Between them, they've done one thing right in their lives, and that thing is Gracie, who is probably having Fritos and Kool-Aid for dinner with Grandma Rita in the ghetto section of Albuquerque. Skye hates thinking about her daughter in a trailer with a swamp cooler and a foldout sofa bed. Would it kill her mother to help? She's too busy with the plastic surgeon, taking trips to some South Sea island Skye pictures as a single palm tree surrounded by sand.

Where is Rocky?

Seven o'clock turns to eight. The snack time bells signal an hour left until lights out. Skye finally admits she has to bag it and heads down the hall with the rest of the inmates. After shooting off her mouth about busting free of this place, she has to spend another night, because they don't let you go unless you have a ride.

"We had vegan Swedish meatballs for dinner," says Nola. "I ate three."

"I heard they use horsemeat in those," Skye tells her just to be mean.

Nola heads to the bathroom, and Skye can hear the water running while Nola empties her stomach. These ridiculous misfits think just because they've been through the worst together in rehab, somehow that bonds them soul to soul. Skye would like to tell Nola, tell all of them, that they need a major reality check: "When we leave there'll be nothing to talk about. Each of us will run as fast as we can to get back to our old lives and try to convince ourselves that we'll stay sober and function. When we fall off the wagon, because the stats say we will, imagine how hard it will be to come back here, to have to admit you failed to everyone. You might as well jump off a cliff."

I'll be different, she tells herself. This time is the last time.

Restless, she walks down the hall to get as far away from Nola as she can. Should she watch TV? No, it's too depressing, and the way she's feeling right now, she couldn't sit still for it. Judge Assmuncher will receive the notification that she's completed the Cottonwoods program. Next comes the mandatory community service or there will be jail time. Everybody and his brother racks up multiple DWIs and nothing happens, but she could go to prison. Skye recalls a time she stopped drinking on her own, a year ago, when she was about to sign a lease on a one-bedroom apartment and put Gracie in preschool. Then Rocky blazed through town, tracked her down, and in a couple of months she'd lost her security deposit, her job, and her white-knuckled sobriety.

Outside, the coyotes are wailing. They have families, friends, and talk every night, like a cell phone plan with unlimited minutes.

Duncan, who walks the halls at lights out, stops where she's sitting, using the wall to hold herself up. "Skye," he says, "why don't you find a bed and call your ride tomorrow?"

"I can't," she says, refusing to look at him.

"This doesn't have to be a setback unless you make it one," he tells her, and reaches out his hand for her to take. "I'll always be here for you as your counselor. You're going to do fine. Maybe, eventually, outside this place, down the line, we can be friends."

"Duncan Hanes," she says, ignoring his soft, dark hand covered with rings and silver bracelets. "Something I've always wondered: Did your mother name you after a cake mix and nylon stockings?"

"Skye," he says, and shakes his head.

There is nothing she can say that will hurt him.

Her first month here, she'd pegged him as a not-very-bright, New Agey Indian. After a week of her smart remarks, he gave her a toothbrush and some scouring powder and made her clean the bathroom floors. All that touchy-feely horseshit hid a holier-than-thou control freak. Every single group meeting, he picked on her. *Let's hear what Skye has to say. Come on, Skye, surely you have more of an opinion than "Whatever."* She worked her Steps, cleaned the floors, chopped onions (where she met the vanilla Jack Daniel's chef), and everywhere she turned, there was Duncan. It isn't until tonight that she sees what all this has led to. He's fond of her, wants to be friends. This same man watched her vomit through her nose in detox. You can't have a person like that for a friend. "Me and the wall are doing just fine, Duncan. Go away."

At nine thirty he comes back. "H.A.L.T.," he says.

Don't get hungry, angry, lonely, or tired . . . The Twelve Step staircase is built of acronyms. "Thanks for ruining a perfectly good word for me," she says.

"You're welcome," he answers. "You planning to sleep in your boots?"

"What if I am?"

"Nothing. I love your boots. Just looks uncomfortable, is all."

She laughs. "After all the crap I've been through here, you think sleeping in boots will break my spirit?"

He squats in front of her and she can smell his smell, which is coffee and cedar, as if somewhere else he secretly builds furniture. He places his right hand on the toe of her boot and rubs the dust off. He looks her in the eyes, and she can't stand it. Duncan has seen her at her worst, sobbing, confessing her sins. He says, "Down the hall, room ten is empty."

After he's enough steps away from her, Skye gets to her feet, feeling hollowed out, like the awful spaghetti squash they serve here. Tasteless, pointless, it's instant compost. Nobody will eat it, not even Nola, and a dinner plate filled with only forty-two calories is like Christmas to her. She walks quietly down to room ten and stands there a moment. Tonight was supposed to be a real bed. Gracie in her arms. The doorknob feels icy on her hand. She walks to the bed nearest the window, lies down on top of the covers. The moon comes up big and silver in the night sky, but she doesn't close the blinds because that would make it too dark. Nothing but prairie out there. Whatever desert creatures are out, they're being stealthy about it.

Just like every night since she landed here, she thinks about Gracie's Marilyn Monroe hair, as fine as corn silk. Ten months ago, Skye gave Rita a long list of dos and don'ts. Eggs give Gracie a rash. Don't ask me why, but she's terrified of parrots. Don't let her go anywhere without her inhalers. If two puffs don't make her better, give her the Proair HFA. Never run out of it, or you'll have to go to the ER. Her favorite bedtime story is *Star Wars*, and if you don't make the Ewok noises, she'll scream her head off. Don't bother buying her a doll, she likes to cut them open. No stuffed animals. Whatever's in them triggers her asthma. What if Gracie has decayed baby teeth from drinking Mountain Dew for breakfast? Gracie could almost put words into sentences that told a story. Will she have established F-bombs and SOBs in her vocabulary? Will it be up to Skye to eradicate all that?

Gracie the magpie. Little Miss Chatterbox. The Queen of Questions. What is rain? How many times you jump on one foot afore you sink into the ground? Where China lives? How a car can drive up a hill and not do falling down? Where are all the candy trees? Are bears afraid of each other? Her little-girl scent, cotton candy and shampoo, a pinch of dirt. Painting each of her five tiny fingernails took only one brushstroke of polish.

Once it is opened, behind that door are the not-so-great memories, too, like the time she forgot her sweet daughter at the Guadalupe BBQ. Gracie slept through it, but Milton never let Skye forget it. That wasn't as bad as the car accident that followed. She was drunk, but had to drive only a few blocks to get them home. She could handle that.

But Skye forgot to turn on the headlights. A coyote ran across the road and she instinctively swerved into the other lane. To avoid the truck that didn't see her—the Mercedes is black—she swerved back and misjudged the distance, hitting a wall. The air bag deployed, but Gracie wasn't buckled into her car seat and broke her wrist. Yes, it could have been worse, but wasn't the broken wrist bad enough? The tow truck driver took the Mercedes to Lobo and Lalo, the mechanics who took care of the Mercedes. The cop put Skye in the back of his car, but the worst part was letting Gracie go with the social worker.

Skye didn't intend to be a bad mother. It was just all so frustrating and difficult, and the skills she needed to excel at that job versus the stuff she'd memorized in school were galaxies apart.

From the start, she had been determined to do a better job than Mama. She made sure Gracie knew how much she loved her. But on this extra evening at Cottonwoods, part of Skye wonders if maybe the best thing she could've done was give her daughter up for adoption and go on to Stanford. Rocky couldn't have put Gracie up for adoption while she was in Cottonwoods, could he? If so, she'd hunt him down and flay him alive. Cover him in salt and leave him in the desert for the birds. From there, her regrets and worries bubble up beyond her control. She wishes that she hadn't gotten the chef fired. What if she can't be in a relationship and stay sober? Life without sex is a terrifying thought, but it's been nine months and she's still here, which means it's possible, just not much fun. If Mama gave her the money she spends on lunches each month, that would pay for Gracie's allergy medicine and fill the Benz's tank for a year. Would it have killed her to take Gracie? To hire her only grandchild a nanny? To cut back on her traveling for just a few months?

Apparently so. Oh, God, she needs something to calm her down or she'll be no good tomorrow. Duncan would offer her chamomile tea.

Just before she falls asleep, she thinks of Daddy, gone since her twelfth birthday to God knows where. If she knew where he was, he'd help her out. Well, maybe he'd help. It depended where he was on *his* drinking. Her letter to him sits in some post office carton marked "Undeliverable." She starts to doze off, drained, and those crazy images that come between waking and sleeping crowd her mind and then morph into dreams, where a person can change into a bird, drink forever, fly blind, make love, and nothing bad happens. Then, what feels like a minute later, she feels Duncan's hand on her shoulder and hollers, "What the hell are you doing in my room?"

Duncan helps her sit up. He waits until she's all the way conscious before handing her the duffel bag of belongings she came in with. Then he walks her to the lobby. "Are you throwing me out in the night?" she asks, near tears, as the gravity of Rocky not showing hits her. "Do you want me to hitchhike?"

"Skye," he says.

Her steps feel leaden. With each one, she has an accompanying thought: Maybe I won't find Rocky. Maybe he won't give me Gracie. Maybe I'll just have a drink.

Duncan points out the lobby windows into the darkness and says, "I believe your ride's here."

As her eyes adjust to the dark, she searches the moonlit-landscaped driveway for Rocky's silver truck. It's not there. Instead, there is a man on a horse, ponying a flashy leopard Appaloosa alongside. Funny, how he looks so much like her Appy, Lightning. The white of his hide shines like chrome in the moonlight, and she gets a lump in her throat. She stumbles out the door and hurries forward as the rider tips back a cowboy hat that she knows has a horsehair band held together by the first silver buckle he ever won, for calf roping, when he was eleven years old. It takes her a full minute to find her voice, to dare ask, "Daddy? That you?"

He pats the empty saddle on Lightning just like in the old days, inviting her up.

Chapter 2

THE DAY BEFORE Skye was released from rehab, Margaret Yearwood had done some waiting herself. She sat on the couch in Dr. Silverhorse's waiting room, across from the wall-sized Storm Pattern Navajo blanket. Until that day, the rug might as well have been wallpaper. Now she could see how lovely it was, and intricate—probably museum quality. After her aunt Eleanor was diagnosed with Alzheimer's, Margaret had sat in this exact spot so many times, holding her hand. Then, her mind had been focused on keeping Ellie calm, turning magazine pages because her aunt enjoyed looking at the pictures, even if she had no idea what the words next to them meant. Aunt Ellie had taken her final journey nearly six months ago, a blessing, really, but when Margaret couldn't stop crying, Dr. Silverhorse had sent her to a psychiatrist, who prescribed antidepressants. The crying stopped, but in Margaret's place was a placid cow that never wanted to do anything except watch daytime TV. She went off the pills and told herself to buck up. Now she was back, to see him for a different reason. It had taken her weeks to gather her courage and make the appointment.

Alzheimer's was the cruelest kind of thief. Aunt Ellie, her mother's sister, had never married or had children. When

Margaret and her sister, Norine, were kids, Ellie had sent them postcards from around the world: Africa, Iceland, Italy, Croatia, France, Ireland, Portugal, Greece, and Spain. Margaret and Nori had fought over possession of them, but in the end practical Margaret had won. In her teens she'd put together a scrapbook showcasing each postcard, including a *National Geographic* foldout world map on which Margaret had marked all the places her aunt had traveled.

Eleanor had sent Margaret and her sister money for holidays, but none so traditional as Christmas. *It's Earth Day, my dears. Use this check to plant a redwood. Winter solstice is approaching. Use this money to buy yourselves cashmere pashminas.* And later on, when Margaret was still married to Ray and things were starting to get wobbly: *I could not let Fourth of July pass without sending you some money for fireworks, darling. Use this money to buy yourself a sexy new nightie.*

Margaret's marriage had ended anyway, the year their son, Peter, turned fifteen. Her ex, Ray, had recently divorced his third wife. Probably she had developed a laugh line or a crow's-foot. When Margaret heard the news, the only emotion she could muster was sympathy for the wife. Ray had to be paying more in alimony than he earned off the dividends of his films. Hollywood was a youth-oriented town, and he was now pushing sixty.

In her sixties, Aunt Ellie had settled in Santa Fe, for the climate and the chance to practice her Spanish, she said. Retired from traveling, she'd whiled away time finishing the *New York Times* crossword puzzle every morning before her first cup of coffee, going to fund-raisers, and working in her garden several hours a day. Her English garden in a southwestern climate made the Santa Fe official garden tour every year. She was always grafting miniature roses and babying her redwood tree, one of two that grew in this dry, high desert town. She created little nooks for the birds to nest in out of odd china cups and those baskets strawberries come in.

When Peter went off to Gallaudet University, Margaret had moved to Santa Fe herself, though out in Eldorado, the planned community some referred to as "the White Reservation"—she couldn't afford the historic district like her aunt. They talked on the phone twice a day, met often for lunch, and had season tickets to concerts at the Lensic Theater. The first indication anything was wrong was her fall, nearly three years ago. Margaret drove to the hospital and met Ellie in the emergency room at Christus St. Vincent's. The young doctor who attended her had taken Margaret aside while an RN put in an IV and prepped her for surgery.

"Your aunt's leg will mend in six to eight weeks," he said, "but she shouldn't live on her own anymore."

"What do you mean?" Margaret asked.

"The stage she's in, she'll require professional home health care."

"I keep an eye on her," Margaret told him. "I just live fifteen miles away."

"I'm afraid I'm not making myself clear," the doctor said, frowning. "Breaking her leg was a blessing. It could have been much more serious. Does Alzheimer's run in your family?"

"Alzheimer's?" Margaret echoed.

"You haven't noticed any signs that your aunt is altered?" he asked as if Ellie's life were a hem that had been taken up.

"Her hearing isn't the best, and from time to time she gets confused, but I haven't noticed any significant changes."

"Come with me," he said, and pulled aside the privacy curtain. "Ellie, how are you feeling?"

Her aunt had a smile for everyone. "I'm just *dandy*," she said, her voice taking on a sarcastic edge. She pointed to the lab tech, who was organizing the vials of blood he'd taken. "Except for that vampire who's stealing my blood."

The doctor smiled back. "You're in the hospital, Ellie. Do you remember breaking your leg?"

The smile widened, then faltered, and Margaret could see the bafflement on her aunt's face. "Yes, you're here to deliver my firewood. It's about time. Don't bring any of that, that . . ." Her words trailed off. "Pinecone! Like you did last year. It's terrible. Spits and burns like crumbled papers."

"I'll make sure I don't," the doctor said. "Can you tell me what year it is?"

"Of course I can. It's 1986."

It was 2007.

"Who's our president?"

"Clint Eastwood. He'll never be a Ronald McDonald."

"Thanks, Ellie. I'll check in on you later."

"I like my firewood stocked neatly, young man," she called after him. "Or don't expect a tipper."

Back in the hallway, tears brimmed in Margaret's eyes. How had she missed this? "What about those new drugs?" she asked the doctor. "I've heard they help dramatically. Can't we try her on those?"

He looked away before answering. For once, the ER wasn't busy. Two male nurses were popping rubber bands at each other. "We can try, but I expect she's too far into the disease for there to be any appreciable improvement. I'll order a brain scan, but you need to start planning for her release."

"What should I do?"

"I recommend assisted living, with a long-term facility attached."

"She can't go home?"

"Not without help."

"What if I move in?"

He shrugged. "That could work for a little while, but believe me, I know dozens of folks who were sure they could handle it and couldn't. It's exhausting. Your aunt can't be left alone, even to sleep. I'll have you follow up with a neurologist. Right now, I have other patients. There will be someone taking her up to surgery any minute to pin those bones back together."

Later that week, while Ellie recovered in the hospital, Margaret straightened up her aunt's house and looked after Nash, Ellie's massive orange Maine Coon cat, quite possibly the most aloof animal that ever lived. Margaret brought along her dog, Echo II, worrying how Nash might react, but he couldn't have cared less. He prowled around the house, crying, as if that would bring Ellie home. As Margaret gave the house an overdue cleaning, she found half a sandwich tucked under the cushion in her aunt's favorite chair. Dirty dishes in the cupboard. Inside the broom closet, she discovered a wad of newspaper tucked behind the mop. Unfolding it, she realized they were crossword puzzles. In some, the blanks were filled in with spidery handwriting, difficult to read. Everyone's handwriting got worse over the years. Some of that could be blamed on computers. But whatever her aunt had written in the blanks weren't letters. It might have been shorthand, that outdated form of note taking, but she couldn't prove it. As she cleaned, Margaret remembered how Aunt Ellie was unable to reach for a certain word in their phone calls over the last year or so, and not all that often, but often enough, she'd confused Margaret's voice with that of her sister, Margaret's mother, who had been dead for decades.

Margaret rented out her Eldorado house and moved into her aunt's full-time. For as long as Ellie was in the wheelchair, they did fairly well, but when Ellie began to get up and wander the house in the middle of the night, Margaret had to hire a nurse. Things muddled along until Ellie's occasional incontinence turned into a daily occurrence. Whenever the nurse tried to change her diapers, Ellie became combative.

After a black eye, the nurse quit, and Margaret found an assisted living situation for her aunt, spending so much money a month that Margaret wondered if she needed to put her aunt's home on the market. But given the economic downturn, the house wouldn't fetch anywhere near what it was worth, if it sold at all.

Ellie lasted about two and a half years after her diagnosis before dwindling away.

When Margaret began forgetting words, having trouble with occasional numbness in her hands and feet, and tripping, she was terrified. The Internet search she shouldn't have done had nothing but dire predictions, and yes, those symptoms could happen to early-onset Alzheimer's patients. Margaret was fifty. She wasn't ready to have this happen. After insomnia settled in, she called Dr. Silverhorse, who had been Ellie's neurologist. Like a lot of Santa Feans, he was a transplant from the East Coast. Once in Santa Fe, he'd changed his name from Silberferd to Silverhorse. He sported a long silver ponytail and a silver bola tie at his neck, but he still wore his yarmulke. "I want you to run every test there is," she told Dr. Silverhorse. "I don't care if my insurance balks at it. I'll pay for it. Just run them all so I don't have to drag this out." And then she bit back the sob that threatened to escape her throat.

"Oy," Dr. Silverhorse said. "There is a saying, Margaret, about borrowing trouble. Perhaps you've heard of it?" But in the end, he relented. That was two weeks ago. Now she was waiting to hear her results.

Staring at the Navajo rug, she realized that had she paid attention all this time, she might have recognized the work of her old friend, Navajo weaver Verbena Youngcloud. Verbena's no-nonsense advice and friendship had sustained Margaret through difficult times. After Margaret left Blue Dog, the artist community where she'd lived until moving to Santa Fe, they'd drifted apart. Now, Margaret didn't even know if the Navajo weaver was still alive. The rug had all of Verbena's trademark idiosyncrasies: brown-and-beige storm clouds in each corner, the margins featuring giant water bugs. In one corner, there was a whirling log no bigger than a pinky finger. The whirling log design was a part of the Nightway chant, a Navajo ceremony. As such, it implied good luck to the Navajo but was generally mistaken for a swastika by anyone unfamiliar to the culture. Weavers had pretty much stopped including the whirling log, but Verbena Youngcloud was stubborn, and it made Margaret smile to remember her. It had to have come from Crystal Trading Post, because they always snapped up Verbena's work. She'd ask Dr. Silverhorse where he bought it.

Memories of her life in Blue Dog flooded her mind. Peter was twenty-five now, married, teaching at Gallaudet, a university for the deaf. But just after his fifteenth birthday, Peter had had an accident. Margaret had organized a family trip to Mexico, even though Ray wasn't keen on it. At the time, she'd thought he didn't want to leave L.A. because of all his pending movie deals. But he'd agreed to go for three days, so down they flew. One afternoon, she'd decided to take a walk, shop a little, and meet up with Ray and Peter for dinner. But when it started raining, she'd come back early and heard her husband on the phone, saying, "I love you with all my heart." Since the words were not directed to her, this had come as a surprise. They'd had the fight of the century. From the adjoining room, Peter had heard them screaming at each other. Distressed, he'd run out into the rain and was gone for hours. Apparently, he'd jumped into a pool filled with stagnant water and hit his head. He'd contracted meningitis, nearly dying.

Peter had survived but had lost his hearing. When the opportunity to attend a school for the deaf in New Mexico came up, mere months after the accident, Peter left their home in Southern California and moved in with the Hidalgos, a couple who'd raised their own deaf children. They opened their home in Santa Fe to the newly deaf teenager, allowing him to immerse himself in deaf culture while he attended Riverwall, the school for the deaf. Margaret, by then divorced from Ray, sold her waterfront house, leashed Peter's dog, Echo I, bought a used Toyota Land Cruiser, and followed him, stopping at the town of Blue Dog a half hour outside Santa Fe, even though Peter insisted he didn't want her anywhere near him. Peter had been furious with his mother for not being able to restore the family and for the divorce, and with the world because he had lost his hearing. He'd refused to consider cochlear implant surgery in part to punish her. But Margaret stayed. For a song, she rented an old Victorian house on the Starr ranch. Until Peter stopped blaming her for the divorce, she passed her time at her easel, painting, and taught herself American Sign Language.

Riverwall School for the Deaf in Santa Fe had helped Peter learn to accept his new life. While he was there, he'd fallen for Bonnie Tsosie, a Navajo-Ponca girl, and had never really dated anyone else. He married her at twenty-two, way too young, in Margaret's opinion. But there was no talking sense to him: Hearing kids never wanted to listen, but deaf kids made an art of it. For two years Peter and Bonnie had been sparring like boxers, one week in different apartments, the next in wedded bliss and contemplating having a baby. Now Bonnie was in Chicago, working for the radio show *Native America Calling*. It was the ultimate irony, Margaret thought, for a deaf woman to work for a radio show. Peter said it was only a temporary separation. Margaret relived her fights with Ray and couldn't help thinking it was her fault for not setting a good example. Sometimes she wondered if society was simply evolving out of the institution of marriage.

And Ray wasn't her only failed relationship. Of course, there was Owen Garrett, the other man Margaret had fallen in love with. Ten years later, the memory was still tender. "I have to go face up to what I did," he'd told her, explaining that he believed he'd killed a man in a bar fight and had been running from it ever since. That implied a prison sentence, maybe for life. He'd left behind his horse, RedBow, and for Margaret, a heart that felt as if it were filled with shrapnel. She'd forced herself to let go, but even after ten years had passed, she wondered every day if he might come back. She could have looked for him, she supposed, but the idea of finding him in prison, or with another woman, kept her from trying.

She'd thrown herself into her painting, then, and actually had a show in the Blue Dog Art Gallery, which also doubled as the hardware store. Moving to Santa Fe was another story, a series of doors shut in her face. When Margaret first moved to the city, she'd applied to join the Downtown Artists' League, which allowed an artist to set up shop a couple of times a year in a parking lot two blocks from the Plaza that generated decent foot traffic. They'd asked her to submit a portfolio. She'd welcomed the chance to update her résumé, listing the places she'd shown and which of her pieces were in private collections. She'd turned in a dozen slides, one large acrylic of cattle, and three oils that were her best work, the paintings she'd done in Blue Dog. The artists were told to pick up their portfolios and wait for a confirmation letter that they'd been accepted. The envelope had arrived two days later, and Margaret had torn it open excitedly. But there in one short paragraph the word *sorry* popped out at her, and she had to sit down and look out the window at the scrubby piñon trees and wind blowing over the Eldorado prairie. She knew she wasn't Fritz Scholder or Donna Howell-Sickles, but she was a fairly decent painter. Not as good as some, but surely good enough to sell watercolors in a parking lot.

That Santa Fe was a good place for artists was the first of many of the city's myths to be shattered for her. Forget even trying the galleries along Canyon Road. The prices they charged were crazy inflated. The downtown galleries carried original works worth up to hundreds of thousands of dollars, not Margaret's kind of art.

Everywhere she went, artists seemed to be hurtling over one another for space. Even the walls of the coffeehouse she went to for a change of pace were covered with art for sale. Most of it was high quality. If no one was going to buy your paintings, then why bother painting?

She'd stopped painting anything ambitious. Instead, she did small watercolors of cacti, horses, Santa Fe window boxes, weather-bleached doors, and gates. Of course she painted the remarkable skies, too, filled with clouds that sometimes lined up like freight trains overhead, but only in watercolor or acrylic. Oil was too expensive to waste on this kind of art. She ran *giclée* prints off a color printer, selling them for twenty-five dollars each online and in bulk to a few gift shops. She had steady customers, and soon she couldn't keep up with the printing, so she hired an outside printer to do the work for her and limited her editions to fifty. It was shocking how decent a living she could make after she took her heart out of the act. Just the sight of one of Verbena's weavings shamed her, because Verbena had obviously continued caring about art instead of ways to make money. This rug, with its vegetable-dyed, tobacco-brown yarn, was a masterpiece.

How could she not have noticed it before?

Occasionally Margaret wondered if her general sense of disappointment in life had something to do with not painting seriously, but maybe that was just part of growing old. Some days, she felt like Nash the cat, out of sorts with everything. Margaret had bought him sardines, catnip toys, a stick with a feather on a fishing line string. He ignored it all. She tried to give him affection, but he did not care for petting and ignored the cat bed she bought, preferring to sleep in the bathroom sink. How could he despise her?

Depression was one thing, but fear of Alzheimer's was quite

another. She mentally reviewed her symptoms: crushing fatigue, intermittent grasping for words, numbness in her hands and feet. She fell down at least once a week. Undoubtedly the onset of Alzheimer's. Dr. Silverhorse would break the news gently and then tell her to get her affairs in order. Already she had a lawyer lined up to create a family trust.

"Margaret?" Amy the nurse called her from her reverie, and she followed the sunny young Latina to the exam room. "You looked pretty deep in thought," Amy said as she had Margaret weigh herself—still 120, after all these years—and took her blood pressure: 130/80, borderline high normal, as usual. "Everything all right?"

"Oh, just planning my errands for the day," Margaret answered. "How are you?"

"Busy," she said. "My youngest girl starts middle school next year. I'm taking some classes at night. Got to keep my hours up, you know? You look good, Margaret. We missed seeing you after your auntie passed."

Margaret saw the tears well up in the nurse's eyes. There was an entire culture around death in Santa Fe, from anniversary obituaries to Day of the Dead artwork and, of course, the road-side *descansos* decorated with artificial flowers and Christmas ornaments, where someone had died from a car accident. "I miss her, too," Margaret said. "Wasn't I lucky to have her all those years?"

"What a good way to look at it. Go ahead and have a seat. Dr. S will be right with you."

Amy left the exam room door ajar. Margaret opened her purse to find her Moleskine, a small, plain paper notebook she used to sketch in. She'd written a list of questions:

Depending on my results, should Peter be tested?

How long will I be competent to make my own decisions?

Will I know when it's bad, or will it happen so gradually I
don't notice?

Power of attorney—is Peter mature enough to handle that?

Should I sell the Eldorado house or put it in Peter's name?

What if he and Bonnie split up? Would he be forced to
sell and have to give her 50 percent of the profits?

Will he take Echo II? If not, could I ask Glory? I'm awful.
She has four dogs already. But she really likes Echo.

Suddenly the ridiculousness of the list made her want to throw
the notebook in the trash.

All weekend long she'd sat out on the portal wrapped in her
shawl, watching spring arrive in Santa Fe. The forsythia bushes
reminded her of drag queens, flaunting their Day-Glo yellow
petals. The lilac bushes that perfumed the air on Ave de Colibri
were heavy with buds, practically groaning with the urge to
bloom. Her neighbor Glory's wisteria was greening up, and soon
purple flowers would follow. Once the nights warmed up, the
solar fountain would turn itself on, and birds would start throwing their predawn raves. And there she'd sat, fifty-year-old
Margaret Yearwood, beholden to nobody, loved by nobody
except her sister, and facing what? Thirty years of assisted living?
Losing parts of herself day by day, the way her aunt did? Becoming
the kind of burden to Peter that she swore she'd never be? No
wonder Aunt Ellie had become combative. Should she move to
Oregon, a state that allowed people to legally end their lives?
What would happen to her life insurance policy if she did? Could
she cash it in before then? Nash the cat would be all right. He

was such an efficient mouser, someone would be glad to give him a home. But who would take care of Echo II? As if the spotty red mutt with the dachshund ears, supermodel-long legs, and heart of the softest gold could hear her thoughts, she had nuzzled Margaret's knee with her wet nose, and Margaret had smiled. She'd never realized how important a dog could be until Ellie died. Echo was the first sentient being she spoke to every day and the last one before sleeping.

Dr. Silverhorse knocked and then entered the exam room. "*Boker tov*, Margaret," he said in his distracted monotone, scanning her file. "I hope you're having a nice morning. Just as I suspected, you're negative for the Apo E. Your blood tests, hmm, I suspect the low vitamin D level is the result of sunscreen, and the giant red blood cells noted are due to a B vitamin deficiency. Take B complex, vitamin D, and of course, calcium. Get the supplements at Trader Joe's. They have the best prices . . ."

"I don't have Alzheimer's?" Margaret blurted out, feeling the adrenaline flood her veins.

Dr. Silverhorse paused. "Just as I told you, no Alzheimer's. However, there is—"

The relief made her so giddy that she babbled right over him again. "Oh, thank God. I've been sick with waiting. I know you told me there wasn't anything to worry about, but I read all this stuff on the Internet, and thank goodness. I suppose you think I'm crazy, but I had to know. I think I'm going to have an ice-cream sundae for lunch, it's all such a relief."

He looked up at her, peering over the top of his glasses. "*Tzipiyah*. We haven't discussed the MRI yet."

And then Margaret knew. It was her own fault, forcing the issue of dementia—her constant worrying had never done her one bit of good. "Oh," she said, that single syllable, a great big zero. This was bad. The breath went out of her. What had he found? A brain tumor?

"Have you ever heard of Dawson's fingers?" he asked.

She forced a grin. "Is that some kind of pastry?"

Dr. Silverhorse sat on the stool and tossed her chart on the counter. "Margaret," he said, and took her chilly hands into his warm ones.

Twenty minutes later she left his office with a dozen pamphlets, computer printouts, the phone number for a support group, and the name of a therapist who knew all there was to know about multiple sclerosis.

Even bad news contained a glint of silver lining. Now Margaret was entitled to have whatever she wanted for dinner. When your entrée was ice cream or an almond croissant, dessert was the moon. For all that everyone griped about sugar, Margaret took the long view. Life was difficult. Sweetness played a vital function. And now, she was supposed to give it up? Dr. Silverhorse said lots of people lived a normal life span with MS. They raised families, climbed mountains, did TED talks, painted masterpieces. Her mind reeled with information. It was actually a kind of relief to finally know, and hey, it *wasn't* Alzheimer's. But a diagnosis of multiple sclerosis made the next twenty or thirty years seem like a very short time.

She drove home, leashed Echo, and walked down Old Santa Fe Trail to Kaune's Market. Echo sniffed every tree, mailbox, and boulder, left pee mail, and of course accepted all compliments and attention that came her way. Echo II had descended from

Peter's first dog, whom Margaret had called "the doggie ambassador" because she could convert cat lovers in mere seconds. Echo II had inherited her mother's finest quality. Echo II was one of the litter that came from the three-legged, blue-spotted dog that belonged to Owen Garrett of the broken-heart episode. Despite the passage of years, the sight of those cattle dogs still filled Margaret with a bittersweet melancholy. John Lennon had once said, "Life is what happens to you while you're busy making other plans," and wasn't that true? "I promise I'll never leave you," Margaret told the dog, hoping that no matter what condition she found herself in down the road, she'd find a way to care for Echo.

Kaune's, first opened in 1896, had managed to hang on despite Trader Joe's and Whole Foods. Margaret tied Echo's leash to a post on the store's portal, a three-foot-wide sidewalk that contained leash hitches and a water bowl. She told Echo to "wait" as she had dozens of times before, and the dog sat quietly, minding. The specialty market was spendy for Margaret's budget, but today was an exception. She bought green chile enchiladas, cherry clafoutis, a pint of vanilla-bean ice cream, and a tin of the imported Dutch cocoa her aunt had loved. How selfish am I, she asked herself, and ordered a small tuna filet for Nash. For Echo, a nice chewy bone with some beef still on it. With every step she scrutinized her gait. Was that left foot a little slow on the uptake?

"You can smell spring in the air today," the clerk said as he wrapped the tuna.

"You sure can," Margaret agreed, keeping her worries out of her voice. "I wonder if it's time to start seedlings?"

"Indoors, sure. But wait until Memorial Day weekend to plant," the clerk answered. "Old Man Winter hasn't let go all the way yet. Do you have fruit trees?"

Though she did not, Margaret nodded and listened to his advice. She paid for her sack of groceries and walked back outside to fetch Echo, who wagged her tail excitedly, because she was just that happy an animal. Margaret peeked in the window of the gift shop next door. For Bonnie's last birthday, she'd bought her daughter-in-law a pair of Victorian glass trumpet flower earrings there but never received a thank-you note or an e-mail. Perhaps the stormy nature of Peter and Bonnie's relationship was responsible. Margaret gave Echo a neck scratch, and the dog groaned her appreciation.

A crack of thunder overhead seemed to split the sky in two. Gray clouds moved in, and a chill seemed to rise from the parking lot. Echo hated thunder and began to tremble. Margaret took off her scarf and tied it tightly across Echo's middle to make her feel secure. Her neighbor Glory had told her the dog needed one of those antianxiety dog jackets. She'd order one today, but for now, this halfway measure would have to do. They hurried the short walk home, hoping to beat the rain.

In the recesses of the Canyon Road yards, patches of white snow still lay obstinately in shade. Soon the empty window boxes would be ready for flowers. The timeless portrait of Santa Fe was white snow against red adobe, the trim color on the houses ranging from that dusty indigo "Santa Fe blue" to turquoise and white and all colors in between. The butcher at Kaune's was right, it would snow again, maybe today. Aunt Ellie had referred to April snow as "a poor man's fertilizer" and pronounced it good for her garden. It must have been true, considering how her plants thrived. But Margaret was looking forward to having the snow gone. Somehow, MS would be easier to accept in the sunshine.

When she made it to Colibri Road, she saw her neighbor Glory Vigil sitting on the front step of her house. Her adopted granddaughter, Aspen, was marching up and down the street, singing. Next to Glory, in a bouncy seat, her five-month-old daughter, Sparrow, was bundled up tight in a pink snowsuit. Margaret babysat both girls often. When Aspen's mom, Casey, needed a break, or Glory had to work late, Margaret said yes, because she remembered how exhausting parenthood could be. Sometimes she told Glory she wanted to keep both girls overnight so that Glory and Joe could get a good night's sleep, finish a conversation, or see a movie.

She waved at Glory as Aspen made a beeline for Echo. "Echo, Echo!" she shouted. "You're wearing a c-c-c-coat!" And she immediately inserted the dog's name into her song. The girl was mental for dogs, talking to them, dressing them up, and always snuggling with at least one at night. Echo wagged her tail and allowed the girl to hang on her as if she were a pony.

"Hi there, Aspen," Margaret said. "And how are you, Miss Sparrow?" Margaret bent and patted the baby's pink cheek. Then she saw the look on Glory's face. "Or maybe I should be asking how is Sparrow's mom, and Aspen's overworked grandma?"

Aspen, the wispy blond-haired seven-year-old, didn't look up from Echo, whose tail was wagging like a wheat thresher. "Echo, yuh-yuh-you needs a new hair ribbon," she said, and pulled hers from her braid. "Now be still," she said, so involved in her play that she couldn't take time to be polite and say hello to her adopted auntie Margaret. Margaret had no problem coming in second to her dog, but it was a little disconcerting how deeply Aspen traveled into playacting. The stutter had begun in September, when the Vigils enrolled Aspen in public school.

Glory sighed. "Miss Aspen received three time-outs this week at school. She insists on kissing a little boy named Gordon whether he wants it or not. Seven years old and already 'macking on the homies,' as her auntie Juniper so delicately puts it."

Margaret laughed. "Poor Gordon."

"Tell me about it."

"How is the speech therapy going?"

"Good. Here's a funny thing. If she sings, the stutter goes away. Weird, huh?"

Margaret studied her neighbor. Something else was going on. She sat on the step next to Glory. "People say I make a very good listener," she said.

Glory smiled, but it was forced. "Okay. Just remember, you asked."

"I'm all ears."

Glory blew out a breath. "You know how people say so long as you're nursing, you can't get pregnant?"

"I've heard something along those lines. I can't vouch for it being one hundred percent accurate, though."

"I think my eggs failed to get the memo."

"Have you taken a test?"

Glory patted her barn coat pocket. "I'm forty-two years old. I've been carrying this test around for a week. I can buck hay bales, train dogs, and plaster a wall while changing a diaper, but I'm afraid to pee on a stick."

Margaret squeezed her hand. "Knowing for sure will help. I'm happy to watch the girls so you can have some alone time."

"No, no," Glory insisted. "I've got to keep busy. Also, I need to tire Aspen out. She must have had sugar at school. She's wound up like a jack-in-the-box. Look at her."

Aspen was spinning in circles. They watched as Echo nosed her, worried. The little girl giggled like crazy and then started coughing. "That's enough, Aspen," Glory said. "Come see Grandma."

"No, I w-w-w-want to play," she insisted, and skipped up the steps to Margaret's house, only to turn and jump from step to step, coughing.

Aspen had been scarily thin when she came to live with the Vigils, but in five months she'd put on weight. She had a heart problem as a result of an illness that had nearly claimed her life only six months earlier. You'd never know it from the pace she kept up, which was high gear day in and out, starting at dawn and collapsing into bed only when her mother, Casey, sat on her.

"Maybe she needs a bicycle. Have you taught her how to pedal?"

"We're waiting for the snow to melt. Do you think she has ADD?"

Margaret laughed. "No, I think she's seven."

"You're probably right. Where have you and Echo been? Walkies?"

"A trip to Kaune's, to pick up dinner," Margaret said. "Want to come in for a cup of cocoa?"

"Not sure if I can muster the energy to get up."

Margaret held out a hand. "Come on. If I can do it, you can, too."

Walking inside her aunt's house—hers now—felt to Margaret like stepping into another world. The wooden floor dipped at the foyer, from years of feet and boots. She wouldn't dream of replacing it. To the right was the massive old sideboard that had come with the house. The full set of blue calico Staffordshire

Aunt Ellie never used sat behind the glass-fronted doors. To the left was the living room, with white plaster walls and a built-in *banco*, a wraparound bench made of adobe and plastered white. Handmade cushions stuffed with horsehair had been there for as long as Margaret could remember. Margaret had sewn more pillows out of one of Aunt Ellie's tattered old rugs. The *banco* culminated in a kiva fireplace, decorated with tile so old that it was worn in places to a matte finish. Walls of built-in book-shelves were filled to the brim with the British mysteries Ellie had loved. Her collection of baskets on the sideboard—*trastero*, as they called them here—reminded Margaret that she really ought to call the museum. There were some incredible examples of basketry, and she'd donate whichever ones they wanted; it would be a shame not to share them with the world. Procrastination was her biggest flaw. Well, that needed to change, as did a lot of things she'd let slide.

"Aspen," Glory called, "come on into Auntie Margaret's house. It's too cold to play outside."

Aspen stamped her snow boot. "I don't wanna."

"We're going to have cocoa," Glory said.

"No!"

"With marshmallows." Margaret beckoned, and Aspen zoomed past them into the house.

Margaret hauled Sparrow and her bouncy seat inside and set it on the floor next to the table. She fetched a clip-on mobile from the baby things she'd bought at the thrift store so she and Glory didn't have to cart toys back and forth when she babysat. She attached it to the table. "Is Sparrow old enough for a mobile?"

"I don't know," Glory said. "I haven't gotten around to reading the parenting manual. I feel so guilty."

Margaret laughed. "People have been successfully raising babies without manuals for thousands of years."

"I never read the pregnancy books, either. Look where that has gotten me."

"You don't know for sure."

"Yet."

Aspen sped by with Echo's leash in her hand. "Echo wuh-wuh-wuh-wants dinner," she announced.

"You know where I keep her kibble," Margaret said, unhooking the leash. "Remember, only one cupful."

The little girl and dog ran through the kitchen to the laundry room, and Margaret pictured just how full Echo's dish would be. Thank goodness she wasn't a food hog. Margaret wondered where Nash was. Probably under her bed, in the very middle, out of Aspen's reach. Nash lived life on his own terms, especially where children were concerned.

"May I use the bathroom?" Glory said, and Margaret laughed.

"Of course, Glory. You don't have to ask."

"I know. I was hoping you'd say no."

"Oh, come on," Margaret said, thinking how much better it would be to have Glory's problem instead of her own. "It's not the end of the world."

"I will be sixty years old before he finishes high school."

"You're positive the baby you don't know you're having will be a boy?"

Glory frowned. "It has to be. I had morning sickness with Sparrow, but not like this. Every time I look in the mirror I expect to see a saltine cracker staring back at me."

"I think they prescribe medicine for that now," Margaret said. "Ask your doctor about it." A rumbling that wasn't quite thunder made them both look up. When the groan followed, they said in unison, "Dolores, go toward the light."

"It's so weird that my ghost moved into your house," Glory said. "Rejected by a ghost. I wonder why? Is it because we have too many dogs?"

"Time Share Dolores, that's how I think of her," Margaret said. "Anyway, she doesn't bother me. I kind of like the company." Margaret could tell her friend was near tears. "Glory, go on, take the test. Splash some cold water on your face while you're at it. I have ginger ale if you'd prefer that over cocoa."

"I want cocoa," Glory said. "If I'm pregnant, I'll have chocolate for every meal."

Then Sparrow cooed, and Glory couldn't stop herself from smiling.

Margaret laughed to see how much in love Glory was with her daughter. She took hold of her friend's shoulders and aimed her toward the hallway. "Go already."

"All right, but if you hear a shriek, you might have to scrape me off the floor."

"Will you just get your butt in there and end the suspense?"

"I don't wanna."

"Now you sound like Aspen. But you're going to find out, and once you do you'll feel better."

Bathrooms in the older Santa Fe adobes were generally tiny compared with the ones in homes built after 1970, but Margaret's bathroom was an exception. Inside was a commode with a pull chain, a pedestal sink, a stall shower, and a claw-foot tub that was a hundred years old if it was a day. Margaret loved to soak in the suds and let her hair fall over the back of the tub. She'd fallen asleep in there on occasion. On one wall was a pierced tinwork mirror decorated on the corners with tiles of a deep blue set against cream. Facing it was a mural by Pop Chalee, the Taos/ Tiwa artist, featuring a string of fanciful rabbits amid flowering cacti and stars. "I love this bathroom," Glory called out from inside it, just as she always did.

Margaret smiled. "Let me get you a clean hand towel," she said, and went to the linen closet. On the way, she passed her studio, previously the guest bedroom. After Ellie died, Margaret had claimed it for a studio because the French doors opened onto the portal, which was bathed in northern light. There stood the larger of her easels, one she hadn't touched in years. On the tray leaned the final horse painting in the series she'd done when she lived in Blue Dog, ten years ago. The painting remained unfinished. The chestnut horse in the painting, RedBow, had become Peter's horse, and then Margaret's when Peter went off to college. RedBow was twenty-two years old now, long retired and free to meander in the pasture adjoining the stable Glory's husband, Joseph, had bought. Joseph was only days away from opening a riding stable for handicapped kids and adults. He'd named his project Reach for the Sky, and it would serve people with both mental and physical issues, as well as juvenile offenders. People recovering from trauma, like Casey, Aspen's mother, who'd been a long-term kidnap victim until just six months ago, would groom and ride the horses. The governing idea was that the work would give them a sense of control and inspire mutual and unconditional love, and that both of these things would allow them to imagine for themselves a future. The responsibilities of caring for RedBow had certainly been good for Margaret's son. And the gelding had fostered in Peter a deep affection for horses that still kept him riding, even in D.C.

Had Owen Garrett never thought of his beloved horse? she wondered from time to time. He might not even be alive, Margaret told herself, though the thought of that was unfathomable to her.

The painting of RedBow she'd started in Blue Dog was done in oil, on a four-by-four-foot canvas panel. The sweet-natured chestnut horse rested his muzzle on a split-rail fence, as he often had in Blue Dog. He loved children and would hurry to the fence whenever he saw one. Next to the horse's whiskery muzzle, she had painted—as planned—a robin on a fence post. Over time, she'd realized the robin wasn't right. One day she'd picked up her paintbrush again and painted over the robin. She'd gotten as far as outlining the image of an albino hummingbird hovering in flight but couldn't finish it. Along with Dolores the ghost, Margaret's and Glory's yards were home to albino hummingbirds that somehow delivered a sturdy mutation: Every year they had babies, some white, others pigmented.

Another painter might say that by stopping at the hardest part of the painting, Margaret had failed to reveal its emotional heart. She saw things differently. If she left it unfinished, the series would never come to an end. She still clung to the happiness she'd experienced in Blue Dog. All it would take was a few more strokes and the bird would transform the painting, but then what?

Margaret blew on the canvas, appalled at the layer of dust. Endings were never easy for her. Relationships, her art career, Peter going deaf. She'd had miscarriage after miscarriage when she was married to Ray. Only Peter came out of their efforts, though she'd dreamed of babies, little girls, running just ahead of her, through flowers and meadows, so often that she recognized and named them. Charlotte, Rose, Katie. Ridiculous. She'd put an unhealthy amount of hope into Peter's eventual children, but shortly after they married, Bonnie had said she didn't want kids— she wanted to make a difference in the deaf world. Funny, Margaret thought, isn't that the point of having kids? But she kept quiet, not wanting to interfere.

A tall gray flat file held her other work. Margaret hadn't opened the drawers since she'd moved in. There was a drawer on her draftsman's desk, too, filled with colored pencils, markers, Conté crayons, pastels, charcoal, and erasers. All of it unused. She should donate it to a school. Against the wall leaned stretching boards with watercolor paper ready for painting. She usually stretched five at a time and filled them up in a week's time. Spring will inspire me, she told herself. Ellie's garden in full bloom would inspire anyone.

The towel in her hand was long forgotten. In its place were thousands of memories, flooding her heart and mind. Glory came into the studio. "There you are," she said. "Come on out into the front room. I'm heating the milk. If we're going to make cocoa, let's do it up right."

"Yes," Margaret said. "Sorry. Lately I've been so absent-minded," she said, knowing it was probably due to the MS.

From the kitchen window they could see Aspen racing around the backyard with the dog. "Hard to believe she has a heart problem, isn't it?" Margaret said. "Any news from the doctor on that front?"

"We're thinking about taking her to Cedars in Los Angeles. It depends on Casey's wishes. I'm an honorary grandma, so I have to walk a fine line."

"How is Casey?"

Glory smiled. "That girl astonishes me. She's nearly finished her GED. Joseph has her working at the stables, helping to design the programs for Reach for the Sky. Casey loves the horses. We trailered Brown Horse down from the pueblo just after Christmas, and her dog, Curly, is already part of the pack. Having Brown Horse at the stable gives her a reason to get out every day. I look at her and think, How tragic to have missed your girlhood. I wonder if she'll ever get over that."

"I'm no psychologist, but between raising Aspen, riding horses, and living with you, she will."

"Seriously?"

"Of course."

"I don't know," Glory said. "After all she's been through."

When Casey was fourteen, two brothers had kidnapped her. They'd kept her in terrible conditions, brainwashed, assaulted, and raped her. Aspen was the result of rape, and Casey had given birth to her while she'd been held captive. Her freedom had come about through her daughter's grave illness, which led to finding her sister, Juniper, Glory's adopted daughter. Watching Casey's progress amazed Margaret. Surviving that trauma had taken real courage—Casey was strong.

While the milk warmed on the stove, Glory and Margaret sat at the table and Margaret jiggled Sparrow's bouncy seat with her foot. "Humans are endlessly adaptable, Glory. When Peter got sick, I wept in the hospital corridor and prayed my heart out, making bargains with God to just let him live. When he went deaf, I thought it was the end of the world. Now he has a lovely wife, a teaching job, and a whole community. The fact is, despite horrible things, people manage to go on."

Glory nodded. "Juniper says that every time she calls home."

"I'd take that girl for my daughter in a minute," Margaret said. "Look at all she's accomplished. Finishing college at the same time others are starting it. So patient with her sister. She's a wonderful aunt to Aspen. And do you know that Chico, her beau, stacked my firewood without me asking? What a thoughtful young man. Casey will get there, too. By the way, how is your mom?"

Glory frowned. "Not great. She's on a new drug. Benlysta? It's given via IV. Took me months to talk her into trying it. I hope it helps. I wish I could talk her into moving out here."

The smell of scorching milk filled the air.

Margaret stood up and went to the stove. "Did you take the pregnancy test while you were in the bathroom?"

Glory nodded. "The directions say it takes ten minutes to develop. I figured if it turned out positive, you'd be here to soften the blow."

Margaret reduced the flame and added four tablespoons of the Dutch cocoa to the steaming milk, whisking it until it turned a rich chocolate brown and adding a tablespoon of honey. "Would it be so terrible to have another baby?" she asked.

Glory laughed. "Picture me running after a toddler while I'm nursing a newborn."

"Well," Margaret said, "I suppose you can consider other options."

"Not me," Glory said. "What if he turns out to be another Joseph?"

Margaret smiled. "Or he could be a she."

"It's definitely a boy," Glory said. "Snips and snails and all that. What is a 'snip,' anyway?"

"Parsnip, that root vegetable, I think. Cocoa's ready," she said. "Go fetch that test and let's have a look."

"Auntie Margaret!" Aspen shouted. "There are f-f-f-fairies in your garden! I seed a million of them."

"I *saw* a million of them," Glory corrected.

"You seed them too?" Aspen asked.

"Never mind," Glory said, laughing as she headed to the bathroom.

"Is that so?" Margaret said. "How many marshmallows would you like in your cocoa?"

"Forty-eleben, please!" Aspen said.

"I'm afraid I only have six marshmallows left. If I give them all to you, then Grandma and Auntie Margaret won't have any. Do you think we could share?"

Aspen stamped her foot.

"Remember, we don't do that at Auntie Margaret's house."

Aspen pouted. "Fine, okay. I will share."

"If you have two, how many does that leave for your grandma and me?"

Aspen counted on her fingers. "One, two. Can I put them in?"

"If you wash your hands first. With soap."

The deed was done, but Glory had not returned to the kitchen. Margaret set Aspen up with a newsprint pad and some erasable markers. "Remember, we only use the markers on the paper."

"I know, I know," the little blond girl said. "Not on the wuh-wull and not on the floor and n-n-n-n-not on the dog. Auntie Margaret?"

"Yes, honey?"

"How sick are you? Are you going to get well?"

Margaret's blood ran cold, the same way it always did when Aspen let out these bits of information that she had no way of knowing. The little girl did it infrequently, but when she did, she was consistently right. It started when she knew Glory had gone into labor, and again when she told Margaret that Echo had an earache, which was confirmed the next day at the vet's. "It's true I am sick," she told Aspen, trying to make light of it, "but not very. I'll be here with you for a long, long time."

Aspen took a slurp of her cocoa. "That's what Dolores said. I loves you, Auntie Margaret."

"I love you, too. Now keep an eye on Sparrow for me, just for a minute," Margaret said, and went down the hall to find her neighbor.

Glory was sitting on the edge of the claw-foot tub, crying.

"Positive?" Margaret said.

Glory nodded. "Is it okay if I sit here awhile, cry myself out?"

"Tell you what," Margaret said. "Leave the girls with me. Go spend some time with your husband. I can give Aspen her bath, and I have instant formula from the last time I sat for Sparrow. Go on home."

"You're the best friend ever," Glory said.

"I consider you the very same."

"Aren't we fortunate to have found each other?" Glory asked her.

"Profoundly fortunate," Margaret answered.

And then she was babysitting instead of feeling sorry for herself. Probably that was the way things were meant to be.

The next morning, Casey came over for the girls. She looked like any other twenty-something in her blue jeans and hoodie, but Margaret knew—perhaps better than anyone—that appearances

could be deceiving. "How are you doing, sweetheart?" Margaret
asked as she placed Sparrow in her carrier.

Casey took hold of it with one hand and clasped Aspen's hand
in her other. "All right. Glory's teaching me to knit."

Her gravelly voice was always a shock to Margaret. "Really? I
love knitting. You should both come over sometime and we'll
have ourselves a stitch-and-bitch."

Casey laughed. "Thank you. We will."

One of the brothers who'd kidnapped her had slashed her
neck. Margaret never asked, but she guessed such an act indicated
they were tired of her and didn't want her found alive and able to
identify them. When she didn't die, apparently the older of the
two brothers took pity on her, and Casey, with courage Margaret
wasn't sure she herself could have summoned, survived. What
could have ended her life had severely damaged her vocal cords.

One of the kidnappers was dead, and the other one had
recently been profiled on *America's Most Wanted*. Someday, she
prayed as Casey waved good-bye. Let him be found, and let the
justice system extract seven years' worth of life from him. It was
only a start, but it would be something.

That evening, Margaret was standing at the sink washing dishes,
wondering how Joseph had taken Glory's news. She knew the
man well enough to be certain he would shed tears of happiness,
but he would also worry. With her last pregnancy Glory had
ended up confined to bed with eclampsia, and now, in addition
to baby Sparrow, Casey and Aspen were living with them. Glory
had told her about Casey's nightmares. Sometimes the flashbacks
of what she'd endured exhausted her for a couple of days, which

left Glory caring for Aspen. If Glory was bedridden for this pregnancy, Joseph would have a lot to do at home while trying to get Reach for the Sky off the ground.

Margaret decided she would start knitting a baby blanket. No, two of them. One blue and another yellow with pink flowers, because no matter what Glory thought, it might not be a boy. She'd make a list of casseroles, go over them with Glory, and then she'd bake them a loaf of bread every week. And cupcakes. Aspen loved cupcakes. Making them meals would be fun and would keep Margaret herself eating properly. Aspen was big on macaroni and cheese, but Margaret's recipe sneaked in grated carrot and zucchini. Margaret wiped down the zinc counters and put the dishes away in the cream-colored cupboards with the black hinges. The farmhouse sink was chipped, the chrome fixtures worn to copper in places. Margaret would never change a thing about it. She heated up water for tea and was about to sit down with the new Robyn Carr novel, *Moonlight Road*, when the computer trilled, indicating someone was trying to Skype her. It had to be Peter calling, or his wife, Bonnie. It couldn't be her sister, Nori, because she was in London.

She sat at the computer on the small desk in the living room. She logged in and clicked on Skype. A fuzzy picture of her son showed up on the screen. He was wearing one of those woolen beanies kids favored these days. She clicked to change the view from a window to full screen. "Hi," she said, signing as she said the word.

Hi, Ma, he signed. *How are you?*

Peter could still talk fairly clearly, having lost his hearing so late, but mainly he signed. He tried his best to fit into the deaf culture, but Margaret sensed there was always a bit of tension there. There was a huge rift that Margaret didn't understand between those who were born *deaf* versus those who had lost their hearing. The bridge that could connect the two worlds had yet to be built.

I'm good, she signed back. *What's up?*

OK I visit for spring break?

Yes, she signed. *Bonnie too?*

She watched the smile he put on his face. *Not this time. Busy at work.*

Something wasn't right. *When will you arrive?* she signed. *Coming into Albuquerque or Santa Fe?*

Santa Fe. Probably tomorrow, OK? I'm flying standby.

Tomorrow? That surprised her. *Of course. Everything OK?*

Everything OK. No worries.

OK, she signed back. But she didn't believe him. *How long can you stay?*

A week. OK?

OK. She smiled back. *Anything else?*

He shook his head no, then signed, *I'll text you my flight time. See you soon.*

She waved good-bye as he did to her. Click. Off. End of conversation. The computer screen saver returned to Gustave Baumann's woodcut *The Bishop's Apricot Tree*, one of her favorite New Mexico paintings.

Margaret took Echo out for a nightly pee, and as usual, the dog sniffed every corner of Ellie's garden, finally choosing her favorite spot, a patch of gravel alongside the house. Margaret patted Echo's head, and once they were inside, she locked the back door. She ran a bath and soaked in the tub for an hour, reading a book touting a low-fat diet for multiple sclerosis patients. It was one of several that Dr. Silverhorse had suggested, and she'd picked them up at Collected Works bookstore, one of her favorite places to sip coffee and shop. The women who ran things, Mary and her mother, Dorothy, had such a wonderful eye for books and for the greeting cards and gifts they carried at holiday time.

At first, the diet sounded austere and hard to follow. Margaret was used to eating pastries and the occasional steak, but those indulgences would have to go. Nothing was too much to give up if it gave her better quality of life. Dr. Silverhorse told her to read a couple of books, try out the diets, and if none of them helped, they'd discuss medication. Steroids were the most often prescribed drug. The side effects included mood swings, insomnia, weight gain, and lowered immune response. No, thanks, Margaret said to herself. I will make the diet work.

With Peter coming to visit tomorrow, she'd have to do a big shopping at the market. Peter ate as if his stomach had no bottom. The good part, she told herself, was that now they'd both be eating vegetarian. Swank's diet for MS said saturated fat was limited to 20 grams a day. She'd have to start reading labels and buying organic. The hardest thing would be finding the right moment to tell Peter about the diagnosis.

She set the book on the sink and got out of the tub. Echo tried to lick the water off her legs as she always did. "You silly girl," Margaret said as she dried herself off and put on her flannel Nick and Nora pajamas. She made most of her other clothes but splurged on these pajamas, which came out in new styles twice a year.

While she brushed her teeth, she took a good, long look at her face, noting the wrinkles and spots from sun damage. People complained about getting old. She never would again. She wanted every day she could get, especially now that Glory would need her help. "Put a kind thought into your mind the minute you wake up," her aunt Ellie used to say, "and send that little bit of cheer out to the first person you see. Good works, like good thoughts, improve life for people on both the giving and receiving ends." As always, it hurt a little to think about Ellie, the closest thing to a mother she'd ever had. Mother was stern and standoffish, but Aunt Ellie gave great hugs and told bawdy jokes. A small part of Margaret had always wished Ellie were her mother, and she knew Nori felt the same way.

Despite worrying about the impact MS would have on her life, and how to tell Peter, Margaret couldn't keep her eyes open. She was emotionally spent from yesterday's news. Echo waited, as she always did, for Margaret to start snoring, and then she climbed up on the bed, inching her way closer. For some time now, Margaret had faked snoring just to witness Echo's approach. She put her arm around the dog and went to sleep.

DOLORES

O F A L L O U R senses, emotion and memory persist the strongest. Now imagine the parts of your brain that are never used. After the corporeal death of the body, those places come to life. How I am, and where I live, makes it easy to pass through years, to fix on certain events, and occasionally, never often enough, to mete out a small justice.

Remember the maid who slowly poisoned the husband who'd killed his wife? You're wondering if I had anything to do with it, aren't you? So what if I did? There's more to tell about what had happened at the moment of the wife's death. As the firewood came down on her neck, her pain transformed into a sense memory of the farm boy she had loved in England. Their first kiss. The afternoon light that came through the barn window. The innocent way the boy had gone to her father, his employer, to ask for her hand. Her father's outrage that a common person had thought such a union possible. He'd forced her to marry the trader instead, a man of means, and a better station. *I forgive you*, she said to her father as she passed from this world to the next.

When news of her death came, her father realized his mistake.

Inside his head, a bubble formed and exploded. This is how it arrives sometimes: A stroke delivers peace. Mercy requires a second death.

Forgive me for loving you, she said to the boy, who'd been fired from his work and sent off without a penny. *I hope you found someone else to love with all of the passion you showed me.*

Even you, I forgive, she said to her husband.

The horses went wild-eyed when he went into the stables. They knew what he'd done to the only person who'd treated them kindly. So did the maid. In her culture, such acts required consequences. For a week she made the daily bread, prepared the dinners, and cleaned the adobe. When she finished with her work each day, she went to the empty barn to stand in the blood-spattered dirt, feeling the energy of fear that lingered, the point of no return. In her culture, there was a ceremony that could have helped him, but she could tell he was not the kind of man who would believe prayers, songs, and sand paintings could help. The trader would have no peace. When he crossed over to the spirit world, his trip hastened by the maid's cooking, his father-in-law was there to greet him. I don't know what transpired between them, but there are consequences for every action.

Tonight I remain fixed firmly in the present. Next door Margaret is sleeping deeply, exhausted by the worry over her illness. A reunion she could never imagine is coming her way. Meanwhile, her son, Peter, is recovering from the five drinks he'd had instead of eating dinner. He's passed out and misses every hurtful message from his wife.

Why haven't you answered my messages?

We both want the same thing. Make it simple. Sign the papers and FedEx them to me overnight.

You were a terrible husband. I faked every orgasm. You don't even deserve to be loved.

Every message she sends hides another message, a secret she won't reveal until the papers are signed. But he knows already. It cuts him worse than any blow.

Next door at Glory's, everyone is asleep except Casey. Her fear has handicapped her rest. She can sleep only on her right side, facing the door, in case it opens. The dream she has most every night is turbulent, not of this earth. When she startles awake, there is a period of vertigo as she struggles to believe she is safe.

I nestle close to her, wishing she could feel me. Sometimes, when I press, I can steer her away from the bad dreams. Sleep, dear girl, I tell her. You escaped. This family, they love you and will help you find your way. You have a beautiful child who understands the realm in which I exist. She'll grow out of it, but for now she has no boundaries, so listen to her. Remember, you have Brown Horse, and your dog, Curly. The woman who died in the house next door loved her horses just as much. Rely on your dog and she will comfort you. Dogs are knowing beings. And I know this: The man who hurt you is on his way to be judged. When he arrives at his destination, all your tears and sleepless nights will end, because he will end. Those of us here will make certain of that.

Deep inside Glory's womb, arm and leg buds are growing. Outdoors, the hummingbird is building her nest. I linger by the dresser, a weathered old pine thing with layers of varnish and paint, cleverly sanded and roughed up so that the age of the dresser becomes its best feature. Age begets wisdom.

Chapter 3

T HE NEXT AFTERNOON, Margaret sat at her easel, painting a watercolor of two bluebirds perched on a wooden fence. She added sunflowers, the bright yellow and gray-brown centers depicting a summer day, and in the distance, the outline of an adobe house. She set it aside to dry and lifted the next board stretched with paper, just waiting to be filled up. On this one, she painted an adobe house with a blue wooden gate. In front of the gate she added terra-cotta pots and had just begun to fill them with geraniums when a door creaked. Echo looked up, raising her hackles. Was the door in her house or Glory's? She walked through her house, wondering which door it was because she didn't remember leaving any open. But the door that led to the garden wasn't shut. She must have left it open this morning when she let the dog out. It could have been knocking in its jamb for hours. Once she started painting, she tended to tune out the world.

Echo nudged past Margaret to the open door. The dog's hackles smoothed down as soon as her paws hit the pathway outside. Margaret saw that the honeysuckle, which had been thick with leaves and buds yesterday, now had two yellow blooms. The sweet fragrance was faint but intoxicating. Then she heard the buzz of her cell phone from the kitchen counter, indicating a text. She turned and rushed back up the steps, losing her balance and falling to her knees. Lord, it hurt. Echo was at her side instantly, whining and nudging her with her nose. "I'm fine," Margaret told the dog. "Just a scraped knee." The fall had torn her painting jeans. No great loss. When she got up, she held the banister as she made her way into the house. She was limping, and she knew Peter would notice. She grabbed a cold gel pack and sat down, placing it on her sore knee while she read his text.

Plane arrived early. Can you come get me?

Of course, she text-messaged right back. *About half an hour, OK?*

OK. ILY, Mom.

I love you, too.

Forty-five minutes later—the city was tearing up Cerrillos Road again—she arrived at the small commuter airport, where instead of punching a parking ticket, you went to a kiosk and left money in an envelope, the amount depending on how long you intended to be away. Peter stood by the glass door and waved when he saw her. Good, she didn't need to park. She could stay in the car and he wouldn't notice her stiff leg.

She popped the lock on the passenger door, and he opened it. "Hi, honey," she said, taking her hands off the wheel to sign.

He was chewing gum. He sat down and pointed to his left ear, grinning.

What the hell? Was the pale blue earpiece a cochlear implant?

Margaret couldn't help the disapproving expression that came over her face. Why hadn't Peter told her he was undergoing surgery? Peter did everything the hard way, and he rarely called except when he was in trouble or needed money.

"Don't look at me like that," he said out loud. "It's not like I got a tattoo, Ma. The only thing that's changed is I can hear you."

She pulled him close and hugged all six feet of him, including the backpack on his lap. Moms were always the last to know anything important. She pulled back. "You could have called," she said, automatically signing as she spoke. "Would it have killed you to let me know you were going under anesthesia?"

He shoved the backpack to the floor in front of him. "No way. That would have spoiled the surprise." He twisted around to the backseat in order to hug Echo, who was beating her tail triple time, trying to climb over the seat to get to him. "There's my girl," he said, and Echo began that yipping, keening whine she did whenever she saw him. A reminder that Margaret came second, always had, always would.

"Echo Louise the Second, I missed you oh-so-much," he sang, and she rolled over to show him her belly.

Margaret shook her head as he reached back to ruffle the dog's fur. "Peter, I wish you'd let me know you were having surgery. Did everything go all right?"

"Of course it did. Look at me. I'm strapping and healthy, all that. You worry too much. Want me to drive?"

"Not right now," she said, not wanting to limp around the car to switch seats. "You must be tired, so just relax."

"I slept on the plane."

"I can't imagine how. Those commuter jets have no legroom. School going all right?" she asked.

"Can we talk about work later? I just want a real spring break. No students e-mailing me, no meetings, just quiet."

Well, you came to the right place, she thought. She drove back to Ave de Colibri, and though traffic was light, he still managed to nod off a couple of times on the short trip. He probably does need a nice, quiet vacation, she thought. I'll let him use the car. Maybe I should give it to him. After her fall today, she was thinking maybe there wasn't as much "normal" time left as she had imagined. If the MS got bad this early, she should stop driving. God, what next? Near tears, she parked in the carport that barely fit a car, let alone her ancient Land Cruiser.

Indoors, Peter spit out his gum and put it in the trash. He leaned against the kitchen counter while Margaret made coffee. "Look in my mouth. Way back, the molar on the right side." He opened wide and showed her what looked like black plastic covering one tooth, held in place by a retainer.

Margaret smelled alcohol on his breath. Maybe he'd had a drink on the plane to numb his fear of flying. "What is that? A temporary crown? You're awfully young to need one."

"Nope. It's a study I volunteered to be part of. With the cochlear implant, I can hear with my left ear. This device conducts sound from the bone in my left ear to the one on the right, allowing me to hear with my right ear, too."

"What study?"

"Does it matter? Mom, I can hear. Both ears."

Years back, a surgeon had told Margaret the auditory nerve in Peter's right ear was likely beyond help. She'd thought, One ear is better than none, but he'd obstinately refused the surgery that would allow that ear to function. It had taken her years to accept that it was his choice to make, not hers. Clearly he'd finally changed his mind. "Does language sound like you remember?"

"It seems tinny, but hey, it's been ten years. I'd still know your voice anywhere. And I can listen to music. I just have to remember to charge the apparatus."

"Peter, I'm floored."

"It's not that big a deal," he said, but his smirk told her otherwise. He sat at the table.

"Well, I'm very happy for you. Is there anything special you'd like to do while you're here?"

"Ride Red. Hike Bandelier. Eat home-cooked meals." He smiled at her hopefully.

"I'll cook whatever you want. Just give me a shopping list."

"I can cook, too," he said.

"I know you can. So, where's Bonnie? She couldn't take some time off work to join you?"

Peter scratched Echo's neck, and the dog groaned in pleasure. Ignoring Margaret's questions was an art form Peter had developed since adolescence. She opened the fridge, and the dog got up. The sound of Echo's toenails on the linoleum sometimes drove her crazy, but if the dog had a single bad attribute, it was going nuts when someone had to trim her nails. Margaret needed to take her to the vet and pay them to do it in order to keep the peace, but she hadn't made time. Now that Peter was here, maybe he could take her.

Margaret looked out from the fridge. "I can tell you right now, there's sprouted bread and lemon tarts in the freezer, almond butter and one leftover green chile enchilada. I haven't had a chance to go to the market yet, so we could go out to dinner. La Choza? Plenty of restaurants within walking distance."

"Maybe I'll just have a cheese sandwich," he said.

Peter still ate dairy, which Margaret was supposed to remove from her diet immediately. He'd been a vegetarian since his early teens, which she blamed on a school report on factory farming. She always thought one day he'd pick up a burger and that would be the end of it. But he'd stuck to his principles, and just look at him, so trim and healthy, with a bloom in his cheeks.

Echo whined. "Why don't you take her out for a quick walk? The air will do you good. Meanwhile, I'll fix you a plate."

"Sounds good," he said, and stood up.

And when your stomach's full, and you're ready for a nap, I'll tell you my news. The diagnosis. How I fell today. Why I'd better stop driving.

Chapter 4

S KYE PRESSED THE button on her watch, and the face shone blue. Two in the morning, officially Friday, thank God. It felt to her like anytime, any year, anyplace out here. Or some kind of dream landscape, maybe. But her dad had come for her. After ten years not hearing from him, he was like a stranger to her, but here he was. What Skye remembered about the day her father left was this: She'd just gotten home from school, lugging her books in the pink backpack he'd bought her for the new school year. She didn't have any homework because she'd done it during lunch. She didn't have many friends. Other kids didn't like her because she was smart, always getting the top grades on tests and winning spelling bees. She also tended to hit first and try to work things out later, which did not go over well with anyone. Nobody sat with her at lunch, so she figured she might as well get her homework over with so she could spend the weekend riding her horse. She was twelve and a total barn rat. Not one horse, not even that insane Arab her teacher owned, scared her. When a horse bucked, she made herself limp as a sack of potatoes, hung on to its mane, and knew all she had to do was wait it out. A tired horse gave you a better ride.

Back then, she thought about horses constantly. How to improve her skills and win more blue ribbons in gymkhanas, the monthly riding competitions. Learning tricks. Did she want to be a trick rider more than she wanted to be a veterinarian? It was a tough choice. Why not do both? The veterinary degree would prove to be most useful, but training on the weekends seemed possible. When Mama and Daddy were seriously fighting, like lately, she had to think of something besides their yelling or go crazy. Horses it was.

Her parents were the kind of married people who never actually engaged in normal conversation with each other. Instead, they threw barbs and guilt bombs that would explode later. Daddy would come home from shoeing and say, "I picked up six new clients," by which he meant this month the bills would be paid on time. Mama's response should've been, *Good for you, and congratulations, because I know how hard you work*, but instead she'd say, "And when are you ever going to mow the lawn? Our house is the shabbiest one on the street."

"I can do it, Mama," Sara would say, but her mother wanted her dad to do it, because that was his job. This particular afternoon, it was clear to Sara that they'd been going on like this for some time. She heard them from the front yard—Daddy's rumbly low bass and Mama's screeching—which meant their neighbors could hear, too. Sara stopped on the porch before going in. When she heard the sound of plates breaking, her daddy opened the door. He was carrying a duffel bag. There were shorts hanging out of it and the zipper wasn't pulled all the way.

He looked at her for a second, as if he were considering taking her along, but then he looked away and hurried toward his truck. Skye watched him throw that duffel in the bed and start up the engine as if it were a race. If he had just stopped and told her what was going on, she might've felt different, understood, in a way.

He didn't even say good-bye.

Still on horseback, she heard the whir of a truck on the highway, though she couldn't tell how far away it was in the early morning darkness. The air was cold on her face, and her nose ached from breathing in the chilly air.

Her father's face was in shadow. Every once in a while the flare of highway lights caught on his belt buckle. He had attached a replacement tire for his truck to his horse's saddle, along with a bedroll and God knew what else. It made him look homeless. It had been years since she'd heard one thing from him—and somehow tonight after midnight he shows up at Cottonwoods? "Daddy?" she asked. "How'd you know to pick me up?"

"A phone call from your mother."

"Are you kidding me?"

"No. She phoned to say you needed a ride back to Santa Fe."

Well, that was the last answer she expected, which made her all kinds of curious. Was Mama listening to her phone messages after all? "You and Mama, how long have you been speaking to each other?"

"We've kept in touch occasionally. Yesterday was the first time we talked on the phone. So that makes it a total of one day." He laughed.

Lightning whinnied, sending thrills up Skye's spine the likes of which she hadn't felt in years. Being on a horse woke up muscles she forgot existed. Her riding posture kicked right in. She loosened her reins so that Lightning could make up his own mind about the bit. That had always been their unspoken agreement. She'd be light and kind; he'd give her a nice ride. Haul out the spurs or a riding crop, even if it was for show, and she'd find herself dumped on her butt without having ever felt him buck. "Lightning," she whispered, and leaned forward to smooch him on the neck. He smelled exactly the same, a touch of vinegar to that sweet, dusky horse musk.

Her dad had been quiet until she asked a question. What should she say next? Where the hell have you been? Everything's forgiven and I love you? She felt her temper getting riled, and she shuddered under her hoodie sweatshirt, cold. Her goose bumps had goose bumps. "I have another question."

"Let her rip."

"What am I supposed to call you? Father? Dad? Sir? My hero? How about asshole who disappeared from my life? Bad Dad? What?" Her heart felt as if it might bust open with anger. "I never thought I'd see you again and now you're here in the middle of the night, which casts a certain dreamlike quality on things."

"I can see how that would happen," he said.

She gathered her thoughts, trying to put them in a logical order, and *boom!* Her temper exploded. "Damn you, anyway! Now I have to readjust my feelings on everything. Feelings always get me into trouble. That's what got me drinking and using in the first place. I've been sober nine months. If I slip because you showed up, well, I'm going to kick some ass your way."

He reached over and patted her hand where it rested on the pommel of an Australian stock saddle. Her father preferred them over western saddles and rarely rode any other kind. She wondered where her western saddle had gone to. "Just hearing you say that means you won't."

"How do you know?"

"Experience. You go right ahead—call me the Asshole if it'll help you stay on track with your sobriety. Now that I'm here, right beside you, I ain't going anywhere ever again except to the afterlife. Probably take me to the end of my days to make up for leaving you, but I'm by God going to. In no time at all you'll be sick of me."

Skye stifled the sob that threatened to bust out of her chest. In group, back at Cottonwoods, the endless weeping of other drunks and addicts made her irate. Duncan always stopped group to allow the person crying time to get it all out, to travel to the source of the trigger, which was often some ridiculous moment from childhood that didn't mean anything important. "Losing a spelling bee? Wetting your bed? Seriously?" Skye blurted out one day. "That's ancient freaking history. Delete it from your mind like a computer file."

That afternoon, Duncan took her off bathroom-cleaning duty and sent her to crafts class. Pottery: throwing clay on the wheel. "Dude, you're making a mistake," she said. "I have no art skills, no desire to create anything, and frankly I'd prefer cleaning toilets."

"Nah," he said. "This is where you belong."

He wouldn't let her quit. For months she worked at that clay stuff, making lopsided bowls and ugly cups that cracked in the kiln—instant trash. One day, it was finally going well, and right there on the wheel in front of her she had done it, made something that was not half-bad. So what happened? She broke down sobbing. Her muddy, chapped hands left clay on her face like clown makeup. She ripped the perfect bowl from the wheel and squeezed it through her fingers until it was ruined, and out of her came this primal howl that released the floodgates. Duncan stood in the doorway watching her, and for the rest of her life she would hate him for that. Wasn't it enough that he'd watched her detox? That she'd slipped? Smarted off? Would he not allow her a single shred of dignity?

The next group meeting, he told the story of the Long Walk, a tragedy that took place during the Civil War yet was entirely separate from it. His voice remained steady as he spoke. "General James Henry Carleton, commander of the New Mexico Territory, right around here, near Four Corners, had success-fully exiled the N'de, or Mescalero Apaches, so took it upon himself to solve what he called 'the Navajo problem.' Pitting tribe against tribe, he ordered the Diné villages burned, wells poisoned, crops trashed, and livestock killed. Some ten thou-sand five hundred Navajo were marched four hundred fifty miles through winter and summer to Bosque Redondo at Fort Sumner. If you straggled behind, you were shot and left to rot. Some women were taken as slaves, and children stolen from their families. Smallpox, dysentery, and pneumonia ravaged the tribes. Of the ten thousand or so who started out, maybe eight thousand survived."

Skye was looking at her rehab-issued ugly slip-on tennis shoes at the time, doing her best to block out his voice and almost succeeding, which was a mistake, because Duncan had freaking radar for that kind of thing.

"Skye?" he said. "Look at me."

She lifted her head and was surprised to see tears coursing down his cheeks while he maintained his poise. God, was there anything worse than seeing a full-grown man cry? "Look, I get it," she said.

"What is it you get?" he asked.

"That it's awful, that persecution happens, only the strong survive, what the hell else do you want me to say?"

"Right this second? I'd like to know what's in your heart."

"You want to know what's in my heart? All right, I'll tell you. I'll freaking tell all of you. Half of you are whiners, plain and simple. You," she said, pointing to Duncan, "should be ashamed of yourself."

"Why?"

"How can you minimize something so terrible, turn it into an anecdote for a bunch of worthless alcoholics and addicts?"

He waited a beat, never a great sign, she had learned, and he said, "History is evidence of cultural extermination. Culture is built on dreams. Dreams become art. Art comes from the gods. Tell us about learning to throw pottery."

He just *loved* making her cry.

"I'm sick of you already," Skye said to her father. "What is it? Three A.M.? I can't even see your ugly old mug, and the horses probably can't see where they're going, either."

"Never said I was handsome," her father said. "But you are just about the prettiest girl I've ever laid eyes on. People love to say, 'She favors her mother,' or, 'She's got her dad's ears,' but honey, you are a hundred percent your own self."

Skye could not admit how happy she was to see him because in equal parts she also wanted to slap him. "Oh, shut up," she said. "Compliments aren't going to make me forgive you."

"Didn't expect them to," he said. "Just saying what's in my heart. It's up to you to say your piece."

What's in my heart? It was like he was channeling Duncan. "There're some things about me you should know," she said. "It's way too much to say in one conversation."

"I read your letter a hundred times. I got so I could fill in the blanks."

. He laughed that same old chuckle she remembered from childhood.

"I even talked to Mr. Duncan a time or two. Heard about the night you were in the hospital. I was worried sick."

"He called you?"

"I am your next of kin."

"He shouldn't have. I'm over eighteen—I'm a legal adult. It's supposed to be confidential! That's a violation of HIPAA or some damn thing. After I beat the shit out of him, I'm getting a lawyer."

"You almost died."

"I did not."

"Yes, you did. Maybe you should take a look at the doctor's chart."

Beneath her, Lightning trembled as her temper rose. She breathed out, trying to stem the anger.

"Now, Skye, before you explode, listen. He was doing us both a kindness. He cares about you and wants more than anything to see you succeed. That night might not have gone by the book, but he's invested in you, just like I am. He helped me see my part in all this when I was inside. I wasn't a good father to you."

"A kindness? Breaking the law is more like it. And what do you mean 'inside,' anyway? Inside of what? Were you in the hospital or something? Next are you going to tell me you're dying of cancer?"

He let a minute go by. "I went to prison."

"Excuse me?" All the air went out of her lungs. She had to gasp to take it all in. If I ever needed you, Higher Power, this is the time to show up, Skye thought. She waited, bit her tongue, but he didn't say anything and she was out of words. God stayed in his heaven or did whatever he did when he wanted you to figure things out on your own. They rode along in silence, listening to the sounds of the night and the crunch of underbrush the horses were trampling. She was on her beloved horse, and right there next to her was her father. Who was an ex-con. For *what?* She pinched herself to make sure this wasn't a dream she was having back at Cottonwoods, the kind that always made her wake up in tears, with Nola, that crazy, bone-thin bitch, trying to freaking hug her. Skye was not, had never been, nor would ever be, a hugger.

Unless the hugger was Gracie. Her throat went thick.

The moon was a crescent in the heavens, and every couple of seconds, it seemed, there went the silver streak of a shooting star. On one of her last nights at Cottonwoods, she'd sat on the portal watching the night sky. Nola came out to sit with her. "Stars are angels rebelling against God," she said.

"If you truly believe that shit," Skye told her, "you will be stuck on Planet Crazy for the rest of your life."

"Has anyone ever told you that you're very intolerant of others' belief systems?" Nola said.

"Nola, I'm telling you this for your own good," Skye said. "I've spent almost a year living with your wackadoo worldview. How many years have you been here? And yet I am rejoining the world and you're not. Why is that?"

"Duncan says it's because I can't accept my program."

"Sometimes Duncan is full of shit. Stars are made of hydrogen and helium. They explode like a nuclear bomb. Fortunately for us, this takes billions of years, otherwise we'd all be dead of electromagnetic radiation. By the time they hit our atmosphere, they've turned to dust. There are no angels out there. They are made-up shit to keep you from taking responsibility for your life. That is all I have to say on the subject, and I hope you listened, because apparently nobody here has the cojones to tell you what your problem is. Stop believing in all that mystical crap, Nola! Crystals are rocks. They don't have souls. They are just rocks. Like everything else in this world, they come from dust or turn to dust. The End."

She hadn't taken it back that night, and only now did it seem a little mean. Just a few hours with her dad and all the anger she felt toward him seemed stupid, too. Her father had been locked up and she hadn't even known. "What did you go to prison for?"

"Assault."

"What kind?"

"The kind where two drunk people start throwing punches, and one of them thinks it's a good idea to bring a pool cue into the mix."

"Whoa," she said, thinking, That's hard-core. They rode on for a few more minutes. Then she said, "It's been a rough day. I'm tired. How long is it until we get exactly where we're headed?"

"A ways. My plan was to come and get you in the pickup hours ago, but turns out my tires weren't on board with the idea. That's what happens when you garage a car for a couple of years. When I got the flat, I realized I didn't have a spare. I couldn't leave the horses long enough to get some help at a gas station, so

I saddled up and ponied yours alongside. We got our tire and then we rode parallel to the highway. I'm sorry it took me so long. Sometimes things just happen."

"What I meant was, now what are we going to do? Where are we going?"

He stopped his horse. "We can throw down our bedrolls here and call it a night," he said. "Or we can ride all night to my friend Joe's house, then throw our bedrolls down on his floor, and sleep all day tomorrow. Might have to sweep his floor first. He's not the tidiest creature."

"Do you even know where we are?"

"'Course I do," he said. "I've ridden this part of New Mexico more times than I can count. It's up to you when we stop. Let me know your druthers."

Druthers? Who used that kind of language in the twenty-first century? Underneath her, she felt Lightning shiver, wondering what was happening. Skye shivered, too, and pulled the string on her hoodie tighter. All day the heat had about killed her, and now it couldn't be more than 35 out. Maybe all this *was* a dream. Maybe they'd just ride until the end of the earth, she and her ex-convict father, until they fell off along with the meteoroids and burned into dust. All she had left was frayed nerves. "Old man, you got a smoke on you?"

"Quit that a long time ago. You should, too."

Skye nodded, though it was too dark for him to see her. Actually, she'd quit smoking when she got pregnant, and she didn't really want one now. Smoking was just something to pass the endless time without having to talk, or worse, *feel*, and it was dangerously close to a drug, if a legal one. They moved on.

Ten minutes later, her father stopped his horse. "Sugar, we aren't making as good time as I'd hoped. I recommend we throw down the bedroll and call it a night. It's another five miles to Joe's house, and the horses are tired."

She thought of Gracie, waiting for her, crying herself to sleep. "But you have the tire. I'd rather keep going."

"It's hard to change a tire in the dark."

"You have a bedroll. I don't."

"Then I guess it's a good thing I brought two bedrolls." Her father dismounted and waited for her to climb down. She stared back at him, her hands on Lightning's reins.

"I ain't Charlie Manson," he said. "I'm your father. I was an idiot when I drank, getting into fights with anyone that looked at me sideways. Which is one of the reasons I don't drink anymore."

"Not even champagne on New Year's?"

"Not even."

Skye swung her leg over Lightning's right side and slid down. "That person you busted up, was he okay?"

"After he got patched up, thank goodness. I got enough bad stuff on my conscience without adding the burden of taking a life. He was hurt pretty bad, though. For a year I tried to live with it, keeping a low profile. Then I turned myself in, pled guilty to assault, and was I ever lucky. The guy I hit came to court and asked the judge to be lenient."

She patted Lightning's neck to say thank you for the ride. "Why would he do that?"

"I can't say. I suspect he had a lot of time to think while he was healing. Maybe he realized the fight started because back then, every time he opened his mouth he felt compelled to insult whoever was nearby. Maybe he found Jesus. Who knows? All I can say is I'm grateful. Instead of sitting in the cell for the remainder of my days, I have the opportunity to reunite my beautiful daughter with her daughter."

At the mention of Gracie, Skye felt that lump back in her throat. She turned away, unbuckled Lightning's cinch, and lifted off the saddle and blankets. They hit the ground with a thud, despite her efforts to lay the whole business down easy, to avoid spooking the horses. Her dad was much better at it. She watched him take off their bridles and replace them with halters, and then ground-tie them so they wouldn't wander. He fetched them both feedbags, and while the horses ate, he checked their feet with a penlight, making sure nobody had thrown a shoe or picked up a stone. Then he brushed them both with a rubber currycomb and wiped it against his jeans to get the hair off.

"Why'd you get in the fight in the first place? I thought the furthest you went with stuff like that was yelling."

He looked up. "Alcohol. I stopped drinking right after the fight. Fell off the wagon once or twice, but since I went to prison, not a drop. I go to meetings whenever I can. As you know, it's not easy. And unfortunately, nobody wants to hire an ex-con. I'm getting a little long in the tooth for roadwork and construction, but I'll take any work that comes my way."

"What about shoeing horses?"

"When someone wants me to, I do it. A lot of younger shoers out now. They do the job faster than I care to, charge less."

"All right, Daddy," she said. "We don't have to talk about it anymore. Thank you for being honest with me."

He unrolled the sleeping bags and she unzipped one and sat

down. She yanked off her boots, shook the dirt off them, and tucked them in the foot of her bag out of the reach of scorpions. She hated scorpions. Getting stung once, on her butt no less, was enough for a lifetime. "This reminds me of camping when I was a kid," she said, though back then she'd never experienced this jittery, lost feeling that made it impossible to relax. She wanted an OxyContin tablet more than a glass of vodka, but either would do. Both would be better.

Skye had loved camping and fishing with her dad, even if she never caught anything. She felt sorry for the worms, so he ended up having to bait the hooks. He pan-fried the fish they caught in bread crumbs and bacon grease. They tasted better than any restaurant food she ever had. Her daddy had come for her, even after his truck threw a tire. He had come on horseback, and he had cared enough to fetch and bring her horse, so that when she settled down in Santa Fe and her sobriety was wobbling, Lightning would be there for her.

"You hungry?" her dad asked.

"Not really."

"Too bad, because I have some beef jerky and chocolate. Plain M&M's. I remember those being your favorite. Probably you outgrew them."

"Hand them over. Otherwise I'm going to have to commit larceny, and then where will we be? Two unemployed ex-cons."

He laughed. "Now that's the girl I remember. You know, once we get to the truck, I'll drive you wherever you need to go, Skye. I have a little money saved, and it'll get you started. I want you to be happy. I want you to stay sober, but that's up to you. Other than that, whatever you need, if I can help make it happen, I'll try."

She could hear the snuffling of the horses, some night bird complaining, and the faint *whoosh* of cars in the distance. Any of that was preferable to listening to Nola pray her New Age prayers and waking up to her stupid chanting, *I name it, I claim it, and so shall it be.* "What I want . . ." She paused to take hold of herself, willing the telltale break in her voice to go away. "Is my little girl back. I don't care about anything but being a good mom."

"'Course you do. You don't have to tell her who I am, but I'd sure like to meet her."

"Why wouldn't I tell her who you are?"

"My record isn't all that good."

"Oh, Daddy. Just stop." Emotions were exhausting. Any second her eyes would close and she would be dreaming. It had been a shit day. But on the plus side, she wasn't at Cottonwoods or anywhere near Nola. In group, Duncan had let people get angry and vent, but by the end of the day, he asked everyone to forgive one another and mean it. His favorite quote about this wasn't Navajo at all: "The first to apologize is the bravest. The first to forgive is the strongest. The first person to learn from it becomes the happiest." Smart-mouthed, Skye asked, "What brilliant Navajo said that?" And he surprised her by disclosing that the quote came from Nishan Panwar, an India Indian kid on Facebook.

Skye thought she said, *Don't be ridiculous. Gracie needs a grandpa as much as she needs her mama. It takes a village, remember?* And that he replied, *Thank you.* But she might have dreamed it.

The ground was hard and cold when the sun came up. Skye's back hurt, and as she rolled up the sleeping bag, she noticed a rock directly under where her shoulder had been. Funny, but she swore she could smell the sunshine, heating up the rabbit brush and piñon trees. She didn't know the proper terminology for the phenomenon but felt sure there was one. Lightning was there, but her dad and his horse weren't. She didn't have time to wonder about that because she heard the sound of her dad's truck. "Camping in April is for Boy Scouts," she said, first thing, more to herself than to him.

Her father had ridden his horse back to his truck, changed the tire, put the horse in the trailer, and driven back before she woke all the way up. He gave the horses some hay, poured a gallon jug each of water into a bucket, and let them drink. "We've got to get to a feed store soon. I didn't plan on this taking more than a day."

She stretched her arms and rubbed at a kink in the small of her back. "First Starbucks we see, I'm ordering a triple shot with whipped cream on the top."

"Joe makes coffee so strong you can stand a spoon up in it. Get those fancy boots of yours on and let's hit the road. Looks like today will be another scorcher."

Skye rolled up the sleeping bags. "All I care about is picking up Gracie."

"Well, so far there's nothing to get in our way," her dad said.

The five miles went quickly in the truck. Soon they turned on a dirt road that was bumpy enough to make Skye hang on to the seat. They were on reservation land, where a few of the houses were halfway decent and others not so much, with old tires strewn about and broken-down cars with weeds growing through the engine compartment. Skye counted reservation dogs—called "brown dogs" by the residents—wandering around and thought of spanking the shit out of the kids who were throwing rocks at them. Skye almost asked her dad to stop the truck but didn't want to waste a minute getting to Gracie. One rangy female followed alongside the truck for the longest time, barking, then turned away. They came upon a weather-beaten mobile home set up on cinder blocks. Next to it was the skeleton of a decomposing five-sided hogan, quite a bit of twisted chicken wire, tumbleweeds, warped plywood, and enough broken glass that it reflected like glitter in the sun.

"We're here," her dad said, and opened the truck's door.

"Why?" Skye asked. What could possibly be the reason for stopping at a place this wrecked? "Can't we just book it to Burque?"

"Got a few things to pick up," her dad said. Before he did anything else, he unloaded the horses. He led them into a corral that had seen better days. Inside was a swaybacked white mule that looked older than time itself.

"Think the horses will be okay with that animal?" Skye asked.

"'Course they will. Joe's had that mule since before sliced bread got invented," he said. "And he loves it, so don't make any nasty comments. By the way, the mule's name is Lightning, just like your horse."

Skye just stared.

"That was intended to be facetious."

"How? Funny or ironic?"

"Your choice. Check the water trough, will you?"

"There's water in it," she said. "It's mossy green in places. I think I see a fish."

After he unsnapped each lead rope from the horses, he walked over to look at the trough for himself. "What do you know? Filled for once. Joe must be on the wagon."

"Great," Skye said. "Just what we need, another alcoholic."

An ancient blue heeler with three legs came out from under the trailer and started barking. Her dad squatted, and the dog came toward him, spinning in circles with excitement. "Hopeful Jones," he said. "You old cuss. I didn't expect you to be waiting for me. You must be twenty years old."

"Don't insult your elders," came a voice from the trailer's door.

The man was possibly the skinniest Indian Skye had ever seen, wearing a faded red AIM T-shirt, surfer board shorts, and cowboy boots. His black hair was braided into a ponytail that reached down to the small of his back. His skin was so pocked and scarred and his face so craggy that all he needed was a head scarf and people would mistake him for Keith Richards. This must be Joe of the strong coffee, she thought. Sure doesn't look like someone my dad would fraternize with. His grin was pure happiness.

"Ya hey," Joe said. "If it ain't my old *biliganna* white-man friend, showing up with an *asdzaa nizhonion* as usual. You're an old man, Owen. Who's this pretty young thing hanging around your saggy ass?"

Owen? Skye's dad's name was Bill.

"She's my daughter, you old fool. No smart remarks, you hear me?"

Pretty soon they were both laughing like hyenas and the dog was licking her father's face. Skye could not imagine what they found so hilarious, but the dog really needed a bath. When Joe motioned for them to come in the trailer, she reluctantly followed. "Welcome to *La Farmacia*," Joe said.

This guy was a druggist? Doubtful. With men, everything was generally in plain sight in the place they lived, and she saw nothing medical here. Rocky's story, for example, came in the form of an equine syringe he used over and over, as if horses didn't get sick from dirty needles. Joe Yazzi's interests were apparently historical protests, like AIM, the political movement that had ended long before Skye was born. As long as presidents needed FBI security, Leonard Peltier would never get pardoned. Among Joe's protest signs: *Payback for Indian Boarding School. Address the Broken Treaties. No Fracking on Reservation Land.* Skye didn't know exactly what that last one meant, but she didn't care to find out. She sat at his rickety kitchen table. Spread over every inch were screwdrivers, a hammer, various pincers, a can of WD-40, and the guts of some mechanism she couldn't identify. She picked up a metal part that reminded her of a Lego. Nothing about it said druggist.

Joe said, "I see you're interested in my time machine. I'm going to patent it and get rich."

"I know what you should do with all the money you make," Skye said.

"What's that?"

"Redecorate."

Her dad came into the trailer, the dog by his side. "Joe, stop messing with my daughter and heat up some coffee for your old friend. Also, if you have any hay I could feed my horses, I'd be happy to give you some greenbacks."

Joe cackled, his voice and appearance aged by cigarettes and booze. "I'm going to call Lefty right now," he said. "He'll bring a bale right over. All my mule can eat is Quaker Oats. Once a month I borrow Lefty's truck and drive to Costco, buy me a pallet." In the middle of all that junk, he retrieved what looked like the latest-model iPhone. Skye looked around the place, trying to reconcile the fancy phone with the worn-out furniture and dented metal percolator on the two-burner stove. Where had her dad come across such a person, and furthermore, what made them friends? Maybe he'd been in prison, too. The three-legged dog lay down on an old blanket. Stumpy-tailed heeler, the blue variety. Her dad had a dog with three legs? She would have thought he'd put an animal like that down.

Clearly there was a lot more to her dad than she had assumed.

When the men went outside to wait for the hay, Skye found the bathroom, then kind of wished she hadn't. She shut her eyes while she peed so she didn't have to look at the filthy towel hanging from a hook on the wall. The bathroom was worse than she'd seen at any bus station she'd ever been stranded in, even outside of Joplin after the tornado. She dug around under the sink for TP, saw a dusty canister of Comet and a sponge, and started scrubbing. When she finished with the sink, a quarter of the cleanser was gone. She opened the gross shower curtain. Men living alone saw nothing but the water coming out of the shower head. Mold was simply not in their visual field. She scrubbed, trying not to see more than one inch at a time. Then she did the toilet.

Next, Skye pulled aside the torn window curtain to allow some light into the bathroom. She saw her dad and Joe leaning against the corral fence, laughing and feeding the horses as another pickup drove off. She envied the way men could pick up friendships wherever they had left off, no matter how many years passed. After she'd married Rocky, the few friends she'd had pretty much disappeared. They went off to college, or got jobs in New York, or got married to guys with normal jobs and had their babies—planned ones, not by accident.

Her dad and Joe were out there so long, she went back to the kitchen area to make the coffee herself. All Joe had was a big can of ground Folgers. No cream or even powdered milk, but there was a ten-pound bag of sugar. While she waited for the water to boil, she picked up Joe's iPhone and tried Rocky's number. Nothing but a full mailbox message. What if he'd taken Gracie and run off? What if she never saw her little girl again? She tried what she thought was Rita's number, but her closest guess turned out to be, of all places, a tire store. Near tears, she cleared a space on the table, laid her head down on her arms, and cried herself to sleep.

She woke up cranky, with a sore neck. Joe and her dad were playing cards at the table beside her. Her dad was dealing. Joe let his cards sit facedown in front of him. "I got a feeling about this hand," Joe said. "Bet me something worthwhile, like your truck."

"Hell, no," her dad said. "That old truck of mine has never let me down, other than throwing a tire now and then. Everything I own in the world's inside it."

"Then bet me something else," Joe insisted. "How about your Levi jacket with the sheep fleece lining?"

"A, it would fall off your skinny old carcass, and B, I won't bet you a dime unless you offer me something worthwhile in return. You've had the excellent companionship of my dog for the last ten years, and since I been here you got fifty dollars of mine for the hay, not to mention exciting company. Tell me some rez news. Is Verbena still weaving? How's her daughter, Minnie?"

Joe looked away. "*Those ones.* A car accident."

"The both of them?"

Joe looked up toward the ceiling, which Skye saw was holding a cobweb contest. "Gone."

"Sorry I asked," her dad said.

"Ah, cheer up. I'm still here. And it's about time for my herbal treatment. I'm happy to share."

Skye turned her head and stared at him. "No way am I sitting here while you smoke marijuana and cause me to fail a drug test."

Joe smiled. "Beauty speaks! No need to fret over legalities. I got a prescription for it."

"Well, I don't."

He lit his pipe, took one hit, and put it out. "Ah," he said, exhaling slowly. "Hits the spot all right."

"What spot's that?"

"The nerves in my legs. Got some painfulness, you know?"

"Did you leave me any coffee?" she croaked. Her arms smelled like Comet, and that cloud of smoke Joe exhaled smelled like something that had been run over. She waved her hand. "Why does pot have to smell so bad?"

Joe took the pipe out of his mouth and set it on the table. "Last time I saw you, Miss Sara Kay, you was still in diapers. Now you're a full-grown woman. Thank the powers you don't take after your dad. He's a nice guy, but he has an ugly old mug I wouldn't wish on the dog."

"It's Skye now, and you shut the hell up," she said. "That right there is my dad you're talking smack about."

Joe raised his eyebrows. "*Aieee!* Got her snake-charmed already. So, Owen. How was the pen? They having you punch plates or what?"

Who was Owen? Was it some kind of nickname? Skye knew she needed coffee before asking that question.

"Nah," her father said. "Since I was a model prisoner, I learned how to train service dogs. It was a bundle of fun compared to working in the laundry, where I was the rest of the time."

Joe laughed. "Steamed your pores open, *init?*"

Her dad laughed, and Skye watched the two men joke with each other, close as brothers. All these years her dad was a fuzzy memory to her, and the real thing turned out to be so different, she had to make room for it. "How long have you two known each other?" she asked.

Joe overturned his cards and dropped them on the table. "Man, is my good old Injun intuition off today. This is the worst hand in the history of Bicycle cards." He got up, poured Skye coffee, fetched an open can of sweetened, condensed milk, and set it on the table next to her cup.

"Doesn't anyone ever answer a question around here?" Skye said.

Joe laughed. "I was getting around to it. Shoot, has to be twenty-odd years now. Your old man and I used to calf rope together. They called us the cowboy and the Indian. Man, we were good. Kills me that I can't ride no more. My spine is disintegrating. Of course, so's my mule's. What a world, eh?"

"You been to see the sawbones?" Owen asked.

"Surgery's a waste of time. Nothing they can do except plug me full of pain medication, and I been sober two years now, so none of that for me. If it comes from a plant, smoke it. If it's made in a plant, refuse it. I got everything I need with the *farmacia.*"

"Pain pretty bad?" her dad asked.

Joe smiled. "It's not something I look forward to every morning."

"How do you get by?" Skye asked.

Joe held up his pipe. "This, when it gets bad. Otherwise, I use my Jedi mind tricks. I think of the best sex I ever had. So many choices! Might take hours! Or I take my mule for a walk, talk to the dog, stroll down memory lane, or make a sandwich. I love me a fresh sandwich. What else do you need in life?"

Owen snapped his fingers and the old heeler got to his three feet, rear end wagging, and headed toward the table.

"That dog," Joe said. "He's one heck of a listener."

Skye could tell the Indian loved him.

"I got to say, I didn't expect to see him alive," her dad said.

"Yeah, prison can make you *hopeless*."

"Very funny," her dad said. "Dog's name is Hopeful," he explained to Skye.

"On account of he was the only pup out of the litter to wag his stump when he saw your dad's face," Joe said.

Skye compared the limping Indian and her dad and saw they weren't much different. Both looked rode hard, both were wearing old clothes, but Joe's ponytail was neatly braided and her dad's hair was recently cut. "Which one of you wants to explain to me who this 'Owen' is?"

Joe whistled. "That's one for your dad."

Her dad squatted and used his fingers to comb the dog. Just like any heeler, whatever time of year, he was blowing his coat and clots of hair drifted about freely. For a long while Skye just stared and waited while her dad focused all his attention on the dog.

Joe tapped her arm. "Sleeping Beauty? Need a refill?"

"No, thanks. My heart's going like a jackhammer. What's in this stuff? Doubt I'll sleep for a week."

"High-test coffee and herbs. It's a secret blend only us Navs know about," he said.

"This better not make me fail a drug test," she said.

"Relax. Some creosote and yerba buena." He winked. "Thanks for tidying up my lavatory."

Skye ignored the wink. "You have something personal against cleanliness?"

"Women's work," he said gruffly, and then laughed at her outraged expression. "Got you going for a minute there. Do you realize what a great guy your dad is? He saved my life more than once."

"I was wondering where all your scars came from. Were you guys fighting buddies or something?"

"Mine are courtesy of the U.S. Armadillo," Joe answered. "Thought I was gonna be a warrior for my country. Famous, like the code talkers. Turned out I was duped by the Man."

"Hence all the protest signs?"

"Nah, the sign carrying is just a pastime. Mainly I enjoy whipping up all the cowboys down at the Walmart. I focus my attention on herbs and native plants for old-timey medicine. I operate the rez *farmacia*."

"Somehow I can't really picture you and my dad being friends."

"That's because he's a different guy from your childhood dad. Bill Sampson, he wasn't much good, I hate to say. Owen, he's the real warrior in the game of life."

Skye thought that remained to be seen. "And his dog?"

"Hope's the most useful dog I ever met. He's killed, let me think, four or five rattlesnakes? Got 'em nailed to a board, somewhere around here. Tourists buy the skins for making belts. Anybody got a gopher coming into their garden, they borrow Hope, and poof! Bunch of dead gophers lined up. Not afraid of nothing."

"Hope? He looks older than you. How's that possible?"

"Them heelers are tough like a dingo. I expect someday he just won't wake up. I'll miss that old bugger when your dad takes him back."

"Where the hell are we going to put a dog?" Skye said. "Mama's pied-à-terre has only one real bedroom. One of us is going to have to sleep on the floor."

Her dad shrugged. "I won't be there that long." He got up and walked outside, the dog following.

Joe said, "Hope don't take up much space. He's an easy keeper. Sleeps under the trailer. Feeds himself hen's eggs, shells and all, when I forget to feed him."

"How can you forget to feed a dog?"

"Does he look like he's starving to you?"

Skye sipped her coffee, which tasted like melted butter-pecan ice cream thanks to the sweetened condensed milk. She was grateful for the caffeine rush and the sugar, but instantly nervous at how good it made her feel. If it felt good, she immediately wanted to overdo it. *That's addiction talking*, Duncan would say. She sat across from this crazy Indian, drinking away a full pot of coffee as if that were natural, and all around her were packets of "herbs" and pot smoke. She listened to Joe's explanation of each herb's properties, pretending to be interested, and watched while her dad trailered up the horses. She and Joe joined him outside to discover that the wind had come up fierce enough for her to shut her eyes. It was throwing sand around like wedding confetti. They were about to head out when her dad began a conversation with the dog.

"Here's the deal," he said, bending down on one knee like he was going to propose. "If you want to stay here, I'm good with that. I been gone a long time, long enough for you to change alliances. But if you want to come along, that's all right, too. I will feed and water you before myself, and I promise I won't leave you again until one of us heads to the Pearly Gates. Up to you."

And the crazy thing was, the dog cocked his head as if he were thinking about it. He went back to Joe, head butting the old Indian on the knee, then turned and leapt into the cab of the truck.

"Traitor!" Joe said, laughing. Without saying good-bye, he went back indoors and shut his door. At least for now he has a clean bathroom, Skye thought.

Her dad laughed. "Scoot over," he told the dog. "Otherwise how am I going to drive this bucket of bolts to Burque?"

Skye got in the passenger side. "I still want to know who this 'Owen' is."

"Long story," her dad said.

"Last time I checked, it took five or six hours to drive to Albuquerque."

"I don't know if that's enough time," he said.

"I ain't giving up, Daddy."

"That's readily apparent," he said.

While Skye watched the scenery go by, her father apparently collected his thoughts. When they drove past the turnoff for Cottonwoods, she gave it the finger.

"Girl, you need to put a governor on that temper of yours."

"I inherited it from you."

"There's this saying, maybe you've heard of it? 'Do as I say, not as I do'?"

"Your dog smells like cow pies fresh out of the oven," she said.

"I agree. First dog wash we come to, I'll give him a bath."

Skye rolled down the window and yawned, hoping the fresh air would help a little. Instead, grit carried by the wind flew inside the cab and went right in her teeth. "Oh, yuck!" she said, spitting.

Despite the coffee, Skye fell asleep hard, her head against the window. Her dreams were filled with Joe Yazzi in some kind of flying machine and her dad holding the string to a kite that turned out to be that smelly, three-legged heeler dog. When she next woke up, they were in Taos, at an Allsup's. Her dad was filling the tank and the trailer was gone.

"Where're the horses?" she asked.

"Left them at a ranch near here that boards. Don't worry. Once we're settled, we'll come back and get them."

"Well, I might've liked to say good-bye."

"I can drive you back."

"Never mind." She went to the bathroom (nice and clean) and then walked back to her dad. "Can I have a couple of bucks?" she asked.

"What for?"

Her cheeks reddened. "A box of Red Vines."

"Sara, that stuff is bad for you."

"It's Skye now, *Owen*. S-k-y-e. It's not like I'm asking for vodka. Though if you want me to be totally honest, that sounds even better."

He sighed and reached into his back pocket for his wallet. "Hate to tell you, but that feeling never goes away."

Skye accepted the five-dollar bill and said, "Don't crush all my dreams at once." She turned and walked back to the convenience store, feeling his eyes follow her. Didn't even get to say bye to Lightning. Even though she hadn't seen her dad for ten years, she had to take his word for it that her horse was safe. Son of a biscuit. As she scanned the aisles of candy, she thought of Gracie. Why did they put everything bad for you right up front, at kids' eyes' height, and make it affordable? Maybe if she ate only half the box, she wouldn't gain any weight, but truly, her body was screaming for sugar, anything to soften the edges, and candy was legal.

Back in the truck, she struggled to pry open the ungodly tight cellophane on the box, wondering whose marketing idea that was. Imagine if you made it to old ladyhood and had arthritis. This could take all freaking day. Then her dad took the box from her and stuck a key into it, making a rip. "Thanks," she said.

"My pleasure, so long as I get a couple of those whips."

"You're as bad as me, aren't you?"

"'I taught the weeping willow how to cry.'"

Skye laughed. "Yeah, right. You and me, we're potatoes in the patch."

"Huckleberry friends."

"Grapes in the bunch."

"Which make a healthy lunch." He started the truck and put his head out the window to check for traffic. He was always a good driver. She remembered when he used to let her sit on his lap and steer. Dangerous, but it was fun.

The licorice itself was slightly stale, sharp on the edges, which was perfect. Some folks liked aged wine; Skye liked licorice past its shelf date. She ate one stick in mincing pieces, while next to her the dog drooled. "You're not my problem," she said, but ended up giving him half a vine anyway.

"That was kind of you," her dad said.

"You I am not talking to," she answered.

"What the heck happened in the last twenty seconds?"

"I've got one word for you. *Owen*," she said.

He sighed. "Fine, I'll tell you, but you're not going to like it."

"Do I look like I'm worried about liking it?"

"So long as that's settled," he said. "The name Owen means 'warrior.' Garrett is for Patrick Garrett, the unsung hero who killed Billy the Kid."

"Tell me the rest of it."

He talked about fresh starts, cutting ties with the past, pushing guilt out so that hope could settle in its place, and she mulled it over in her mind. Before she knew it, they were in Albuquerque, surrounded on the east side by the Sandia Mountains, home to the balloon festival, and north to south, crouched over the Rio Grande, the river Duncan called *Tó Ba'áadi*.

Chapter 5

AT NINE THIRTY Saturday morning, Margaret opened the door to check on her son. In D.C., where he lived, it was already eleven thirty A.M. She'd been up for two hours, finished the *New York Times* crossword puzzle, and done one load of the laundry he'd brought. His clothes were appallingly worn and faded, his pants shiny at the knees. Peter, always a clotheshorse, had come a long way from that, and she wondered why. After last night's dinner, without asking, he'd fetched a bottle of wine and opened it up. This morning, she'd found the empty bottle in the recycling. Was he hung over? Was he still breathing? How did she summon the courage to ask him about his drinking? Was that even appropriate? He was twenty-five years old.

She found it consoling to see that the adult Peter slept the same way he had as a teenager, before the accident. Facedown, feet hanging off the mattress on her convertible couch, a stranglehold on his pillow as if it were a life preserver. Echo II had curled up between his legs, her head resting on his thigh. The dog looked up at Margaret, wagged her tail, but made no move to jump off the bed for breakfast.

Margaret didn't mind. Peter had a way with animals. When he was a boy, he brought home nestlings, a baby chipmunk, and then one day, Echo, the puppy who waited by the front door until he returned from school every day. Peter wasn't like that with people. Echo I had been the one to bring him back from the coma he'd suffered as a result of meningitis years ago, and his bond with animals had only grown. In Santa Fe, half the population would say it was being in the coma that caused it, that he'd come so close to the spirit world that he'd returned to the living profoundly altered.

Out the kitchen window she could see gray sky, overcast. No real clouds, just wisps of darker gray scudding along. Snow? Calling Glory might be an intrusion, but sending her an e-mail would not. Margaret was anxious to know what Joseph's reaction was to the unexpected pregnancy. The Vigils were like extended family to her. She logged on to her computer to check her mail. There in her in-box was a message from Joseph with a link to his website. It was finally up—his cousin's nephew's friend had been building it over the last three months. Glory had said Joseph was tearing his hair out trying to get the kid to take down the raucous music he insisted would make their program appear "sick," which meant, as near as Glory could figure, "cool." Joseph said the music made him want to put a bullet into the computer monitor. Margaret laughed to herself. Nothing at the Vigils' ever ran smoothly, but a messy, sprawling family in which someone was always laughing or crying was the kind of family Margaret had hoped to have herself. She clicked on the link.

Reachforthesky.org ran across the top of the site, with tabs for drop-down menus. In the background was a beautiful New

Mexico sky, postcard blue as far as the eye could see. They'd posted a gallery of photos. Margaret clicked on one of RedBow, Peter's horse. *Red is a quarter horse/mustang and at age 22, our most senior citizen. From rodeo to trail horse to lesson horse, Red's done it all. He loves tiny tots and trotting, and will dance for apples.*

Margaret smiled.

Dressage wasn't dancing; it was work and required hours of lessons, but dancing made for better copy. Peter had taken lessons from a trainer for four years. The horse seemed to thrive on learning. The *passage* and flying lead changes were beautiful to watch. Peter had looked stunning in his riding habit, and Red was handsome with ShowSheen emphasizing his muscles and his mane plaited into braided knots. With his tail braided, too, no one would ever guess he'd once been a team roping horse allowed to grow shaggy.

Next Margaret clicked on a photo of Aspen with her gap-toothed grin. She sat on Brown Horse and wore a pink riding helmet and matching gloves. Next to her stood her mother, Casey, one hand on the horse's reins and the other at her side. She looked just to the left of the camera. She had a hard time making eye contact. The bandanna she wore around her neck looked perfectly appropriate. No one would ever suspect it hid the scar on her neck from her horrible injury. Glory had mentioned they were exploring surgical options to minimize the scar, which made people seeing it for the first time gasp out loud. But first came the delicate vocal cord surgery, which would hopefully return her voice to a normal range.

In another photo, Joe looked dangerously handsome in a pair of chaps, leading Juniper on a Palomino named Dollar Bill. Reach for the Sky took retiring horses, provided they had gentle natures, were not excessively lame, and could see out of at least one eye. There was even a photo of the two barn owls that made their nest in the ceiling of the barn. The whole enterprise sounded so exciting to Margaret. It was all due to Juniper's sister, Casey, who'd benefited from this therapy when she came to live with the Vigils. Yet they made no mention of Casey's involvement except as a parent and volunteer. The testimonials they posted focused on the results of the programs, not the traumas they served. She read on.

> A handicapped child's environment is a daily reminder of what he or she cannot do. At Reach for the Sky, we strive to show the opposite. From the first time a child is on top of a horse, looking down, he learns to see the world differently. Developing a relationship with a horse removes significant barriers and inspires mutual trust. Our staff psychologists are also riders. Through a unique combination of equine-related therapy, horsemanship, recreation, and fun, we are dedicated to improving the quality of life for adults and children with disabilities and physical and emotional trauma.

Margaret had met the psychologist who was responsible for Casey's reunion with her sister. Ardith Clemmons had twenty years of social service experience, and given her conservative blazers and pearls, you'd never guess that in her youth, she'd been a trick rider on the rodeo circuit. Who better to tell someone to get up, dust yourself off, and get back on the horse than Ardith Clemmons?

Margaret saved Joe's e-mail, bookmarked the website, and composed an e-mail to Glory.

How'd it go? Hang in there. Nausea can't last forever. My son
Peter showed up last night. I can't believe you haven't met him
yet. If only he'd been able to come for Ellie's funeral. Anyway,
I'd love for you to meet him before he heads back to D.C.

XO Margaret

Margaret wasn't usually one for hours of web surfing. She didn't use
Facebook other than to showcase her work, and the same went for
Instagram, Twitter, and YouTube. But e-mail was essential, especially when it came to selling her prints. Gift shop orders came in
weekly. She sold on Etsy, OOAK, and her website, margaretwood
.com. She'd left off the "year" in her name, because she wanted this
site to be about selling prints, not "art." A dubious difference.

While she waited for Peter to wake up she had some time to
waste, so she looked at MS sites and joined a chat room for
newbies, though she couldn't imagine what she'd say in one. *I'm
terrified?* After a few minutes of reading scary medical histories,
she took a walk down virtual memory late, looking up websites
she'd bookmarked long ago. Advanced Bionics, Inc. The NIDCD.
YouTube. She figured she alone was responsible for at least a
thousand hits on the video "29-year-old hearing for the first
time." How she had longed to give that experience to Peter, and
here he'd done it on his own, after ten stubborn years of silence.
Now her son would hear it all: traffic noises, birds chirping, a
voice whispering, "I love you." She wondered if he'd told his dad
about the cochlear implant yet. Maybe this would make a difference in their troubled relationship. If Ray became more a part of
his son's life, it would make her happy.

Next she visited another favorite video. Her fingers typed,
"Extreme Sheep LED," and hesitated over the arrow icon to start

the video. Watching felt illicit, like drinking alone. Nobody knew how often she watched it except the computer's browser history, but it was so frequent that she felt a sense of shame— there were much healthier activities she could indulge in than watch videos that reminded her of Owen Garrett.

The first time was right here, at the small desk in her front room. It was her first Christmas in Ellie's place, sans Ellie. Margaret had pared down considerably when she left California, but in those couple of years in Blue Dog she'd acquired more stuff. Now that she was living in Ellie's smaller house, she decided another paring down was in order. Nobody was going to come to a winter garage sale. Whatever wasn't essential would go to Look What the Cat Dragged In, a thrift store that benefited shelter animals.

So there she was, by herself on Christmas Eve, culling shoes she hadn't worn in years and old boot-cut jeans that weren't in style anymore into a trash sack. There was no one to prepare an elaborate meal for; Bonnie and Peter were spending the holidays in D.C. and Margaret had sent out their presents a month ago. Her sister, Nori, was in London, working, and Margaret, usually just fine on her own, wondered where the tears were coming from. She sat at the computer to check her e-mail before she went to bed. Nori had sent her a link to a YouTube video, a cat climbing a Christmas tree or something. Nori was the cat person. Of course, once Margaret watched it all the way through, up popped a slew of video suggestions she might enjoy. Christmas carols, home movies, cats and dogs decorated with bows. Echo II sat at her feet, agreeable to whatever Margaret suggested. "Why not watch other people's lives if you have none of your own?" she asked the dog, who beat her tail happily against the old wood floors. From Christmas carols to reenactments of Joseph and Mary's trek to Bethlehem, she landed on a video of Welsh sheepherders who'd rigged their flock with LED lights. When they whistled, their border collies moved the sheep, creating a green Christmas tree with a white star on the top. The star wavered side to side, because the sheep wearing the white lights apparently did not relish their position at the top of the tree, and that made her laugh. Margaret thought about Owen Garrett on horseback. That three-legged heeler dog of his was responsible for knocking up Echo I. To allow the dog to run off his energy, Owen would saddle up his horse and whistle to the dog—his name was Hope—to move twenty sheep around the pasture until he was tired. She must have watched the video fifteen times that night. Outside it was blizzarding and everyone had hunkered down for the holidays.

It wasn't as if her loneliness were self-imposed. She'd tried to make friends here. She'd joined a bookstore reading group, but the members of that group didn't really talk about the books so much as they gossiped about whoever hadn't made it to the meeting. She met a nice woman—also an artist—while waiting in line to pay taxes. They struck up a conversation and seemed to have a great deal in common, so Margaret impulsively offered her phone number, inviting her to have coffee sometime. The look the woman gave her in return was searing. Did she think Margaret was trying to hit on her? Anything Margaret said made the situation worse. She didn't want to lose her place in line, so she spent the rest of the time pretending to check messages on her phone. Such awkwardness. It brought back the embarrassment she'd felt in junior high when she'd tried to befriend one of the popular girls. For a week, they'd pointedly shunned her, and even though it had happened long ago, she never forgot the unbearable feeling of being deliberately excluded.

Margaret attended a women's networking luncheon at the Hotel Santa Fe, a lovely place with kiva fireplaces, soft leather armchairs, and excellent food. They also had a free parking lot, which was scarce in the downtown area. There was chicken salad for lunch, followed by panna cotta for dessert. During coffee, the various businesswomen introduced themselves to the group. This took over an hour, and by the time it ended, Margaret was dizzy. How many acupuncturists, massage therapists, caterers, professional organizers, and therapists who specialized in color therapy, the way of the whale, the dolphin mind, the wolf path, and phases of the moon she hadn't known existed could there be in this town? Not to mention more yoga instructors, shamans (shawomen?), poets, novelists, biographers, ghostwriters, and filmmakers of every sort than she could imagine. There were twice as many artists as the rest of the women added together. Every single one of them had a story like hers. They sold their work at the flea market, but you had to get on a waiting list to join and pay a fee. The farmer's market also allowed an opportunity for art, but the percentage they took made it not worth the effort. Become a museum docent or work in an art gallery, they suggested. Press your business card on every person you meet.

The art scene was so competitive that the other artists only seemed to be seeking valuable contacts and connections. No one else seemed to be interested in trying to build true friendships, and Margaret couldn't imagine trusting any of these women with her innermost secrets. They weren't the give-you-a-hug, be-there-for-those-times-when-you-need-an-ear type. Those kinds of friendships had seemed gone forever, until she met Glory, two years ago, when her family moved next door. And Glory was nearly a decade younger than her.

Margaret learned if you were a single woman in your fifties, either you had massages at Ten Thousand Waves, ate lunch out every day, or shopped your way into finding friends. That wasn't Margaret's scene. At the training schools in town, she took advantage of low-cost massages. The students needed someone to practice on, and Margaret felt starved for touch. She needed to tend to her body, remind it that kind touches existed, even if there were no soul-deep kisses or passion. She shared laughter with Glory, but Glory's hectic life meant that sometimes weeks would go by where they said nothing more than hi and bye to each other. The thing she really missed—and there wasn't a friend on earth who could provide it—was sex. At age fifty, how did you explain that to someone without sounding like a pervert? She was forced to rely on her memories of what it was like to make love with Owen Garrett ten years ago, on his creaky-spring twin bed in a bunkhouse that was so often visited by mice that in their afterglow they'd inevitably hear a snap when a trap went off. "Reckon I'm fighting a losing battle," Owen often said in his bass voice. "The best I can hope for is reducing their numbers." That was what she missed the most: being held in a man's arms, satisfied, and happily discussing mice in the grain bin.

After the sheep video ended, she tried to come back to earth, but it was easier to let herself fall gently into memory. Her sheepherder may have been rough around the edges in appearance, and in trouble with the law, but he knew how to coax Margaret out of her head and lead her into her body. He didn't have any tantric moves or engage in fancy tricks with his tongue. He made love the way he laughed, with a deep, rumbling pleasure that seemed to emanate from his belly and resound through his entire body, pouring joy into hers. Passion was different for every woman. She'd had her share of we-can't-wait-let's-tear-our-clothes-off-immediately encounters with her ex-husband, Ray, and even with the sheepherder at the beginning of their affair. But after that, she and Owen had settled into the comforting, routine, missionary-position type of lovemaking. When he ran his fingers through her hair, it was as if he ignited some hidden erogenous zone. They had always begun there. Then he'd kiss her, sharply, hungrily at first, almost crushing his mouth into hers, and move his hands down her body, so softly, his fingertips barely brushing her breasts. He teased her into a kind of fever with those slow touches everywhere. He'd take hold of her inner thighs, gently prying her legs apart and using his thumb to make circles where they met. And once he was inside her, he moved agonizingly slowly, the exact opposite of her ex, Ray, who rushed the whole encounter, wanted it over with in as little time as possible. How did men learn all that? she often wondered. Porn? *Penthouse*? Did they shut their eyes, picturing that perfect fantasy-woman's body? What happened when they touched the ordinary one in their bed?

She pressed replay on the sheep video and paused it on the close-up of the Welshman on horseback. She could see his hands holding the reins gently, how he leaned forward to tell his horse which way to turn. That was the part that reminded her of Owen. They'd gone riding together only a handful of times, but she'd noticed the way he held his reins with the lightest grip, as if he carried on a constant conversation with his horse's mouth. He listened and adjusted, probably could have let go and the horse would have continued on the way Owen wanted to go. That was what she missed, being touched by someone who was entirely in tune with her needs.

"Mom?" Peter said, yawning in front of her. "What are you thinking about? You were like a million miles away."

She quickly turned off the screen, smiling at the sight of her grown-up boy in sweat pants and a Gallaudet T-shirt that had seen better days. "What to make for breakfast."

It was rare she got the chance to cook for anyone besides Glory's tribe, who seemed to live on Frito pie and spaghetti. She had a few Meyer lemons in the fruit bowl, so why not use them to make pancakes for Peter? While he read the paper, she grated the lemon rind and removed all the seeds, then squeezed juice into the mix and the remainder into an ice tray to save for another time. She rinsed blueberries, chopped pecans for the batter, and browned MorningStar Farms vegetarian sausages in a frying pan. The smell had always been what caught Peter's attention, but now he could hear the cooking sounds along with the aroma. It was close to eleven o'clock when she set the plate down in front of him. He set aside the newspaper. Echo was parked under his chair.

"You sleep okay?" she asked.

"Like a rock."

"Do you take your implant out, or do you sleep with it?"

"Out. It has to recharge all night. Plus, sleeping in silence makes for a better night's sleep."

"That makes perfect sense." She took a pancake from the stack for herself and spread it with butter. "What time is it in D.C.?"

He handed her a napkin. "I don't know, lunchtime?" He picked up his fork.

"Did you want to check in with Bonnie?"

He frowned at his pancakes. "Do you have any maple syrup?"

"Oh, sorry," she said. "They're so sweet, I usually just have them with butter. Sometimes Devon cream."

"Have me arrested for liking maple syrup," he said.

The comment surprised her. Was it meant as a joke, or was it as hostile as it sounded? She got up from her chair to go to the fridge. "It's no problem," she said, trying to distance herself from the tone in his voice. The fridge seemed to always be on the brink of empty when her son was around. She fetched the tin of Canadian maple syrup she kept on the lowest shelf. It was pricey stuff, but she splurged, because it would last her a year. Peter, however, would go through the tin in a week, especially if she cooked like this every morning. "Here you go." Sure enough, he poured a rather large puddle over the stack of pancakes, drowning out the subtle taste of lemon and the tart blueberries. She watched him inhale the food and sipped her coffee. "What's it like?" she asked. "Or are you already so used to it that you don't think about it?"

He chewed and swallowed. "What's what like?"

She pointed to her ear.

"Oh, hearing." He smiled. "It's incredible. When they turned the cochlear implant on, I bawled like a baby."

Margaret warmed her hands on her coffee cup. "I wish I'd been there. I also wish you'd let me know you were going under anesthesia. You know, things can go wrong."

"Mom!" he exclaimed. "For crying out loud, am I not an adult?"

"Of course you are, Peter, but it was a general anesthesia, right?"

"And you knowing that would have helped how?"

Echo whined beneath the table. Peter reached down to give her a neck rub. "Sorry. I just, you know, wanted to do it on my own."

"I respect that," she said. But it still bothered her. "Why now? Why not years ago when the doctors said—"

His nostrils flared and Margaret knew she'd asked too many questions.

He set his fork down. "I didn't tell you because what if it didn't work? If I'd gotten your hopes up, and then wrecked them all over again, I wouldn't be able to take it."

She could see the tears in his eyes. "I see. I'm sorry for pecking at you, Peter. Everything turned out fine. Let's not argue while you're here, okay?"

There were a million things she wanted to say, but she chose to be quiet rather than be honest and get her head bitten off.

Peter sniffled and the tears retreated. "That first night, I couldn't bear to go to sleep. I was up until four A.M. on iTunes, listening to all the music I missed. And eating potato chips, listening to the crunch."

She smiled. "I can imagine."

"Yeah, but who knows if it will last? That's why I signed up for the Stanford medical trial for my right ear. I know, I know. It's a crapshoot, but what do I have to lose, really?"

Margaret set down her coffee cup and reached for the pot, to refill it. "What are you talking about, Stanford?" Had he told her already, and she'd forgotten? Was it the MS?

"I told you last night."

"So tell me again."

"Stanford's got a stem cell program trial coming up. They're already using the treatment in South America. It's amazing, Mom. They harvest cells from your forearm, where the hair grows. They tweak them in the lab, and get this—they regenerate a *pluripotent* hair cell for the inner ear. I'm on their list for my right ear. There's too much damage for a cochlear implant, and while the tooth cap helps, this could work all on its own."

"It sounds thrilling. What was it like the first time you heard Bonnie's voice?"

Peter blotted his mouth with a napkin. He pushed his plate away and looked straight into his mother's eyes. "Jeez, Mom. Just come out and ask, why don't you?"

Her cheeks flamed. "I didn't mean to pressure you. But I noticed you weren't wearing your wedding ring and I just wondered—"

He folded his arms across his chest, never a good sign. Echo got to her feet and plunked her head into Peter's lap, watching his face nervously. "You're a fine one to talk. You don't tell me everything, do you?"

"What are you talking about? I—"

He cut her off. "Are you sure you really want to know?"

"Of course I do. I love you and I want you to be happy. You know that."

Peter made that scoffing noise he used to make when he was fifteen. Translated, it meant, *You hopelessly lame parent, I wish you could hear yourself like I do.* "You were against us getting married in the first place."

"Not against it, Peter. I just didn't see what the hurry was."

He shook his head and sighed.

"What?" she asked, dying to reach out and touch him, but knowing that with Peter, what felt right to her often turned out to be the wrong thing to him. "You can tell me anything. And if you don't want to talk about it, I won't bring it up again. Cross my heart."

He unfolded his arms and picked up the Waterford crystal salt shaker. "You were probably right. The thing is—" His voice broke, and he set down the shaker and stopped speaking. He went straight back to signing. *Arguments. Jobs. Children.*

Margaret signed back, feeling that pit in her stomach widen. *Sorry. Prying. I'll shut up.*

"Mom," he said, "it's not your fault. Marriages break up for all kinds of reasons."

"What do you mean, break up?" This had gone further than she thought. "Are you contemplating divorce?"

"Actually, it's already under way."

"No counseling?"

He picked up the salt shaker again and turned it so that the sun reflected through the crystal, throwing rainbows across the yellow kitchen. "Too late for that. But don't worry, we're totally amicable. It's just a matter of signing papers. It will be over before you know it."

She couldn't help thinking of her mother's diamond ring she'd given to Bonnie. It was the closest thing she had to a family heirloom. Surely Bonnie would return it. "What if you separate for a while?"

He laughed and set down the shaker and looked out the window. There was a pine siskin in the tree outside, complaining that the feeder was empty. "Mom, she moved to Chicago. How much more separated could we be?"

"I knew she got offered that great job with *Native America Calling*, but I thought it was temporary."

"This is why I didn't tell you! I knew you'd act just like this."

"Like what? Concerned for my son?"

He frowned, and she caught a glimpse of the burden he was carrying. "There's a big deaf community in Chicago, and an even larger Native community."

"But you teach at Gallaudet. Surely there are a few Native students there for her to make friends with."

Peter sighed. "Mom, it's kind of like it was with her reservation family. I'm welcome there, but I'm always going to be an outsider."

"But isn't that what marriage is about? You take vows and form a bond and you become each other's family?"

Echo whined again, and Peter stopped talking long enough to reassure her with more neck scratches.

"Surely she still loves you."

He winced. "Not anymore."

"I don't understand. What changed?"

"Look. Bonnie has a full-blood Creek boyfriend. He was also born deaf. Apparently she has had other boyfriends I didn't find out about until recently. Other couples might be able to repair that kind of damage, but here's the deal, Mom. She doesn't want to."

"But you love her."

"Of course I still love her! I would have done anything for her!" He set down the salt shaker so hard that the white grains inside jumped.

"Peter, I'm so sorry."

"Yeah, well, I was planning out when and how to break the

news to you, but since you know, I guess I'll just lay the rest on you now. I'm taking a leave from teaching. Could I move home until I get settled?"

Margaret was still processing the multiple boyfriends information. She guessed this was why she hadn't received a thank-you note from Bonnie for her birthday present. Frankly, Bonnie wasn't one for etiquette, which at first Margaret chalked up to cultural differences. Peter had written all their wedding thank-yous. Bonnie was a little spoiled, Margaret had confided in Nori, and Nori had said in that sarcastic way of hers, "Gee, ya think? She reminds me of those horrible children on *Toddlers & Tiaras*." There were times Margaret watched Peter and Bonnie together and thought, Good Lord, she orders him around like he's her servant. Is that how marriage is supposed to be? Because Margaret sure didn't know. When she'd asked Bonnie to help her do something, Bonnie always refused, saying she was too tired. When they shopped, however, she had no problem at all asking for nice clothes or expensive belts to cinch in her already tiny waist.

"You're always welcome here, Peter. Do you need an attorney?"

"No, she got one. All I have to do is sign papers."

Margaret tried to hold her tongue but couldn't. "Now you listen to me," she said. "I'm your mother and I admit I'm prejudiced, but I have to tell you, I can't think of a single divorce in history that went smoothly. It's either a financial nightmare or an emotional nightmare, often both. Blame always rears its ugly head, and anger. Sometimes an angry spouse decides that money makes a nice Band-Aid."

He snorted. "Bonnie's not like that."

She gave him her gimlet eye. "Even if all you have an attorney do is check over the documents, that is money well spent."

"What if I don't have any money to pay one?"

"What about your job at the university? Isn't legal aid part of your benefits package?"

He pointed to his ears. "This has caused some problems. I was a term professor. The reason I'm taking a leave is because they didn't renew my contract. So I'm officially looking for work elsewhere."

Oh, my God. All those years he'd put in at Gallaudet. "Santa Fe's a rough job market in the best of times," she told him.

"I have an interview at Riverwall."

That was the deaf high school Peter himself had attended. "Riverwall? I doubt it has the university pay scale."

"Mom, you think I don't *know* that?"

"Of course not. I was just thinking out loud. I apologize. But what if you don't find anything here?"

"Then I'll go somewhere else."

"Such as?"

"Jeez, could you be any more negative? I'll move back to California. I'll go to London and mooch off Aunt Nori. There you go, plans B galore. Happy?" He stood up and pushed his chair in. It squeaked painfully across the floor. The dog inched farther under the table.

Margaret put her head in her hands and sighed, then looked up. "Peter, stop it. Since you're an adult, and so am I, we'll conduct ourselves like adults. You can stay here for as long as you need to. I think the guesthouse would suit you better than the guest room, but you'll have to clean it out—it's filled with boxes. And there's one condition. I insist my attorney help with the divorce. No, don't look at me like that. Aunt Ellie left me some money, so I can pay for it. You need counsel."

"Fine. Now can we talk about something else? Because I'm kind of done talking about me."

She felt ready to pop, she had so many questions. How was a mother supposed to parent an adult son? "Of course," she said. "After breakfast, would you like to go shopping? I couldn't help but notice you need some new clothes, and if you're going to stay here"—she smiled and tried hard to mean it—"then we should shop for a new mattress. That pullout couch in my studio is old and lumpy."

"No argument there," he said, rubbing his neck. "After my shower, though."

He waited until she stood up from the table and hugged her, kissing her cheek. He signed, *I love you*, and then he gathered his dishes and carried them to the sink. Margaret watched him wash them, using actual dishwashing *soap*, versus rinsing off the worst and leaving them for her the way he usually did. He set them in the drainer to dry, threw away his napkin, and shut the cabinet that held the trash can. Echo followed his every step.

From down the hall she heard the radio switch on. That was a first, too.

"Will you stop looking at me like that?" Peter said when they stopped for coffee at the Starbucks across the street from the Plaza.

"How am I looking at you?"

"Like I'm some poor rejected waif who's lost his way."

"I'm not—"

"Yes, you are, Mom."

"Well, I'm sorry. I'm having a hard time with all this." What she didn't say was, *Thank goodness you didn't have children.*

"I'm grateful that she ended it. Why stay married to someone who cheats on you? Life's too short for that. Wouldn't you agree?"

You mean like I stayed with your dad, Margaret said to herself, wondering if that was the subtext of Peter's words. Parents were supposed to set an example. She had held on to hope they could work things out until Ray got that girl pregnant, hadn't she? But she also never married again, and maybe Peter thought his life was going to turn out like hers.

She thought all those things in the time it takes to lift a grande latte to her lips, sip, burn her tongue, and set the cup down. She'd ordered Peter a venti mocha, herself the latte, and a grande chai, suspended. "What's that for?" Peter said as they sat at the table.

"The guy playing guitar outside, or any other homeless person who asks for it."

"Seriously?"

"Chai has the most nutrients." At Peter's expression, she said, "Look, sometimes I do this, okay?"

"Why?"

"It makes me feel better, all right?"

"Mom, for crying out loud, the dude with the guitar probably lives in an apartment with a fifty-inch flat-screen."

"I don't care. He's somebody's son and it's cold today."

"Yeah, and he could always sell his guitar to buy his own coffee and get a job."

She wanted to ask, *When did you get so bitter?* When had he gone from a smiling young man with enthusiasm in every step to this? When Bonnie cheated on him, that's when. Instead of plying Peter with more questions, Margaret walked around the Plaza with him. Of course he wanted to stay there all day, listening to the musicians on the stage, a Spanish group trying to sound like Los Lobos, maybe back when they practiced in garages and performed at parties for free. Music had been a huge part of Peter's life before he lost his hearing. It made perfect sense that he had a lot of catching up to do, so she sat with him and tried to reconcile everything he'd told her, obsessing a little over her mother's ring. Could she ask for it back? Or was it better to let it go? It was one of two things she had of her mother's, the other being a small Van Briggle flower vase, packed away since the move.

Maybe the divorce was a good thing. Peter's life would be wide open in a way it hadn't been since he was a child. Bonnie had always gotten her way. Had that held him back? A simple divorce, he'd said. He has no idea what he's in for, she thought. They may own nothing but furniture and clothing and have their outstanding student loans, but Peter doesn't see things the way someone who's been through it does, she told herself. Beneficiaries to life insurance policies. Cobra medical insurance coverage from the college. *Alimony.* The word struck fear into her heart. For all he knew, Bonnie was preparing to whale on him for everything wrong with her life, punishing him for having the surgery. She might even be considering a move back to the reservation. The two of them in the same state. How would that work?

"I always thought you wanted children," she blurted out between songs, while the musicians took a short break.

Peter looked straight ahead. "I did. I still do."

"And Bonnie?"

"She hemmed and hawed and finally I confronted her. She told me she did want kids—just not with me."

The mother in Margaret was instantly livid. "Why not?"

"Calm down."

"I'm calm."

"No, you're not. You're freaking out."

Her heart beat like hammers in her chest. "All right, I'm calming down."

"This might sound crazy to you, Mom, but I understand where she's coming from. If Bonnie has a child, she wants it to be born deaf, you know, into her culture. I don't have the gene that carries deafness. Because I can't guarantee a deaf child, she doesn't want children with me."

They sat and listened to the music for another half an hour or so, though Margaret couldn't tell what the band played. She was boiling with rage and sorrow and was, most of all, stunned that the girl Peter loved had hurt her son in such a cruel and selfish way. *I want Mother's ring back*, she told herself. *I want those beautiful earrings I splurged on.* A coin-shaped place in her heart burned so hot over the stupid earrings she'd given Bonnie. She wanted to snatch them out of her ears. Margaret didn't want to wear them—mauve glass trumpet lilies were much too frilly for her, but not on Bonnie, who had sloe-brown eyes and thick black straight hair Margaret coveted. She didn't want someone who'd been unfaithful to her son to have any beauty in her life. She tried to take the long view, the old the-worst-people-need-our-compassion point of view, but maybe she just wasn't that generous a person. All she could see was the head of a hammer coming down onto the glass earrings. *I want back every kind word I ever gave that girl. How dare she hurt my son?*

She looked around at the people wandering the shops. They were mainly tourists, because few people who lived in Santa Fe could afford to actually shop here. She herself visited Mimosa and Cowboys and Indians in order to get ideas for clothes, and then she shopped at Santa Fe Fabrics, the store next door to Dulce, a coffee and pastry place she loved. She sewed clothes up on her old Singer machine.

The sun had come out for a few hours. The trees were budding. Actual leaves were unfolding. But the still chilly afternoon wind whistled through the Plaza, causing her to tighten her scarf. Spring is a fickle lover, she thought, and turned up the collar on her coat. Nothing is ever guaranteed. She knew that as well as anybody. But somehow when it comes to your kids, that sort of acceptance goes out the window.

When the music ended, Peter said, "Mom? Would you mind if I dropped you back at home, and went to see my horse?"

Just like when he was fifteen, she thought. Embarrassed to be seen with his mother. "Sounds great," she said, smiling, handing him the keys to her old Land Cruiser. "What do you want for dinner?"

"Anything," he said.

"Come on. Let me cook for you. What are you craving?"

"How about your eggplant lasagna? I haven't had that since the last time I saw you."

Margaret was surprised. "I wrote out all your favorite recipes and gave them to Bonnie before you got married. I kind of thought Bonnie had learned how to make it."

"I did the cooking. Hey, I'll cook for you, too. You know, earn my keep while I'm here. I promise."

Margaret bit her tongue as they walked to the parking garage. He beeped open the car doors and she slid into the passenger seat, reaching for the seat belt, her right hand suddenly weak and causing her a moment of despair. She pulled at the strap with her left hand and managed to get it latched.

It was a perfect time to bring up the MS, but she couldn't bring herself to spoil his smile and the way he was singing along to the radio.

While Peter was at the stable, Margaret went onto Craigslist to look for a bed. The price of mattresses in local stores was insane, and maybe a used one would be in good enough shape. However, she accidentally clicked on employment instead of furniture, and what popped up first was Joe's ad.

> Reach for the Sky, a handicapped horseback-riding program, is seeking to hire a full-time barn manager. You will tend two dozen horses, be responsible for feeding twice daily, mucking stalls, grooming, arranging veterinary care, and shoeing. A background in social work, education, or related fields is a plus, as is being bilingual. Candidate must have a familiarity with horses. Experience working with youth, the handicapped, or challenged is desirable. A strong sense of ethics, and an understanding of the at-risk population we serve, is essential.

> This position includes free board in our newly renovated bunkhouse and boarding/feed for up to two horses of your own.

> To apply: Call for appointment. Bring a résumé outlining skills and provide a minimum of three references. Tell us why you want to work with horses and children to young adults.

Thank you for your interest in Reach for the
Sky. Visit our website to learn more about our
programs and other available positions.

Didn't that sound like a terrific job? Margaret thought. You
couldn't find kinder employers than the Vigils, and there was a
bunkhouse to stay in—she remembered the casita on the Starr
ranch down to the tiniest detail. The picnic-style wooden table,
mismatched salt and pepper shakers, a deck of cards, always a
yellow bottle of horse liniment or a roll of Vet Wrap nearby. The
bleached cow skull that hung on the wall was the real thing, not
something you paid a decorator hundreds of dollars for. The blue
tack box chest at the foot of Owen's bed was always latched tight.
She never once peeked inside it, but she'd always wondered what
he kept in there. Pictures of his family? His father's tools?

She remembered the careful way he made his bed every day
and the worn Indian blanket he used as a bedspread. She could
still hear the mattress springs creak their accompaniment while
they'd made love there, when they were trying to keep their tryst
a secret from Peter. She could almost feel the roughness of Owen's
hand against her skin. The scar on his face. The secrets he carried,
including the one he'd left her over: *I hit a man with a pool cue. I'm
pretty sure I hit him so hard he died. I have to go away for a while so I
can come back here and be Bill Sampson, not Owen Garrett.*

But he hadn't returned, had he? Not even for his horse. Then
Peter went straight from high school to Gallaudet, and, needing
company, Margaret had moved to Santa Fe and lived her life,
such as it was, never putting herself in the position of being
asked out on a date. She painted, tended her aunt, sold prints,
and, except for the Vigils, kept to herself. Verbena Youngcloud's

rug in the doctor's office had brought back so many memories. She should look for Verbena, even if it was just to thank her for being such a good friend all those years ago and apologize for not keeping in touch. Margaret sat down at her small easel and started painting a new watercolor that would reproduce beautifully, appear ordinary, and offer a springtime garden, a birdbath with a bird perched on the lip, or something equally pedestrian. Maybe a cow skull on an adobe wall, she thought. Those sell out quickly.

She worked, mulling over memories, until she heard a car pull up next door at around four thirty. Moments later, the phone rang.

"Margaret?" Glory said before Margaret had time to say hello.

"Glory? How'd it go?" In the background she heard kids playing, Sparrow fussing, and dogs barking, but somehow Glory was an island of calm in the middle of it.

"Joe went out of his mind. You'd think I'd brought about world peace instead of getting accidentally pregnant, for the *second* time."

"So you're going to have the baby?"

"Of course. If I can keep it."

"You'll keep it."

"If I have to stop working, or be on bed rest, if it turns out anything like when I was pregnant with Sparrow . . . well, that's why I'm calling. I'm going to need your help. But only if you're up to it, okay? We fully intend to pay you a little each week."

"Oh, hush. You know I'll be glad to pitch in however much you need me to. Tell me what you want me to do. Babysit every day? Make supper?" It was so exciting that Margaret could hardly wait to start. "This is going to be so fun."

"Now don't you make me cry, Margaret Yearwood. Right now I am held together with tissues and hormones. So your son arrived out of the blue? What's that mean? Good news, I hope."

Margaret looked out her window. A blur of white zoomed by the forsythia. "Glory, she's back! The albino hummingbird." She stretched the phone cord as far as it could go to follow the bird's path to the crook of her redwood tree. "I wonder where she'll make her nest this year? I hope it's in my tree."

"No fair. You had her last year, so this year it's my turn."

"You make it sound like I bribed her. It's up to the bird."

"Can we forget the bird for a second? None of this is why I called. On the way home from school Aspen told me that you're not well. What's wrong?"

All it would take was two letters. It would be such a relief, having it out in the open. But if she told her neighbor before she told Peter, he'd probably be furious. She took a breath and looked for the hummingbird, but she'd flown out of sight, probably gathering the tiniest of twigs to build her thumb-sized nest. Maybe she'd already built it. After age fifty, Margaret simply could not cry and still have a productive day. "I meant to tell Peter first," she finally said, "but I haven't found the right time."

"Margaret, you're scaring me."

"It's only MS."

The phone cord seemed to gather weight under all that silence. "*Only?* Margaret, no. That's serious."

"This is why I wanted to tell you in person, Glory. It's not even noticeable except on the MRI. Very early stages."

"It sounds bad enough to me. What is the prognosis?"

How did she answer when she didn't even know herself? "I'm fine right now. It was a shock to hear, initially, but really, there's nothing major going on."

"When will Peter be home? I want to meet him."

"I suppose when he's hungry. He's gone to the stable to ride Red."

"Joe just left for the stables. I'll call and tell him to look for Peter. Come on over and bring the dog. I've got blackberry scones in the oven, and yesterday I made sweet-potato dog treats. Now that I have permission to get fat, we'll eat butter and sugar and carb out."

Margaret laughed. "I'll be right there."

Dolores smiled as she drifted from one yard to another. The hummingbird had done exactly as she asked. Now it was time to check in on the writer up the street.

Chapter 6

FRIDAY EVENING, THEY arrived in Santa Fe. On the stone steps in front of Sheila's casita, Owen stopped behind Skye and whistled. "Canyon Road. This is prime real estate. I had no idea your mama had got this rich," he said.

"Well, that's the positive outcome of getting married five times," Skye said.

"Five?"

"Okay, four so far as I know, but with Mama, anything's possible. She isn't exactly talking to me at the moment."

"What did you two fight about?"

"Does it matter?"

There were two doors, the carved wooden screen door, painted with hummingbirds and hollyhocks, and behind it another door, this one made of old wood that looked as if it could have been part of a pirate ship a century ago. "It's not all that fabulous, Daddy. Do you know what a pied-à-terre is?"

"Some kind of ballet dance?"

Skye burst into tears. "Gracie was going to take ballet lessons," she said.

"And one day soon, she will."

"I thought for sure she'd be at the Trailer Ranch."

"I know," her daddy said. "We'll find her. Tell me more about the peed-off terrier."

She sniffled and rubbed her eyes. "It's pronounced 'pee-yayed a tare.' It's French and means a little place, a temporary stop."

"I like peed-off terrier better."

"Well, don't ever let Mama hear you say that. She's so proud of having a home here."

"For the record," he said, "I was just trying to make you laugh. Think any movie stars live around here?"

"Doubt it. There are much nicer houses in Hyde Park, or on Museum Hill, or in Tesuque." Just saying the name reminded her of the man who'd paid for her to turn her life around. There had to be some way to thank him. Although Milton, her old boss, wouldn't be happy if Skye showed up.

The lock was fussy, and after much jiggling of the key, she was ready to scream. "What in the Sam Hill is the matter with this thing?"

"Probably a third generation, copy of a copy," Owen said. "Hand it to me. When I worked for Rabbot's Hardware in Blue Dog, I used to cut keys. Sometimes the originals were so worn the duplicates required some handwork filing to get them to talk to the lock."

Skye had stopped crying, but she'd probably start again. Where was Rita? How could she just leave with Gracie like that and not tell Skye where she was going? Apparently tears had a mind of their own, because here came a new flood.

"Darlin'," her dad said, "if I was you, I'd go to bed early and get a good night's sleep. You're gonna need it for tomorrow when we get to work looking."

Skye, twisted up with all kinds of emotions, flung some mean-
ness his way. "Well, I'm not you, am I?"

"True enough."

"I'm sorry." The last time Skye had cried like this, she was
looking at a plastic stick that showed two lines, indicating she was
pregnant with Rocky's child.

"Here is why I know women are the stronger species," her dad
said. "When it comes to a woman and her child, she will hike
through quicksand to get to her. And you will do that, too.
Albuquerque was just a starting point. You're stronger than you
think. Joe Yazzi used to say that the reason only women were
allowed to have babies was because they could cry, whereas men
just got constipated and broke things."

Skye dropped her duffel bag on the porch. "If I was looking
for profound truths, that old hermit Indian wouldn't be the
person I'd turn to."

"You're awful hard on a guy who's been my friend for many
years." He finally got the lock to turn. "There we go. We need to
get some WD-40 in that thing. Probably a market would have it."

Once the lock finally gave, Skye pushed ahead of her dad to
go in first. "I have to pee," she said, blazing past him. The
house smelled like some horrible Christmas candle had mated
with dryer sheets. She opened the bathroom window before
she sat down to pee. Although she was proud of her sobriety,
and her dad's, it was unfortunate timing. One of them needed
to take the edge off, which would make everything go easier,
particularly in a five-hundred-square-foot house with one
bedroom and one bath. Even a half tab of Oxy would sure hit
the spot right now. She wondered if the bottom of her purse
had one.

"Wash up and get ready for bed," her dad called out to her. "I'll see if there's anything to eat."

Though it wasn't very late, Skye took his advice. She stripped down and turned the shower on as hot as it could go. She cycled through vague memories of her early childhood days. When she was a toddler and her dad gave her baths, he always made sure to put in bubble-bath powder. Just like Gracie, she'd never wanted to go to bed, either. She was always afraid she'd miss something. There had to be a reason parents poured cocktails and put on music once the kids were in bed. Gracie fought sleep so hard, sometimes Skye had to rub her back for an hour.

After her shower she dressed in a pair of her mother's silk pajamas and found a matching robe. La Perla. Navy silk with gold trim. Wow, that had to cost a week's worth of groceries. Her feet were too big for her mother's slippers, so she put on fuzzy socks and walked out to the main room to look around. She'd been here only once before, and that time she happened to be a little bit drunk. Okay, maybe a lot. And she might have thrown a couple pills in the mix, too. But Mama was hard to take sober.

Her mom had yelled at her in front of the other guests, saying Skye had ruined the housewarming by showing up "altered." Skye had known that the only way she could go to the party was "altered," and Mama was plenty "altered" herself, on gin and tonic, and said so.

The place was small, but everything in it was high-end. The floor—red Saltillo tiles with small blue ones inlaid at the corners—had been scattered with kilim rugs. The adobe walls were stark white. A weathered, rustic console table piled with leather-bound books sat in front of an Indian rug on one wall. Sheila didn't read, so the books must've come via a decorator. A

Moroccan-style light fixture with amber glass panes hung over one of those pigskin tables that made Skye cringe: *Come sit at my dead animal skin table!* There was a wall mirror framed in some exotic scrolled wood, and the typical Santa Fe paintings you'd expect to see: a *giclée* Miguel Martinez Latino Madonna, a stunning Frank Howell grandmother print, and one of the clouds rolling in over the prairie. There was an original painting, too, of an old Victorian house in the middle of nowhere.

Not one inch of this place had escaped Sheila's relentless decorating. It was too perfect. No rough edges. Skye let her eyes stare off into the middle distance while her dad puttered in the kitchen end of things. The appliances in the kitchenette, a Bosch dishwasher and Viking stove, sure were a waste: Sheila did not cook. There were two sets of cupboards, too, and a butcher block that looked as though a family in Brooklyn had been chopping pastrami on it for generations. Skye bet her life it had been used only as a place for Mama to set down her Louis Vuitton purse.

"There's soup, beans, and some of that instant rice that tastes like glue," her dad said.

"Soup," Skye responded, and sat on the couch, the weariness from crying hitting her hard. She might fall asleep before the soup was hot.

Their first stop had been the Trailer Ranch in that part of Albuquerque that made Skye wish she had a concealed-carry permit. Turned out Rita Elliot hadn't lived there for months, and no, they didn't have a forwarding address or recall if she had a little girl with her. There was rap music booming, and a few of the residents were giving her a look she didn't like. Their uniform seemed to be wife-beater undershirts and baggy pants hanging halfway down their asses. They sported those metal chains hanging out of their pockets, as if whatever they cuffed to inside the pocket was potentially fatal. Another group of *vatos* stood around a different trailer, smoking cigarettes, making her want one. Their movements were jittery, as if they were high on something, probably crystal meth, which made Skye feel superior since she'd never tried it. Rocky smoked it occasionally. She'd met people at Cottonwoods who'd done crack for years. Their brains were emptier than a Halloween pumpkin, their teeth yellow and broken. Once they found out the Trailer Ranch was a dead end, Skye's dad had hustled her back to the truck, locked the doors, and driven that hour-long drive back to Santa Fe in forty minutes flat.

She watched him appraise his ex-wife's cozy little second house while the soup heated. He walked around the room, exploring. The Moroccan lanterns. A *Yei be chei* Navajo rug on the wall, the figures clutching cornstalks. He inspected an old Chief's Phase blanket that looked faded and worn, as if it had weathered over a few hundred years. "I hope your mama didn't pay too much for this," he said, "because it's a fake."

"So long as it looks good, I doubt she'd care," Skye said.

"I have to say, I feel a little sorry for her, always trying to make her life appear important by cluttering it with things." His eyes lit on the painting of a house, and he walked over to inspect it. He shook his head. "Well, I'll be a monkey's uncle."

"What is it, Daddy?"

He turned to her, his face stricken. "I'd recognize this farmhouse anywhere. It's on the Starr ranch, in Blue Dog. I spent a couple of years caretaking from the bunkhouse on that property."

"What are you saying? Mama bought the painting to make you mad?"

He shook his head. "Nothing of the kind. It's a coincidence."

"Don't lie to me, Daddy. I can tell by your face it's a lot more than that."

"Just seeing this triggers so many memories."

"Is the soup ready? I'm beat."

Her dad poured soup into mugs and brought one to her. They sat at the pigskin table, using paper towels for napkins. Skye blew on her spoonful and then swallowed. Nothing had ever tasted this good. Her dad drank his from the mug.

"Life in Blue Dog was peaceful until the day Maggie Yearwood moved in. I'd thought I was done with women."

"Ew," Skye said. "Is this story going to have old-people sex in it?"

He walked over to the painting, took it down from the wall, and brought it over to the table, where the light was better. "She painted this."

"Mama? Seriously, she can't even get her eyeliner on straight."

"I wasn't referring to your mother," he went on. "I was referring to Margaret. She must have painted this after I left. What a great mom she was to her insolent, teenaged son. She put up with more than I ever would."

"Daddy, you make her sound like a saint."

"She was, so far as parenting that selfish son of hers. He punched me in the mouth once."

"Did you hit him back?"

"Nope. He needed to hit me."

"This is crazy. How could a painting by Saint Margaret end up here in Mama's house? That's Lifetime movie material."

"You know how New Mexico is. The small-town vibe."

She laughed. "Did you just say *vibe?*"

"I'm not that old, Skye. Go on to bed. We can continue the story tomorrow."

She set down her mug. "I'm not tired anymore. Tell me now."

After her father laid out the details—what year it was, how long he lived there, the motley sheep he kept—Skye could picture Margaret hanging laundry outside and smell the fresh hay in the wind. Somehow, the painting of the weathered house seemed full of the whole, lonely story. Margaret's dog, Echo, who'd gotten knocked up by three-legged Hope on the first day Margaret arrived at the Victorian farmhouse that was too big for her. Her deaf teenage son, Peter, who refused to live there with her. The day Owen left, asking the deaf kid to care for his horse but getting a knuckle sandwich instead. Owen leaving before Echo had even whelped her pups. When Skye's father finished the story, he rubbed Hope's head, paying particular attention to the ears.

Skye yawned. "So why don't you look her up?"

"It's been too long. I'm sure she got on with her life."

"Daddy, don't be stupid. If she meant that much to you, if the only reason you left was prison, she might still be pining for you."

"Nah, I'm sure she found some decent fella. She's too pretty to stay single."

Skye leaned on her elbows. "Isn't it up to you to find out? Finding Gracie's my priority. Without her, my heart doesn't work right. Seems to me that painting is like a sign. Do you know how much I wish I had something like that to help me find Gracie? I'll call Mama and ask her where she got that painting. Even if all you do is find out that Saint Margaret's happy, it still seems worth it to me. How long a drive is it to that Blue Dog? Maybe she still lives there."

Her father took their empty mugs to the kitchen area. He ran water in the sink and washed the dishes. "You could help dry," he said.

"There's a dishwasher."

"I figured it was a waste of water to run it for two mugs, a pot, and a spoon. Isn't Santa Fe always in drought?" He stood there drying the dishes, ignoring her question about Blue Dog.

Skye looked at him through new eyes. "You've changed, Daddy. The guy I remember wasn't afraid to take a risk."

He sighed. "I heard from Joe that the ranch house was torn down. So she isn't there. The fellow who bought it built a new house. Probably has those granite countertops and the crown molding nonsense everyone has to have nowadays. What is it they say? Open floor plan? Stop pestering me and go to bed."

"I won't until you promise to look for her. Shit like this happens for a reason. You have to find her. It's like it's in the stars for you. Romantic."

"It's a coincidence. The chances of Sheila buying this painting from the artist may be astronomical, but it could just as easily have come from a secondhand shop. Everywhere you turn in Santa Fe, there're consignment shops filled with stuff from estate sales. Seems like too many people come to Santa Fe to die."

"You think Mama bought that for herself? Daddy, she wears leopard print!"

"You know something? You're not a kind person when it comes to your mother. How did you end up like that?"

Skye punched his shoulder. "Even if I started now, it would take until the wee hours for me to explain."

Her father rubbed his arm. "Want a cup of cocoa? I saw some in the cupboard."

"Yes! Are there marshmallows?"

Drinking her cocoa while her dad took his shower, Skye sat on the floor in the bedroom, brushing his smelly dog. Like every cattle dog she'd ever known, Hope was shedding. She gathered balls of hair in a pile at her feet, listening to him groan in pleasure. Despite his current state of dirtiness, she was growing fond of him. Lord, there was enough hair here to knit Shrek, the cartoon ogre, a sweater. She listened as cars drove up Canyon Road, idly wondering how much Mama's place was worth. Probably a million. And she didn't even live here or rent it out. If she could afford multiple houses, why couldn't she help Skye out, just a loan to get herself settled? Or at least let her stay here until she got back on her feet? She balled up the dog hair and took it out to the kitchen, placing it in the trash under the sink. She watched the dog turn four circles on his three legs—no easy feat—lie down, lick his boy bits until she wanted to kill him, and go to sleep.

The stoicism of animals had always intrigued her. The ridiculous idea that animals don't remember pain, which some behaviorists argued, seemed like a convenient way to rationalize beating your dog. If she'd gone to vet school, that would have been one of the first questions she'd ask: *Do animals remember pain?* Did Hope remember having four legs? He seemed to get along just fine. And his choice to go with her dad, after it had been ten years? The fact that Hope even recognized him seemed miraculous, but it didn't surprise her. The dog was twitching in his sleep, yipping softly every now and then, and she wondered what he dreamed about. Killing gophers? Chasing sheep? Wild rez dogs threatening his domain under the ratty trailer? Or did he dream about familial and pack bonds?

Images of her childhood pets rushed through her mind: Bun-bun, an Easter gift, who'd lived ten years. She'd taught him to use a litter box. The pet store turtles that got sick right away and died. She'd taken them back to the store and told the clerk who sold them to her that he was a worthless piece of coprolite for selling sick animals and she hoped he rotted in hell. Looking back, she decided maybe her reaction was over the top; but her anger had been justified—nobody should ever mess with a child's love for a pet.

Her fascination with animal behavior began early in her life, when she started observing the social order of horses in the riding ring. Her riding instructor used a gray Morgan named Sultan for guided trail rides. He always had to be in front. Then there was his buddy Tonto, fourteen hands—barely taller than a pony—and the oldest horse in the barn. But all he had to do was pin his ears to make Sultan walk away.

Not often did Skye allow herself to think of how her life could have been if she hadn't gotten pregnant. If she'd gone on to Stanford, she'd have finished her BS and be in the second year of vet school by now. Would she have gone to Davis, staying in California? Or would homesickness have won out, prompting her to return to Colorado, where the state university had a good program? Maybe she'd have gone to Ithaca, New York—despite the horrible winters—and met some other guy, married him, gone to Europe, opened a practice together, or any one of a hundred things besides turning into an alcoholic single mother who needed almost a year of rehab to finally kick booze and pills. *Learn from your past, and then move to the future,* Duncan would say, like it was that easy. Duncan and all his advice. Now that she had some distance from Cottonwoods, she saw him differently. He was Navajo, so maybe the things he said came from his upbringing, not a need to proselytize. Maybe he really did care about her, but how could he? What a horrible career he seemed to have, trying to get people to kick, watching them detox, slip in sobriety, or overdose and die. She felt sorry for him for about two minutes, thought of his laugh and how the sound of it made her uncomfortable someplace deep down. It wasn't until just this moment that she realized it was because it reminded her of her dad's laugh. Then she remembered her dad saying they'd talked on the phone, and that made her mad again, embarrassed, really. At least her dad hadn't witnessed her detox. That, Duncan had said, would stay between Skye and him for all time, which meant even if one person forgot about it, the other one remembered.

Skye turned over on the bed and hugged one of the down pillows. Like all four of her wedding cakes, Mama's bed was made of layers: On top of the memory foam mattress lay a feather bed. The sheets were linen, the duvet silk, and the down comforter far too warm for this time of year. Shams, patchwork quilts, lacy this, and tatted that were piled up everywhere. The bed was as white as an albino foal she'd once seen delivered. A single pickled-pine night table stood by the bed, and a skinny metal lamp was decoratively rusty, but the creepy shade looked like more stretched animal skin. The wooden vigas in the bedroom ceiling looked hand-hewn. Her dad was right. The house was trying so hard to be classy that it verged on becoming a joke.

Skye heard the shower turn off and got up for a glass of cold water. Looking for ice in the freezer, she found a bottle of vodka. She couldn't believe Sheila had left booze in the house, knowing her daughter was coming out of rehab. After all of Skye's screwups, Mama still wouldn't accept that Skye was an alcoholic. Rowing her boat down the river Denial was Mama's specialty. The glass was frosty and Skye felt the pull so viscerally that her hands shook. "Gracie," she whispered, and poured the contents down the sink.

"Good for you," her dad said. He was dressed in a clean shirt and his same old jeans.

"Daddy," Skye said, "you take the bed. The sofa's fine enough for me."

"No," he said. "I'm taking the floor."

"Dammit all, will you just take the bed and go to sleep?"

"I prefer the floor. You need the bed for a good night's sleep. We have to make a plan to find Gracie in the morning. You gotta be fresh."

"And you don't?"

"I'm a tough old buzzard. I'll be fine."

"Okay, I'll take the bed." Skye thanked him even though she knew she wouldn't sleep much given her worries.

"I'm going out to my truck to get the sleeping bags," Owen said, and the dog got up and tried to follow him out the door.

"You stay," her dad told Hope, and the dog turned around. It killed her how loyal that dog was.

Skye walked over to the bedroom window so she could look out at her dad. He did just as he said, no sneaking a cigarette or a drink. He behaved like the trustworthy man he apparently was now. There had to be more like him in the world. Sliding under the covers at long last, Skye smelled lavender. Probably her mom had paid someone to sew sachets into special pockets. She tucked herself in and pulled a box of tissues on the nightstand closer in case of night crying. She opened the single drawer and found a note pad and a pen, a Cowboy Bible, one hideous chandelier earring, and a nearly full jar of La Prairie cellular cream, which, according to the ingredients, contained platinum. Seriously? She opened the lid, stuck in a finger, and rubbed a fair amount on her face.

What a life, never having to look at price tags. Maybe she'd use up the whole thing, see if Mama noticed.

When her dad came back inside, she hollered, "I changed my mind about making the list to find Gracie. First thing tomorrow, I'll call the police. You know, they have those alerts, like AMBERs."

She heard her dad unrolling the sleeping bags. "I'm not sure this would qualify for one of those alerts. Plus, the agreement you and Rocky made—you paying him five hundred a month to let you have custody—was off the books. Might not turn out in your favor."

"What about hiring a detective? Are they like lawyers? Do they let you pay on the installment plan?"

He walked into the bedroom. "In Santa Fe? I doubt it," he said. "Listen to me, please. Once you involve the police, there's no turning back. A detective is going to do the same things we can, and it won't cost us more than phone calls and gas money. Let's explore options for just one more day. Maybe we should earn a little money before we go the detective route. I'm down to my last couple hundred."

"What's that supposed to mean?"

"We should get jobs."

"Jobs? Are you serious?" She threw the note pad at him. "It's my little girl I'm talking about. How do I know she's safe? What if she's cold, or hungry? It's like Rocky and his mama disappeared into thin air. She's my daughter. My baby. Oh, my God, what if something happened to her? What if she's been hurt or molested or even—"

"Calm down, Skye." He picked up the note pad and smoothed out the pages. "We'll find her. We'll go to the library and do some research on the computer. We can look up perverts, too. Whatever you want. We're going to find her. Tomorrow, we'll start with the Pro Rodeo Cowboys Association. I know a couple folks there. And then we're going to look through the yellow pages until you remember the name of that lawyer who's handling your divorce. You have to stay strong, honey. Night is the worst time to make big decisions. You make a big move now, I promise you'll regret it in the light of day."

"More of that AA bullcrap," Skye said.

"Maybe sounds like that to you, but it works for me—and it's been working for you. Try to keep positive. Say the Serenity Prayer."

"I won't. It's stupid."

"Didn't you read the Big Book in that place?"

"I skimmed it."

He laughed.

"What? It was boring and old. Written before television was invented."

"If I shut my eyes, it's like you're eight years old," he said. "Pout out to here, scraggly pigtails."

Skye blew her nose into what she suspected was a five-dollar tissue. When she dropped it on the bed, her dad picked it up and wadded it into a damp ball. It reminded her of the time Gracie was sick with the flu. Skye felt more like a janitor than a mother. "Give me that tissue."

"It's all right. I'll throw it in the trash."

Her dad yawned. He was tired, and Skye felt all dried out. "I'm sorry, Daddy."

"For what?"

"All day I've been mean to you. It's just that everything hurts so much."

"I know, darlin'. Now go to sleep."

He left the room, and it wasn't a minute later she heard his gentle snoring. Maybe sleep was an audition for being dead, and the older you got, the easier sleep came to you. All she knew was there was nothing more to do now. She turned onto her right side, thinking about that painting by Margaret. An empty house, full of stories. How did a painter accomplish that?

Skye woke Saturday morning with the sun lasering into her eyes. Her head pounded. I have a crying hangover, she told herself as she staggered out to the front room. Her dad and the dog were nowhere to be seen. She looked over that painting Lady Love had done. It had featured in her dreams, but she couldn't recall the details, only that the house had so many rooms she was lost inside it.

When she'd taken a shower and dried her hair, she peeked out the window. Sixty-five degrees, according to the thermometer outside the peed-off terrier. Hope was back, chewing a bowl of kibble. "Dog, where's my dad?" she asked. "Where's Owen?"

The dog continued to eat. Maybe he was deaf in addition to being ancient. Skye dressed and went out the front door, expecting to see her dad pulling weeds or doing some other chore, but he wasn't there. Just Sheila's ridiculous garden sculpture that had looked like a coat stand surrounded by boulders last night. Today Skye saw it was one of those awful metal contraptions, two figures made up of abstract shapes with holes where their hearts should be. A discreet plaque noted the title: *Mother and Child*. That was irony. What a waste of perfectly good metal, she thought. An early morning jogger went past, heaving breath. God almighty, Skye thought, I'd rather be fat than work that hard. Women had voted out curves a long time ago, but the trouble with being skinny and muscled was that it made you crabby or like Nola. Which was worse? Her dad's truck was gone, and she hoped that meant he was finding the nearest Starbucks and bringing back a venti Americano with four extra shots.

She went back in the house, sat on the couch, and leafed through a *Phoenix Home & Garden*. The dog had finished his kibble and was now engaged in washing his privates, something he apparently did at least five times a day. "Must you?" she asked. What a disgusting noise. She fetched the yellow pages from the drawer in the kitchenette in hopes of finding the lawyer Rocky had hired to do their divorce. Following the category "Astrologers," there were twenty-six pages of attorneys to serve a city of sixty-eight thousand residents. She pored over the firms from AAA Lawyers 'R Us to Martinez & Sons, but she didn't recognize a single name.

Hope settled down in the same sunbeam that had jarred her awake. Santa Fe was no place for a ranch dog. Hope needed that den under Joe Yazzi's trailer to sleep off the remainder of his days, not a town filled with visitors, tourist sites, and traffic. She wondered what would become of her dad. Would he disappear again? Had he disappeared already, leaving her with the dog? She looked through the cupboards, searching for a coffeepot or even some instant. There were teabags, yuck, and a microwave to heat up the water. With no milk or cream it tasted just awful, but she drank it like medicine, desperate for the caffeine.

As soon as she had finished the cup, the dog got up and went to stand by the front door. Maybe he needed to pee. She fetched his leash and was about to head out when the door opened, and there was her dad. An aromatic box of Whoo's Donuts was in his arms and, balanced on top, a Starbucks bag. "Thank goodness," Skye said, taking the bag. "I was about to call 911. Your dog heard you coming like five minutes ago. How is that possible when he's a hundred and forty years old? Never mind, don't tell me. 'Them heelers are tough like a dingo,' right?"

"Having never met a dingo, I can't say. Hope's intelligent. Do you like doughnuts? I bought a dozen. Half of them are maple and bacon. Sounded pretty good to me, so I bought all they had."

If she could have stood the emotions, she might have hugged him. "Daddy, you done good. Now let's drink the coffee while it's still hot."

Already high on sugar, they made phone calls while finishing the doughnuts. The road crew boss, Chuck, didn't have any leads. "Rocky win the lottery or something?" her husband's former boss asked her. "Not that I know of," Skye said. She called four of his friends, and three of their numbers were no longer in service. That was the trouble with cell phones, Skye decided. Everybody dumped their landlines, and as of yet, there wasn't a cell phone directory. Miguel, the guy who usually hung around Rocky at rodeos, didn't have too much English. "Rocky?" Skye said. *"Hasta las vista?"* Miguel laughed, so she knew she'd butchered the Spanish. After that, she handed the phone to her father. "I can't do this anymore," she said. "You try for a while. I'm going to rest on the couch."

Her dad plopped the yellow pages in her lap. "Start again at A, and read every single name. One of the lawyers or firms is bound to ring a bell."

Her dad called the PRCA, the Professional Rodeo Cowboys Association, and said, "They have a message option," he said, pressing the number three on his cell phone.

Skye dropped the yellow pages and stood by her dad, tilting the phone so she could hear when to talk. For the first time, she allowed herself to hope. But her optimism dwindled when the message option sent them to voice-mail hell that led nowhere but back to the extension stating they were closed. She wanted to scream. Her father pressed zero, and finally it went to an answering machine. Skye would have let loose a freight train of swear words, but not her dad. "I'm looking for a bull rider, Rocky Elliot," Owen said. "It's urgent that I get in touch with him. A four-year-old child is missing. Please call me back at your earliest convenience." Then he rattled off his number, twice, to make sure they got it.

Skye sat back down on the couch and picked up the yellow pages, determined not to cry. If the lawyer wasn't under the B's, then maybe he was under C. Hope got up from the rug and came to her, head butting her knee. "I'm busy," she said. "Go talk to Daddy."

Her dad hung up the phone and snapped his fingers. The dog

butted Skye once again and reluctantly returned to Owen. "Find your jacket and let's get a change of scenery."

"No, you go. I'll wait by the phone."

He patted her hand. "We've given everyone my cell number and I'll have it with me. The air will clear your head. Dog needs a walk. We need a break. I don't know about you, but I need some protein. All that sugar gave me a buzz that's turning into a headache."

"But what if—"

"What if, what if. Sara, you're killing me here."

"How many times do I have to tell you, *Owen*? It's Skye."

As they started up Canyon Road, memories flooded her mind. Snow at Christmas. Taking Gracie out to see it for the first time. Her pink snow boots, her wide-eyed wonder, little mittened hands reaching for the falling flakes. The smell of piñon wood burning, carolers on Christmas Eve. Soon she was snorting back tears.

"Aw, honey," he said. "We'll find her. From what you told me about Rocky and his mama, neither one of them would neglect that child." He patted her back, and she leaned all her weight against him, just about knocking him over.

Her dad was too old for her to be leaning on. It was crazy for her to think he'd drop all his business just to help her. "Soon as we pick up the Mercedes, you should go on your way," she told him. "Do your own stuff. Find Margaret."

"Your business is my first priority. I'm here because I want to be. So enough of that. Let's grab some lunch at the place up the road."

For the first time, Skye understood why her roommate, Nola, purged. "I'm sick from all those doughnuts."

"No, you're not. You just need real food, and so do I." He pointed to the Teahouse restaurant, on the left side of the road, with a couple of cars in its parking lot. "We're already here."

"All right," she said, "but I don't want you spending all your money on me. Let's split a sandwich."

He smiled. "I believe I can cover two whole sandwiches while we plan our next move in this caper."

Overhead, tree branches were busting with leaves that would carry them through the hot summer. Already the servers were wearing T-shirts and miniskirts. Her dad was old, but he looked like she remembered him, that easy grin, the crinkles at the edges of his eyes. "Daddy," she said, "where have you been all my life?"

He leashed the dog and tied him to a bicycle rack. Then he took off his hat as they went into the Teahouse to grab a table. "Oh, making one stupid move or another. Guess it took me sixty years to get a smidgen of wisdom. But earning it is better than having it just show up." He laid his arm over her shoulder and pulled her close for a hug.

When Skye was ten, when she was still Sara Kay, she clomped around the house in her cowboy boots loud enough to wake the dead. Her dad could tune it out; her mother seemed to take it personally that she had zero skills in the manners department. Sheila found some ridiculous "etiquette seminar for young ladies" and enrolled her. The lessons took place in LoDo, a part of Denver that was pretty ritzy now, but it hadn't been back then. The class was held in the banquet room of some hotel that had seen better days. Later, it would be torn down and replaced with a Westin. Sara Kay was positive she was going to despise these afternoons, which included tea, stale pastries, and the nasal voice of Mrs. Wadsworth, a stocky old lady who wore flowered dresses that hit her midknee. It was probably for the best, Sara thought; Mrs. Wadsworth's legs could pass for sugar pine tree trunks. Sheila attended the first meeting, but after that, she just dropped Sara off and went shopping, and once or twice she'd come back with flushed cheeks and wine on her breath. At the second meeting, the young ladies listened with attention. "Girls," Mrs. Wadsworth said, "how many of you dress for dinner?"

Sara had snorted with laughter, imagining, like all of the other girls, her parents naked. Mrs. Wadsworth had given her the major fisheye and said, "Sara Kay, perhaps you'd like to share with the class what you find so amusing?"

"No, ma'am," she said, thinking that would be the end of it.

Mrs. Wadsworth picked up her clipboard that held the forms each girl had filled out in cursive writing. "I see here that your father's occupation is listed as farrier. Can you explain what exactly that entails?"

"He shoes horses, ma'am."

"What an unusual career choice that is in this day and age." Mrs. Wadsworth smiled ever so slightly. "Girls, any of you have a father who shoes horses for a living?"

"My dad's a physician," one girl said. Another said, "College professor." And still others: "Attorney" and "CEO." Every single one of the occupations stung like a wasp. Sara wanted to staple that old biddy's lips shut. But the damage was done. Finally, when they returned to the subject at hand, most of the girls said they dressed up on Sundays, for church and breakfast in a nice restaurant, or when they stayed at a grandmother's house. Candy Pierce said, "Oh, my mother and I love to dress up and go shopping, or to see a fashion show. And it's good practice for when I come out."

"Come out of what?" Skye asked. "A coma?"

Candy smiled. "When I'm introduced to the world, you know, as a debutante."

"Very good," Mrs. Wadsworth said.

Sara made a note to look the word up later. For now she'd shut her mouth and pretend that made sense.

"It's always helpful to practice one's manners," Mrs. Wadsworth said, cocking her head and looking directly at Sara. "The idea is that one can better her station no matter what background she comes from."

Sara felt her face go crimson. She wasn't a crier—she hated crybabies—but her eyes welled with tears.

Later, while practicing the proper way to sit down, a girl named Kaitlyn nudged her knee into Sara's under the table. She had French braids and the cutest navy-blue jacket, more like a blazer, really, fitted at the waist. It made her look at least fourteen years old. Sara looked up miserably, but Kaitlyn winked at her. "If your dad's a farrier, you must ride horses, right?"

Sara nodded. "I have a Leopard Appy, Lightning."

"Where do you board?"

"Cherry Creek in Aurora," Sara whispered to her.

"Me too!" Kaitlyn whispered. "Want to go riding on Sunday?"

"I don't know," Sara said. "I might be all tied up with dressing for dinner."

Kaitlyn laughed out loud, and here came Mrs. Wadsworth, who pulled her up by a shoulder and said, "Clearly you two should not be sitting together."

Even across the room, having a friend made manners class tolerable. Kaitlyn, of the beautiful, perfect teeth, white-blond hair, and adorable clothing, wanted her to go on a trail ride. The rest of the class went by quickly. At home that night, she did exactly as Mrs. Wadsworth instructed. She asked her parents if they could dress for dinner every Thursday night.

"Why Thursday?" her father asked.

"It could be Wednesday or Sunday, if you'd rather. You know, just to practice my manners."

"I think that's a lovely idea," her mom said. "What do you think, Billy?"

"I think I've got to go shopping."

All his shirts were flannel, which always felt soft when he hugged her.

Since things were proceeding so well, she had another question. "Daddy, why don't we have a horse trainer?"

"What would we do with one of those?" he said, laughing. "You have Valerie, don't you?"

"She's just a riding teacher. A trainer can teach you how to ride to win."

"Last time I checked, we all knew how to ride. Red and Lightning are pretty good at it."

Sara made sure to leave three uneaten bites on her plate, because a girl needed to show she could leave something behind. She pushed her chair in after dinner. Then she began clearing the plates.

"Don't you dare laugh at that little girl, you big old has-been Okie clodhopper," her mom said when Sara was in the kitchen, rinsing the dishes to put into the dishwasher. They had to know she heard them. Her mom said, "I'm trying to help her fit in with higher-class people so she can have a better life than this. Hell's bells, Billy. It's the basics of etiquette. Good manners. Something you never learned one iota about."

She knew her dad felt bad hearing that. It was as if her mother's words were blunt arrows with poisonous tips.

"I apologize, Sheila. If it's that important to you, find me a book on it and I'll do my best to learn how to act higher-class."

Sara peeked around the corner. Her mom's withering stare told the whole story. Her parents' marriage had seemed rocky as far back as she could remember. They fought with hushed voices, and then they made up all lovey-dovey, but it never lasted.

At the stables the next weekend, Sara discovered there was another side to the riding school, where girls wore English riding pants and black leather knee-high boots. They "posted" the trot, which looked crazy to Sara, on hornless saddles and wore those National Velvet hats that her dad referred to as brain buckets.

On Sundays, Sara started going with her dad when he shoed horses. She rode Lightning with a fleece bareback pad rather than let Kaitlyn see her crappy old western saddle. It had belonged to her dad when he was a kid. Kaitlyn taught Sara "leg leads," the difference between "cantering in hand" versus the lope. Lightning caught on quickly, but when it came to jumping the fences, he refused every single one.

"You should ask your parents for a Haflinger," Kaitlyn said, "or maybe a Lipizzaner."

"What are those?"

Kaitlyn's laugh was like listening to tinkling bells. "You must not have a Breyer horse collection."

"I never heard of that."

Kaitlyn gave her a history lesson. Haflingers descended from wild horses that once roamed the Alps. They were first imported to the United States in the 1960s. Some went to Canada, others Illinois. They were strong and had a steady temperament. "You know the history of the Lipizzaner, don't you?"

"Yeah, of course," Sara said, making a note to look the word up at home.

Kaitlyn said, "Thank goodness. Otherwise I'd have to spend another hour explaining all that. Prince is half Lipizzaner, but his line goes back to Maestoso. He was born in Slovenia. That's in Europe."

"How did you get him here?"

"My dad had him FedExed."

No way, Sara thought, but she said, "He's really pretty. You're so lucky."

"You want to know why Prince wins at horse shows?"

"Because you're a great rider."

Kaitlyn laughed. "I wish. He was trained in *haute école*." Sara looked at her blankly. "You know, the Spanish Riding School, where they teach Lipizzaners to perform 'airs above the ground.' Watch this. *Le passage*."

Kaitlyn gave Prince her right leg, no kicking or anything, a gentle press Sara might not otherwise have noticed. She laid the rein on his neck. Sara could convince Lightning to move sideways, but it took reins and a swift kick. After that first thing, Kaitlyn began cueing Prince to change leads. The horse looked as though he were skipping. How was she doing that? Sara had no idea a horse could do that. It looked like ballet.

Kaitlyn walked Prince back to where Sara waited. "He was trained to perform to Strauss's *Beliebte Annen Polka*. Once he hears the music, he practically does the routine himself. The only move he can't do is the *levade*. That's why he was so cheap. Only eight thousand. When I grow out of him, Dad promised to buy me a mare, and she can have babies." Kaitlyn reached into her jacket pocket and fed Prince three sugar cubes.

That Sunday, after shoeing horses all day, her dad showered, shaved, and put on his nicest pants and a new white shirt. He even dabbed on some of that awful cologne Sara had given him a couple of Christmases back, because what do you give a dad, other than a new razor, when he already had one of those? Her mom had roasted a chicken. At the table, her dad said, "Sheila, that is a right pretty flower arrangement."

"It's called a *centerpiece*," her mom said, and snapped open her cloth napkin and laid it on her lap. "Let's all say grace."

"What's grace?" Sara asked. Her mom said, "It's a blessing to show we're grateful for all we have."

Her dad said, "It's a prayer, like your mom says, but the word has more than one meaning. Grace also means making your way with dignity through difficult circumstances."

Her dad hadn't ever gone to church that she knew of. She waited, wondering if grace was silent. Then her father said, "Bless this meal and we who are about to eat. Amen."

Sara echoed him. Surely her mom would be nicer to him for doing that.

Her dad cut up the chicken and served her mom first. Then to Sara, he said what he always did when they had chicken: "Guess what?"

Sara was supposed to reply, "Chicken butt." It was their special routine. But she couldn't say that anymore because it was bad manners. "I'll have a drumstick, please."

He looked at her funny but gave her what she wanted.

Halfway through dinner, she piped up, "Can we trade my western saddle in for an English one?"

"What's wrong with your saddle?"

"It's not English."

Her father set down his fork. "I learned to ride on that saddle. It was made by a great saddle maker, Clint Mortenson."

Sara knew—she soaped it clean every time she used it. "It's a great saddle, Daddy, but to learn how to jump, you need an English saddle. A hunt seat."

"Jumping," her dad said, flatly this time. "Lightning's the best cow pony I've ever seen. He'll take you over a ditch when you need him to."

"Not fences, Daddy. But with the right saddle, he might."

"Sara Kay, he's a western horse. You can do pole bending, run barrels with him, and even calf rope."

"That's another thing. Kaitlyn says I should get a Haflinger mare or a Friesian gelding."

"What about Lightning?"

Sara looked down at her plate, then up at her mom, who was pouring another glass of wine, her mouth already pursed up for the fight that would come later. "We could find him a good home."

Her dad about choked. He folded his cloth napkin, laid it on the table, and then said, "That was a lovely dinner, Sheila. Excuse me." He got up from his chair and walked out of the room.

Her mom reached over the table and placed her hand on Sara's. "You keep on aiming high, girl. I'll talk to your dad."

But that night in bed, imagining Lightning headed off in a trailer to God knew where made Sara feel as if there were a wind wailing inside her stomach. She did love Lightning. He loved her, too, and that soft nickering he breathed into her neck was better than anything, even candy. He liked apples and carrots, especially the green parts. She couldn't sleep. Down the hall she heard the angry tones of her parents arguing.

Daddy: "I saved a whole year to buy her that horse," he said. "I did a ton of free work for the breeder. Why are you trying to force that perfectly fine little girl into that kind of crowd? We can't compete with that. For crying out loud, I shoe their horses. I told you from the get-go I had my doubts about this finishing school business. She says please and thank you. She writes your mother thank-you notes. What else is there to learn?"

Mama: "You really have no idea, do you? You boneheaded lummox. You'd probably be happy if she went straight from bubble gum to chewing tobacco."

Daddy: "I surely would not. Why else did I quit? Sheila, we can't pay for all those things she's asking for. Giving her high-falutin ideas is only going to break her heart. Shoot, if she wants to go to college, it'll have to be a state school or a hefty scholarship . . . Sheila, wait. Don't push me out of my own bedroom."

A door slammed. Her dad's footsteps padded down the hall-way that led to the living room. Sara heard the squeak of the old couch's springs. She tiptoed down the hallway to see what was happening, and her dad crooked his finger for her to come sit beside him. She stood in front of him and whispered, "Are you and Mama getting a divorce?"

He patted the couch beside him, and she sat down and began fiddling with the fringe edge of a throw pillow. "Here's the thing, Sara," he said. "English saddles cost about two grand for a cheap one. Lightning cost eight hundred dollars. The fancy horses you're talking about? Some of them cost more than this house."

"Kaitlyn's only cost eight thousand."

"I don't make that kind of money, peanut."

"What if you got a better job?"

He pressed his lips together in a firm line. "I don't have the education. I shoe horses all year round. I work construction. I'll never make that kind of money unless we win the lottery."

"But I want to ride English."

"If that's what you want, I will make it happen. We can work out a deal with Valerie." Valerie was their stables manager and riding instructor, and she taught all the kids to ride western. "I'll see if I can trade her some work for English riding lessons. You could borrow a horse until we sell Lightning. That sound okay?"

Sell Lightning. "I guess so."

The next time her dad was shoeing at the stables, he did Prince, Kaitlyn's Lipizzaner. Kaitlyn's dad insisted on holding Prince's lead rope, which her dad didn't like all that much, because sometimes a horse spooked. He liked to have the horse cross-tied, because that was safer, but he went along with it.

"If you do a good enough job on Prince, maybe you can do our other horses," he said. "Of course, with five horses, we'd appreciate a group rate, or discount."

Kaitlyn's dad was a stockbroker. Even his casual shoes had tassels.

Her dad didn't say anything for a while. "How much does one of these horses run?" he asked.

"For you or your daughter?"

"My daughter," he said. "I'm a western rider, came from a long line of cowboying, raised Sara Kay the same way."

"You could get a learner horse for about five grand," he said. "If she wants to show to win, you're looking at a minimum of forty grand. Anything under that and you're invisible to the judges."

Sara couldn't see it, but she knew her dad's jaw dropped open. When her dad finished shoeing Prince, Kaitlyn's dad said, "Here's a twenty for your trouble. You could put it toward your daughter's horse fund, eh?"

"Drop me out front," Sara told her mom at the next etiquette lesson. She waved, watched her mom drive away, and then went to the atrium of the hotel, where she sat for forty-five minutes looking at a tree that looked as if it would rather live in Hawaii. Did trees get lonely? Then she pulled out her *Pocket Dictionary of Horses* library book and read for the remaining hour of class. When it was over, she trailed behind the girls who had attended. It worked for two lessons, but then her mom tricked her, arriving early to watch the end of the class. When Sara emerged from the atrium and came to the lobby, her mother grabbed her by the arm. "I spent good money on these lessons," she hissed. "You are going to attend those classes if I have to drag you myself."

The remaining classes went by in a blur. Sara learned how to offer her hand so a gentleman would shake it, and about situations where she shouldn't offer it. She learned to make a lopsided swan out of a cloth napkin, to cross her legs at the ankles, to lift a teacup with the all-important outstretched pinky. Then they started walking lessons, the reason her mother cursed her to this circle of hell in the first place.

"Sara, suck in your tummy," Mrs. Wadsworth scolded her.

"But it hurts," Sara said.

Mrs. Wadsworth put her hands on her hips, which she did whenever she was appalled by a girl's major faux pas. "That's the way of the world as far as women are concerned, so you'd best learn to live with it." Then she turned to the other girls, the ones who weren't infested with cooties. "Girls, remember to tell your mothers to bring their checkbooks next week. We'll be starting part two of our program."

That Sunday, earlier than she ever got up, Sara made sure she was dressed in her Wranglers and one of her dad's old shirts so she could go with him to the stables. On the drive there, he said, "Your mama told me you cut some of those classes and now you don't want to take advanced manners, or whatever it's called. Why? I thought you liked going to them."

"Those girls are nothing but a tribe of skags."

"Your mother would skin you alive for using that word."

"Daddy, promise me you won't make me go back. I hate it. The girls make fun of me. They're stupid. I don't belong there. I already know how to say please and thank you and I tiptoe now. Please, can you make Mama understand?"

He nodded. "I'll try my best."

"Thank you."

A few miles later, he said, "I may have found a buyer for Lightning. A nice client's little girl wants something flashy to barrel race. They offered twelve hundred. With that kind of money we could put a down payment on an English horse for you, and I could take a loan out for the rest. What do you think?"

Sara screeched so loudly that her dad winced and put a hand over his ear. "Don't you dare sell Lightning! I love my horse." The sobs that came out of her were huge and wet, complete with dripping snot and an instant headache, another introduction to how things in the world went for women. "Nobody else knows what he likes, and he loves me."

Her dad handed her his bandanna. "I'm heartened to hear it. Unless we mortgage the house, I can't afford one of those big-time horses, but if that's what it takes to make you happy, I'll try."

"Hell, damn, and shit, no, I don't want that! I want to ride western for the rest of my life."

"I did not know you could talk like that. It's fine this once, but cut it out from now on, okay? Truth be told, I'd prefer you stay clear of those inbred sociopaths."

"You mean Kaitlyn and her dad?"

Her dad laughed and laughed. "No, sweetie, I'm talking about imported European horses. You think Europe sends their best horses to the U.S.? Hell, no. They're importing the worst of the breed, and getting rich off it."

As the miles peeled by, Sara thought about how close she'd come to betraying her daddy, and worst of all, her horse. It seemed like something you could try to forget but then found out you couldn't. Worse, the second you felt sad or embarrassed, it rose to the surface like a bubble. Like Mrs. Wadsworth. Like hearing your mother yell at your dad for not measuring up to her idea of a husband. "I love Lightning," she said. "Just so you know, I'd never sell him, not even if I was poor, or homeless. I'd live in a tent so I could keep him. I'd skip lunch, even dinner, to make sure he got fed."

Her father nodded and kept his eyes on the exit sign for Cherry Creek.

"There is one thing I'd really like to do, Daddy."

"What's that?"

"Set fire to those stupid white gloves and that awful panty hose Mama says I have to wear. Really, Daddy. All that money and what'd I learn? Nothing."

"Now, now," her dad said. "It wasn't all bad. And you did learn how to walk more quietly. How about after we're done shoeing, we stop by Dairy Queen to get a Blizzard, wreck our dinner, huh?"

She laughed, thinking of how appalled Mrs. Wadsworth would be, because overeating led to an overly rounded *tummy*. Shit, damn, and screw, she said to herself. Mrs. Wadsworth can go to hell, the old bitch.

"Price for a sandwich has gotten out of control," Owen said as he folded his money back into the clip he carried and returned to their table at the Teahouse with their coffee drinks. He picked up somebody's discarded newspaper and opened it to the want ads. "Skye, honey? I'm not sure I can find work in this town," he said. "Maybe in Española, or farther out. You all right with me being an hour away?"

"Sure," she said, caught up in remembering the horrible etiquette lessons. By now, Mrs. Wadsworth was probably pushing nettles out of her grave because the daisies all had committed suicide.

"You know, down south, there might be more opportunities to put my trades to use. I learned how to train dogs in prison. Doesn't seem to be much of a market for training assistance dogs here, however." He handed her the newspaper. "Read me the want ads," he said.

She looked up and her lower lip trembled. "I don't feel like it. You read them to me."

"I would if I could, but I can't."

"Did you forget how to read?"

He looked away, hurt.

People at the other tables were laughing, happy, not having stupid, petty arguments. Once he had regained his composure, he answered. "I love to read. But I stepped on my reading glasses this morning, and I haven't had time to buy another pair."

"Daddy, I'm sorry. I'm such a brat."

"I reckon you have a right to be bratty, but I don't think it helps anything."

The sandwiches arrived. Open-faced roast chicken nested in a salad of basil and tomatoes. "Let me know if there's anything else I can get for you," the server said.

Skye set down her coffee and said, "Daddy? Guess what?"

"Chicken butt?"

At her dad's smile a great weight lifted off her soul. She leaned over the table and kissed his wrinkly old cheek.

"Well, I don't know what I've done to deserve that, but I'll take it," he said.

She cut a piece of chicken and tomato and sighed at the taste. So far, the want ads were mainly for nurses, educators, and businessmen. Then she saw it. "Listen to this one, Daddy. A stable running horse programs wants a barn manager. Can you imagine how many applications they'll get from idiots who think that's an easy job?"

Owen wiped his hands on his napkin. "Circle that in pen. Now read me the number." He took out his cell phone and dialed as she recited it. The message he left was perfect. When he ended the call, he smiled at her. "Soon as we get back to the *peed-off-terrier*, I'm going to write down all my skills and you can check the spelling for me. I don't give a hoot how many people apply. That job is mine."

Owen stood up while Skye bussed the table. "I know, I know," she said. "It's the waitress in me. I can't leave a dirty table."

"I was going to say that's a lovely habit to have."

When they walked outside, the wind blew through the trees, bringing with it the scent of sage and piñon. Her dad untied Hope's leash and fed the dog the crusts he'd saved from his sandwich. They walked down Canyon Road, looking at the red adobe, the fences worn by time and weather, galleries interspersed between historic houses painted the color of the mud they came from. Windows and doors were the shade of blue Santa Fe was famous for but had bleached in the sun and ranged from turquoise to indigo. When they arrived at a street called Ave de Colibri at one end and Colibri Road at the other, one of those alleyways tucked sideways between Canyon Road and Acequia Madre, Skye noticed the houses there were smaller, less fancy than the others. "Wonder what they cost?" she mused.

"A pretty penny," her dad said.

"Daddy, look at your dog." Hope was barely keeping up with them. His three-legged gait looked so uncomfortable, it made Skye want to pick him up and carry him. "Poor guy, he's exhausted."

Owen bent down and rubbed the dog's ears. "I reckon the downhill grade is too much for him. I got some Absorbine in my truck."

"You still use that? Chapman's doesn't stink, and it comes in a gel. You should buy some when you run out of that old sideshow crap."

"Well, excuse me all to crazy. Absorbine has worked fine for me for many years. Matter of fact, I rub it on my own lower back, and I'm still standing."

They stopped to rest a minute, and what looked like a brown rez dog came racing out the front door of one of the houses. Hope wagged his stumpy tail, and the brown dog lay down in the road, showing Hope her belly.

"What do you say, Hope? Is she girlfriend material?"

"Daddy, really. What a thing to say!"

"I'll have you know Hope was once in great demand as a stud. He threw beautiful pups."

The two dogs had a little confab, and Skye looked at the house the dog had come from, the front door ajar. At each window, blue-painted window boxes waited for spring. Then a woman—possibly forty, but no older—hurried out, balancing a baby on her hip. Her hair was silver, not gray, and Skye could tell it had gone this color way earlier than it did in most other people. "I'm sorry," she said. "Curly! Come on in the house right now. I hope she wasn't bothering your dog," she said as she walked closer, trying to get Curly's attention. The woman smiled grimly. "One of my daughter's dogs. She opens doors. The dog, I mean."

Her dad smiled. "A dog that smart will settle down some if you teach her tricks."

The woman nodded. "I know you're right. I used to train all my dogs, and then she came along." She looked down at the baby. "Now I'm lucky if I get time to brush my teeth."

"Cute baby," Skye said, looking into the child's big eyes. "What's her name?"

"Sparrow."

"What a perfect name," Skye said. "How did you decide on it?"

The chubby baby was drooling onto her bib, blinking at the new people she'd just met. "It's a long story. But it seems to fit her, doesn't it? Everyone says her eyes are hazel, but to me they seem gray, the color of a sparrow's feathers. Curly, come on," she said. "Enough bothering these people." Curly was on her feet now, and major sniffing was taking place. The woman sighed. "We need to get her spayed."

"You know, I do some dog training," Owen told her as he took hold of the dog's collar. "Don't suppose you'd have any use for that service? Or maybe a dog walker?"

"Actually, a dog walker is exactly what I need. Do you have a card?"

"Not on me. I can give you my phone number, if you have something to write on, and write with."

"Sure." She looked down at the dog as if she were trying to figure out how to manage getting her leashed, all that and the baby, too.

"Let me hold the baby for a second," Skye said. "Come here, little Sparrow." The woman handed her over, and Skye felt the same thrilling sensations of holding Gracie for the first time.

Memories she'd taken for granted—days gone by that would never come again—washed over her.

The woman leashed the dog and patted her pockets. "I don't have a pen with me. But I have one inside. Can you come in, just for a second? Then I can put the baby down and get the dog out back. You must think I'm out of my mind. I'm not, I swear, just pregnant—the stage where your brain is in a fog and you cry at the least little thing. Come on, my house is right over here."

"Skye?" Owen said.

"Coming." This woman had an adorable baby and another on the way, and she lived in a house that could have come from a fairy tale. How did people get that lucky? Skye followed her up the steps and into a great room with flagstone floors, a groaning bookshelf, a playpen, and so many toys scattered about that it looked like a baby store riot. Her dad took the runaway dog to the French doors, let her out, and two larger dogs, a border collie and a mutt, immediately greeted Curly while Hope sat there, uninterested.

"Thanks so much for helping," she said. "I'm Glory."

"Skye. That's my dad."

"Talk about a beautiful name. Did your dad name you?"

"He's really great with dogs," Skye said, sidestepping the question. She took one last inhalation of that powdery, baby scent before placing Sparrow into the playpen. "Me, I prefer babies."

"They do have an appeal," Glory said, "especially when they're clean and happy." She pulled open a desk drawer and took out a yellow Post-it note pad and a chewed-up pen. "I hope it still has ink in it," she said, shaking it.

Owen wrote down his phone number and "O. Garrett." "I hope I can be of service to you. Seems like you have your hands full."

Glory laughed. "You don't know the half of it. My older girls, my dog walkers, are either at work or at college. I'd be happy to hire you to walk the big ones every couple of days."

"The big ones?" he asked, gesturing at the three dogs outside racing around one another. "Does that mean there are others?"

She whistled. "Eddie!" Around the corner came an Italian greyhound. "He's perfectly normal," she said, "so don't worry about how thin he is. It's a sight hound trait."

The little dog was wiggling his butt off, trying to get Glory to pick him up.

"Miniature greyhound?" her dad asked.

She nodded. "Italian."

"I've trained full-size greyhounds, smart dogs. I don't believe I've ever seen a greyhound this small."

"It's a toy breed. He's full-grown. I got him from a shelter."

Eddie walked around the three-legged heeler, observing.

"It's my pleasure to walk whichever dogs you want," he said. "Just tell me how long a walk, what kind of exercise, and I'll tucker them out for you." He walked toward the front door, his tripod dog following.

The second Skye had let go of the baby, the hard-to-ignore desire to use had risen steadily. How great it would feel to have an OxyContin or three, a drink of anything—even a baby Valium would help. There was nothing like it when a drug kicked in and blunted everything that was difficult or painful. She loved when the hurry-up-and-feel-the-calm hit her like a rush, the relief from the constant anxiety that bubbled in her veins. When she looked at Glory, she felt certain the woman could tell what she was thinking.

"It was nice to meet you, Skye," Glory said. "Owen, put a business card up at Kaune's. Santa Fe's a real dog town. Most people around here shop there. And everybody works, so I bet you could get new clients in a week's time, or less."

"Will do."

Skye walked toward the door, following her father.

He stopped just below the steps, staring at the house next door. He had one hand up as if to shield his eyes from the sunlight, but it wasn't sunny out at all. He looked back at Glory, about to say something, just as the sounds of a fussing baby began.

"Well, that's my cue," Glory said, then hesitated. "Owen? Clearly, I'm nobody to talk, but you should know there's a leash law in this part of town. It's a fifty-dollar ticket."

"Thanks."

Skye watched her dad reach into his jacket pocket, pull out a leash, and hold it in front of Hope. The dog delicately took the leather in his mouth and turned to walk back in the direction they'd come.

Glory laughed. "Get video of that on your smartphone, and it would make a great advertisement for your services, Owen."

"Give me a ring and we'll set up a time."

"Great," she said, and walked back to her house.

"Daddy," Skye said, "what the heck were you staring at?"

"Just before the baby started crying, I swear I saw a girl standing right there. Dressed strange, like an old-time Indian in deerskin and feathers, long braids." He pointed to the little bit of yard in front of the house next door. "Hope even growled at her. He never does that."

Skye frowned at him. "Daddy, there isn't anybody there."

"I swear there was. She was looking right at me."

"Really. And what did the Indian lady say to you? 'A rocky vineyard does not need a prayer but a pickax'? 'There is nothing so eloquent as a rattlesnake's tail'?"

"Where'd you hear all those Navajo sayings?"

"From Duncan Hanes, drug and alcohol counselor, and reciter of Navajo proverbs. The asshole who broke confidentiality and called you, breaking laws left and right. You'd only see an Indian woman dressed like that if someone was making a movie, in which case the streets would be blocked off."

"Call me an old fool, but I saw her."

"You've had a lot of coffee," Skye said. "You're probably dehydrated or something. Let's go back to Mama's. Your dog needs a nap."

"Me too."

"Daddy?" Skye said. "Wake up, I made dinner. Go wash your hands."

Owen rubbed his eyes. "I can't believe how long I slept. It's dark out. What're we having?"

"Skirt steak. Or else you can have scrambled eggs. I walked down to Kaune's and bought us a little food while you were sleeping. But soon, one of us needs to go actual shopping, and you're the one with the money. And more coming, since you got a dog-walking job. I need to check in with somebody about my community service, but I really thought I'd have found Gracie by now. Hard to commit to a schedule if you might have to break it."

"Honey, give me a minute to get my bearings." He got up, straightened his sleeping bag, and walked toward the bathroom.

The dog usually followed him everywhere, but he was fast sleep on the Persian rug.

Skye fixed their plates and got extra napkins, an old habit from feeding Gracie, who liked to personally "interact" with her food, which meant fingers, not silverware. Owen came back into the room, his hair slicked back and his face washed. He sat on the couch. Skye handed him his plate.

"This looks good."

"Wait until you taste it. There was a bottle of soy sauce, some frozen green chile, and a jar of jam in the fridge, not a lot to work with. I think I should call the cops now. I've run out of places to look and people to ask. While you were in dreamland, I looked all the way up to the letter *H* lawyers' names in the phone book. Not one of them rings a bell."

"Where's the rodeo this time of year? Texas?"

"Yeah. Then I think it goes to California."

"Hmm," Owen said. "Tomorrow, after my job interview, let's head to the library to use one of their computers. Chances are, we can find his name on the roster. Unless he took a season off. But maybe a name will ring a bell, give us someone else to call."

"I thought of someone else while you were napping."

"Who?"

Skye blew out a breath. "Well, it depends on the time of year, and how much money Rocky won, but he has this friend, kind of. A dealer."

Her father was dipping his skirt steak into green chile. "A dealer in antiques or what?"

She couldn't look at him. "Cocaine."

"Cocaine? I thought they drug tested at rodeos."

"Yeah, they test the horses."

Owen set his fork on the edge of the plate. He didn't say a word.

"Daddy, say something. You know cowboys—to them it's nothing more than a way to kill the pain and keep riding."

His mouth was set. "Last time I checked, it was codeine you used for pain, not cocaine. Did you use it, too?"

All Skye could think of was how ridiculous she must have looked when she was high. The higher she was, the surer she'd been that she could hide it. It was also the wrongest idea she'd ever had. "I know you're disappointed in me. I'm disappointed in me. But I admitted my problem. I dealt with it. I imagine I'll be dealing with it the rest of my life."

He reached over and touched her cheek. "I'm sure you're disappointed in me, too. Waste of time. I'm no one to judge anybody for anything. So where do we go from here?"

Skye set down her fork. Her appetite had vanished. "Rocky said when he got too old to rodeo, he wanted to get a little place in Truth or Consequences. Or maybe he went back to Oklahoma. He has a cousin there. Jared or Jerry, something like that."

Her dad finished his steak. "You're a good cook. You took a skirt steak and made it taste like a T-bone. That requires talent."

Skye stared at her plate. "A miracle, more like it." The hunk of cooling meat made her want to eat nothing but vegetables. "If Rocky went someplace like T or C, it could be a good thing. Like maybe he got a job and put Gracie in school."

"I've been there. It's a one-horse kind of town, and I mean that in the best way. Everybody knows everybody, looks out for everybody. Shouldn't be too hard to find him if he's there. Especially if he's as good at bull riding as you say. That's rodeo culture. People fix on one cowboy and follow him like golf fanatics follow Tiger Woods."

Skye snorted. "Rocky had groupies all right. He dressed the part. He'd wear these custom-made American flag chaps, his flashiest spurs, and his hat was always beaver, a high-end quality, marked XXXX. The groupies loved that. You might have liked him, before all the drugs."

Owen stood up and put his hands on her shoulders, feeling the knots and massaging them. "Every one of us has made a mistake like that at one time or another." He walked over to the painting.

Skye set her plate down for Hope, who got to his feet and stretched out his remaining front leg like a yogi. "You talking about yourself?"

It was as if he didn't hear her. That painting had him rapt. She saw in his expression that her dad was lost in memories again. He was thinking about Margaret, apparently his one true love. "Daddy? Did you hear what I said?"

"Yeah," he said, and took the dishes into the kitchen. While he stood at the sink and scrubbed the plates, Skye read the want ads again. Slim pickings. Tomorrow she'd pick up the car, and then she could really start looking for her little girl.

DOLORES

I'M SPENT AS a sheet of wet newspaper from that appearance. I'll have to rest. For days. Time is running out. I had to make sure Owen saw the house. It was the only way. Men aren't so . . . easy to reach as women. Women are more willing to see things that don't make sense because their bodies are used to magic. Men need snakebite to loosen them up before they accept the otherworldly. But this Owen doesn't drink. Which makes it hard.

Next, I'll show him his horse.

The relationship between a man and a horse is sacred. It's easier to love an animal than another human. Give-and-take is easy when you don't speak the same language. And yet there are men—lost, afraid, and unable to allow the emotions of happiness and sorrow to coexist in their souls—who take their rage out on the animals.

I imagine that every single animal is welcomed into the realm without question. That they go straight to water and will never be thirsty. For some, there are seeds, and for the orangutans and parrots, perfectly ripe fruit. For the horses, beneath their hooves, the timothy grass never stops growing.

Chapter 7

A T S E V E N A.M. on Sunday, Skye was up, dressed, and
finishing her eye makeup, listening to her dad pace across
the flagstone floor, champing at the bit to get to his job interview.

"Jeepers, Daddy, you aren't meeting him until nine, relax!"

"I can't help it. I want to get there early enough to check the
place out. Make a good impression."

Skye laughed. "It's not like you're taking a test, it's a job
interview."

"Shows what you know, Sara Kay. I got a mess of handicaps,
the first one being my age, the second one being my age, and the
third one—"

"Don't call me that. Let me guess, the third being your age?
Just drop me at the mechanic's," she said in her pre-coffee raspy
voice. Everyone said cigarettes wrecked your pipes, but apparently so had booze. Soon enough, Skye couldn't stand her father's
nerves. "Fine. We'll go early. I hope the mechanic's open. Where's
the damn dog?"

The answer was, already in the truck. Hope spooked her a
little, seeming to sense whatever was going on, but then that was

what had interested her in animals in the first place: their ability to figure shit out before a human did.

Once they were driving toward St. Francis, her dad seemed calm, but the dog kept licking his chops, so Skye knew otherwise. Lobo and Lalo's Mechanics was a Quonset hut, but they did great work cheap. The OPEN sign was lit. "Thanks for the lift," she said as she opened the door to go pick up her mother's Mercedes. She'd had it since she was seventeen years old, so she guessed her mother didn't want it back. "Go knock 'em dead at the interview."

"I ain't leaving until that car starts up and I see you drive away," he said, holding the passenger door open.

"Then I guess I'd better haul ass. Lobo, where are you?"

Lalo, Lobo's five-foot-zero twin brother, walked over. *"Buenos dias, Señorita Sara,"* he said, handing her the keys.

"Muchas gracias, Lalo. But call me Skye. I'm not the same woman who dropped off this car. Say *hola* to Lobo for me. And tell him *muchas gracias* for letting me store my car here."

Lalo opened the door of her mother's Mercedes, and Skye smelled the misery she'd left behind locked up in there. Empty bottles, fast-food wrappers, and some clothes she'd planned to take to the dry cleaner ten months ago. Guess she could throw them away now. She put the key into the ignition, turned it, and waited for the rumble of the motor, but there was nothing, not even a click. Skye's dad sighed, and he waited some more. She turned the key three more times and then gave up. Her Spanish was not the best, but she managed, *"Qué hace el motor* every day?"

"Sí, sí," Lalo said. *"¡Qué hacer arrancar el motor cada día!"*

"Well, then why the hell won't it start now?"

Lalo's face reddened as he popped the hood, exposing the massive German motor inside. *"¿Podría ser muchas cosas, batería esta muerto?"* He looked at various wires and held up one cable with a frayed end. *"¡Esos malditos ratones que mastican en el cableado!"*

"Lalo," Skye said, "I have only *poco español. Lo siento. Despacio.*"

By now, her dad had shut off his truck and come to take a look. "He says the effing *ratas* chewed up the wiring."

"What am I supposed to do about that? Set a mousetrap on my carburetor?"

"Hola, Lalo," her father said, and shook the man's hand. *"¿Por favor, reparar el cableado?"*

Lalo nodded. *"Si, no hoy. ¿Tal vez mañana?"*

"Bueno." Owen took the keys from Skye and handed them to Lalo. "Just get in the truck, Skye. The car will be ready tomorrow."

"What'd you tell him?" Skye asked once they were on the road.

"To please fix the wires the mice chewed."

"Mice? I thought you said rats?"

"Rats, mice, what's the difference?"

"You should slow down, Daddy. There's bound to be a speed trap nearby. I ought to know, I got enough tickets in this town."

"Skye, you're giving me a headache. Please, can you just be quiet for ten minutes?"

"Well, pardon me," she said, leaning as close as she could to the passenger window. On her lap she held the bag of apples her dad had insisted on taking to the job interview. "Like bringing flowers, or a bottle of wine to a dinner," he'd said.

It was raining lightly—always something to cheer for in New Mexico—but soon it turned to wet splatters of snow, hitting the windshield like the spit wads kids used to throw in elementary school. Her stomach growled because they hadn't taken time for breakfast.

"Can I have one of these apples?"

"No," her dad said.

"You really think he'd notice one apple was missing?"

"No, I think you ought to wash the apple off before you eat it. Chemicals in everything these days."

"All right. Soon as we get there, I'm taking one because I'm hungry." *And angry, lonely, and tired?* she heard Duncan say. *H.A.L.T.*

Oh, shut up, Duncan.

Skye wondered if Gracie was awake, having her Cheerios and drinking from the little sippy cup she refused to give up. And who was feeding her breakfast? Rocky? Rita, while smoking a cigarette at the kitchen table? As they drove down Rodeo Road, heading toward 599, she noticed a few changes in the city's business end. In the mall, Mervyn's, where she could find the best panties, had gone out of business. Just down the road, there were another couple of car dealerships, a Kohl's, and a Walmart.

They headed across the intersection to Airport Road, toward the more rural community of La Cienega. There adobes dating back to 1700 stood in the shade of ancient cottonwood trees that turned to gold every autumn. But fall was a long way off, and while summer had seemed just around the corner, today it was raining, then snowing, and now it was dry again. Make up your mind, Skye thought. Overhead, the skies were ridiculously blue, as if the snow and rain were all in her mind.

They passed by the Santa Fe Trailer Ranch, cousin to the one Rita had lived in while in Albuquerque. It was a little village of singlewides set in the dirt, followed by a large lot filled with old RVs, a few "canned ham" aluminum trailers, and, scattered like precious gems among the rock, those silver bullets, the Airstream trailers she loved. The hills behind La Cienega were the site of many petroglyphs, dating back to the 1300s. Skye had hiked there herself, years ago, but Gracie had never seen them. She couldn't wait to show her daughter the petroglyphs and tell her stories about them. And everything else she'd missed doing with Little Gee. As the road curved, they passed a sewage treatment plant that hopefully was upwind of this yet-to-materialize stable/riding school. The *arroyo* on the other side of the road was dry, choked with salt cedar. They were less than a mile outside of La Cienega when she spotted the sign for the stable: *Reach for the Sky! A horse-centered therapeutic facility.* "Daddy," she said.

He clicked on his blinker. "I see it."

She could sense the nerves her dad was feeling. At his age, was he up to this kind of work? Lifting bales, grooming twenty horses a day? Shoot, he'd fallen deeply asleep after that walk up and down Canyon Road. Which kind of broke her heart because then she had to admit he was getting old. By the time they made their way down the winding gravel road, the sun cast a rosy light against an old, corrugated metal barn undergoing repairs with what looked like a decent-sized crew and lots of pickup trucks. He parked the truck next to a yellow Land Cruiser. Cool old car, Skye thought. A man came out of the barn to meet them, leaning heavily on a four-pronged cane.

"Wait in the car," Owen said to the dog.

"Don't mind me," Skye said. "I'm just chopped liver."

Her dad waved at the man, and she watched them shake hands.

Somehow Skye had expected the man interviewing her father would be massive and burly, the type that worked out every day and ate an entire pie for lunch. Instead, he was a slim guy—not bony, but not muscled out, either. He moved as if he were in pain, and as if it were that pain that kept him lean. His blue jeans were too nice to be working clothes and his shirt wasn't western cut with a yoke, just a plain chambray work shirt. He had short dark hair, a firm jaw. He was part Navajo, she could tell, but something else, too. The guy had a slight military air about him, so maybe he'd gotten injured in the service, hence the cane.

Owen and his interviewer went inside the barn, which left her with the dog, who was now sitting at attention, looking out the open window to where her dad had disappeared. "Relax, Hope. Chances are he'll get turned down in five minutes and be right back."

While she waited, Skye looked in the glove box and found only the registration, some receipts for gasoline, and a left glove she recognized as the one her father used when shoeing horses. Skye had no watch to see how long he'd been gone. All she had to go on was the rising sun and her empty stomach, which was now feeling downright hollow. And damn it, she'd forgotten to take an apple like she'd planned to. She dozed off, then jolted awake at Hope's whining.

"Need to go tee-tee?" Skye mumbled, and then realized it was how she talked to Gracie, not this three-legged charity case. She sighed and got out of the truck, yawning. "I'm going to see if they have a vending machine somewhere around here. You stay here, Hope. Hear me? Do not go into that barn or I will personally put you on a leash for all time."

The dog cocked his head at her. Maybe God knew what he was thinking, but Skye sure didn't.

Hammers and saws were at work somewhere inside the barn, and judging by the number of pickup trucks, there were construction workers inside. She couldn't help but think of Rocky, back when he did that kind of work. He stayed off drugs when he worked construction or on the road crew. One of the workers' trucks had a set of chrome-plated bull testicles hanging from his trailer hitch. That'd be real funny until a cop pulled him over and gave him a ticket because they were illegal, even in places like Oklahoma and Montana.

The men were building new stalls for the horses, she guessed. And where were those horses? Walking away from the noise, she checked out two good-sized arenas. There were a couple of Porta Potties and several equipment sheds, those metal prefab things you could buy at Home Depot. At her barn in Aurora, riders rented them to hold saddles and tack. Reach for the Sky had everything but a vending machine. She wandered over past the largest riding arena fenced with white pipe. Next to it was a covered arena, metal roofed like those northern New Mexico houses. Kind of spendy for a stable. She climbed the board walls and peered over. Here were the horses, wearing breakaway halters, milling about. She counted fourteen. Nothing to write home about, but solid candidates for a facility for the handicapped. They were bomb-proof and would never scare, once they got used to the kids.

Out beyond that was a wide-open space that culminated in the petroglyph-laden hills. She rested her arms on the rail, remembering the hours she put in training Lightning to become the best barrel-racing Appaloosa in the state of Colorado. Such good times. Too bad she hadn't appreciated them more. Even all this time later, put fifty-gallon drums in an arena, and Lightning would gather his muscles and run the cloverleaf. Thank goodness for horses, because riding had kept her hormones in check for a good five years. Without them, she might have become pregnant at fourteen.

Far in the distance, there came a rider, barely hanging on his horse, which was at full gallop. The horse must have been poky on the way out and now it was barn sour on the way back. Once an older horse knew it was heading back to the stable, it often decided to gallop home. The most stubborn animal, one that balks at trotting, could suddenly get fleet feet in its rush to get home.

Skye jumped down from the fence, curious. There was plenty of time to watch him, check out his seat, assess his faults—one of which was not keeping his elbows in. *Chicken arms—bwak, bwak,* Valerie the riding instructor would say when she taught riding lessons. *Bwak, bwak,* indeed. He transitioned to a trot, then a walk for the last hundred feet. He knew what he was doing, even if his riding style wasn't the best. He must have taken lessons. The chestnut horse looked vaguely familiar.

The rider neared, and then Hope leapt out of the truck and took off running toward him. "Dammit all," she cursed, and sprinted after Hope. "Get back here, you little weasel!" she said as she huffed along, trying to catch him. How could her dad have a problem dog? Hope should be used to horses; he'd have been around them day after day. Skye had an advantage, given that she had the requisite number of legs, and finally she overtook the gimpy dog. She caught him by the collar and yanked. The rider came toward her, and she was too out of breath to say, "Not horse-friendly!" He appeared to be around her age, a little older, and she stared at him, feeling her armpits dampen from exertion. If he didn't wear a hat, his sandy hair would bleach white in the high desert sun.

"That cannot be the same dog," he said.

"Excuse me?" she asked. The dog was remarkably strong, pulling her toward the horse.

"Hopeful?"

Skye was still catching her breath. "How would you know that?"

"We're old acquaintances," he said as he dismounted. He led the horse over to a Q-line Equestrian hot walker, shiny red, with four arms you could clip horses' lead ropes to in order to cool them down. It looked like an umbrella that had lost its fabric. He removed the horse's saddle and bridle, fitted him with a blue halter, and connected him to the equipment. Man, that horse reminded her of RedBow, her dad's old horse. The guy clicked the ON switch and the hot walker began to turn, forcing the horse to walk and cool himself down. He came toward her, carrying his tack. "Long story. I guess there are other tripod heelers, but this one I know. Your dog? Did you get him from the shelter?"

"Belongs to my dad."

The young man's face changed from friendly and open to something else. His tone went from friendly to accusatory. "Really," he said flatly. "Where is he?" He dropped the saddle and tack and rolled up the cuffs of his long-sleeved shirt. "Tell me where he is."

She didn't like the tone of his voice. "Why? Do you work for a collection agency?"

He looked away. "I just want to talk with him."

"I doubt that. Look, I don't know you from Adam, and clearly you don't know me, but one thing that's true is my dad's a stand-up, honest person, so if you have a beef with him—"

"Where is he?"

"Jeez! He's in the barn getting interviewed for a job. And don't you dare go in there and ruin it."

He picked up the saddle, placed it over the railing, and started to walk briskly toward the barn.

Skye grabbed his arm and hung on. "Back off, Roy Rogers. Tell me what the problem is, starting with your name. I'm Skye."

He shook her arm off, looked up at the sky, and wailed, "How can life be this unfair?" He crossed his arms over his chest, then pointed at the hot walker, where Hope had taken up residence, watching the chestnut horse go in circles. "See that horse? Did you know he once belonged to your dad? Did you know he abandoned it?"

"That's Red? My dad would never—" It slowly dawned on her that this guy was Margaret's son. Margaret, who painted the picture of the house that seemed busting with stories.

"Hate to burst your bubble, honey, but he did."

Skye hated being called "honey" or "sweetheart."

Before she could say so, the guy went on. "That loser. If it weren't for me, this horse would've been sent to the glue factory years ago. I paid his board, his medical care, and I schooled him for years. When I went to college, my *mom* paid for him to be fed, ridden, shod, veterinary visits, you name it." He pointed to his chest. "You know what that makes me?"

Skye couldn't help laughing at his indignation. "From here it looks like a bloviating a-hole. Am I close?"

Peter threw his arms up in the air. "You're just like him."

"I take that as a compliment."

He stared at her, and she noticed the blue earpiece above his left ear. What the hell was that all about? Was he part Cylon? Meanwhile, Hope waited patiently by the hot walker, studying Red's progress. "My dad's horse looks cooled down," Skye told him.

"My horse," he said, pointing at himself again. The gestures he intended to be dramatic came across as childish. *"Mine."* He stomped back to the hot walker, unhooked the horse, and began leading him toward the barn. Skye picked up the saddle and followed him. Hope loped alongside them as best he could.

"They're still making a racket with the power tools," she said. "Maybe you want to turn him out in the indoor arena until that's all done."

He huffed. "RedBow is bomb-proof. I've worked with him on that."

"Well, la-ti-frickin'-da for you. I'm sure he's that way because my father trained him first, because whatever you think of my dad, and I don't care to know, he is a real horse whisperer. And a great farrier."

The guy sighed and kept walking. His steps could have used Mrs. Wadsworth's finishing school. He moved purposefully, heading toward a showdown. At the stall, he checked the horse's feet one last time, while Skye put the saddle up on the rack. Hope lay down by the stall and, like a pretzel, rested his head on his back leg. "Never caught your name," Skye said. "Or is that classified information?"

"Peter. Not that it's any of your business, but I plan to have a little *chat* with your father, once he leaves the office. And whether he gets the job or not, I plan to tell Joe Vigil, who I met yesterday morning, exactly how that son of a bitch left his horse behind and never sent so much as a penny to take care of him."

"When he tells you why, will you stop being such a rageaholic?"

"What?"

"You heard me, Pete. Rageaholic. You act like a little kid who dropped his ice-cream cone and can't believe the universe won't give him a new one for free."

"Fine," he said, "call me whatever name you want. It's proof you're uneducated and that you have no manners."

"Me?" Skye said. "Looked in the mirror lately? What a miserable human being you are. Didn't your mama teach you how to be nice?"

He pointed at her. "Don't you of all people say one word about my mother. Your so-called father," he said, showing his bottom teeth, "left my mother high and dry ten years ago. Talk about manners. I can see you learned from the best."

"You know what?" Skye said. "You can fuck the fuck off, you whiny little prick."

Behind them, someone cleared his throat, and Skye turned around to see her dad with the crippled guy. "There a problem here?" the crippled guy said.

"No," both Peter and Skye said at the same time.

He held up his cane. "That's a relief. I was afraid I'd have to use some cane-fu on you two. I like everyone happy around my stable. Not a discouraging word, as they say." He smiled at Owen, and Owen smiled back.

"Skye, meet Joseph Vigil. My new employer." Owen looked at Peter. "Son, you have grown into a strapping young man. I believe I owe you some money for my horse."

"Not your horse anymore," Peter sputtered. "Eminent domain."

Her father patted Peter's shoulder, and Skye was surprised that Peter didn't immolate. "Let me say hello to Red and then we can talk. See the two plastic lawn chairs over yonder? I'll meet you there. Over the years I've come to believe that any disagreement can be better settled when sitting down."

"Come on, Peter," Joe said, steering Peter toward the office. "I could use your opinion on a couple of things."

Skye followed her father into the barn. Red started whinnying the moment her dad set foot over the threshold. Hope was lying down by the stall gate, cleaning his boy parts again. As Skye watched her dad move toward the horse, the horse leaned across the gate, whinnying, stretching his neck as far as it could go. Red pressed his head into her dad's outstretched arms like a lover. "I know, I know," he said, opening the gate and entering the stall. He turned, and Red took the bandanna in his back pocket out with his teeth. "He still remembers," her dad said, bringing an apple out of his pocket and feeding it to the horse as a reward.

Skye, still hungry, felt the absence of those ten years cut her like a knife. The horse knew her dad better than she did. She turned and walked out the barn door because she couldn't take one minute more of this reunion without feeling her heart break. And what would Gracie think of her, having been there one minute and gone the next? She'd rather take *ratas* poison than know the answer.

Peter was seated in the first chair, closer to the office doorway than the other one. He didn't even look up at her as she walked by.

"Skye," Mr. Vigil said. "Come on in here a minute. I'd like to tell you about our program. Who knows? You might decide to volunteer."

A great idea, she wanted to say, *giving away my time for nothing.* Whatever. Maybe I should have stayed in rehab, she thought as she sat in the folding chair next to his battered old desk. Already it was covered with dust, and it wasn't even summer. Mr. Vigil poured her a cup of coffee from a machine that looked past due for the bone pile. He reached under the desk to a dorm-sized fridge, took out a cardboard container of half and half, and pushed it across the desk to her. She dumped too much into her coffee, in the hope that it would silence her growling stomach, and then had to try to drink it without spilling.

He gestured toward the phone, blinking madly in its cradle. "See that? I have an answer machine filled all the way up with messages from everyone wanting this job. But I could tell the minute I heard your dad's voice that he was my barn manager. Him showing up early, that impressed me. His experience with livestock, horses, and his time in the pen, that sealed the deal. Most folks would hide that. Not your dad. He told me up front that he understood if it was a deal breaker, but that he was an honest man and wanted everything out in the open. Decided I'd hire him right then and there."

"You're an ex-cop, aren't you," Skye said.

He smiled. "How could you tell?"

"I'd say haircut, for starters." She pointed to the note pad by the telephone. The pad had the Albuquerque Police Department insignia on it. "That clinched it."

He laughed again, his eyes crinkling shut.

"I have a question," she said.

"Ask away."

"I was wondering about employment opportunities."

He nodded.

"Maybe you need some help around here?"

Joe leaned back in his chair. He frowned. "Our budget is already tapped out, and we haven't even opened yet."

"I'm sure it is," Skye said. She knew she shouldn't have pressed right after this man had hired her dad. "Never hurts to ask. I have to fulfill some community service hours anyway. Maybe I could do that here?"

Joe smiled. "I'm interested. What kind of work have you done with horses? Or are you experienced with kids?"

For a moment, Skye's throat seemed to close up. Once you became a mother, you were pretty much experienced at everything. "You might say kids are the heart of who I am."

The phone rang and Joe ignored it. "This facility will be serving handicapped children. Some of those handicaps are going to be on the inside. How are you with troubled children, or adults for that matter?"

Skye thought about that. "Takes one to know one."

"Good answer," Joe said.

"So far in my life I've only had a couple of paying jobs. I was a server at Guadalupe BBQ. Before that I was mainly a barn rat, mucking stalls and selling sodas at horse shows in exchange for lessons, feed, and boarding. Plus, I make great instant coffee."

Joe laughed. "I like a person with a sense of humor."

"Just like my dad, I can pick up a bale of hay and tell you how many ounces it's short."

"Ah," Joe said, steepling his hands together. "You admire your father."

Skye set down the cup. "We've both made our share of mistakes, but all that's in the past. Maybe he told you, I'm trying to get my little girl back."

"Oh?" Joe nodded, as if he were saying, *Tell me everything*. And she darn near did, but she felt compelled to go outside and check on her dad and Peter.

She swallowed hard, determined to end this conversation on a positive note. "And I will find her, no matter how long it takes." She pressed her hands on her jeans. "If there's a way for me to complete my community service here, I will work twice as hard as anybody else. If your riding instructor calls in sick, I can teach everything from trick riding to barrel racing. I can sense when a horse is going to colic, or founder, or needs to be turned out to run off the bucks. When a horse goes rogue, I know how to get people out of the way. I don't smoke. I don't waste time. I do a good job at whatever I'm supposed to do." Except for mothering, she thought. I seriously messed up at that.

"From this side of the desk, it sounds good. You're a determined young woman. I bet you'll find a paying job in no time at all, but in the meantime we'd be happy for you to do your community service here. How are you set for friends?"

She shrugged. "I'm kind of a loner."

"Then you have to come by my home and meet my two older daughters."

"Sure," Skye said, with absolutely no intention of doing that. She had finished the creamy coffee and her stomach was settling down.

"Would you be up for leading a group on trail rides?"

"Sure."

"I don't have it firmed up just yet, but it's in the plans. Let me get back to you when I've figured it out. How's that sound?"

It sounded like the first bit of luck to happen to her in so long that she was overcome for a minute. Just as she began to answer, there was a crashing sound outside, and both she and Joe Vigil jumped up to see what was happening.

Chapter 8

BEFORE SHE CROSSED the threshold of the office, Skye knew she'd pegged that Peter right—a rageaholic who didn't mind punching senior citizens—because her father was on the ground, blood at the corner of his mouth. He looked puzzled, as if he had been standing there one minute and was on the ground the next. In the palm of his hand he held a molar.

"Stop it!" Skye said, trying to get between them. But Joe took her arm, holding her back. Considering the cane and his limp, she was surprised at his strength.

"Don't," he said softly. "Sometimes, with men, the only way to work things out is with fists. Clearly these two have some history."

Owen stood back up. Peter threw punches every which way, while her dad blocked most of them. Then Peter got lucky and landed a blow on Owen's cheek, and Skye was horrified to see her father stagger back a few steps while he absorbed it. For the first time, he looked old to her. He regained his footing, and she felt herself cringe for the blow that was coming, but he picked Peter up by the shoulders and unceremoniously dumped him into the lawn chair with a thud. The breath rushed out of Peter, and he sat there, gasping, trying to get it back.

"Now," her dad said, "sit your behind down and we'll talk like civilized people."

Peter started to get up from the chair and Owen used one meaty hand to push him back down. "Breathe," he said. "That's right, nice and slow."

Then Owen sat down, too. He pressed the bandanna he carried into the corner of his mouth. Already a bruise was forming on his jaw, and what looked like it would be an epic shiner. The three-legged heeler came barreling around the corner, standing between Peter and Owen. "Late to the party, Hope," Owen said, "but I appreciate you showing up all the same."

Joe Vigil was laughing. He elbowed Skye. "If only we had some popcorn," he said. "This is better than a Hollywood movie."

Skye looked at him, surprised. That was not the response she expected, given the man's seemingly gentle nature. "Are you serious? He's like forty years younger than my dad. This isn't a fair fight."

"All the fireworks are over," Joe whispered. "Now they'll talk things out. Watch and see."

"That dog!" Peter said.

Owen studied his displaced molar. "Roots and everything," he said. "I guess I don't need to see a dentist after all."

Joe Vigil said, "We all done with the fists? Yes? Time to get some ice on your eye or it's going to swell shut."

"I'm fine," Owen said.

"I'm going to the convenience store and getting some ice anyway," Joe said, leaning on his cane, heading to his car. "Anybody want chips? Nuts? McDonald's? I'm buying."

"We already have a couple of nuts," Skye said. "I'd love a Coke. Maybe some red licorice."

"You got it."

"Thanks for taking such good care of Red," her dad said in his gravelly voice. "Horse looks great."

Peter stared at Owen. "Oh, sure. Show up after all this time, and expect to take the reins like nothing happened. Red is my horse. You abandoned him."

"I seem to recall that I asked you to take care of him, not to be his owner. Believe me, I came as quickly as I could. Only reason I headed here first was to gain employment. That's what I was doing until you jumped me. You were a punk when I left you, Peter. Breaks my heart to see that you haven't changed in that respect."

"I'm a punk? You're ten times worse than that. You're, you're—," he sputtered, searching for the term he wanted.

Owen cleared his throat. "I recall you once referring to me as a *Bonanza* extra. I have yet to hear an unkinder remark, so why don't we leave it at that?"

"No way, dude. You've put on weight. You could pass for Hoss on *Bonanza* now. So where the hell were you?"

"Prison."

Peter whistled. "Prison, whoa."

"When did you get your ears fixed?"

"Recently. So, Hoss, did you ever intend to contact my mom?"

Owen slid the molar into his shirt pocket. "'Course I do. I had to get myself squared away first. Namely, a job, so I can buy the gas to drive to Blue Dog to find her."

"Too late, asshole."

Owen's face fell. "What do you mean? Oh, Lord. She didn't pass away, did she? Or worse—did she move back to California?"

Skye wanted to slap the smirk off Peter's face.

"Nope. She's right across town. But last night I couldn't sleep, so I got up and messed around on her computer. She bookmarked all these sites on MS. Then I found the pamphlets. I confronted her. She's sick. Show up now and it'll look like a pity fuck."

"Don't use profanity in front of my daughter," he said.

Peter forced a laugh. "She swears worse than I do! Pack your shit and hit the road, Hoss. Last thing my mom needs is another round with you."

"You shut your pie hole or I'll shut it for you," Skye said. "My dad works here, you don't."

In the quiet that followed, Skye noticed that the construction workers had stopped hammering and sawing to watch the fight. All but one had bet on Peter to win from the looks of things, because everyone was handing one guy their ten-dollar bills. The guy who'd bet on Owen, a tall blond fellow rocking a sleeveless T-shirt, was raking in the dough. He saw her looking and wolf-whistled at her. "If you value your nuts, you won't do that again," she said, loud enough for them all to hear. His buddies all laughed and turned to go back to work.

From the barn came a whinny. Both her dad and Peter turned to look at the same time, nearly cracking heads. "He's got more muscle on him than I've ever seen," Owen said. "What were you feeding him?"

"Alfalfa pellets," Peter said. "He lost a couple teeth and that was it for hay. I put him on senior feed and vitamin supplements. He really likes a hot bran mash and massage."

"Well, who doesn't?" Owen said, and laughed. "I guess I owe you a pretty penny for all that. I hope I can reimburse you over time. Five hundred dollars a month work for you?"

Peter's frown returned. "I'll say it again, Hoss. You don't owe me a dime because Red is *my* horse. I've been caring for him for ten years, and I'm not giving him back."

Owen stood up. "In the Bible, King Solomon suggested that two women claiming to be the mother of the same baby should settle their problem by cutting the baby in half. The true mother backed out of that deal. So I guess that means you can keep Red," Owen said. "Since I'd hate for anything to harm my horse."

Peter laughed. "Don't try to pull that Jedi shit on me."

Owen chuckled, and Skye listened to his laugh: He sounded like Wilford Brimley, who did the diabetes commercials.

"Are we done fighting?" he asked Peter. "How about we revisit this issue at a later date? May I please have your mother's telephone number? And her address?"

"No."

The yellow Land Cruiser pulled up. Joe reached his hand out the window, handing a bag of ice and a six-pack of Coke to Skye. "They only had black licorice, so I didn't get any. No more punches?"

"Not a one," she said. "I think they're both tired out."

"Then I'll be heading home. Owen, glad to have you on board. Fill out those papers I left on the desk. Skye, there's a waiver for you, too. I've left two keys and the gate code. Owen, see you tomorrow."

"Thanks," Owen said. "Peter? Her address, phone number?"

Peter shook his head, then seemed to think better of it. "You know what? Whatever reception you get you deserve. We might as well get this over with so we can get on with life. Follow me."

Owen turned to Skye. "Honey? You mind driving? I can't see much out of this eye."

"Daddy, put some ice on it, for crying out loud. You should go to the ER and get an X-ray."

"I've been in enough fights to tell when I need medical help. I'm fine."

Peter walked toward *another* Land Cruiser, Skye noticed. Santa Fe was lousy with these cars. Up came the wind again, blowing grit around. She wanted to take a bath in lotion.

"Please reconsider, Daddy."

"No way. This here is my bargaining chip. I fully intend to let it bloom. That way Margaret can see there's not a mark on her son."

Peter turned around. "You're senile. My mom is going to take one look at your mangy old ass and shut the door in your face."

"We'll see about that. Accept the consequences for your actions, Peter. Same lesson you were learning ten years ago. Haven't gotten too far, have you?"

"Do you need to stop at Denny's for the early bird special, now that you're a senior citizen?"

Owen smiled.

"Daddy, are you going to let him get away with that?" Skye said.

"It's all right, Skye," he said, patting her icy hand. "One day he'll learn that no one escapes Father Time. Black eyes fade. Teeth, however, can't be put back in." He hollered out, "Your mom will make you pay for my dental visit."

Peter yelled back, "Doubtful! I'll bet you ten dollars she's madder at you than me."

"Ten dollars? Be serious. How about we bet Red? Whoever wins keeps the horse."

"No way!" Peter hollered. He pointed at the heeler, wagging the stub of his tail. "I still don't believe that's the same dog."

Owen yelled back, "What are the odds of me having two heelers with three legs in one lifetime?"

"With your lifestyle? I'd think pretty good."

"I think I liked you better when your ears were busted. What kind of flowers does she like?"

"Flowers? Seriously? As in, 'Sorry it's been ten years, here's some daisies'?"

"Roses," Skye said. "White or pink ones. Red is tacky."

Peter looked at her dad with a smirk. "If I lose you, take Cerrillos toward the Railyard. Make a left on Guadalupe. Turn right on Paseo de Peralta, and head up Canyon Road. Then look for Ave de Colibri. It's number 105."

Skye looked at her father. "Number 105? We were standing there yesterday. Right next door. Where you had the hallucination."

"It wasn't a hallucination, Skye. I saw that Indian girl as clear as I'm seeing you now."

"Well, you also just got punched in the head, so that's not a real strong argument."

"Can we just go, please?"

Peter slammed his car door and started his engine.

It had been quite some time since Skye had driven a column shifter. She stalled the truck twice but got it on the third try.

"If I ever needed a drink, today would be the day," he said.

Skye shifted into third. "If you get one, then I do, too."

"Am I an idiot to bring her flowers?"

"You'd be an idiot if you didn't. We'll stop at Trader Joe's before we see this mysterious Margaret. When I lived here, they had the best flowers."

Owen said, "Her son isn't worth two shits, but she is really something."

"So why didn't you write to her from prison, you jackass?"

"Haven't we been through all that?"

"Daddy? Let me ask you something. How often do you want a drink?"

"Every day of my life."

That was extremely disappointing news. Skye sighed and drove toward Cordova, where Trader Joe's was located. The wind was blowing trash across the road, empty McDonald's wrappers and plastic bags. There really wasn't anything else to say.

Chapter 9

WHILE PETER AND Owen were reacquainting themselves, Margaret was clearing out the casita for Peter. She raised her arms above her head and leaned forward to stretch her back. She blew out a breath, surprised at how tired she was after opening only one box. She'd been there since breakfast, trying to make sense of the space while Peter was out riding RedBow. Ellie had put these boxes in storage before she got sick. When she died, Margaret had cleaned out her rental space, canceled the contract, and moved the boxes out to the casita, since the house had no garage, only a carport. They were stacked three deep, and no matter how many Margaret moved, it seemed there was always another one behind the last. She had the overwhelming urge to get rid of them without opening a single one. Professional organizers say that if you haven't used something in a year, you don't need it. But what if she missed something special? Something that could change one's mind about life? Ellie had lived into her eighties. She'd been through the Second World War and had traveled the globe long enough to pick up some treasures. Margaret decided to keep looking.

"I promise I'll spend the day helping you clean out the casita," Peter had told her that morning, after he blew up over her diagnosis. He was unloading all his stress, especially the divorce stress, on a handy target. "I want to ride Red," he'd finally said, "and then I have a few errands to run." A good idea, Margaret thought, time to cool down. But these errands must have taken him to Timbuktu, because hours had passed and he still wasn't back. Worse, she'd found another wine bottle in the trash this morning, so his drinking wasn't just a onetime thing. Wine wasn't water except in the Bible, and the concept of "hers" seemed to be lost on him. At some point, they'd have to talk about it, but she wasn't sure he could handle any more bad news in one day.

He'd been using her computer and had looked at her browser history. He left a tab open, a medical site that discussed treatment options for people with MS, and when she saw what he'd found, she knew there was nothing to do but talk about it.

At first, he'd refused to look at her. Then he got angry. "Why in the hell did you not tell me about this?" he said. "How long have you known?"

"I was diagnosed the day before you called to tell me you were coming home," she said. "I've barely had time to process it myself."

"That's wrong. Normal people would call their kids. Immediately."

She wished she had the nerve to say, *Just as normal kids undergoing surgery for a cochlear implant would call their moms.* "Peter, don't freak out," she beseeched him instead. "I can't bear it just now. Dr. Silverhorse said I'm in the earliest stages. Sometimes my feet get pins and needles, and occasionally I trip. I have to make sure

I follow the diet and get enough rest. And avoid stress," she added, hoping that was a big enough hint to get him to calm down.

"Mom," he told her, "call Dad."

"Whatever for?"

"Because he lives in California, and California has the best doctors. You'll never find that in this place," he said, sweeping his arm as if Santa Fe were as small as her house.

"I like my doctor," Margaret replied. "He said there's nothing else to do for now. At some point I'll probably try some medicines, and I've already made an appointment for physical therapy. One thing I know for sure, in the future I will need physical help on a regular basis. A cleaning person, maybe even a gardener."

"I can do that stuff for you."

Maybe, she thought. "I can't imagine that day will come anytime soon. But in the meantime, I've decided to quit driving. You can take my car. In fact, it might make sense, after the divorce, of course, to transfer it to your name."

His eyes filled with tears. "Mom?"

She patted his hand. "Come on now, Peter. It's not that bad, it's just something we need to plan for eventually. Now go ride your horse, and when you get back, change into clothes you don't care about so we can get the guesthouse clean and ready for you."

Suddenly the emotion caught up with her, and she felt wrung out. "I need to lie down for a half hour."

"That's about how much time it will take me to run a few errands," he said, and left in a massive hurry, taking his cup of coffee with him.

As soon as he went out the front door, Echo settled down across the doorway to the guest room/studio. "Fickle," Margaret told the dog, who wagged her tail and would wait there all day for him to come back. Why should her son be any different at twenty-five from how he was at fifteen? Well, there were lots of good reasons, but Peter had never been the kind of son she could chart by consulting Dr. Spock. She woke up forty minutes later, surprised to discover that she'd slept. Maybe she needed to nap every day. But Peter wasn't there when she woke up, and he still hadn't returned.

Margaret pushed aside a couple of cardboard boxes. It was after eleven, and she'd skipped breakfast. Though her stomach growled, she didn't go inside to make lunch because surely Peter would be back any moment. She called his cell phone, but it went straight to voice mail. Besides the wine issue, he had forgotten to feed Echo this morning, which was a rather inauspicious beginning to their agreement that he'd pitch in around the house. She sighed, and then she opened another box, sneezing at the dust. When Peter secured a job, should she make him pay rent? How much? Was it enabling if she didn't? The casita seemed smaller than she remembered. But renting was a huge market in this part of Santa Fe.

Why hadn't she rented it before now? Laziness? Or was she afraid she'd attract a psycho tenant? Or had she subconsciously kept it vacant for when her sister got tired of London? Nori did everything gung ho until the day she was utterly over it. Margaret could have turned the casita into her painting studio, but now that Peter was here, he'd be better off out here in the guesthouse, coming and going as he pleased, than he would in the main house with her. Should she make dinner for two every night? What if he brought a girl home to spend the night? Was she feeling huffy about the idea of him staying because she was settled into her own routine? Was that selfish, or just growing older?

Motherhood had never been easy. Motherhood never ended. One day a year celebrating mothers wasn't enough. It should be the other way around, one day we *don't* celebrate, 364 days we do.

When Peter contracted meningitis, she was sure she was going to lose him. He'd lain there, comatose for weeks, and the doctors weren't optimistic. She'd read to him, played music—which she later knew hadn't reached him because he'd already lost his hearing. Some days she just sat there staring at him, afraid if she shut her eyes, he'd stop breathing. Nothing changed until the day she sneaked Echo I, Peter's dog, into the room and shut the door behind her. The dog was a basket case at seeing her human. She had jumped on the bed and straddled Peter, licking his face over and over. Later that day, he'd moved his hand, and his eyelids had fluttered open. He was able to track the doctor's penlight for a full four minutes. That was when he started his journey back to the living. Margaret had made a promise to herself: She would never forget how precious Peter was, even when he was acting out or yelling at her. Now those particular chickens had come home to roost.

She opened another box filled with coffee table art books. She wasn't up to picking through them just now, so she pushed it aside and wiped her hands on her blue jeans. Behind the box, leaning on its side against the wall, was Aunt Ellie's aluminum walker. It was a short-lived tool, but seeing it made Margaret's throat close up. Should she give it away or put it aside for herself? How long would it be before she needed it?

She opened a third box. Oh, for crying out loud, it was filled with adult diapers. Surely they could be of use to someone besides her. She'd take them to the Rosemont on Galisteo, a place she wasn't ready for and hoped she never would be. She lugged the box down the steps to the portal and set it away from the fence so Peter wouldn't smash the gate into it when he opened it.

Tears ran down Margaret's cheeks and she wanted to scream. Maybe age fifty was supposed to make you feel mortal. A year ago, she might have wished time would pass more quickly. Now she wanted it to slow the heck down, and for everything to stay the same, so she could catch her breath. She reminded herself that she'd had fifty good years before MS, and that was a blessing. She tried to maintain "a cheerful heart," as Glory would say. Glory should know, with all she'd been through: losing her first husband so early, adopting those girls, the unexpected babies, health issues of her own. Glory's husband, Joe, was in pain 24/7 from the shooting that had injured him and killed his best friend. Yet she never saw him without a smile on his face. Whenever she asked him how he was doing, his answer was, "Margaret, I'm so blessed I can't believe it."

Aloud, Margaret said, "In case anyone's listening, I'm grateful Peter is here. I'm thrilled he can hear again. I hope he gets the job at his old school and finds happiness." Then she felt silly. But while her own dreams and goals might be curtailed by the MS, her dreams for Peter would not.

Margaret ran her thumbnail down the brittle tape of box four. The gummy adhesive had dried out. What was once flexible tape had turned to brittle flakes sharp enough to cut, and naturally, she poked one of the shards below her thumbnail. Surprise, the box held more art books! In the middle of them, however, was a small gift edition of *The Virginian* by Owen Wister. Strange, because Ellie never read anything but British mysteries. Margaret tucked the small book into her jacket pocket. Underneath, wrapped in tissue paper and marked "keep," there were so many letters she couldn't count them. The stamps went from a penny postcard up to ten cents to forty-five cents. Some of the envelopes were that old airmail blue, the tissue-thin fold-and-seal kind. Some were plain envelopes, yellowed at the edges. She tucked the letters into her canvas shopping bag from Trader Joe's. She'd look them over later. It seemed crass, but her first idea was that she could sell them on eBay. Artists were always looking for old-timey cursive writing for projects. Weird, how letters had become an artifact. Glory said they didn't even teach cursive writing in school anymore.

Next she found Aunt Ellie's old English riding boots, which evoked a memory of her aunt on a horse, jumping fences with a smile on her face. The boots were thick with dust and needed a good saddle soaping, but they were gorgeous, and Margaret and her aunt wore the same size. A mouse or two had gotten to them, she discovered when she turned the left boot upside down and out fell the telltale dryer lint and dried grass that made up a nest.

It started to rain, and Margaret sat and watched it hit the windows, thinking of her aunt working in the garden, a grin on her face, chattering to her plants, Nash the cat rubbing up against her. Why couldn't she have lived her last years in peace, without the Alzheimer's? It didn't seem fair at all that the disease had robbed her of everything. Maybe a person would be better off dying in her sleep. Should Margaret get a DNR order on herself? How did those things work, exactly? How did a person know when to let go?

The rain that had started five minutes ago stopped. There was no evidence of wind, but the single-pane window in the casita began rattling. "Go towards the light, Dolores," Margaret muttered. It struck her—what would Peter make of the resident ghost? She'd been remarkably quiet for a couple of days, no doubt bothering Glory and Joe. But when she saw an opportunity to "noodge," as Glory's mother termed it, she took it. What did it mean? That Margaret should spend ten thousand dollars on replacing windows? Was Margaret messing about in Dolores's territory? Were there more artifacts to uncover, like the *retablo* devotional painting Glory and Joe had unearthed when they built their addition?

Minutes ticked by, and Margaret kept at it, removing the few things she wanted to keep. In addition to the book and letters she'd found, there was a perfect Lalique vase shaped like a trumpet flower and some turquoise jewelry marked "mine #8." It was "dead pawn," which meant the pieces had been pawned but never redeemed. The turquoise was that stunning sky blue you found in really old pieces. In a shiny black box with French words written on it—*pour la femme qui sait ce que les hommes apprécient*—she found a pair of unworn seamed black stockings, so old that they were popular again. By lunchtime, Echo had given up her watch for Peter and come out to the casita. She nudged Margaret in the knee, which meant *Walk me.*

"All right," Margaret said. She gathered up the letters, the boots, and a book on Chagall. She took care going up the back steps, and once indoors, she washed her hands and face, taped a Band-Aid over the paper cut she'd forgotten about, and strapped on Echo's harness. The dog was in the throes of what Peter referred to as "chopper tail," wagging so hard that it kind of broke

Margaret's heart. By now Echo probably thought seeing Peter was a dream. It was a good time to walk—the lunch hour for most people. After two in the afternoon, the traffic would pick up, and as people left work for the day, it would only get worse.

"Just a short one today," she warned Echo as she opened the front door. Before they could take a single step, she saw her Land Cruiser pulling into the carport. The driver's-side door opened and Peter emerged. Then came an old black truck with one of those split-screen windshields from the 1930s or 1940s—very Santa Fe. A pretty blond girl Margaret didn't recognize got out, and it wasn't until the passenger-side door of the truck opened that she realized this was no neighborhood entrepreneur selling firewood or asking for work. Either she was hallucinating or the man walking toward her carrying an armful of peach-colored roses was Owen Garrett. Her hand went instinctively to her pocket, touching the book. Echo jerked the lead from her hand, rushing toward Peter, and Margaret tried to stabilize herself by placing her right foot forward, forgetting the loose brick on the middle step. She fell, breaking the fall with her left hand.

The next thing she knew, three human faces and one dog's peered in closely. Too closely: It was making her claustrophobic.

"Mom, are you okay?" Peter babbled. "Should I call an ambulance?"

"Don't be ridiculous," she responded. "I'm perfectly fine. Physically. Though I'm worried I'm hallucinating." She looked directly at Owen. "Where did you come from?"

"Help her up," Owen said in a voice she'd recognize anywhere, taking hold of her right hand. "Better get some ice on that wrist."

Margaret stared in wonder, her lips parted a little. The blond girl brought her a small plastic bag filled with ice for her arm, but honestly, Margaret felt no pain as she sat on the ground. She had heard Owen's voice, so it wasn't a vision—it was real. She focused on him as he smiled down at her, his craggy face just as she'd known it ten years ago, although there was an addition to his scar in the form of a black eye. She reached out to touch it but was distracted by the scent of the roses in his arms, which was overwhelming and dreamlike—she couldn't take in air quickly enough.

"Help me inside," she told Owen.

While she leaned on him, he led her to the old Rawnsley sofa she'd found in a consignment shop and reupholstered herself in a San Miguel Pendleton blanket. She'd lugged it from Blue Dog to Eldorado, and now to Santa Fe proper. Ten years ago, she and Owen had sat on this very piece of furniture, talking and kissing, and now Margaret had to pat herself to make sure she was in one piece, that all this was real.

"You," she said, pointing at Peter, who stood in the doorway with the dog. "Take Echo for her walk."

"Leave Hope here," Owen said. "He didn't do too well yesterday."

"And when you get back," Margaret said, "clean up the back yard—I put some boxes out there while I was cleaning the casita."

"You sure you're okay, ma'am?" said the blond girl, her hands on the doorjamb while chilly air blew in.

"I'm fine. Could I have a glass of water?" Margaret asked her, and without speaking, the girl bolted to the kitchen.

After Margaret drank half a glass, she looked up at the girl. "Are you Sara Kay?"

The girl nodded. "I go by Skye now. It's nice to meet you. My dad has told me about your art, and your time in Blue Dog."

Margaret smiled. "Please call me Margaret."

"Sure thing, Miss Margaret. I think I'll tag along with Peter if that's all right."

"Why wouldn't it be?" Margaret asked, and the look Skye and Peter exchanged told a story all right.

"Come on," Peter grumbled.

Margaret turned to Owen and poked a finger into his chest. "You disappear for ten years," she said, her voice wobbling, "suddenly materialize, and what? You expect me to be happy to see you? I'm furious."

"I thought you might be. I missed you every single day."

"Don't you sweet-talk me. I am immune to compliments. Where were you? Why didn't you write?"

"I meant to. I just didn't know what to say. I have a hard time with words. The right ones, anyway."

Peter and Skye headed out, shutting the door behind them so quietly that Margaret was surprised. She turned to Owen. "I hope they stay gone for at least an hour, because I have a lot of questions for you."

"Fire away," Owen said, embracing her and smiling as if they had all the time in the world.

Such assumptions! Her pride hadn't been injured; it had been *maimed*. Words died in her mouth. He kissed her on the forehead, both cheeks, and placed his hand on the small of her back, murmuring, "Maggie, Maggie . . ." Ten years' worth of tears began coursing down her cheeks.

"I was released a week ago," he told her, still holding her close. "I had to help my daughter and find employment—you were next on my list. I'd planned to start asking around in Blue Dog, but here you are."

He'd been in prison, all this time. Her chest filled up with sorrow, imagining the years, how slowly time must have passed. But on the heels of sorrow came anger. "You are a complete jackass," she said. "Do you know I thought you were dead?"

"Sometimes it felt that way, being in prison."

"What happened? Did that man you hit in that fight die? Did they charge you with murder?"

"Easy, Margaret. He lived. He talked to the judge and said the minimum sentence for aggravated assault was all he wanted, because he said he was guilty of starting it." Owen touched his lips to her neck. Probably someone younger than Margaret would have made him wait, held him at bay until all her questions were answered. She knew he expected her to vent. But as a fifty-year-old woman with MS, she now knew time was a commodity, and there was so little of it. She kissed him back.

So much had changed in ten years, including desire. She didn't need a sloppy tongue kiss. The trembling pressure of their lips together was more than enough to say what each of them meant: *I loved you then, I love you now, we can do this forever.* She broke away and touched his face, felt the swelling around his eye tenderly.

"Did you learn nothing in prison about avoiding fights?"

"I didn't lay a hand on the other guy," he said.

"Somehow I doubt that. Who did this to you, and why?"

Owen laughed and shook his head. "Let's just say you raised quite a fighter."

"Peter? Are you kidding me?"

"I am not. He didn't give me quite the warm reception you have. It's just a hunch, but he was already looking for someone to hit, I think, and I just happened to be handy."

Margaret sighed. "He's going through a really hard time. Divorce," she explained. "But that's no excuse. It's like my son has a doctorate in anger, not a master's in comparative literature." She ran her fingers through Owen's beard, which was grayer than she remembered, but then so was her hair. "It's exactly the way I remember it," she said, "so soft." She leaned into his body, smelling hay underneath the roses. "Where did you run into Peter?"

"At my new place of employment. Reach for the Sky. You're looking at the new barn manager."

Margaret gasped. "The Vigils live next door to me. Joe and Glory. Are you serious?"

He laughed. "Yes. Next door, you say? I think I've met her—silver-haired woman, rez dog named Curly, tiny greyhound?"

"That's Glory."

"Where I'm staying, in my ex's casita on Canyon Road, one of your paintings is hanging on the wall. Took my breath away when I saw the Starr farmhouse. My daughter says it was a sign."

"Your daughter is brilliant," Margaret said, running her hand over the sleeve of his flannel shirt.

When Owen pressed his hand to the small of her back, the sensory memories of their past came pounding back. This touch was a signal, the prelude to making love.

She started to say, "Wait—," but Owen interrupted her.

"Right now, let's be selfish, Maggie. Don't we deserve that?"

Under his hands, she felt as if her skin were softening. Light and love coursed wetly through her veins, making her dizzy with desire. How strange to feel that wanting again. The ten years they'd spent apart disappeared. Owen sighed, her breath grew ragged, and she felt she could not get close enough. "Bedroom," she said, but he shushed her, already pulling her there as if he knew the way all along.

Hope followed.

Skye and Peter walked carefully along Canyon Road, stepping up onto narrow curbs when cars came by, stopping to look into gallery windows. "Echo, huh?" she said. "Where'd her name come from?"

"If you know your Greek mythology, you'll remember Echo was a nymph. She abetted Zeus in his extramarital pursuits, until Zeus's wife, Hera, found out. Hera decided to punish Echo by taking away her voice, by only allowing her to repeat what was said to her. Or am I telling you something you already knew?"

Skye matched his smug little grin. "Oh, pardon the hell out of me for not being your intellectual equal in matters that make no difference," she said. "What are you? A professional student?"

"Close," Peter said. He stopped to untwist the leash from his leg. Echo kept turning around to look at Skye, as if to say, *Where did you come from?* Her ears were pricked forward the same way Hope's were when they were driving to Albuquerque. Apparently both dogs thrived on adventure. "As a matter of fact, I am a college professor."

"What do you teach? Fairy tales?"

"It's called comparative literature. Folktales, fairy tales, urban legends, and magical realism."

"Really? Sounds like bedtime stories to me."

"Is being snarky in your DNA or are you just bitter?"

"Bitter? What do I have to be bitter about? I'm just your

everyday happy and sunny twenty-three-year-old just out of rehab and trying to find her missing daughter."

Peter whistled. They started walking again. "Please disregard my comment." He gestured with his free hand, nearly hitting a tree branch. "I guess I'm just annoyed at your father showing up, and I'm transferring that irritation to you."

More college words, Skye thought. "Your mom didn't look too annoyed."

"Duh. I noticed."

"Plus, you were the one who started the fight."

Peter sighed. "I named my first dog after a nymph because I was a geek who had few friends in high school. This Echo," he said, pointing to the dog, "is not the original, by the way, but one of her pups. I named her Echo also because it made sense, as if she was an Echo of her mother. And she kind of is. Very sweet-tempered and affectionate. By the way, your father's mangy dog, Hope?"

"What about him?"

"He's Echo's dad. Fortunately for me, she takes after her mother, not her dad."

"You are the touchiest bastard I've ever met," Skye said, running her hand along an adobe wall with exposed brick, rounded and worn by the elements.

"Have you ever considered that maybe you bring out that quality in people?"

"All I did was speak my mind."

"You certainly do that," he said, and laughed. "Often."

Neither one of them said another word until they came to the crest of Canyon Road. On the other side of the street, El Farol was no doubt setting up tables for the dinner crowd. Skye was beyond hunger now, and she was itching for a drink. She wondered if the servers would mind if they brought Echo indoors, just long enough to order a Coke, because maybe if she poured an icy Coke down her throat, it would squelch the desire for alcohol.

But no, the truth was the taste of Coke made her crave rum. "I have an idea," she told Peter. "How about we head back to my place, give the old fogeys some time to get their freak on, then get something to eat?"

"God, could you think of a more disgusting way to phrase that?" he said.

"Oh, pardon me. I had no idea you were so uptight. Let me put it delicately, then," she said. "Let us allow our respective parental units to make splendiferous, meaningful, tidy love in private, so we don't have to listen to their cries of passion."

Peter said, "I seriously doubt my mother would allow your father, after ten years, to—didn't you see how angry she was? She's probably slapping the shit out of him as we speak."

"Now *there's* a fairy tale," Skye said, and laughed. "They're lovebirds, like on my cowboy boots." She lifted one to show him.

Peter said, "I noticed your gaudy footwear at the stables. They don't look very practical."

"Where is it written that everything has to be practical?"

"I hope my mom is all right. She could've broken her wrist."

"So take her to the ER for an X-ray."

"I was thinking more along the lines of calling her neurologist."

"I'm sure she'll be fine," Skye said, remembering Gracie's wrist in the tiny pink cast. "If it's broken, it'll heal in six weeks or so."

"My mother, in case you haven't noticed, is a painter."

Skye looked at him. Could he be any more annoying? "Dude, I'm not blind."

They had walked by the river, made a lap around the Plaza, stopped to listen to music, bought coffee at Starbucks, and walked by the Palace of the Governor's, before walking back toward Canyon Road. Two hours had passed by the time they made the turn for home, Skye looked in the shops that would soon be closing for the day, drawing out the walk long enough to give Owen and Margaret some alone time. Just the sight of the Railyard made Skye purse her lips and recall the feeling of going headfirst into the Mercedes's windshield. A *whoosh* as the airbag inflated and the gasp she made when it punched into her stomach, because her seat belt wasn't fastened. The smack of her forehead against the glass as it shattered, like thousands of snowflakes that refused to fall. Her nerve endings had shut down because of the shock, but she didn't pass out because Gracie was in the backseat. Her mother-radar had kept her vigilant. "Gracie," she had said, "honey, you all right? Talk to Mama . . . Gracie, answer me! . . . Gracie!" She couldn't get out of the car fast enough and had torn her shirt on the twisted metal. She listened hard for the little peeping voice and couldn't hear it over the screech of sirens. Finally, a whimper: "My arm hurts, Mama." That broken bone had been all her fault. Oh, God, just the idea of it made her sick to her stomach.

Skye and Peter passed the Chalk Farm gallery, one of her favorite Santa Fe places because it was dog-friendly, filled with plants, a fish pond, and a waterfall, and it wasn't your run-of-the-mill *artsy art* gallery.

"You ever been in here?" she asked. "It's a cool place. Not like the la-ti-da galleries."

"I live in D.C."

"Near the White House?"

"Everything's near the White House when you live in D.C."

"Have you ever seen the president?"

"As a matter of fact, I went to his inauguration."

"Wow. You must be somebody important. Did you tell him a fairy tale?"

"Hardly," said Peter. "I was invited because I was deaf."

"So I guess the music was wasted on you," Skye said, snickering, "because your ears were still broken."

"Does your sense of humor come from a different planet?"

"Sorry. I know that's a touchy area. On the way over here, my dad filled me in on your hearing. Why didn't you get your ears fixed earlier?"

"Because I was a stubborn asshole."

"Ah, finally you say something I totally agree with," Skye said. "You are not hopeless after all. Had my doubts there for a while. So, you gonna give my dad his horse back?"

"Absolutely not."

"You live in D.C., where you teach students about fairies. Why do you need a horse? Do you do those Civil War reenactments? Hey, there's my place," she said, gesturing to the tiny adobe. "Come on in. Have a glass of water. Maybe that'll cool your jets."

Peter shook his head. "I really hope you don't have any siblings."

"I don't. Why?"

"Because I seriously doubt the world could handle another person like you."

"Yeah," she said, smiling. "I am a one-of-a-kind, amazing,

no–bullshit, don't–mess–with–me only child." She opened the door and turned on the Moroccan lights, which glowed like honey, casting light on all her mother's treasures. "Have a seat," she said. "Let me see what there is to drink or eat." She opened the fridge, looked in the cupboard, and said, "Your choices are coffee or water."

"Then I guess I'll have water."

Skye brought a bowl filled with water and set it in front of the dog first. Echo wagged her tail and sniffed it before she drank.

While she filled two drinking glasses, Skye noticed that just like her dad, Peter went directly to Margaret's painting. She wondered whether Peter was a painter or did something artistic. Probably he painted fairies or whittled little garden gnomes. She laughed, then handed him his water and sat on the couch.

"What's so funny?" he asked.

She laughed again. "If I told you, I'd have to kill you."

"You are the most unreasonable person I've ever met," he said, and sipped his water.

"Thanks. I try." She tried to imagine him in a jacket with suede elbow patches, talking about Little Red Riding Hood. "You have any money?" she asked.

"A little. Why?"

"Because I think we ought to go out to dinner and I don't have any money."

"How are we going to get there?"

She pulled her father's keys from her pocket. "It's not that long a walk to your mom's. We could shut the dog inside and drive somewhere in my dad's truck. Go get McDonald's or Lotaburger. I'll pay you back, I promise."

He looked at her as if she were speaking Welsh, that crazy language without vowels. "Fast food?"

"Why not?"

"Because it's terrible for you."

"You want to walk back up the road to El Farol?"

"No. I'd like to go somewhere to eat that has healthy food and more than one vegetarian option."

"So order a freaking salad. McDonald's makes salad. Or I can eat the burger and give you the bun. Frankly, I don't understand vegetarians. The cavemen ate meat. They started everything and led to us. It's natural."

"Oh, my God!" Peter exclaimed. "Who are you and where did you come from?"

Skye thought of Duncan, chiding her. *You need to dial it down, Skye. Not everyone runs at Mach one. Causes misunderstandings.*

She sighed. "All you need to know is that I'm newly sober and my first priority is getting a job and finding out where my soon-to-be ex-husband stashed my four-year-old daughter."

"I'm getting divorced, too."

"Got kids?"

"I wish."

"Trust me, it's better you don't. It hurts like you can't believe."

Peter was looking at her in a different way now. Revealing her embarrassing truths should have made him steer clear, yet it seemed to have the opposite effect. He leaned toward her, looking as if he wanted to kiss her, and she jumped up from the couch. "Did you not listen to a word I said? Turn up your hearing apparatus already. Let's go to La Choza. It's got cheese enchiladas and the most awesome red sauce. I will pay you back."

*

"Your daughter, Skye," Margaret said, snug in Owen's arms, their clothes on the floor. His dog was making a nest in them. "What a stunner with that blond hair, and her smile. Does she take after your ex-wife?"

"Skye doesn't take after anyone," he said. "God gave her beauty. But don't let that fool you. She's a hellion."

Margaret laughed. "Owen, she has your eyes and your nose, how can you not see that?"

"I stepped on my glasses." He rubbed his hip and winced. "My hip hurts. Does yours?"

"Not yet. I'm sure everything will hurt in the morning, but right now, I can't feel anything except how happy I am. It feels like my body is singing. Want me to rub your hip?"

He laughed. "Tempting. I can think of a few other places I'd rather have you rub, but not until I get my strength back. How's your wrist?"

"Sore." Margaret sat up and pulled the sheet to her breasts. "And I'm starving. I forgot to eat breakfast, lunch, and what time is it?" She reached for the alarm clock on her bedside table. Owen kissed her left breast as she leaned toward the nightstand, and she looked at him. "Owen, really?"

"Can't help it," he said. "It was on an intercept course."

Margaret laughed. "Stop that! I'm going to make us some scrambled eggs. Or I think I have pasta. I can make a tomato sauce. That okay with you?"

He smiled at her. "I will eat right up whatever you fix and ravish you again. Only if you let me help you make the dinner, though. And sometime we should talk about the multiple sclerosis."

So Peter had told him. She turned on a bedside lamp. "I'm

fine right now," she said. "But my doctor says symptoms will progress."

Owen turned her face to his. "I will be there every step of the way."

Margaret leaned into his hand, feeling the warmth and kindness. "That's a long road, Owen. Part of me wants help. The other part is just so damn angry this had to happen." She looked out the window to the casita, which was dark. All the boxes were sitting next to the gate where she'd left them. Damn it all, did Peter ever listen? Where was he? "For now I need to eat right and rest."

"So no flamenco dancing?"

She laughed. "Owen, how can you joke?"

"And I suppose that means no more trapeze swinging, climbing Everest, or marathon runs?"

"Right now? It's more like not doing anything when I'm tired. And no doughnuts."

"That does it," he said. "I can't love a girl who won't eat doughnuts. It's just unheard of."

"Telling Peter didn't go well. I'm pretty sure that's why he hit you."

"I agree. That young man needs to learn anger management." Owen stood up and reached for his shirt, which was half under the dog. "Hope, move, damn it. I can't walk around the house half-nekkid or I'll scare the furniture."

"Would you care for coffee?" the waitperson asked as she cleared the dishes from their table at La Choza, including Peter's third jumbo margarita glass.

"I think it's a little late for coffee," Skye said to the woman. "Peter," she whispered, "give me your wallet. I need to pay for our meal and leave a tip big enough to make these people forget about your ridiculous behavior."

"I wanted an after peef."

"What?"

"Apter reef," he said, slurring his words. "Aw, shit. I want another drink."

"Shh," Skye said. "There are families with kids in here. Don't wreck their night, too."

"I'm thirsty," he stage-whispered. "How's that?"

"After three massive drinks there is no way you are thirsty. I'm going to remind you of that tomorrow morning when I bang pots and pans in your face to wake you up."

"You're so pretty," he said. "Just pretty, pretty, pretty! I want to kiss you."

"Of course you do," she said. "You're drunk. But since you're my friend now, I'm offering you a shortcut here. I have a suitcase full of problems. You don't want to kiss me to *kiss* me. You want to kiss me for the same reason you hit my dad. To show me who's in charge and to avoid dealing with your own rude behavior. So resist the urge, Professor. Believe me, you're better off. Right now I'm sure I look like a way to work your yayas out, and then forget about them. But I am not—nor will I ever be—that chick. *¿Entiende usted?*"

"But you're so pretty!"

A plastered Poindexter. That was just what she needed. Somehow she had to haul this marinated hulk out of the restaurant and get him into her dad's truck. She hoped he didn't throw up, because that was not her department. Child barf, yes. Adult barf? Nobody's but her own.

"I'm real sorry," Skye said to the host at the entrance. The place was packed with people hoping to get a table. "Excuse me," she said, moving through the throng of hungry people. "My friend doesn't seem to be getting along on his feet too well. First person who helps me get him to that truck gets five bucks."

A burly guy stood up immediately. "Want me to fireman carry him?"

"That would be great."

He picked Peter up and hoisted him over his shoulder. The host followed them out the door and onto the sidewalk, complaining. "I'm supposed to call the cops when someone gets that drunk. If he drives, our restaurant can get fined."

Skye wagged the keys. "He isn't driving, I am." The burly man dumped Peter by the truck, where he promptly sat in the dirt. "Here's your money," Skye said, taking it out of Peter's wallet. There had to be at least two hundred dollars inside. Professors must get paid pretty good.

"Can you throw him in the truck bed?" she asked.

"That's illegal," the host said.

Peter was now groaning a little. "Well, I can't have him puke up front, so I'll call a cab."

"They can take up to an hour to get here."

Skye shot a withering look at the host. "I'll call," he said quickly. "See if I can hurry them up." He pulled out a cell phone and dialed. "I'll stay here until you get him in the cab, but I'm not helping. I have a bad back."

"Whatever floats your boat," Skye said, leaning against the driver's-side door. Peter slumped at her feet, and within a few minutes, he was snoring.

"So," Skye asked the host as the minutes ticked by, "any openings for servers?"

He lit a cigarette. "You never know. We get a lot of turnover in tourist season. I can get you an application."

After fifteen minutes, Skye had filled out her application and learned that the host had four children, liked Mumford & Sons, and was also an artist, like everyone else in Santa Fe. She explained about her fruitless search for Gracie, and the man nearly cried. That was Santa Fe for you, filled with empaths and soft hearts.

"I hope you find her, mija," he said when the Capital City cab arrived.

"I will," Skye said, though she wasn't sure about that at all.

The cabdriver got out. "If he yorks in my cab, you're paying for it."

"Here's ten bucks even if he doesn't." Damn, it felt good to give away money. Why not? It wasn't hers. Skye helped the driver buckle Peter in. "Do not move," she said to Peter. "If you so much as reach for the buckle, I will personally remove the parts that make you a man."

Peter smiled and babbled some more. Lord, even in her drinking days, Skye had been able to handle a couple of jumbo margaritas just fine. What a weakling. "Follow my truck," she told the driver. "We're only going a couple of blocks—105 Colibri Road off Canyon."

He nodded. "I know where it is."

"Don't worry, girl," Skye told Echo as she drove back to Margaret's. "In a couple of hours he'll be all right. We're almost home."

Parking the truck where it had been before, behind the Land Cruiser in the carport, she honked the horn twice. She leashed the dog and let her out of the truck. She stood in the light of the cab and hollered, "Daddy!" just as the door opened. Her father came out, his hair wet from a shower, she guessed. "Peter's smashed and I need help getting him inside."

Her dad nodded. "Take the dog in and let Margaret know."

Inside the house, Margaret stood at the stove, stirring something in a frying pan. It was the first time Skye had been alone with her, and since the woman was clearly wearing nothing but a bathrobe, conversation didn't come easily.

"Does your son have an alcohol problem?" Skye asked. "He got wasted at dinner."

Margaret set the spatula on the counter and turned off the burner. From the look on her face, the answer was yes. "I'm sorry you had to see that," she said, starting for the front door, but Skye took her arm.

"Daddy can handle it. Let's get the bedroom ready. I recommend you put a bucket on the floor. He's really drunk."

They looked at each other for a moment. The glow emanating from Margaret released heat the way a bad sunburn did. "A funny way for us to meet," she said.

"Not to me," Skye said. "I could write the book on funny."

Margaret smiled. "Well, we can talk about that later. I guess I better go open the foldout couch for him."

"I'll help," Skye said. She followed the plaid flannel robe down the hallway and into what looked like her painting studio. "My mom has one of your paintings," she said. "I wish you could have seen the look on my dad's face when he saw it. You must be pretty special."

Margaret smiled and removed the cushions from the couch. "So's your father."

"Well, there you go," Skye said. "We're going to get along just fine, Margaret, because I agree. Tomorrow morning, I'll be over at five thirty sharp."

"Whatever for?"

"I'm going to take Peter to his first AA meeting. After that, he's on his own."

"Thank you," Margaret said. "Your father told me about your daughter. If there's any way I can help, please let me know."

Chapter 10

THE NEXT MORNING, Skye joined hands with strangers she didn't know and chanted "Keep coming back because it works when you do and it won't when you don't."

"So that's how you get sober," Skye told Peter as they left the AA meeting on Rosina Street and Isleta, at the Friendship Club. "And from here on out it's up to you. I need to focus on finding my daughter."

Peter had put on his sunglasses. "I need a nap," he mumbled.

"No, you don't," Skye said. "You need a Coke, a couple aspirin, and then you need another meeting. There are meetings practically every hour in Santa Fe. Come on, let's get a soda or some coffee. Then I'll walk you back to the Friendship Club."

"Please," he begged. "Dump me in an alley and let me die."

"Aw, that's just the hangover talking. Come on. It's a nice sunny day and the birds are chirping. Let's go in this diner and get some bottomless Cokes and yummy bacon and eggs with wiggly yolks."

"Skye, I have to go to the restroom," Peter told her as soon as they were seated at a booth near the courtyard.

"I don't know where it is. You could ask the waiter."

He stood up and made his way to the front, walking as though every bone in his body were hurting. The waiter pointed, and Pete limped down the hallway. Skye remembered plenty of mornings like that. Waking up only to wish she had died in her sleep.

While she waited, she retrieved her note pad from her hoodie pocket and reviewed the list.

Maybe the lawyer's name was Church?
Call PRCA back—see if they have a record of the upcoming
    events Rocky's registered for.
Find Rocky's dealer.
Drive to T or C?
Give up and call the cops.

The diner was directly across the street from Guadalupe BBQ. Skye was a mouthy waitress, always ready to laugh, even when the joke was on her. It made her really popular, which resulted in great tips. But as good as that memory of her apron pocket stuffed with money was, Guadalupe BBQ was the scene of the crime: the place she'd once left Gracie curled up on the floor of Milton's office, sleeping on a ratty blanket. Skye had forgotten her—not for a moment, but for an *hour*.

She'd been in a hurry to get downtown after her shift ended at ten. Catfish Hodge was playing the blues at Vanessie's piano bar. She found a great parking spot on Water Street and stumbled through the door, thinking that even though she smelled of fries and onions, she looked good in a denim miniskirt, a navy tank top, and her Old Gringo forget-me-not cowboy boots. The place was crammed. She found a place up front and ordered a Dos Equis and a double shot of tequila, trying to relax. Between work, Gracie, and Rocky coming and going, her schedule was always so crammed that her mind was never truly at rest. Maybe she needed a Xanax. She found one in the bottom of her purse, picked off the lint, popped it, and swallowed. Every time another worry nagged at her, she ordered another shot, followed by a beer. Catfish Hodge and the Hillbilly Funk Allstars wailed through "Like a Big Dog Barking" before Skye remembered—*holyshitholyshitholyshit*—that this was her night with Gracie and she'd left that sweet girl in Milton's office at Guadalupe. She pushed her way through the crowd, tripped, and landed in some guy's lap, apologized, pushed some more, and finally, crying, told the bouncer, "Get me out of here!" Lord, bouncers weren't paid enough. The way he picked people up and out of the way made her want to kiss him. It took a while to remember where she'd parked her car. She threw up in the street, wiped her mouth, ignored the horrible comments made by people walking by, and gunned the Mercedes's engine. God bless German engineering—it took her about three minutes to get back to Guadalupe, where she parked crookedly on the street, begging Jesus that no harm had come to her baby. Milton was waiting at the bar, and Gracie was fast asleep.

"Nice to see you finally remembered you had a child," Milton said.

In her mind, Skye was saying, *ThankyouGod*, but a different story came out of her mouth. "You shut up. Rocky was supposed to pick her up."

Milton sighed. "You're a terrible liar and a worse parent."

"Yeah, maybe, but at least I'm not a judgmental asshole."

She'd never forget the look on Milton's face, sorry for her, sorrier still for Gracie. He grabbed her keys out of her hand so fast that they left a burn. "You sit down and drink some coffee."

"I'm fine to drive," she said.

"No, you're not." He poured her a cup and watched her drink it down black.

Gracie's head lolled to the side. What with all the yelling and partying that took place at Skye and Rocky's, Gracie could sleep through anything.

"There," Skye said. "Coffee all gone. Now give me my keys, please."

Milton marched her to the curb and shut the metal gate behind him. He was hard-core on drunks, because Guadalupe had once been fined a whole weekend without liquor sales when another server—not her—served a minor. The BBQ had lost thousands in earnings. Milton fired that waiter, then turned around and sued him for damages.

At the car, he said, "Here's the deal, Skye. Without me here to wait for you to show up, you could've lost her. People are crazy. Pedophiles are everywhere. Bad shit happens all the time. I'm the only thing standing between you and felony child endangerment, *capice?*"

Milton was a professional at making people cry.

The coffee was hard on Skye's stomach after vomiting and all the booze, and her nerves weren't helping matters. She stroked Gracie's pink cheeks, trying and failing not to sob. "I'm okay, Milton," she said. "I swear I can drive home. Straight home."

He didn't say anything. She figured he would be over it by tomorrow. She placed a sleepy Gracie into the car seat she'd nearly outgrown, there in the right rear backseat, the safest place for a child to be. She was sure she'd locked the straps, too, but apparently she'd imagined that part. She got into the front seat. Milton leaned down and she stuck her head out that window. "Now what?"

"You're fired."

"Milton, no. This will never happen again, I promise. Please let me finish out the week. I need the money."

"Two days," he said. "That's all. I'll have your last paycheck ready by then."

Just one more horrible memory to add to all the others.

The speed limit in the Railyard was like twenty-five or even twenty in places. But she was drunk and angry and pressed her foot down on the gas pedal a little too fast, fishtailing up the street toward Alameda. She made a right, intending to double back toward Canyon, when out of nowhere a shadow of a dog seemed to stop right in front of her. She swerved into a retaining wall, hitting it hard enough that the radiator buckled, and she could smell the coolant. When she looked up, she saw it was a coyote, disappearing into the rabbit brush.

Dwell not in the past, but in the moment. The present is what matters, Duncan's voice whispered in her ear. Duncan listened calmly to even the most heinous acts people had committed thanks to alcohol and drugs. He never once changed his expression, *because at Cottonwoods we don't judge, we're all equal.* Skye smoothed her skirt and let out a flinty laugh—this was the same stupid denim skirt she'd worn that horrible night. There hadn't been a drop of blood on it. The blood had been in the backseat—Gracie's.

"Here you go," the waiter said, breaking her reverie. The man set down Skye's eggs and coffee and Peter's Coke.

Where in the hell was Peter? Maybe he'd gotten sick in the bathroom. Passed out, even. She pushed her hair back behind her ears and called the waiter back. "Did you see my friend come out of the bathroom?"

"Nope. You want me to check?"

"If you wouldn't mind. He wasn't feeling well."

The waiter smiled and left. Skye sipped her coffee. It was better than the AA coffee, but ditch water pretty much was, too.

The waiter came back. "I knocked, opened the door. Nobody's in there," he said.

"He must have walked out the back door," she said. "I'm sorry. He was supposed to pay the check. I have a dollar. Can I mail the rest to you?"

He sighed. "Just go. It's okay this one time."

She jaywalked across Guadalupe Street and straight into Guadalupe BBQ, bypassing the outdoor tables and heading straight to the bar. That's where Peter would go, the nearest bar, to get a little hair of the dog to ease his headache. The restroom was directly across from it. She knocked, opened the door, and found it empty, too. Dammit! He was messing up her plans. And she basically had dined and ditched, which was a terrible thing for a former waitress to do.

She turned back and the bartender was right there.

"You need a drink?" he said, smiling.

What a question. "I have a dollar in my pocket. Could I have half a Coke?"

He grinned, eyeing her up and down. "I'll even add a couple of cherries."

"Thanks. I'm thirsty." Peter was probably halfway home by now. What was the old saying? "No good deed goes unpunished"? She watched the guy handle the soda hose and wondered how old he was. Freshly twenty-one, she bet. Give him a Santa Fe summer in the food industry and he'd go back to college willingly.

He plucked three cherries from the prep table container. "I'm Brad."

"Nice to meet you, Brad."

"You new in town?"

"Nope. Coming back after a time away."

"Anything else I can get you?" he said, leaving the end of that sentence open, as if the main reason women went into bars in the daytime was to have a freaking love encounter with a stranger.

She started to stand up but changed her mind. Milton and Rocky were friends. "Is Milton around? He knows me."

The bartender cocked his head sideways the way her daddy's ancient dog did, only Hope didn't smile like he wanted into her pants. "Yeah. I'll go find him."

While he slipped out the doorway, Skye studied the liquor bottles behind the bar, lined up like crown jewels on the wooden shelves. The liquid glistened, some of it crystal clear and looking as harmless as water inside glass bottles pretty enough to use as vases. Others were deep amber and yellow. They could have been magic potions, and boy, did they ever feel like it to begin with.

She sipped her Coke and waited. When the bartender returned, Milton was behind him. Skinny Milton, in his cigarette leg jeans and a Hawaiian shirt with a dizzying print she had to look away from. He frowned at Skye and said, "Oh, hell, no. You put down that drink and head back to whatever rock you crawled out from under. The last nine months have been nice and quiet, which I determine to be directly related to your absence. Brad, remember her face because this one is eighty-sixed from the establishment permanently. If she isn't out of here in five minutes, call the cops." He turned to go, but Skye stood up and took hold of his arm.

"Jeez, Milton. I'm not asking for my job back. I'm trying to find Rocky. I came by to ask if you'd seen him."

"Oh, sure," he said. "That's how it always begins. Just this one little favor and pretty soon I got ATF fines and sting operations and feds breathing down my neck."

Milton watched too much television. "When did I ever ask you for a single favor?" Skye said.

He barked a short laugh. "Do you really want me to answer that? Because we could be here all day."

Skye ducked her head, embarrassed. "Look, could we start over, please?"

"Why? Is the story going to be any different?"

She made herself look him square in the eyes. "I've done some really stupid things. I'm the first to admit it. But I'm going on nine months sober and I just want to find Rocky, that's all. Answer one question and I'll be on my way. You seen him or not?"

Milton studied her up and down, but not the way Brad had. He was the kind of boss who'd call you Muffin Top and tell you to lay off the fries if your skirt was tight that week. He wanted all the servers smiling all the time, even when someone dumped a plate of chili on your lap. Every woman who worked here thought he had a BMI calculator where his heart should have been. He tossed a napkin and pen her way. "Leave your number with Brad. If I hear from him, I'll let you know." He walked away, just like that.

Skye laid down her dollar.

"On the house," the bartender said, pushing it back toward her. "Not only are you pretty, but anyone who gets a rise out of Milton has to be hella fun, too," he whispered. "Everyone who works here thinks he's made out of Terminator parts. This one gal, Lily, she yells out, 'Metal!' every time he comes out of his office."

"Yeah, I've attended that particular rodeo," Skye said. She took her wallet out of her purse and flipped to the photos inside plastic sleeves. There was one of Rocky holding Gracie, back when staying married to him sounded reasonable. She plucked it out of her wallet and held it up. "This guy look familiar?" she asked.

"Sorry."

"How about the little girl? Blond, about four?"

Brad shook his head. "I know everybody from the smoked-out meth heads to the Euro trash. Can't say I've ever seen either one of them."

"Well, thanks anyway. I appreciate your time," she said. "You headed back to college, Brad?"

"School is pointless. I'm a screenwriter," he said. "Just paying the bills until my script gets green-lighted."

"Good luck with that," Skye said. She hoofed it out the patio and turned right on Guadalupe toward the river. The day had started out nice, but now clouds were moving in to gray up the sky. Duncan would say *nahodoołtį́į́ł*, meaning "the rain has not yet commenced, but would soon."

She didn't know where Peter was. Probably getting daytime drunk. Well, she couldn't stop him. She hoped it wouldn't take a wreck for him to see the light. Especially with his mom already stressed out, ill and everything. It was Cottonwoods that made her take the time to deliver Peter to an AA meeting—Step Twelve: Spreading the message—and now she'd lost hours out of her day when she could have been searching for Gracie.

Skye hadn't planned to revisit the scene of the crime, the retaining wall she'd plowed into, but here it was. It looked as if nothing had ever happened to it. She walked down the street to the wall, put her hands on it, and pushed. It was solid, probably reinforced with rebar, which only made her more ashamed at how fast she'd been driving.

She crossed the street and leaned over the metal railing to see the stream of water that was the Santa Fe River. It smelled kind of rank. You had to feel sorry for the river, which had been shunted this way and that instead of being allowed to go the way it wanted. First it had been diverted for the archbishop's garden, and then the swamp on Burro Alley was inconvenient, so the marsh had to be routed out as well. On the river's bank, she saw a few homeless guys, one sleeping or maybe passed out, hard to tell. No Rocky, though. And no Gracie. She racked her brain to think of potential places he could be. The place that kept coming back to her was Truth or Consequences. Sometimes, when he was sober, Rocky spoke of getting a few acres there, growing chiles, and breeding horses. She needed the Mercedes running and reliable so she could drive down there. Maybe her dad would lend her the gas money. Maybe she could host a few of those trail rides for Mr. Vigil and ask the riders for tips. She wouldn't ask Peter. He probably had enough money to help her out, but although he'd been too impaired to notice the five dollars here and ten dollars there she'd handed out from his wallet last night, he'd put two and two together sooner or later.

She walked back to Sanbusco Market Center on Montezuma Avenue to get her dad's truck. World Market still had free parking. That overpriced shoe place was still in business. There was the insane towering standing sculpture that held a truck the same year as her dad's.

Not that it would do any good, but she wanted to shout, *Rocky, where are you?*

DOLORES

THE BOY, PETER, had a cell phone buzzing with messages inside the pocket of his blue trousers. Like every man I've ever seen, he has trouble with snakebite. He lay facedown on the floor of the casita, right where there had once been a garden for growing the three sisters: corn, beans, and squash. As if he were rock and the plants could grow around him. The dog sat beside him. I sat next to her. Soon, she was asleep, too.

As much as I try to shut myself down, I can't sleep. But I don't miss it, not really. I see them sleep and try to remember what that felt like. The cell phone began to buzz, like a tiny box of bad news.

I wanted to see the messages, so I caused the window to rattle, which made Peter turn over, which in turn made the phone fall out of his pocket. I studied the messages. Many of them were invitations from someone named Big Fish. He wanted the boy to upload or upgrade or play, play, play. A warning kept appearing: *Battery low 10%. Dismiss?* There was one message from Bonnie. It had a paper clip, indicating an attachment. The message read: *Atty. papers att. We both want the same thing. Sign & return ASAP.*

Beep! Here came another message from Bonnie. *You are a terrible person to make me wait like this. Karma will get you.*

Living humans are so mean to one another. I wondered if I should wake him up, but then I saw his eyelids flutter. Behind them, his eyeballs were busy, dreaming. The best thing about being who I am, besides talking to Aspen, who was once so close to the realm that she can still hear me, is entering human dreams. This was Peter's:

He was inside her apartment, waiting. That feeling. Anticipation. Didn't he message her every night just to tell her how much he loved her? Didn't he fly to Chicago every weekend?

Including the one weekend she told him not to.

Bonnie was away on a weekend retreat for the crew of *Native America Calling*. He'd surprise her, fly out, and be there with dinner all made when she arrived home Sunday.

Waiting in her living room. The door opened: Bonnie with an Indian guy who looked like Russell Means, one of Bonnie's heroes. Their arms linked. Signing. Kissing. Heading to the bedroom. Peter stood up. The Russell Means man stepped back from Bonnie, which made her notice Peter. Her face, shocked, mouth raw from kissing, lips frozen into an O. The man with her signed, *Sorry.* Peter signed back, *She's all yours*, and walked out the door. Then he was in Revolution Brewery, a bar, drunk. His phone vibrating across the bar like a puck in an air hockey game. Bonnie messaging him. Then he was flying back to D.C. He started calling ear surgeons. Found one that would see him that week. The surgeon who ended up doing his implant wrote on a note pad, *I don't understand why you waited so long.*

Peter answered him: *Never had a good reason to until now.*

Chapter 11

H ERE IS THE thing about being the mother, Margaret
reminded herself bitterly as she scrutinized her refrigera-
tor's shelves that evening: No matter how heinous a day you've
lived through, whether you're feeling up to it or not, you still
have to make dinner. You have to get up, get dressed, look in the
fridge, and pull something together out of nothing. If it's just
you, you can eat Brussels sprouts sautéed in a slab of butter, with
leftover breakfast bacon crumbled on top. Or half a loaf of bread,
slice by slice of cinnamon toast. But when you have a child, even
a grown one, you have to at least make pancakes, or the world
order collapses. However, you can't make pancakes for dinner
twice in one week. You can't make a soufflé without going next
door to borrow eggs from your neighbor, who is likely having a
much worse day than you. When you're this tired, you can't risk
your neighbor asking you to babysit, when you're not even up to
chatting. Margaret stood at the stove while the gluten-free pasta
boiled—a whole box, so there would be leftovers. I can't cook
like this every day, she thought. It makes me too tired. Maybe she
should make double batches of everything and freeze half for the
days when she didn't feel up to cooking. She had opened a jar of

green chile and was grating carrots, zucchini, and Dubliner sharp cheddar, all of which would end up in a nice, filling casserole her son would inhale. Skye had borrowed Owen's truck to drive out to Las Vegas—New Mexico, not Nevada—way out past Pecos and Ilfeld, to look for friends who might possibly know Rocky's whereabouts. Owen had borrowed Margaret's Land Cruiser to trailer his horses from Arroyo Seco, north of Taos. He might not be back for dinner, he said, so go ahead and eat if he wasn't back by seven. Margaret couldn't wait for the moment he returned, when they could retreat to her bedroom, shut the door, and act out scenes from all the Robyn Carr romance novels she'd read in the last decade.

Margaret melted some Irish butter into a saucepan, sprinkling in oat flour to make a roux. As soon as it began to brown, she added almond milk and watched it thicken. When it was consistent, she'd dump in the cheese and whisk it to perfection. She looked in two drawers for her favorite whisk but couldn't find it. *That's what happens when you have to share your space with someone. Everything gets put away wonky.* She tried a fork. The real effort was making sure the mixture turned glossy and smooth as you beat in the cheese, a sauce instead of lumps. Her arm was already tired. It would have been so much easier with the darn whisk.

She ladled the lumpy cheese sauce over the vegetables and pasta and put it in the oven to brown the crust. She was counting off the minutes when she heard the back door open. There stood Peter, looking as if he'd slept in his clothes, which he probably had. She could smell the alcohol on him before she turned around. "I made dinner," she said, unable to stop signing just yet but catching herself when she did. "We need to talk, Peter. Not just about Owen, but about your drinking."

He sighed and started to speak, but Margaret interrupted him. "Go wash your hands and I'll dish this up. We'll eat first."

Echo was under the kitchen table, her usual spot when Margaret ate. Margaret watched Peter shuffle down the hall. He looked exhausted. She felt just as exhausted. Why did life pull these pranks with such exquisitely poor timing? Here's your long-lost lover. Tonight's entrée, MS, comes with a side order of grown-up son with a drinking problem. And for dessert? A new MS symptom: always feeling as if she needed to pee. Or was it a bladder infection? Sex that many times in one day had a price. She listened to the bathroom water running and waited for Peter to be done so she could use it.

They ate salad and pasta without talking. Peter got up and filled his water glass twice. When he finished his plate, she got up and took some chocolate mousse out of the fridge. It wasn't homemade, but she just hadn't had the energy. She squirted Reddi-wip on top and set it in front of Peter.

"I don't think I can eat that," he said.

"Oh, you'll eat it. It might be from a box, but I still made it for you," she said. "And while you're eating, I have a few things to say."

He stirred the whipped cream into the mousse, waiting.

"If you're staying here, even in the guesthouse, there will be no more getting drunk. Apparently you made quite a shameful scene at La Choza last night."

"So what?" he said. "Lots of people drink a little too much now and then. What's the big deal?"

Margaret looked up. "Seriously? I live in this town. I go to La Choza. People talk. This morning you went out to an AA meeting, which must have helped tremendously, because you've been drinking all day. You didn't use to drink like this, so why are you doing it now? Is it something new? Do you really think your work won't be affected?"

He scowled. "Bonnie's pregnant."

Margaret put her hand to her heart. "Is the baby yours?"

"I don't know whose it is, but it's not mine."

"So you didn't tell me the whole truth about the divorce. Why not?"

"Guess I just didn't want to admit the baby was real."

Margaret put down her spoon. "Is there anything else you're not telling me?"

Peter wouldn't meet her eyes. He picked up his spoon and began to shovel the mousse down his throat as if it were medicine. She sighed. "Whatever it is, I hope you'll tell me in time. You can do the dishes. I'm going to take a bath. And stay out of my wine. If you want a drink, ask."

Later that night, Margaret looked up at the vigas above her in the bedroom ceiling. Parts of the house went back two hundred years, and she suspected the vigas, hand-peeled log beams that came from standing dead spruce, were probably that old or older. Between the beams, white plaster arced from log to log. How difficult it must have been to create. The wind rattled her window as if it were storming outside.

"I could replace those windows with double panes," Owen said. He was propped up against the pillows, Margaret in his arms. His husky voice was a creaky sound that made her think of the groaning of wooden ships.

She asked the question that preyed on her mind. "Why didn't you write to me?"

After a minute, he answered, "Truthfully? I figured a clean break would free you up for a decent man, one who deserved you, could properly take care of you."

"Owen. Listen to me. I can take care of myself. There is no man on earth who could take your place in my heart. What we had, what we *have*, is something special. Or didn't you see things that way?"

"'Course I did. I still do." He stroked her hand.

"Thank goodness for that." She wondered what he thought of her fifty-year-old skin, which had become softer and looser in the decade since they'd parted. She'd cut her long hair, too, and there was a lot of gray in it now. Well, he was older, too, and there wasn't time to lose. "Will you move in with me?"

"That's a wrinkle I have yet to figure out," he responded. "Fact is, I'm supposed to live on site at Reach for the Sky. It's a good job for me, managing Mr. Vigil's barn. It makes use of every skill this old farrier has to offer. "

"You mean you have to sleep there? Every night?" She shut her eyes when she said that, not wanting him to see how badly she wanted him here instead.

"Somebody has to be there to watch the horses. Make sure nobody breaks in. You could come with me. Be like the old days."

Owen's bunkhouse at the Starr ranch hadn't been far from her rented house. His quarters were small, but there was a toilet and a sink, hot and cold running water, even a solar shower. It could have been a lifetime ago. "Is there a bathroom?"

"Nope. Outhouse and cold water."

"What with the MS, and Peter, I think I have to stay here. When do you start?"

"I'm already working, but I don't have to live at the bunk-house until the fund-raiser gala. But don't worry. We'll figure out how to make this work. Now that I have you back, we're not going to do this halfway. We'll find a way. Who knows? Maybe after a while I can hire someone to do nights part of the week."

"I'm worried about Peter. He's drinking too much."

"And I'm worried about Skye. If she doesn't find her little girl soon, she might have a slip."

"You mean drinking?"

"Or pills. She wants to borrow a couple hundred dollars from me to go look for Gracie. I'm going to have to ask Joe for an advance on my paycheck. Not the best way to start a job."

"I can help some."

"No," he said. "You've got your hands full with Peter, and taking care of yourself. It pains me to say this, but I think I have to call Skye's mother."

"For money?"

"That would help, but most important, those two have got to mend fences. What happens if Skye doesn't find Gracie? What if this thing is dragged out for years? I'm going to encourage Sheila to come to Santa Fe."

"That makes sense."

"Lord, I hope so. Maggie, I've missed so much of Skye's life. I can't let her down anymore. I have to make amends. I have to stay close enough to them that we can have Sunday supper, so I can watch Gracie sometimes. Have a real family again."

What about me? Margaret thought. Don't I get to be your family? She nodded. "That's important."

They kissed. Margaret tasted coffee and green chile, and a dash of sadness. Owen's beard brushed her forehead. All she wanted to do was close her eyes and feel his warmth and never have to be apart again. She held his face in her hands, tenderly cupping the place that Peter had hit him, which had turned all colors. After all this time, the sex was still great, but she never remembered it being this strenuous. She laughed inwardly and stifled a yawn. She bet each of them was waiting for the other one to say, *Can we go to sleep now?*

Life was different. And she had a feeling it was only going to get weirder.

Margaret copied the messages from Peter's phone by hand. He'd left it on the table last night after dinner. As far as she could tell, he hadn't gotten drunk last night, but who knew what he had out there hidden away in the guesthouse? She had awakened at three A.M., feeling like she needed to pee. Then came a headache. She'd found the aspirin, chewed two, and made herself a cup of herb tea. Peter's phone was just sitting there, beeping like an alarm. When she picked it up, she saw that there were twelve text messages. All from Bonnie.

Message one: *Please sign papers, notarize, and send overnight.*

Message two: *There's no reason to drag this out.*

Message three: *Why haven't you responded to my texts?*

They grew in nastiness.

Message four: *You're probably out whooping it up with some girl. Don't you have any respect for me? I will make sure everyone knows what a prick you are.*

Five: *I hope you're not hiring a lawyer. Remember, I can still ask for alimony.*

Six: *Every single one of my friends thinks you're an asshole.*

Seven: *You are an asshole. I put up with you longer than I should have.*

Eight: *You could never understand deaf culture because you weren't born into it.*

Nine: *I never loved you.*

Ten: *You don't deserve love.*

Eleven: *I'm not returning your mother's ring.*

Twelve: *I am going to punish you.*

The Twelve Steps of Divorce, Margaret thought. She considered deleting them before Peter could read them, but that wasn't right, any more than invading his privacy was. The part about her ring was upsetting. She told herself, It's just a ring. But it was a ring that had belonged to her mother. Why was Bonnie so angry when she was the one wanting the divorce? Regardless of who the baby's father was, she was technically married to Peter. And Margaret knew that deep down, she was just as mean as Bonnie, because the thought of dragging the divorce out until the baby was born just tickled her pink.

At breakfast the next morning, Peter picked up his phone. "There it is. I was starting to worry that I'd lost it. Where's Owen?"

"Working at the stable. Peter, I have something to confess."

"Now what?" he said.

"I read your texts from Bonnie. You need to show them to the lawyer. Otherwise, I have a feeling you're going to be paying alimony and child support. Look," she said, setting down a plate of toast and scrambled eggs before Peter could complain. "I'm paying for the lawyer, so I get a say. You need to go on the offensive. I've been where you are, the injured party. Your father—"

"Mom, I don't want to know any horrid details about Dad cheating and your failure to keep the marriage together. I don't want to get into that nightmare again."

Margaret was stunned. "*My* failure? Do you still blame me for that divorce, like you did when you were fifteen years old? You know what? Do whatever the hell you want." She flung the frying pan into the sink, and the hot metal hissed. "Don't you ever talk to me like that again. You're still my son, even if you are grown up. And I'm your mother. I'm sure it makes no difference to you, but I love you, and I want the best for you and you're acting like a twerp."

She stomped down the hallway into her studio, shut the door after herself, and ripped the watercolor she'd been working on from its board. She pushed the small easel away and brought back the easel with the unfinished oil painting of the horse. She was going to paint that effing hummingbird and be done with this painting for once and for all.

Peter stood outside the studio. "Mom?"

She squeezed shades of white onto her palette, starting with Titanium, Flake White No. 1, a touch of Zinc, and finally, a color she'd never used before, Cremnitz, a lead-based paint she'd had Nori send her from London. "I'm working, Peter. Go away."

"Sometimes I can be a real asshole," he said.

Margaret was glad he couldn't see her smile. "Yes, you certainly can. Now get lost. I plan to be in here all day," she said. "I'm sure you can find something to occupy yourself with."

"Mom? Are you mad? Do you want me to move out?"

Well, of course she was angry. Stupid question. "What I want is for you to do the chores we agreed on, starting with emptying the trash. You promised to take Echo for walks, and to feed her, and so far you've done that once, and only because I reminded you."

"All right," he said. "Listen, I'll make dinner tonight. Do you have fresh garlic, Parmesan, and tomatilloes?"

Oh, Lord. He loved spicy food, curry and habanero peppers, marinara sauces made crunchy with way too much oregano. If a recipe called for one clove of garlic, he'd put in the entire bulb. "No garlic, no peppers, and Parmesan on the side."

"All right."

"No more watching cartoons in the daytime. You're twenty-five years old. And call the damn lawyer and make an appointment!"

"Okay."

Just like that, while yelling at Peter, Margaret had painted the white hummingbird. She'd captured the curve of its beak and the motion that separated it from everything else. Of course, it needed finessing, but that would come in time. She picked up her favorite brush, the hog-bristle Manet-Soies Pures from France. She'd waited all her artistic life to have a use for it and now she did: painting iridescent hummingbird feathers.

Yesterday, after returning from Las Vegas with no leads on Rocky, Skye had gone to Goodwill and bought herself a pair of running shoes for five dollars. With a little bleach and scrubbing, they didn't look that bad. Today she planned to sell her Old Gringo forget-me-nots to Home on the Range, the custom bootmaker in Santa Fe, near the courthouse. It was killing her to let them go, but the money she'd get would finance her trip to Truth or Consequences.

She tucked cardboard into the shafts, then wrapped each boot with tissue paper. She set them into the box they'd come in, nearly overcome with the memory of buying them. It had been the PRCA Rodeo Finals, and Rocky was winning huge amounts of money. He'd hired a babysitter for Gracie, given Skye a thousand dollars, and told her to go shopping. When she'd discovered the Old Gringo Trunk Show, she'd stopped in her tracks, and later, a thousand dollars poorer, she'd walked out with the most beautiful cowboy boots ever designed. All day she'd walked around the booths, and people had stopped her to ask her about the boots so often that she wished she'd taken business cards and handed them out.

It killed her to put the box into a canvas Trader Joe's bag she found in the cupboard. She loved those boots as though they were a person. She set the bag on the floor and picked up the new cell phone her dad had bought her. If she was lucky, they'd net her five hundred bucks, half their value. But money was what she needed, and five hundred, though a good start, was not enough to get her own place, feed Gracie, get her school clothes. She pressed number three on her speed dial, and it rang twice and then went to voice mail. "Y'all've reached my message thingy. So, either I'm traveling, shopping, or having too good a time to pick up! Leave a message, y'hear?"

Mama's voice had gotten all Texas since she'd married that plastic surgeon. Probably he had fixed up every inch of her by now. Skye hoped he wasn't just another loser Mama had latched on to, to take whatever she could from him before abandoning him for something better.

After the beep, she said, "Mama, I sure do need to talk to you. I'm not in trouble. I'm out of rehab and in Santa Fe and I have a lead on a job. Please call me back." She recited her cell phone number, and then she looked at Margaret's painting and burst into tears. "Mama," she said in a choked voice, "please, please, please, will you call me? I don't know what to do. I can't find Gracie. And I'm not ashamed to ask you for some money to finance my drive to Truth or Consequences to look for her. I know I'm a disappointment to you and I fully accept that. But Mama, Gracie is my little girl. You're her grandmother."

She ended the call and walked to the kitchen window, her shoulders rounded, her neck feeling as if she had a yoke across it. Damn the early morning sun breaking through the cloud cover. Damn the nice weather. Double damn her father being happy and in love, things she'd never know again because she'd messed her life up so bad.

She opened the fridge and looked at the half-price day-old bagels and store-brand orange juice she'd bought. Bagels probably had like nine thousand calories, but so what? She wasn't having sex with anyone. That got her thinking again about the Cottonwoods rules, and Nola, and Duncan. Crazy place, Cottonwoods. Crazy roommate, Nola. Crazy Indian dude trying to make her well through a bunch of stories.

On the morning of her departure, he'd knocked on her door before dawn and said, "Even when you leave here, promise me you won't sleep past sunup."

"Why not? What if I'm working nights? Will that offend Grandfather Horny Toad? Or invite a skinwalker into my house?"

That same I-love-everybody smile. "No, Skye. It's because you'll miss everything."

She took out two bagels and the carton of orange juice, deciding she'd bring breakfast to her dad. She shut the fridge door, walked across the room to fetch the newspaper, and then just like that a name came to her—Diego Iglesias, JD, the judge who'd handled her DWI. Who'd given full custody to Rocky. Why hadn't she thought of this earlier? Surely the judge's office had Rocky's contact information.

Hell with Home on the Range.

On the way to Reach for the Sky, Skye used the five dollars she'd lifted from Peter's wallet—he owed her that—on gas. How stupid does it feel to drive a Mercedes and not be able to fill the tank?

As she turned onto Airport Road toward the stable, a snake was crossing the road, so she slowed down. Big one. Duncan said snakes were a "manifestation" of the Lightning People. "Never run over a snake," he said, "or you will have bad luck for seven years." Must be a broken mirror snake, she figured. Down the newly tamped driveway to the stables, she recognized Peter's Land Cruiser. Awesome, because she wanted to yell at him for leaving her downtown yesterday morning. She practiced what to say as she parked between it and her dad's truck.

She walked into the barn, where the horses were busy eating. Leaning against the barn wall was a sack of feeder carrots, so she shook out a few and broke them into pieces, petting the muzzles of the nosy horses who looked up from hay flakes or pellet feed. Joe let Owen board two horses as part of his pay, and when Skye came to Lightning's stall, he nickered. "Hello, handsome," she whispered to her horse as she unlatched the door and went in. They visited for a long time, and Skye checked his feet and his legs, picked the boogers from the corners of his eyes, and brushed him until his black spots were as glossy as patent leather. Even after all this time he still let her hang on his neck and slide up on him, bareback. He didn't even so much as twitch. She lay down across his back until as much of her as possible was touching her horse. He kept on eating. She ran her hands down his neck, feeling the muscles and then the throb of his pulse. An average horse's heart weighed ten pounds, an astounding fact in itself, but Secretariat's heart had weighed in at twenty-two pounds. She imagined having a heart that size. All it could hold, room for life's ups and downs, gains and losses. If there was a God, why hadn't He made human hearts the biggest of all? After a while, she slid down and said, "Finish your Wheaties, buddy," and locked the stall door behind her.

The bunkhouse door was closed, so her dad was probably out taking his morning ride. Instead of knocking, she tried the knob and the door opened. Her intention was to grab some paper, leave him a note, and tell him about the judge. But there he was, butt naked, with Margaret underneath him, the two of them having what looked like old-people sex.

"Sorry," she said, backing away, wishing she hadn't seen either of them, especially her dad, naked. Skye stumbled back to the Mercedes, her face purple with embarrassment. In less than a week he'd found a job, a place to live, and somebody to knock boots with? At his age? What was fair about that? She started the engine and sped out.

Skye tried to block that picture out of her mind while she drove to the courthouse on Catron Street. At the entrance, there was a turnstile and a couple of security guards. The guy was leering at her boobs, but the female guard was checking everybody's identification. Hoo, boy. I knew I should have brought doughnuts, Skye thought. She held out her driver's license, hoping for a pass, but no luck. "Hold on," the female one said, placing her hand out to block Skye's entrance. "You need to show a jury summons to come in this entrance, or be scheduled for a court appearance."

"I don't have a jury summons. I need to speak to Judge Iglesias. He knows me," she said.

"I'll bet he does," the woman said, rolling her eyes.

That lit up Skye's cylinders. "Yes, that's right, from a previous court appearance. You have an issue with that?"

"Are you an attorney?"

She gestured to her jeans and t-shirt. "Do I look like an attorney? I just need like five minutes of his time."

"I'm sorry," the woman said. "Step aside, please. There are people behind you who have legitimate court business."

"Mine's about as legitimate as it gets," Skye said. She stood on the concrete step and leaned against the handrail as people walked by. Not one of them looked very happy about it. After a break in the foot traffic, Skye returned to the entrance.

"Now what?" asked the same security guard.

"Could I leave a message for the judge? It's really important. There's a missing little girl at stake. My daughter."

The woman softened. "Sounds like you need a police officer or a social worker, not a judge."

Skye bit her lip. "Are you a mom? Look. I'm not trying to bust your chops, and I respect the law. I'm just trying to find my daughter. She's four. My husband disappeared with her. Judge Iglesias awarded my husband temporary custody. I don't have any documentation with me, but I know there has to be some and Judge Iglesias probably has copies of it. The judge might be able to help me find my daughter."

"Step aside, please," the woman said, letting four more people inside.

While Skye waited, she tried to think of another way to come at the problem, but writing or calling the judge would take time, which she didn't have. Then, a lawyer who was dressed in a blue-black suit and an orange Jerry Garcia tie placed his hand on her shoulder. "Couldn't help but overhear your dilemma. As it happens, I know Judge Iglesias personally. If you'd like to write him a note, I'll make sure he receives it."

"Oh, my gosh, thank you. Shoot, I don't have any paper."

He opened his tooled leather briefcase and handed her a sheet of stationery.

She winced. "I don't suppose you have a pen?"

He laughed and took a gold Cross pen from his suit pocket.

"Thank you," Skye said. *Wolfgang Schneider, Attorney at Law,* was printed across the top of the thick, creamy paper in raised, indigo-blue ink. Who named their kid Wolfgang? Did they want to make sure he'd get beaten up on the playground or what? Skye sat on the bottom concrete step and used her purse as a flat surface.

Your Honor Iglesias,

You were kind to me in the past when I came into your courtroom on a DWI almost one year ago. Instead of jail, you gave me rehab. I am happy to report that I have completed rehab and I am over nine months sober. I believe with all my heart that will continue. I know you are a busy man with important cases, but I hope you can give me a minute of your

time. You granted temporary custody of my little girl Grace
Eleanor Elliot to my husband, Rocky Elliot. However, my
husband seems to have disappeared with my little girl. No one
lives at the address he gave me. The phone is disconnected.
Your Honor, all I want is to know my little girl is safe, and to
try to be a good mother to her again. Do you have contact
information for my husband? Here is my cell phone #. You
can call anytime day or night.

> Yours most very sincerely,
> Skye (Sara Kay) Elliot

When she finished, she folded the paper in half and handed it to
the lawyer. "What kind of law do you practice?"

He smiled at her. "Oh, family law, mainly."

"Does that include divorce?"

He glanced at her left hand. She couldn't even remember what
happened to her engagement ring. Probably she let Rocky pawn
it for entry fees or he spent the money he got for it on drugs. "It
does indeed. You in need of a divorce lawyer?"

"It's possible."

"I'm happy to give you a free consultation. Or to recommend
a colleague."

He was good-looking, but there was no time for flirting. That
was like asking King Kong whether he wanted one banana out of
the bunch. "Could I have a card and get back to you later?"

"Sure." He handed her two of his cards. "Write your contact
information on this one, and the other one is for you to keep.
Divorce can be a tricky business, I know. Best of luck," he said,
and after she handed him the card, he went into the turnstile
she'd been blocked from.

"Wait! I still have your pen," she called, but he was gone. Skye put the pen in her purse, saluted the security guard, and walked away.

The giant cottonwood trees around the buildings in this part of town made the grassy lawns look like something out of a movie set: the perfect place for anyone stuck working indoors to escape to at lunch hour, enjoy a peanut-butter sandwich, and recharge for the afternoon. In a movie set there, someone like Wolfgang Schneider would hand her a pen, they'd fall in love, and before she knew it, she'd have a baby on the way and be living in a cute little Pueblo-style adobe with a yard for Gracie. "Focus," she told herself, realizing how completely stupid and romantic that was. Pretty much the same thing had happened with her and Rocky, and what had that led to? This moment right here. A clueless mother walking down the sidewalk past the courthouse where she'd been a defendant.

Sad as that was, she admired the way the tall trees cast shade over the sidewalk and how spring had brought warmth to the days, enough to feel it on your face. That high desert air was hell on the complexion but sweet and clean in your lungs. Good, clean air was just what she needed—she still wanted to scour out the horror of seeing her dad and Margaret naked.

Skye passed Home on the Range but decided that could wait. The idea of haggling back and forth for a decent price for her boots was too much. Her cell phone rang just as she reached her car.

"Hello?"

"Hi, Skye."

"Mr. Vigil?"

"Yes, it's me. I have a trail ride set up for tomorrow if you can get here by noon, and a private ride after that for one-thirty. The group gig pays fifty dollars. The single pays thirty-five. I'm sorry it's not more."

"That's all right. Money's money."

He laughed. "Don't forget: Tomorrow is the night of the gala. We agreed you'd be there, right?"

She thought it over. One more day of not looking. "All right," she said. "But right after the gala, I have to go to T and C. Just for one day."

She knew she couldn't drive all over the state looking for Gracie if she had no money to fill her gas tank, so this would help. She thought of her dad, being in prison all those years. All the mean thoughts she'd entertained, certain he was remarried, had all new kids, was happy when she wasn't. She thought of all the times she'd goaded Nola into throwing up. What the hell was the matter with her? She got in the car, put her head on the steering wheel, and cried. Look at me, she thought, squirting girlies. Last time I felt like this I was pregnant. She prayed she could escape having a sex talk with her dad. But really, what was he thinking? Old people were supposed to be over all that nonsense.

Chapter 12

WHEN SKYE HAD shut the door, Owen and Margaret sat up laughing until tears ran down their cheeks. "What are the odds?" Owen said.

"Quite good, apparently." She kissed Owen and giggled. "Let's have dinner tonight. What time do you get off work?"

He frowned. "I have a meeting with Joe about the gala, and I need to stow the equipment he's bringing. Plus, there's a load of hay coming and who knows when it'll show up. I have to be here to sign for it, then stack it in the barn."

"You have to eat dinner sometime."

"Yes, and ordinarily that would mean a cup of soup heated in the microwave."

She sighed. "But I want you to see my painting. I think it might be the best thing I've ever done."

"And I want to see it. But this is the start-up, Maggie. We'll be busy until after the fund-raiser. You'll come to that, right?"

"I already agreed to sit the Vigil kids. Maybe I can come for the beginning."

"After the gala, we'll find a way. I'm not letting you go ever again."

Margaret smiled, began to slide her arms into her bra. Owen stopped her. "Don't cover up just yet." He leaned forward and reached for her, cupping her left breast in his hand. "My goodness, you are just as beautiful as the day I first met you."

"That's ironic."

"Why?"

"Because I had more clothes on then."

"I remember those red panties like it was yesterday. And your legs, three feet of wonder. You, running from the water spout to the dogs. I'll never forget that. Don't suppose you still have the red panties?"

"Owen, be serious. That was ten years ago. That particular pair wore out."

"Can I ask from what?"

She gave him a gentle punch. "From normal wash and wear, you dope. I haven't had any lovers."

"Can you come back later tonight?"

She shook her head no. "I'm babysitting tonight, too."

"You sure that you're up to it? That seven-year-old is a handful. And what will you do if the baby cries?"

She laughed. "I'll feed her or rock her or change her diaper. Believe me, after Peter these two seem easy. I'm going to feed them dinner, pop in a video, do their laundry, read them a story, and then collapse. Glory's last pregnancy was high-risk and I want to help out as much as I can."

She ran her hand along his craggy jaw, bristled with whiskers. "What are we going to do, Owen? You have to stay on site here and I have obligations in town. How are we going to work this out?"

"I'll think of something. You get on home and do what needs doing. Take your time driving. I love you, Maggie Yearwood."

She hooked her bra shut and pulled on her shirt. "I love you, too."

"We won't dwell in the past. We'll enjoy what we have right here, right now, and tomorrow will work itself out."

Margaret touched her cheeks as she drove from Owen's, feeling the chafed skin from his whiskers and all that kissing.

At home, she smelled something she couldn't immediately identify. She went to the kitchen, found Echo snoozing on the rag rug. Her water dish was full. She'd clearly been fed. The dog always left about a half cup of kibble in her bowl, as if saving for a rainy day. Margaret gave her a quick pet and told her she was a good dog. She called out for Peter, but he wasn't home or in the casita. There were, however, dirty dishes in the sink with gunk stuck on them. So much for her lecture. Ah. The burned smell was due to the coffeepot being left on, with barely a quarter cup of coffee remaining. She was lucky to come home and find it before the glass cracked. After putting her kitchen to rights, Margaret took a shower and changed into gray leggings and a Henley top. Echo followed her from room to room, knowing that when Margaret moved with purpose it often implied a walk or being left home alone. Either way, treats were involved. Margaret dried her hair, set the brush on the pedestal sink, and looked at her dog. "You can sure turn on the tragic, can't you? Fine, let's get your leash. But we're only going next door. You can play with Glory's dogs."

She rapped on the Vigils' door, then tried the knob, and it opened. "Glory?"

"In the bedroom," she called out, and Margaret followed her voice through their home, impressed, as always, by the way it revealed the family's inner selves—baskets, books on the shelves, pieces of pottery here and there, old furniture, and the painting of clouds done by Joe's cousin. It looked like a trompe l'oeil window outdoors from where it sat on the mantel.

Glory was dressed in yoga pants and an Albuquerque Police Department sweatshirt several sizes too big for her. She sat in the middle of her bed, working on folding a mountain of laundry.

"That is a lot of clothing," Margaret said.

Glory sighed. "Sometimes I feel like making a deal with Rumpelstiltskin. There's always one load in the wash and one in the dryer," she said, making a face. "I expect to be doing four loads a day for the next eighteen years."

"In retrospect," Margaret said as she sat down and began folding baby onesies, "those will seem like the good old days. Where are the kids?"

"Oh, I put them all into foster care," Glory said. "It was either that or kill them."

Margaret said, "I know you're kidding. But all I can think is how Owen's daughter would do anything if it helped to find her little one."

"Oh, sweetie, I'm sorry. I can't joke around without putting my foot in my mouth. Aspen is at school. Joseph took Sparrow to the pediatrician for her next round of shots. I hope he remembered to ask for baby pain medication. Otherwise we'll be up all night. Hey," she said, "did you get a facial or something? You're glowing, but your cheeks look abraded. Remember when my sister had that bad reaction to dermabrasion?"

Margaret could hold it in no longer. "Glory, Skye walked in on us!"

Her friend laughed. "I'm so glad you have your beau back. I'll speak to Joe about getting a lock for the door. But, one thing?"

"What?"

"Details, girlfriend."

Margaret laughed. "Seriously?"

"Oh, yeah," Glory said. "I get to live vicariously through your romance, and I don't have to worry about getting pregnant because I already am. What's better than that?"

An hour later, Margaret was lying on Joseph's side of the bed. She had fetched Glory herb tea, boiled some eggs, and put together a platter of carrot sticks and Brie wrapped in phyllo dough, warm from the oven. They looped the gooey cheese around the carrots and savored the moment. The dogs were all played out, and were snoozing on the floor next to the bed. Margaret had just finished telling Glory about Skye's name change. "She said Sara Kay was the name of a spoiled brat. Skye, she insists, is wide open to all changes."

"Kids and their names," Glory said. "Juniper made such a big deal out of changing her last name to ours. We had a party. Want to know something strange?"

"What's that?"

"Casey asked to take our name, too."

"It isn't really all that remarkable," Margaret said. "Everyone who meets you wants to be a part of your family. Can I be Margaret Vigil?"

"Sure, join the party. Pretty soon the state will be filled with nothing but Vigils. Actually, we have a pretty good start on that already."

"How's the little Vigil who's incubating? What did the doctor say? Are you taking a leave from work?"

Glory shrugged. "Not yet. Everything appears to be fine. My blood pressure is normal. All she said was to watch my diet, drink gallons of water, and no getting upset at anything."

"Well, that's good, isn't it?"

Glory said, "Yes. This time around, I'm trying to mark every moment. I started a journal. I look forward to the ultrasound. As soon as I see the heart beating, I'll be fine. I'm a little worried about how I'll manage two babies—Sparrow and the unnamed one—but seeing that little pulse, the heartbeat, there's nothing like it."

Margaret squeezed her hand. "I'm so happy for you. Where's Casey?"

"Today she has her therapist appointment. Afterwards, she walks to Aspen's school to pick her up. They have a snack at the café and some alone time. She should be back any minute."

"How is she doing in therapy?"

"Joe could probably tell you more than I can. Casey smiles a lot more now. She's still seeing Ardith Clemmons, the therapist she met in Española. Ardith gives her 'homework' to do. Write in a diary, help with the handicapped riding program, and learn to make a few meals. It's all directed toward getting her to socialize beyond our family, eventually."

"That sounds promising."

"And difficult. We try to keep things positive around here, you know, as much as we can. It's just . . ."

"Just what?" Margaret prodded, brushing a lock of stray silvery hair behind Glory's ear.

Glory yawned. "Excuse me. You can see it in her face sometimes. She is reliving something horrible. I try to draw her out, but she won't talk about it. Breaks Joe's heart. Mine, too. I swear, Curly, that dog of hers, is psychic. She somehow knows when Casey is struggling and she goes directly to her."

"You may have come late to the game, Glory, but you're a first-rate mom, through and through. Now take a little nap while I put these clothes away."

By nine-thirty the next morning, Skye was champing at the bit to do something, anything. She had already tidied up the casita and ironed her good jeans and a white shirt for the gala. It was as dressed up as she could get, because there was nothing appropriate in Mama's closet. She'd go in to Reach for the Sky early, earn more hours off her community service. Clean up the barn. Groom the horses. Help decorate. She had to fill the hours of her day until her lessons.

She worked up a good sweat in the barn and then got ready for her first trail ride. She led four young men who were in treatment for juvenile offenses around the ring and then a quarter mile on a trail. When they first arrived, they were throwing gang signs and cursing. She thought about taking them back to Mr. Vigil. Instead, she remembered something Valerie had taught her when she was introducing new students. She handed them halters and ropes and said, "Catch a horse."

"By ourselves?"

"That's the idea," Skye said. "It's easy. You're all strapping young men. Go find one you like and put the halter on it. Then bring them over here, so we can go over how to saddle them."

Oh, those big bad juvenile criminals turned into little boys instantly. Valerie was right—this approach worked every time. She held back a laugh after one of them put a halter on upside down. Within ten minutes they were calling her ma'am and willing to do whatever she told them. She rode in the back of the line of horses so she could watch them. When she asked, "Who's up for galloping?" she was met with silence. They weren't after speed any more than she had been in her childhood days. Back then it hadn't been about going fast. It was about the view. From atop a horse the world was different. She was in her own domain when she was on horseback—without bullies or arguments between her parents—and a slow trail ride allowed her imagination the time to transport her into another realm. Now it made her smile to see this in the boys. On the turnaround point on the trail, the boys argued over whose horse was better.

"RedBow," said Paul, the boy closest to her.

"Little Mac," Julio said. "He's the nicest. Plus, he's the color of *oro*. Gold."

Skye smiled. Some kids saw a Palomino and that was that.

Once they were back at the barn, she showed them how to groom the animals and then allowed them to feed the horses carrots. She heard some sniffling and knew that these gang boys had discovered that unconditional love did exist in the world, and that one place to find it was in the company of the horse. The van driver arrived to take them back, and two of the toughest-looking boys cried as they said good-bye to the horses.

"Keep racking up those good behavior stars," Skye told them, waving. "Then we can do this again." Skye had spent the hour blissfully free of worries about Gracie, but the second the boys were packed off, she was eating her guts again. She checked her cell phone every two minutes in case the lawyer called, trying to think where else she might look. Oklahoma? How much gas would it take to get there? Could she stand taking a bus?

After they left, she asked Mr. Vigil for the fifty dollars, and when he told her the treatment center hadn't paid yet, her heart sank along with her morale.

But soon it was almost time for her second trail ride. All Joe had told her was that the client's name was Opal and that she would be bringing her own saddle. Skye was more worried about her bringing a checkbook.

Because the gala was to begin at five P.M. sharp, the stable was a hive of activity. What with trucks unloading tables and chairs, and a shrill young woman with a clipboard directing the flow of traffic, Skye was concerned the horses would be jumpy. The party planner, about Skye's age, pointed men carrying tables in one direction, while another group with chairs went inside the barn. "No, no, no!" the woman yelled. "They go outside! The heaters, too!" The workers scurried around like confused ants, and Skye felt sorry for them.

The fact that the sky was gunmetal gray did not appear to faze that woman at all. Skye was relieved not to see her dad. The first ride had taken a ton of effort, reducing her energy level by half. She made the decision to put both a bridle and halter on Coconut, a white gelding who had chestnut ears that looked like a child's cap. He also had the requisite chestnut shield on his chest, making him a true "medicine hat" paint horse. The history of the medicine hat horse was one of Skye's favorites. Duncan had told her that the Plains tribes believed the horses, born so rarely, had supernatural powers. The only people allowed to ride them were tribal chiefs, medicine men, and the best warriors. But it wasn't just the Indians. Cowboys went nuts for paint horses, and medicine hats were frequently stolen, particularly the mares. Not Coco. He was gelded, past anything but this, quiet lessons, the occasional trail ride. She fastened on his bridle and bit and rubbed the horse's withers, checking to see if he was lame. Next time she'd have Opal do everything, but today it was better to do the bridling herself.

"Let's go earn me some money, you monsters," she said, walking Lightning and Coconut out of the barn. She could feel the barely controlled jitters in both animals. Even safe, bomb-proof horses liked a nice, quiet barn, dinner on time, the occasional carrot, and no surprises. Skye hoped none of them would flip out at the gala. She waited by Joe's office. The ride was scheduled for one-thirty, and Skye expected Opal to be late, what with crosstown traffic. But there she was, right on time, getting out of a Cadillac SUV, wearing a sparkly sequin scarf and a matching pink shirt that could have been designed by the late Nudie Cohn, that outrageous Ukrainian tailor who'd made clothes for Elvis and Porter Wagoner and ZZ Top. Rhinestones on embroidered cactus. Loopy white piping on the sleeves. There was no other designer who did things that cool except for Old Gringo.

Immediately Skye felt guilty for not selling her boots and teared up.

From the waist down, Opal was all business in tan English riding breeches with suede patches inside the knees. She was carrying the most beautiful English saddle Skye had ever seen. Its curves and decoration were classic and simple, but the quality of the leather was what made it perfect. The woman looked so thin and moved so slowly that Skye doubted she'd make it another foot with that saddle, let alone survive a trail ride. She put on her best smile anyway and walked toward her.

"You must be Opal. I'm Skye, and I'll be taking you on your trail ride today. Would you like me to saddle your horse? His name's Coconut."

"Oh, no. I can do it," Opal said, shocking Skye by swinging the black saddle and sheepskin pad up on Coco as if it were nothing. She sneaked a sugar cube to him, and Skye pretended not to notice.

"I could use a little help with the girth, though," Opal said. "Damn arthritis."

Skye twisted the leather strap inside itself. "That's quite a saddle," she said as they walked their horses to the gate.

"It's a Passier," Opal said. "I bought it in Germany."

"It looks really comfortable."

"I admit, it's awfully cushy on my old bones. Yours is a Muster Master Australian stock, isn't it? Boy, does that bring back memories. I used to ride in Australia when I was a young lady."

Opal really got around. She looked as if she were in her eighties, wore the awesome clothing—perhaps the real thing—had been to Germany and Australia, and now lived in Santa Fe. Skye admonished herself for judging Opal before she met her. This elderly lady was not at all what she'd expected.

Opal smiled at Skye and reached out to touch her cheek. "Honey, if you don't mind me saying so, you have black mascara streaks running down one side of your face. Would you like a La Fresh Travel Lite? I don't go anywhere without them." She reached into her pants pocket and handed one over. "Now this may sound crazy to you, but Preparation H cream is great for taking down eye swelling. If I were a nosy person, I'd ask who is the rogue who caused your tears."

Skye laughed. "Good thing you're not nosy."

"Just tell me, male or female?"

Skye smiled wider. "Uh-uh. Opal, if you tell me your level of riding, then we can go on our way. Sounds like you've had lots of experience."

"I haven't ridden for several years," Opal said, "but I'm sure it'll come back to me. I was brought up on a horse ranch in Lexington, Kentucky."

Was there anywhere she hadn't been? Skye checked Lightning's girth strap again, to make sure it was tight. "I guess I wonder why you want a trail ride—not that I'm complaining—if you have so much experience?"

"Oh, it's not for me, not entirely. It's a trial run for my girls' group, the CFOBs. Every month one of us poses a physical challenge for the group. So far we've done hot-air balloon rides during Albuquerque's festival, zip lines at Angel Fire, hang gliders, and a most unfortunate BBQ where Adrianna served us grilled rattlesnake. Trust me, it does *not* taste at all like chicken. I wouldn't give that to my dog. I hid my serving in her potted mums." She laughed, a tiny tee-hee only older women could get away with. "Anyway, now it's my turn to pick our activity, and I thought this sounded like a fun way for us to get some fresh air, provided we can keep our wigs on."

"Wigs?" Skye echoed.

"Side effect of chemo."

"Oh, my goodness," Skye said. "I'm so sorry."

"Oh, honey, don't feel badly. Most of the ladies are doing just fine. Sometimes you have to push yourself back out into the world," she said, lifting her arms as if she held the whole world in her small hands. "You have to be more courageous in remission than you were during treatment. We created the club so we could keep each other's spirits up."

Skye watched as Opal placed her helmet over her chin-length bob that was black and shiny, with enviable platinum-blond streaks. It didn't look like a wig, but apparently there was some incredible wigmaker on the level of the Passier saddlemaker.

Opal adjusted her embroidered cowboy-style pearl-snap shirt and said, "I'm ready."

Skye couldn't stop looking at the shirt. Sometimes, not often, she'd come across a Double D Ranch brand or Johnny Was shirt at Double Take, a secondhand store down the street from the Guadalupe BBQ. Even used, they cost a lot of money. "So, Opal," she said. "You have such a pretty name. Were you named after a relative?"

"Nope, born in October, named after the birthstone. Papa always said I was his little gem."

Skye pulled up a mounting block with a step attached. "You know how to use mounting blocks?"

"Yes, I do. And I despise the fact I can't get up without help."

"You won't feel bad for long. Everything looks better from the top of a horse."

"How sweet to hear you to say that. My father used to tell me the same thing."

Skye got her settled, then went around Coco to get to Lightning. She walked him forward, coming around Opal's left side.

Opal was focused on the man heading into the barn. "Who is that handsome man?"

Skye thought it best not to respond. Opal was already holding her reins the correct way. Skye was impressed. "Do you need me to go over any of the basics? The emergency stop?"

"No, dear. 'Grab mane and press yourself into the horse's neck.' I remember all that. What a wonderful feeling this is," Opal replied. "Makes me wonder why I waited so long to ride again."

She pointed back over at the man who was now tipping a bale of straw end over end toward the barn. "That fellow is so handsome he could be on the cover of a romance novel."

"Opal," Skye said, "stop looking at that man and pay attention to your horse."

"A girl's allowed to look," she said.

"Not when it's my *dad*," Skye said.

"Oh, my heavens," Opal said. "I thought he was Kris Kristofferson. Will your father be around when my girls come to trail ride?"

"I imagine he will since he's the barn manager. Can we please go now?"

"All right," Opal said. "Just one more thing. Is he married?"

Skye sighed. She stood in front of Lightning and placed two fingers between his ears, and he dropped his head until his muzzle was almost touching the ground. Skye almost put her right foot in the stirrup but remembered a trick she'd taught Lightning years ago. Would he remember? Facing his beautiful spotted muzzle, she planted her legs about a foot apart. Her arms reached toward his poll, and he flexed his neck muscles. She made a kissing noise, and Lightning jerked his head up, and Skye was slightly airborne before she landed deftly on his back, facing his butt. The fact that he remembered touched her in the sore places, but also made her sad. She turned herself around, put her feet in the stirrups, and took hold of his reins. "Let's head toward the gate."

"That was astounding," Opal said. "Can you do that when the ladies are here? Tell them that's how you get into the saddle. They will flip their wigs, literally!"

"I'm not sure that's the best way to inspire confidence," Skye said, "but I suppose it couldn't hurt, so long as they realize it's a stunt."

"No, you have to let them think it's the standard," Opal said, her laugh going from polite to laugh out loud. "You probably think I'm a mean old woman, but honestly, I'm not. I just like to have a little fun."

Skye headed toward the gate with Opal following, then bent down to open the latch, shoo Opal in, and lock it after herself.

"When do we canter?" Opal asked.

"How about we just walk and trot today?" Skye suggested. "Maybe next time we can canter a little. Now, Coco will follow behind me if you make it clear that's what you want. No wandering off trail, okay? Nobody wants cactus spines, least of all the horses. See that rock? We'll ride out to there, turn around, and come back."

"Ah," Opal said. "The Cieneguilla Petroglyphs. That's the perfect spot for a picnic. The girls would love it. We could get Chocolate Maven to put together a proper high tea, spread out a blanket, let the horses graze."

On what? Skye wondered. Nothing grew there besides weeds. "Today we'll just concentrate on getting there and back. Another time we can stop there and hike up to see the petroglyphs or eat chocolate."

"I haven't been up there in probably twenty years. After my Diego died, I just stopped doing things."

Skye listened as Opal poured out her heart, and it wasn't all recipes and cowgirl dreams, either. Imagine, having the love of your life die in your arms. Opal had seen most of the planet, including Antarctica. She told Skye about her daughters, one of whom was a power Realtor, the other an attorney who had a 100-percent win record in her practice. "The old-boy network is terrified of her," Opal said. "They're just the most modern girls you ever could find. I don't think Shannon has cooked a single dinner in her life. Jodie works so much I told her she ought to set up a cot in the courtroom. They hardly ever have a minute to spare. And neither one wants my Haviland china. Then there's the everyday original Fiestaware, two complete sets, and the Stickley furniture."

"What's Haviland?" Skye asked, listening to the creaking of her saddle, thinking of the hidden places she needed to soap up, to get it flexible.

"Oh, Skye. There simply aren't enough hours in the day to tell you the whole, exciting story. The company began in the 1700s, and has a delightfully juicy history, what with cutthroat competitors and the discovery of true kaolin clay in Limoges, France. Artists like Rodin, Dufy, and Cocteau all made a contribution to the china known today as Haviland. It was the White House china during the Lincoln administration. Google it up on the computer sometime. It's as engrossing a story as anything Ngaio Marsh or Dorothy Sayers ever penned."

Skye had never felt so uneducated in her life. "I'm sorry. Who are they?"

Opal posted the trot perfectly until she was up alongside Skye. Then she slowed Coco to a walk. "This will keep you from wrenching your neck to look at me. Darling, they are the most marvelous mystery writers of the 1930s and '40s. On our next ride, I'll bring you some books to read. Or you can pop by my house and pick them up. I live at Waldo and Houghton. I must warn you, I rescue miniature dachshunds, so there's a bit of barking."

"I wouldn't feel right borrowing your books," Skye said. "They sound like they're valuable."

Opal laughed, a tinkling, glassy sound. Even her laugh sounded well informed. "At my age," she said, "I can give things away to whomever I want. After all, they're just things. Besides, knowing you'll read them makes me happy. Think of the discussions we can have."

I just met you, Skye wanted to say, but in the next breath she asked herself, what on earth prevented her from making a friend who was maybe sixty years older than her? "I look forward to meeting your friends," Skye said. "I've been wondering about the 'CFOBs.' What's it stand for?"

"Cancer-Fighting Old Broads," Opal said.

Skye looked at her and raised her eyebrows, suppressing a smile.

Opal laughed again. "Yes. We thought we should have an acronym for our little club."

They were silent as they reached the turnaround point. Skye had to pay more attention to Coco and Lightning here, as they both tended to be barn sour, just like RedBow. "Keep your reins tight," Skye said.

"Is it all right if I trot just a little?"

"I guess so," Skye said, "but keep him on a short rein. Who knows? Coco is an old man, but I've never met a horse that didn't want a chance to get his yayas out."

Opal smiled at her and assumed the formal position of an English rider. She began by pressing her legs against Coco until he sped up, then she slowed him down, as they agreed to a lovely, quiet pace, moving slowly. "Good boy," Opal said, patting Coco's neck. The gait was what Skye's father called a "gentleman's jog." And it was beautiful.

When they were unsaddling the horses after they'd returned to the barn, Skye wrestled up the courage to ask, "Do you mind me asking what kind of cancer you have?"

"Oh, I've been in remission for years," Opal said. She lifted up her wig, revealing a shiny bald head. "I have alopecia."

Skye walked Opal to her car as they set up a time for next week. There would be four riders in all, and Opal asked if she might have a horse with more "pep." Skye would put her on Lightning. She watched her drive away, and thought, *Damn, I forgot to ask Opal for the thirty-five dollars!* As she stepped into the breezeway where she would brush both horses, she overheard her dad talking with Peter. Owen was hauling rented heat lamps outside the barn, placing them every five feet or so. The wind was picking up, and Skye felt certain her dad would be dragging them back inside the barn shortly. "Hi, Peter," she called out. He looked at her but did not wave. The look on his face said *hangover* in flashing neon.

Damn it, Skye thought. *Nothing I said made any difference. I guess if he wants to throw himself a pity party, that's none of my business.* She moved the horses to their stalls, listening to her father and Peter talk.

"I could use some help here, son."

"What do you need me to do," the boy asked flatly, his hands in his pockets.

"Oh, don't tell me. Somebody has a case of the poor-me blues?"

"Don't ask, don't tell," Peter said.

Skye rubbed Lightning's neck, stifling a laugh. "Wouldn't dream of it. Can you help me unfold the tables? I need them set end to end. The tablecloths are in the box over yonder."

"Yonder?" Peter laughed. "Sure thing, Hoss."

A slap of New Mexico wind flew into their faces, flinging grit with it. Skye watched her dad brush the dust off his face with his bandanna. "That wind is giving me no end of doubts," Owen said. "Maybe we should move the party indoors. What do you think?"

"What is wrong with women?" Peter asked, clearly focused on matters other than the weather.

Her dad chuckled. "Other than the fact that they are a superior species, I haven't a clue," Owen said. "If this is about Bonnie, your mom already told me. Getting divorced is never fun."

"Tell me about it," Peter said. "First, she's like, 'Let's just get this over with as quickly as possible, since we both want the same thing.' But we don't want the same thing, and what I want isn't up for discussion. She lives with somebody else. She's having his baby. Now she wants me to give her alimony! She makes more money than I do. What the fuck?"

"Next time you feel like dropping the F-bomb, say 'pinochle.'"

"Why?"

"Because it will sound so ridiculous you'll understand why swear words change nothing. I'm sorry to say, Peter, but the judge will rule in her favor. You might as well get used to it. Now grab hold of that end of the tablecloth and give it a shake."

The moment Peter gave it a snap, Brown Horse let out a panicked shriek and kicked her stall door hard. "Uh-oh," Skye said, coming out of Lightning's stall and going to Brown Horse next door. Someone in her past must have whipped her, Skye figured. "Hey, it's okay, Brown Horse," she said, soothing the horse the way she had Gracie. Sometimes Gracie had a bad dream; other times, after a video, she could remember only the monsters and not the heroes. Just then, a tablecloth blew by the barn, and Brown Horse kicked again, just missing Skye. "That's enough of that," she said, and quickly latched the stall door. Maybe they should move her to the other side of the barn. Santa Fe was famous for wind. As in cartoons, it picked up lawn chairs and umbrellas and tossed tumbleweeds wherever it chose.

"I can't believe the stinking wind," Peter complained, wiping grit from his face. "It's like the whole world is against me."

Owen laughed. "I can hear it now on the five o'clock news. Dick Knipfing, KQRE, reporting live from the gala at Reach for the Sky: 'This afternoon, the wind picked up for the sole purpose of irritating Pouty Petey even further than usual.'"

"Stop making fun of me," Peter said.

"Quit calling me Hoss. I'm going to find the party planner lady. We need to move everything indoors." A car door slammed. "Peter, go see if that's the caterers, would you?"

Peter clomped off, looking about thirteen years old, as if his mother had put the kibosh on his plan to attend a girl-boy party. Though she hated to admit it, sometimes he reminded Skye of herself. And they both had something to cry about—the end of Peter's marriage and Skye's missing daughter. She wanted a life like that of the happily married Vigils, Glory and Joe, who had that cute little baby and another on the way. She had dreamed of veterinary school, and maybe that could still happen sometime in the future. Even if it didn't, she wanted a little house with cherry-print curtains in the kitchen. All she had to do was serve her community hours, stay sober, and find a paying job. She could do that. Right?

Skye groomed the horses, polished tack, and checked all the mousetraps.

"Are you going home to change?" Joe asked her as she put the horses away.

"I guess I am now," Skye answered.

Then she headed home to shower, change, and come right back.

She threw her keys down as she walked in the door, and was unbuttoning her shirt on the way to the bathroom when she heard the front door open. Oh, my Lord, was it Daddy, wanting to talk to her about the scene she'd walked in on? Skye wasn't any more ready to talk to him today than she had been yesterday or the day before. But she might as well get it over with, so they could look at each other normally again. She came out of the bedroom, already blushing, when she saw it wasn't Daddy at all. A familiar-looking woman with a Louis Vuitton roll-along and a matching pet carrier stood in front of her. She was dressed in white slacks, a white blazer, and a white scarf knotted fashionably around her neck. Her small white dog, which looked like a Pomeranian, peered around the woman's legs, took one look at Skye, and began barking as if she were Freddy Krueger.

"Pearl, you hush up right now. I mean it, or you're going back in your crate until suppertime."

"Mama?" Skye said. "Oh, my gosh. You never answer my phone calls. I can't believe you came. You look beautiful."

Her mother set her purse on the couch. "I do own this house."

Skye's stomach clenched. "Does that mean you want me out?"

Her mother stared. "Travel makes me dehydrated. Fetch me a drink, will you? There's vodka in the freezer."

Skye couldn't move. "I'm sorry. I poured your vodka down the sink the day I got here."

Her mother blanched. "That was a specialty vodka! It cost a hundred dollars a bottle. What were you thinking?"

"I was thinking if I didn't pour it down the sink, I'd pour it down my throat, because I am and always will be, I guess, a recovering alcoholic."

Mama said nothing. Skye could see the wheels in her head deliberately not turn. She did not, and would not ever, believe Skye was an alcoholic. In her mind, alcoholics lived on Skid Row and slept in cardboard boxes.

"Look," Skye said. "I can't pay you back for the vodka for a while, but I promise I will. There's a box of wine in the pantry. Why don't you drink that? I have to take a shower, and then somehow get the coffee stain out of this shirt. After that, I'll be out of your way."

Skye turned, and then it happened. Her mother reached out and took her by the arm, the first touch between them in a long time. Skye felt the pull in both directions. She was twenty-three one minute and age ten the next. Apparently a mother's touch rendered a person a child.

"You and I are overdue for a discussion. Sit down on the couch."

Skye stood where she was. "I have to go back to work, Mama. It's a brand new job. If you want to talk, I'll talk to you later."

Her mother's mouth drew thin in a straight line, just as it had before she commenced yelling at Skye's father. "Fine," she snapped, though Skye could see it was anything but. "When do you get off work?"

"Tonight there's a grand opening party there, and my boss insists I stay until everyone is introduced. As soon as it's over, I'm driving to T or C."

"A party?" Sheila asked, eyes gleaming. "What kind of party?"

"It's a fund-raiser for Reach for the Sky. It's at a stable. Dirt, et cetera. You'd hate it." She decided not to mention the canapés, the silent auction, and that her dad would be there.

But it was too late. The party life was her mother's natural habitat. "We can go together. There should be ample time for us to chat while you drive me there."

"I don't know, Mama," Skye said. "It depends on what you want to talk to me about. I have to tell you, I'm feeling pretty fragile right now, what with Gracie being missing." Her eyes filled with tears, and she tilted her head backward so they wouldn't spill.

Mama picked up her little yapping dog and fed her a treat from her purse. "Your father said you changed your name to Skye. May I ask why?"

When had she talked to Owen? "I needed a fresh start after rehab."

Her mother looked her up and down. "Skye, then. Can you guarantee this time you'll stay sober?"

"I can't. Like they say, I just go one day at a time."

"Your track record isn't good."

"You think I don't know that? Shit, Mama. Why do you even bother?"

"Do not curse at me, young lady. Since you haven't done too well on your own, I think I am the one to help you fashion a decent life."

Oh, my God, that sounded so mean. "How do you propose to do that?" Skye said.

"I'm willing to work with you on a mutually agreed-upon payment plan with a low interest rate."

"Are you effing kidding me? A payment plan, *with interest*, is going to help me get my life in order? Jeez, Mama. I thought I'd hit bottom with you, but apparently the well continues down a thousand more feet. I don't need your kind of help. I'd rather stay at a homeless shelter." She wrenched free, went into the bedroom to grab her few clothes from the closet. "I'm leaving now. I'll find somewhere else to stay." She made it as far as the front door, opened it, and Sheila grabbed her arm again.

"Now you just wait a cotton-picking minute," her mother said. "I'm not done here."

In the sunlight coming from the open door, Skye saw that her mother had some wrinkles and a few gray hairs had escaped the dye job. In other words, makeup didn't cover everything. "Make it quick, Mama. I have to go."

Her mother toyed with the bracelets on her left wrist. "What do you plan on wearing to that party?"

Skye held up her clothes. "Since this is all I have in the entire world, this is what I'm wearing. I'll change in the Porta-Potty at the stable. Good-bye."

Her mother took the shirt and jeans away from Skye. "This won't do for a fund-raiser."

"Mama, what the hell do you think? I'm supposed to run out and buy a cocktail dress? I am broke. The last thing on my mind is a dress code."

"While you're showering, Pearl and I will find you something perfect for the party."

"Please don't. If you want to help me, then give me gas money so I can go find Gracie."

They stood there silently, eyeing each other. Skye knew she'd gotten off on the wrong foot the instant she confessed that she'd dumped the vodka. But damn it all, how cruel was it to ask a newly sober person to get within five feet of anything with alcohol in it? Was Mama really that freaking clueless?

Her mother smiled. Was it real or icy judgment? Who cared? By the time the gala ended, Sheila'd probably be back in Phoenix. "It's important to honor your commitments. Go take your shower," her mother said. "You don't want to be late. We'll talk later."

Skye got into the shower and lathered up her hair, trying to get all of the grit out of it. The water hitting her shoulders felt like a masseuse's hands. If Santa Fe weren't always on water rationing, she'd have stood there until the water tank emptied. It freaked her out wondering what the world would be like when Gracie grew up. Would they be trucking water into Santa Fe, the way they were in parts of Texas? Would more wildfires take down the forests? So many heavy issues. She thought over the trail ride with Opal. The woman was extraordinary. She reminded Skye of the people she saw during Fiesta Days, dressed traditionally, wearing all their silver and turquoise. If Opal's friends were anything like her, Skye couldn't wait to meet them. She had the feeling that they might change her life, even if all she did was read the books they recommended.

What had made her mother come all the way to Santa Fe? Why now? Surely by now Skye had left a hundred messages for her. Not once had she called back.

Their troubles had begun in an ordinary way, if you could call pregnancy at seventeen ordinary.

Since it was too late for an abortion, Mama had suggested she give the baby up for adoption.

Skye said she understood that some mothers could do that, but she wasn't one of them. She was having the baby. And keeping it.

Mama said, *You'll regret this forever. You're throwing away your perfectly good life.*

Skye said, *So you're saying I should throw away this baby's perfectly good life to save me some trouble?*

Unspoken between them was the subtext, of how Mama might've wished she'd done the same thing. Neither of them would touch that topic, the mother-daughter nuclear weapon that once fired could never be unfired.

Radio silence for weeks. Mama had finally text-messaged her: *Then you're on your own. Don't come crying to me when everything falls apart.*

She hadn't even wanted to meet Gracie. She did not send a birthday card. Acted as if Gracie didn't exist.

A year went by, and things were falling apart with Rocky. It was the beginning of Skye's own problems with alcohol and drugs. She called her mother once a week, but Sheila would not pick up the phone. When Mama bought the peed-off terrier, she invited Skye to the housewarming party she threw, but not Rocky, and no children were allowed.

It had been the first time they'd seen each other face-to-face in a year and a half. Skye arrived a little drunk. Well, a lot drunk. But Mama was drunk, too. The two of them had a massive fight. After that night, the silence spread out like a snake uncoiling itself in the sun. They began to play the game of Who Will Say Sorry First, and still, no one had lost—or won. What exactly was Skye supposed to apologize for? Her pregnancy? Gracie? Being a little high at the housewarming party? Okay, a lot high. Her entire existence? Maybe it was time for Skye to bite the bullet and say she was to blame, even though she didn't think the rift between them was entirely her fault.

And today? Mama in the flesh? What did that mean? Skye was sure she'd ruined any possibility of Mama lending her gas money. The expression on her mother's face said she was sure Skye would spend the money on drugs. Hard enough to cut glass, that diamond on her ring finger had to be worth tens of thousands of dollars, and all it did was sit on her finger looking pretty. The irony of that fact alone was so ridiculous Skye couldn't measure it.

Chapter 13

"MAMA?" SKYE CALLED as she came out of the shower. She didn't get an answer, but Sheila's suitcase and Pearl's dog carrier were still here, so her mother hadn't skipped town yet.

She was blow-drying her hair, which seemed to take forever, when Mama's little white dog came scurrying into the bathroom and started barking at her. Skye aimed the blow dryer at the Pomeranian and it ran out of the bathroom, yipping, tail tucked. She set down the dryer and pulled on her mother's robe. "Mama," she called.

"Out here!"

The front room couch was covered with shopping bags. So many packages that it looked like Christmas. "Mama," Skye said, "I told you not to do this."

"I just bought you a few things. Here," she said, holding out a dress on a hanger, encased in plastic. "This is for tonight."

Skye shook her head no. "I am not wearing that. Take it back for a refund. I told you—if you're going to spend money on me, please let it be gas money so I can go looking for Gracie. She's the only thing that matters."

"Everything was on sale, clearance, not returnable. Just try it on. I think it will go nicely with your boots."

Skye sighed. "Mama, I am putting on my jeans and a clean shirt and I am leaving the second Mr. Vigil is done introducing everybody."

Her mother's mouth was set. "I'll make you a deal. You wear the dress tonight and I'll pay for your gas to drive to T or C."

"That's blackmail or something."

"It's just a little enticement to get you to wear it. The dress should be bribe enough! Try it on."

What next? Skye lifted the plastic from a velvet dress so dark blue, you could only call it indigo. She hated it on sight, because it reminded her of all the things she'd never be able to afford. It had long satiny sleeves and a short skirt, with embroidered flowers—periwinkle blue, yellow gold, and pink—on the bodice. She pulled off her jeans and T-shirt and lifted the dress over her head. It fit perfectly, but she felt like one of those dressed-up dogs rich women carried around in purses: utterly ridiculous. But if she caved in to Mama's deal, they both got what they wanted, and the expense to her was what? An hour of pure humiliation. She could do it, for Gracie.

Mama was smiling. "It's exactly right," she said, pushing Skye toward the bathroom mirror. She took hold of the cuff of the left sleeve. "Those are called bishop's sleeves," she said, buttoning it so that the loose material overlapped in a generous way. "This design is called the 'Dalia.' Isn't that just the sweetest name you ever heard? And it's made by—"

"I know who made it, Double D Ranch," Skye interrupted. "Even if I have no money, I do have good taste. I sure as hell know you paid full price for this dress. Three hundred dollars,

Mama! Do you have any idea what three hundred dollars means to me? " She stopped and took a breath, instead of telling her. Immediately the tears came.

"Hush," her mother said, leading Skye to the couch and sitting her down. She was frowning. "I can't undo the fact that I put my own needs before yours when I left Colorado. I wasn't there for you when you needed me. However, if we both agree to try, I think we can make the future better. I hope you'll agree to wear the dress to the party, Skye. Just for tonight. Afterwards, if you hate it that much, you can throw it out."

Skye sniffled. Throw it out? Hell, she'd sell it on Craigslist. "What brought about this change of heart?"

Her mother reached down to pet the dog. "Your father and I talked. He's a good man, Skye. I wish I'd seen that earlier."

"Daddy? What's that mean? Are you getting another divorce?"

Her mother picked up a small bag and pulled a bottle of nail polish out of it. "Your father and I respect each other. The state of my marriage is none of your business."

"You're getting another divorce."

"I don't want to talk about it. Now let me paint your nails."

"Aw, Mama. I hate nail polish."

"Then at least let me paint them with clear coat."

All of her life, Mama had been bubbly and joking with everyone from the grocery store checkout person to strangers on the street. If she wasn't out with friends, she was on the phone with them. But if Skye went to her crying about the playground bullies, Mama said, "Push back," and that was the end of it. Skye figured once she turned into a teenager, she'd have a lot more in common with her mother, like shopping, prom dresses, girl stuff. But after Daddy left, Mama devoted all her time to finding and marrying rich, powerful men. Love was never part of it. Skye watched her deftly wield the polish brush. The feel of her fingers against Skye's hand, the dress, maybe this *was* affection to Mama. The closest they'd ever get to a hug.

Of course Mama insisted on coming to the gala. When they arrived at the stable, a few cars were already being parked by a valet. Skye didn't want to be stuck there all night. "Can you please park it so I don't get boxed in?" she asked. "I'll be leaving the party early."

"How am I supposed to get back to my casita?" her mother asked.

"I'm sure you'll find a ride. If you don't, call a cab."

With every step they took toward the barn, Skye hoped her mother would not flirt with Daddy. "He's in love with that painter, Margaret. They're good together. Please be nice to him."

"Why wouldn't I be?" Sheila said. "I have nothing in my heart for your father other than gratitude."

Say it enough times and maybe you'll believe it, Skye thought as they rounded the corner and took inventory of the party setup. The wind was howling, and Skye covered her face to keep from getting grit in her lip gloss. Paper flowers had busted loose from their pots and were flying around and landing in the dirt. The party planner, wearing spiky heels, could not run fast enough to catch them.

The caterers were dressed in black and white and wearing chile pepper print aprons. They were trying to keep the Sterno cans lit, but it was a losing battle. Skye watched her mom retrieve a whistle from her purse and blow it. "Change of plans. We're

moving the party inside the barn. Someone break open a bale of
straw, not hay, and start spreading it on the floor." She pointed to
the party planner. "You're in charge?"

The woman nodded.

"Then get your people started moving things inside. And
hurry. Guests will be arriving any minute. Go!"

When things were under way, the planner hobbled over on
her spike heels to Skye and her mother. "Thank you for saving
my butt. I wondered, though, why do you have a whistle in your
handbag? Do you teach preschool?"

"Good heavens, no," Sheila said. "I don't relate very well to
children until they are toilet-trained and able to speak in full
sentences. That's my 'don't even think about it' whistle. I also
carry Mace. Actually, you shouldn't leave home without it."

Sheila got right to work, adjusting the linen tablecloths and
placing the decorative paper ones atop the linen at an angle. Skye
was amazed at her mother's ability to walk into a room and
organize everyone. This was a side of her mother she didn't know,
and it seemed—for the first time—like one she could learn from.

"Crudités first," Sheila said. "Main dishes last. Where are the
serving spoons?"

"In the van," someone answered.

"Well, what are you waiting for? Go and fetch them!"

The interior of the barn began to transform. The straw under-
foot made it feel intimate and comfortable. One of the workers
was tacking crepe paper to the wall, measuring it so it draped like
a banner. When another worker brought in helium-filled
balloons, her dad emerged from the stalls and said, "Absolutely
no balloons. Even the calmest horse in the world will spook at a
balloon popping."

"But can't you see? Without the balloons, the banners are only one layer," the party planner argued. "Without layers, you don't get texture, and without texture, nothing works! They have to be there."

"I have no idea what you're talking about," he said, waving hello at Skye. "What I do know is that there are nine horses in this side of the barn, and five on the other. I've seen a horse jump out of a box stall when a balloon pops. That kind of panic is contagious. Someone could get hurt. No balloons."

"Can't you just chain them in the stalls?"

Owen threw up his hands. "Holy Mother of God, dear, they're not circus elephants!" he exclaimed. "Liability insurance on a place like this is hard enough to get in the first place. What part of 'no balloons' did you not understand?"

There went the balloons. Layering, Skye thought to herself, I have to remember to ask Sheila about that. And once the balloons were out, in came the band. "Take those amplifiers back to wherever they came from," her dad said.

Skye put her arm through her mother's. "Daddy," she said, "here's Mama."

The first thing he did was take off his cowboy hat. Then he smiled and kissed her on the cheek. "Sheila, you look wonderful," he said. "Thank you so much for coming. It's good to see you again."

"Good to see you, too. The years have been kind to you."

Owen laughed. "Thanks for saying that, but we both know it isn't true. You, on the other hand, look about thirty years old."

"It's all done with smoke and mirrors," Shelia said.

Skye was amazed to see her parents relating on such good terms. Her mom had called her dad the day Skye got out of rehab. Who knows? Maybe they'd talked more than once. It seemed like they had settled a few things. Had he convinced her to come to New Mexico, to help Skye in this search for Gracie? She would have given a kidney to have eavesdropped on that conversation, but she'd settle for the outcome. These two had a relationship she knew nothing about.

"It's going to take me a while to remember to call you Owen," Sheila said. "The both of you with your name changes. But I'm in favor of new beginnings, having made a few myself. Is everything set in the barn, now?"

Uh-oh, Skye thought. She was definitely getting another divorce.

The three of them stood near the bandstand, where musicians were setting up instruments. "Things are fine. Do you mind if I have a private word with our girl here?"

"Not at all. I'll go organize the auction tables." Skye's mother gave her father a kiss on the cheek that lasted a bit too long, and when she walked away toward the stalls, she took her sweet time, allowing Owen plenty of time to study her backside, had he been looking. If her mother made a play for her dad, Skye would sit on her until she gave up. Could you ever really stop loving someone you once took vows with, using that word *forever*? Despite the way things had ended, Rocky would always own a part of her heart. But no way was Sheila going to get between Daddy and Margaret.

The tables were rapidly filling with spa packages, gift baskets, pottery, and silver jewelry. Skye glanced across the room, and there was Margaret with Mrs. Vigil's baby daughter. She was also holding the hand of a little girl near Gracie's age. "Daddy," Skye began, reminded of their awkwardness, "I'm sorry I walked in on you and Margaret. I didn't think—"

He held up a hand. "Margaret and I have a long history, and a future ahead of us, Skye. And I may be old, but I'm not Methuselah."

"I know, Daddy. You guys have the real deal. I hope I can be that happy someday."

He patted her hand. "You will, I know it. By the way, you look beautiful."

"Please, I am barely holding it together. Mama bribed me into wearing this dress. As soon as the introductions are over, I'm hitting the road for T or C."

"Did you hear from that judge?"

"No. I just have a feeling. And it won't hurt anything to poke around."

He frowned. "I wish you weren't going by yourself. Can't you ask Peter to go with you? Or your mother?"

Skye laughed. "In a contest for high maintenance, who would win, Mama or Peter?"

"I see your point. Please drive carefully. There are a lot of drunks out on the road."

Skye said, "Don't we both know it? Listen, I think you ought to invest in a lock for that door," she said.

He chuckled. "Already done. See you later, doll." He started to walk away, then came back and gave her a hug. "It's a tie for prettiest woman in the room. Don't tell Margaret I said it, but I'd vote for you."

"Aw, go polish your boots."

Skye walked back to Mama, who was bidding on the spa package. Each item had a card with a description, its retail worth, and places to enter bids. "Ten Thousand Waves," her mother said. "Maybe we could go together."

With all my spare time, Skye thought.

Sheila took Skye's arm as the guests began arriving. Women were dressed in floor-length broomstick skirts and velvet blouses, sporting squash blossom necklaces that otherwise resided in safe deposit boxes, dangly needlepoint turquoise earrings, and silver bracelets so numerous that they shimmered in the light of the barn. Most of the women wore cowboy boots instead of high heels. The men wore whatever their wives told them to wear, so there were Pendleton blanket jackets in a multitude of patterns, cowboy hats, and western-cut tuxedoes. They were dressed for dinner. Sunday best. It pained Skye to admit, Mrs. Wadsworth hadn't been entirely wrong in her lessons.

"You watch carefully," Sheila said. "Worthwhile philanthropic events in Santa Fe bring out the born-and-raised New Mexicans, not just retired wealthy people. These are the powerful folks you want to get to know."

Mama never passed up a chance to elevate her station. "You look great, Mama," Skye said. "Nobody can rock a little black dress better than you. With your hair piled on top like that, you could pass for Audrey Hepburn."

"Oh, honey," her mother said. "A lot of work and money went into keeping this old body looking young. But thankfully I have a plastic surgeon for a husband. He tells me what's possible, and what he refuses to do. I don't want to end up like that cat-faced woman with the miniature greyhounds. It's a fine line. Now, let's go get a drink."

"You go ahead."

"But I want you to go with me."

"Mama, I can't be around alcohol. I just can't. It makes me want to—"

"You can't live in only one part of the world, Skye. You're coming with me and that's that."

Skye steeled herself and went to the open bar, where her mother ordered Johnnie Walker Blue with cream. Skye tried not to smell it, but one whiff and she felt the anticipation surge through her body. She could almost taste that mellow flavor of aged Scotch, feel the burn in the back of her knees, where it always hit her.

And there Sheila went, shaking the governor's hand and giving a hug to Pop Wilder, whom Skye actually remembered from stories her dad told. Skye had been friendly with his daughter, Lily, the ultimate party girl until she met that guy Tres. Or was it Cuatro? Some Spanish number. Pop Wilder's wife had been in a few made-for-TV movies and some commercials, but Skye couldn't remember what they were for. Her dogs! That was it. She'd been instrumental in getting the dog track shut down, and she rescued retired greyhounds and now, Spanish galgos. Skye wondered if she knew Opal.

Mr. Vigil was leaning heavily on his cane tonight, and Skye watched him take a pill from his pocket and pop it into his mouth. She bet she knew what it was, too. A pale peach–colored 20-milligram oxycodone tablet, which he took for his back pain and Skye had taken for fun. He and Mrs. Vigil were standing next to Margaret, fussing over the baby. "There she is, Mama," Skye said.

"There's who?"

"Daddy's girlfriend."

Sheila stiffened beside Skye. Apparently, Mama was allowed to move on, but not Owen. What did she want him to do? Languish forever?

"What sort of music do you suppose the band will play?" Sheila asked Skye, hiding the disappointment that had clouded her face.

"I have no idea. Hopefully something that won't rile the horses, if Daddy has any say in it."

The room quickly filled as the Bosque Boys began to play their own country-alt renditions of big band songs. Without the amplifiers, the music was low-key, and her dad finally looked relaxed. "I gave every horse a quarter bucket of sweet feed," he told Skye when she saw him next. And here came Mama, back from more mingling to circle Daddy like a mako shark.

"I figured," Skye said.

Her dad smiled. "I also gave them a dose of that hippie medicine Mellow Out that you mentioned. It actually seems to work. I'm hoping it will keep them calm for the duration. Sheila, how do you like Arizona? Those triple-digit summers sit right with you?"

"Heavens, no. We spend the hottest part of the year on Orcas Island."

"Last time I saw the Pacific Ocean, well, I can't recall."

"It's lovely and unspoiled, the Pacific Northwest at its best. Sometime if you'd like to use our cabin for a vacation getaway, I hope you'll let me know."

"Any horses up there?"

Sheila laughed. "Not that I'm personally aware of, but if there are, I bet you'll find them. I can say for certain there are plenty of deer, eagles, otters, and whales. Mainly killer whales, hence the name Orcas."

Skye's father was listening intently. "Doesn't that sound like a piece of heaven. Nice of you to offer, too. I suppose I had better start thinking of where to take Margaret on our honeymoon. Sounds like that might work. Thank you," he said, clasping her hands and giving them a squeeze.

"Daddy!" Skye exclaimed happily. "Marriage?" She could feel the disappointment in her mother like a physical force.

"I haven't asked her yet, but I'm going to," he replied with a grin. "Now excuse me, ladies, I can see someone wants a barn tour." He put his hat on and walked toward the stalls, where a bored-looking teenage boy stood by his parents.

"Pardon me," a fifty-something woman asked Skye, "do you know where the restrooms are?"

"Outside," she said. "You can't miss them."

"Portable toilets at a fund-raiser?"

Skye smiled. "I guess so."

"What do you know," the woman said. "I don't have to go that bad after all."

Skye and her mother laughed, and at the end of the laugh, Skye caught a glimpse of the old mom she remembered from her early childhood. Utterly unprepared, Skye was awash in long-buried feelings that made her heart ache. Christmases, July Fourth fireworks, the good times when the family was whole. She patted her mother's shoulder gently. Her mom mustered a small smile, but that was it. Skye knew her father's talk of marrying Margaret had stung, but how much?

"I think I'll get a refill on my Scotch," her mother said.

"'To ride a horse is to ride the sky,'" Mr. Vigil said in his opening remarks when the business part of the evening began. "I tried to find the name of the author who wrote those words, and what do you know, it turned out to be Anonymous. The most prolific writer in the world."

Everyone laughed.

He introduced his family, starting with his wife, Glory, with her silver hair and apple cheeks. She had that glow of pregnancy about her. Then he introduced his daughters, starting with the baby, Sparrow. He moved on to Casey and Juniper, and his granddaughter, Aspen. When he was done, Glory handed Sparrow back to Margaret.

Margaret looked beautiful; the gray in her red hair shone like silver. She was wearing a blue broomstick skirt and an embroidered top, but it was the concho belt that made her outfit. Skye wondered about Margaret's illness, how they'd handle it down the road. She really wished she hadn't seen her naked, but that was life, and she guessed old people were allowed to have sex if they wanted to.

Her dad, married. That would be an adjustment, because now that Skye had him back in her life, she wanted him all to herself. Having her father around made her ache for Gracie even more than she did already. She looked at Sparrow and Aspen, and she could imagine their little hands in hers and the sweet-sour smell kids had just before you gave them a bath. What if T or C was another bust? What if she never found Gracie? How could a person go on after that?

Margaret waved good-bye to Skye. Probably she had to get the kids home to bed.

Skye walked over to Peter, who shook his head when he saw her coming. "No more nagging," he said. "I can't handle it."

"I wasn't going to nag you. Just wanted to say hello, and tell you that you look spiffy in that leather jacket. Very Justin Bieber."

"Oh, yeah? Nice dress for a garden party and canapés."

"My mother forced me to wear it."

"Mine, too." He laughed. "Going to a party sober isn't much fun, is it? Want to go visit the horses?"

"Can't. I have to wait for Mr. Vigil to introduce everybody. Then I'm hitting the road."

"Sorry I ditched you after that meeting." He blinked nervously, and Skye could tell that apologizing was a big deal for him.

"Getting sober is your choice, Peter. I just showed you where the meetings are."

"So does that mean you forgive me?"

"Nothing to forgive. Once you quit drinking, you'll see. Forgiveness is the easiest thing ever." She placed her hand on his jacket sleeve, picking a piece of straw off it. "I've been thinking about something," Skye added, and pointed to her dad, saying good-bye to Margaret. "Whether you decide to quit drinking or not, Pete, we have to find a way to get along. They're going to get married. You can practically smell it on them. There will be holidays we're invited to. Dinners where we both have to show up. We have to find a way to get along, because we're going to be family."

He frowned. "Only because it says so on a piece of paper."

"Are you always this crabby?"

"I suppose I am."

Skye nudged him with her elbow. "Pete, lighten up. You've gotta roll with the punches, or trust me, you'll never get laid again." Peter stood there with his mouth open, and before she walked away, Skye wished a fly would zip in there.

Mr. Vigil tapped the microphone to get everyone's attention. Skye tensed up, hoping he'd finally get to the staff introductions so she could leave this shindig and drive to Truth or Consequences.

"Tonight I'm surrounded by the most generous hearts in our community," he said. "Our mission with Reach for the Sky is to help struggling children and traumatized adults from all walks of life to overcome difficulties by teaching them horsemanship.

"Phase one of the operation is our riding program for the physically handicapped. To begin with, it will run two days a week. The seeds of phase two have been planted," he continued. "The most important endeavor at Reach for the Sky is to help those with invisible issues, from those who have undergone trauma to juvenile offenders. As you know, hurt manifests in different ways.

"New Mexico has been called 'the Land of Enchantment' since 1879," Joe continued. "It's a great state, filled with history, talented artists, and multiple cultures, but it's also home to a high rate of domestic violence and an unacceptably low high school graduation rate. We hope the programs at Reach for the Sky will make a small dent in those numbers. Already we have one renowned psychologist on staff. We're especially grateful to Ardith Clemmons." He smiled and waved at the therapist to stand and be recognized. "We also have a score of volunteers ready to assist riders. What we need is simple: sponsors, donations, and community support."

This was never going to end.

"That's what tonight is really about," Joe said. "Making this place succeed, and keeping it going. You'll find a brochure in the goodie bag you'll take home tonight as a small way for us to thank you. It's filled with locally sourced items, from my father's Hatch green chile to a Navajo Christmas ornament, a jar of Bucking Bee locally produced honey, and even a signature Reach for the Sky wristwatch, designed exclusively for us by Peyote

Bird. One hundred percent of the earnings will go directly to Reach for the Sky. But enough about that. For tonight, please relax, enjoy the music, and fill yourselves on the wonderful food. Be sure to look over the auction items and bid frequently! The silent auction will end at eight P.M. In the meantime, our barn manager is ready to take you on tours of the facilities."

Then he was done, and people clapped, and the Bosque Boys began to play music a person could dance the two-step to. The party was in full swing, with people talking, eating, and going to the auction table frequently. Skye supposed he wasn't going to introduce staff after all, so she could finally get going. She needed to track down Mama and the gas money she'd promised. Skye saw Opal come in, dressed head to toe in another vintage Nudie Cohn suit. Her jacket was midnight blue, with a sky full of silver rhinestone stars winking from the shoulders, and the pencil skirt was like something out of a black-and-white movie. Her scarf was ivory velvet with satin flowers fixed to it. In her youth, Opal must have been quite the looker, Skye figured, because at eighty she was a grande dame. She waved at her, and Opal waved back. As hungry as she was, Skye ignored the taquitos, guacamole, beans, corn cakes, and rice. She was on a mission. Perhaps her mother was near the barn stalls. Skye walked as quickly as she could, ignoring everything that usually made her linger: the bales of hay stacked just so, the individual horses that nickered for attention, and the smell of the barn, with all its complex scents mingling. It could be bottled as a perfume, but it also had the unfortunate power to make a person cry.

Skye thought of foaling season at her old stable in Aurora, where she rode when she was little. Vets were on call twenty-four hours a day. Lots of horse owners stayed the night, in sleeping bags outside the stalls. In the horse world, birth was an arduous process. So many things could go wrong in an animal so poorly designed for pregnancy. In humans, a breech birth was no longer that big a deal. But when foals came out breech, things could and often did go horribly wrong.

Skye had seen foals taking their first steps on spindly legs, and though the babies were adorable, not all of them made it. A pregnant mare needed nearly as much prenatal care as a woman did. If a cheapskate owner skipped vital vaccines, nothing could make the baby right. But what truly broke Skye's heart was the way the babies were weaned. Nursing was the most bonding of ties, and after the foals grew into colts and fillies, they were wrenched from the mares and moved to the far side of the barn, where they couldn't even see their mothers. All day long, the mares and their offspring called to one another in distress, keening.

Which was exactly the way losing Gracie felt. Cruel. Unnecessary. There was no way to explain how tired she was of nothing going right in her life, of scaling a mountain every day only to find another taller one waiting. Not even Duncan's Navajo stories could put a spin on that.

Out of the corner of her eye, she saw a plastic drink cup someone had set on a hay bale and forgotten about. Skye picked it up and held it under her nose, immediately recognizing a black and brown. The ice hadn't even begun to melt. With tears rolling down her cheeks, she walked over to Lightning's stall and watched him polish off the last of his sweet feed. Her hand was shaking. Here in the barn, where no one could see her, why the hell not drink the drink? It was a party. Everyone else was buzzed, bidding on stuff, all in the name of a good cause. It would be just one small drink. Who would find out? Her mother might have left the party already. It wouldn't be the first time she'd left Skye high and dry. Skye had the cup halfway to her lips and was just about to take her first sip when she heard someone behind her clear his throat.

"Skye?"

She set the drink down on a bale of straw. Both relieved and angered by the distraction, she turned around to see Peter, and he had someone with him, too.

"I wanted you to meet my dad," Peter said. "Skye, this is Raymond Sweetwater, my father, the film director."

Except he wasn't, at least not to Skye. Raymond Sweetwater was the man she knew as Tesuque, Mr. Black and Brown, who ordered the drink every night but never drank it. He had paid for her rehab, and there she was, on the verge of drinking. They looked at each other, and Skye smiled. "How lovely to meet you," she said.

"And you as well," he said, smiling back at her.

A few minutes later, she heard her phone buzz, indicating someone had left a message. Stupid ringer must have gotten turned off. After fishing it out of her purse, she went straight to the message:

Wolfgang Schneider here. Rocky Elliot has a bench warrant in Truth or Consequences. His last known address is . . .

Skye thought, Holyshitholyshitholyshit, my luck's finally turning. She began to look for Sheila in earnest, because she needed that gas money. Or hell, maybe she'd drive for as long as the car took her and then just pull over and walk.

Skye found Mama waiting by the car, clasping her blanket coat around her, looking up at the star-studded sky.

"Mama! Where have you been? I was looking all over for you."

"Just standing here watching the stars," she said. "Making wishes."

That was going to be a discussion for another time. "I finally got a lead on Rocky, so I have to go, like right now. This could be it. If all goes well, I could have my girl back by tomorrow."

"You'll find her," she said. "You always were stubborn, even as a toddler."

"Mama, I don't mean to rush you, but I need that gas money."

Her mother opened her purse and took out her wallet. She took out twenties and fifties and even a few hundred-dollar bills.

"Mama, that's plenty. Listen, do you want to come with me?"

Her mother's eyes glistened in the moonlight. "No. Pearl's waiting for me back at the house. You go on. Text me what happens."

"Thank you for the dress," Skye said, and gave her mother a one-armed hug.

"You do look beautiful," her mother replied, and began to walk back to the party.

·

Chapter 14

SKYE WAS PUMPING gas into the Mercedes at the Allsup's when her cell phone rang. Who on earth could it be, unless maybe Mama had changed her mind? "Hello?"

"Wolfgang here. By any chance is your daughter named Eleanor?"

"Her name's Grace. But her middle name is Eleanor. Have you found her?"

"There's an Eleanor Grace Ellis in foster care in the T or C area. Could be a typo for Elliot."

"Foster care? Man, oh, man, do I have an earful for Rocky when I get there."

"Don't drive angry. And keep in mind you don't know the whole story yet."

"Who on earth puts their own child in foster care?"

"Let me give you the number to call. Got a pen?"

Skye laughed. "As a matter of fact, I have a gold Cross pen with the initials *W.S.* in case you want it back."

"Thank you. I appreciate that, though I have a million of them. Pens are what your children give you when your ex marries a rich guy."

"You're divorced?"

"Isn't everyone?"

"Did you represent yourself?"

He laughed. "Every judge will tell you, 'When you decide to represent yourself, you have a fool for a client.' How about I tell you all about it when you get back? Over dinner?"

Whoa. Well, thanks to Mama, she had a date dress. "Let me think it over. Do your close friends call you Wolfgang?"

"Mainly they call me Wolf."

"That's light-years better than Wolfgang."

She heard him chuckle. "Now that's settled, here is the number for Social Services. You want to ask for Mrs. Rodriquez. Skye, I'm not a hundred percent sure this is your daughter. Even if it is, the return process can take a while. You can't let this upset you. I've faxed paperwork from Judge Iglesias to speed things up for you."

Skye twisted the gas cap closed and got in the car, the phone still pressed to her ear.

Traffic was light, and no drunk drivers seemed to be out. Skye couldn't help wondering where Gracie was, and if she was hungry, or cold, or worse, having an asthma attack. *Damn Rocky anyway, and what the hell was Rita thinking? Where was Grandma? Playing the slots at Fort Sill Apache?*

"Hey, Skye?" Wolf asked, bringing her focus back to the road. "Drive carefully."

"I *am* driving carefully."

"You going to find a motel to stay in until morning?"

"No."

"Why not?"

"I can't afford a motel. I'll sleep in my car."

"Skye," he said, "absolutely not. I've just now made a reservation for you at the Comfort Inn off Date Street."

"What? I told you, I don't have the money."

"I've put it on my corporate card. Right now, I consider you my client. Once the case is settled, we'll talk about repaying me."

"How am I your client? I don't recall hiring you."

"Lawyers are allowed to take on cases pro bono. You go get a good night's sleep, and call me tomorrow. I have to go now. Good luck."

"Wait," Skye said. But he was already gone. She pressed END on her cell phone.

She drove for miles and miles in silence, passing by red rock, the yellow-brown plains covered with rabbit brush, interrupted only by scrubby piñon. The appearance of a cottonwood tree meant there was a water supply nearby, because cottonwoods were water suckers. She smiled to think of rehab being named Cottonwoods, but how close she had come to drinking tonight made her shiver.

The farther south she drove, the drier things got. Small rocks kicked up by passing big rigs dinged her windshield like shrapnel. She hated the wind. *"Nil-chi-tsosie,"* Duncan would say. "It's only a small wind." Maybe she and Gracie should move somewhere else, like California or Hawaii? No, she knew she wanted to be near her dad. Her mother, well, she'd have to wait and see what was going on there.

There was the exit for the Comfort Inn. Skye clicked on her blinker, slowed down, and took the exit. She pulled up to the registration office, shut her engine off and got out. It was warmer here than Santa Fe. Stars were out big time.

She knew for certain that she wouldn't sleep a wink. If I shut my eyes, she thought, she'll disappear again. I can't take the chance.

Chapter 15

MARGARET HAD LAIN awake for hours after the kids were in bed. After stories, a video, cuddles, and kisses, she felt pinned to the couch, unable to muster the energy to go down the hall into the bedroom, but surprisingly awake, mentally. Glory's kids were a lot of work, but the entertainment factor made up for that. Margaret felt an urge to call Nori in London, but she couldn't remember the time zone hours. How was she going to explain everything that had happened in the last week?

She heard the car pull up, the engine turn off, and the driver's door open and slam shut. The gate creaked as Peter headed to the casita without stopping in to say good night. Good for him. He was building his new life, and as a mother it was her role to watch from the sidelines. She thought of Aunt Ellie and the letters she sent, those checks always seeming to arrive at the exact right times. How did Ellie always seem to know? That reminded her of the letters she'd brought in from the casita, which she'd taken from the grocery bag and tucked into a shoebox in her closet without reading. Now was the perfect time to read them. She wanted to know what would make her unsentimental aunt hold on to them for so many years.

She got up, leaning against the arm of the couch until her feet felt steady. Joe had given her one of his hiking canes, saying as if it were perfectly normal conversation, "This is a good starter cane. Bear your weight on the cane as you step with your strongest side. Get used to it for a few days. If it doesn't suit you, then we'll try another. And I think you should start trying to get your handicapped parking sticker. Believe me, those things are lifesavers."

She took the cane into her left hand and made her way down the hall, checking on Aspen and Sparrow, who were sleeping like angels in her studio. Echo was stretched out at the foot of the foldout bed. She wagged her tail and Margaret smiled at her. In her bedroom, she took the shoebox of Ellie's letters out of her closet, opened it, and tucked the lid under the box. She turned, intending to take them to bed, read a few, and then doze off. Who could say? Maybe she would have a lovely dream in which her aunt made an appearance. But she dropped the box, and the first packet of letters fell out, scattering on the floor. "Darn it," she said, trying to believe this was simply late night clumsiness. She sat on the floor and gathered the letters to her, arranging the postmarks by date. The letter that had fallen farthest from her was the last one she picked up. She recognized her mother's handwriting on the envelope at once. Mother had a distinctive way of breaking a single word into two when she wrote in cursive. It had always intrigued Margaret. The postmark was around forty-one years prior. Margaret opened it, and the faint scent of roses came from the tissue-thin pages.

Dear Eleanor,

Ted and I have discussed the matter for a week now. I've prayed about it as well. While I admire you for continuing the pregnancy, I wish you'd learned from your earlier mistake with Margaret. Nevertheless, we've come to a conclusion that we hope will work well for all of us.

We'll send Margaret to Lake Bryn Mawr Summer Camp for three months. When she returns, we'll have the new baby and tell her I was several months pregnant when she left. And that the baby came early.

Margaret smoothed the crease in the letter. What the hell? Was this why Ellie and her mother always seemed on the brink of fighting? In fact, when letters or packages from Ellie arrived for the girls, her mother always wore a disapproving expression and insisted on reading the letters first.

Just as we have done with Margaret, this new child will be raised as our own, unequivocally, and must never know of our arrangement. You can't expect them to grow up with us as disciplinarians without believing we are their parents. If one day you step into their lives and reveal you are their birth mother, they will rebel, have no respect for their elders, and then who can say what path they'll take? If you want them to grow up properly, that simply cannot happen. This has to be a one-hundred-percent parenting situation or none at all. Consider this. If they find out that you're their mother, then surely they'll wish to know who their father is, and that's the whole point of keeping this secret, is it not?

Margaret pressed her hand to her mouth and set the letter down in her lap. She barely heard the rattle of the bedroom window. It was the only window moving in the entire house and there wasn't any wind outside, so it had to be Dolores's work. Margaret sat there on the rug while images played in her mind. Christmases when Aunt Ellie came for Christmas Eve dinner but left before morning. Her father had never liked Ellie, saying her sense of humor was bawdy and inappropriate. The way Nori's laugh sounded so much like Ellie's that Margaret accused her of copying her. She remembered the occasional drawing Ellie scrawled in the margins of letters she sent, one of tide pool life in Maine, another of the Eiffel Tower. How Margaret had sent a drawing back. The out-of-the-blue present of colored pencils from England for Margaret and the Native American wooden flute for Nori. Margaret had made a life being an artist, and Nori still played the flute. There was the birthday she had given them matching turquoise bracelets. Margaret still had hers. She'd wondered why if it was Nori's birthday, there was always a present for Margaret and the other way around? They'd spent a summer riding horses at Ellie's lake house, the prize for a year's worth of straight-A grades. Until Santa Fe, Ellie never really had a home base other than that lake house, but it was primarily a summer cabin. She rented it out but always kept the month of August for them, though Mother, the killjoy, didn't allow them to go except for that one summer.

When her mother was dying of cancer, why didn't she tell them? Dad had followed shortly after, but he didn't say a word, either. Margaret and Nori were grown up, already living independently. What better time was there to reveal their true parentage? Worse, where was Ellie when that happened? Off to China, or Ethiopia, or Nepal? And in Ellie's last few years, not once did she bring up the topic.

Why had Ellie kept the secret long after it no longer needed to be a secret? It struck her like a bolt. The answer was, just as Mother said, because she was protecting their father. Who was he?

Margaret looked up at the window, which quieted immediately. What did she do with this information? Should she wait to read the rest of the letters? Stay up all night and be good for nothing tomorrow? Not with two children in her care. Not with Owen planning to spend the day with her. She placed the letter back into its envelope and reached for the phone to call her sister. She pressed in the numbers for an international call and waited. When Nori answered, she said, "Maggot, what is so freaking important you are calling me at this hour of the morning?"

Margaret said, "Seaweed, just you listen."

On Thursday morning, Skye woke up fully dressed. She looked at the motel alarm clock, blinking twelve o'clock, and for a moment she thought she'd slept in far too late to start this day. But her watch said eight fifteen, so she slid on her boots and brushed her teeth with the complimentary brush and toothpaste they'd given her at the desk when she'd checked in. She accepted the continental breakfast—coffee and a Danish—and got in her car.

It was nearly nine A.M. when she found Rocky's address.

Oddly, it wasn't a residential area. It looked more like a doctor's office, or a medical complex, where a person could get lab work done, see a doctor, and get a recommendation for a specialist, all within a few steps. She parked the Mercedes and read the sign: *Outpatient Clinic, Bio Laboratory*, the names of four doctors, and *Sierra Hills Rehabilitation and Assisted Living*.

Skye felt a chill even before she entered the automatic door, when air-conditioning blew over her like a wave. "I'm probably in the wrong place entirely," she told a woman dressed in flowered scrubs sitting behind the counter. "I'm looking for Rocky Elliot. I was told this was his address."

"He's here," she said, turning away from the computer and getting up to come around the counter. A large TV on the wall was tuned to CNN, but nobody was there to watch it. "Are you next of kin?"

Skye's heart began to thrum harder. "I'm his wife."

"Good. Right now, only next of kin may visit."

"What happened to him?"

The woman smiled her professional smile and did not answer. "He's in room four. I think his mom's in there with him. Want me to announce you?"

"That's not necessary," Skye said, full of fury, angry for so many reasons as she walked down the hall. She wished Duncan were there, so he could squeeze her arm and remind her to H.A.L.T., but this was something she had to do on her own. When she swung open the door to Rocky's room, her fire went out as quickly as it had started, because there on a hospital bed lay Rocky, a long scar laddering down his forehead. It looked as if it had been recently stapled. He'd been shaven bald, and he was connected to machines by wires and tubes. His eyes were closed. "What happened?" she blurted out. "Did he have a brain tumor?"

Next to his bed sat Rita, her mother-in-law, who smelled of cigarettes and looked as if she hadn't brushed her hair in quite some time. She looked up at Skye as if this were any other day in the world. "Traumatic brain injury. They had to operate. Twice."

"I'm sorry to hear that," Skye said, and she was. He was such a handsome cowboy, perpetually happy, but this version of him didn't look anything like that. Keeping her voice even, she said, "Rita?"

"Yes?"

"I've been on quite the hunt trying to find you and Gracie. You said you'd be in Albuquerque. Last night I learned Gracie was in foster care. Care to explain?"

Rita bent her head, unable to meet Skye's eyes directly. "I know you're hopping mad at me, and maybe I deserve it, but my baby was hurt. It was either your daughter or my son. In the end I had to go with him."

"Without trying to get in touch with me? Without leaving me an address, or a phone number? Rita, Gracie is with complete strangers! How dare you do that to your own granddaughter? You dumped her like some unwanted cat at the pound."

Rita leaned forward in the chair, frowning. "What did you expect me to do? Rocky damn near died. Well, he did die for a few minutes, but the paramedics got his heart started again."

"What happened?"

Rita sighed. "Just like a hundred other times, he got thrown by the bull, and knocked out. But then he got kicked in the head." Rita squeezed the tissue in her hands. "He seemed fine at first, talking and laughing, and then, he went from making sense to babbling nonsense."

"Did he fracture his skull?"

Rita shook her head no. "Blood clots. Hematoma, they called it. I forget what else. They sawed him open. They say it might take years for him to get back to normal, if he ever does." She stood up. "Go on and take my chair. I'll go visit the restroom."

"No," Skye said. "Stay here with me. I'll find another chair."

She found one in the hallway, plastic and cheap, like outdoor furniture, but it was clean. The receptionist walked by and said, "Enjoy your visit," which struck Skye as the most heartless thing a person could ever say about a semiconscious man who was likely brain-damaged for life. Skye sat next to her mother-in-law, who was crying silently. Every time Rocky opened his eyes, Rita got up and said his name. He wasn't tracking, and when he did seem to notice Rita, it was clear he didn't recognize her. Every once in a while he made a noise that sounded like a donkey bray-ing, and Skye felt her heart rip in half. They were as good as divorced, but Rocky would always be the father of her child.

"He does that all day long," Rita said, wiping her tears. "I think he's saying something, but I don't understand it yet."

Skye took Rita's hand. They sat there together for a while, and then it was time for Skye to go, to pick up Gracie and start making a reasonable life for her, which couldn't be here. Skye stood up, said goodbye to Rocky and then she leaned close to Rita's ear and said, "Rita, I forgive you."

Skye peered through the window of the social worker's office. She didn't know what she'd expected, but it wasn't this. The metal desk, covered with papers held in place by a painted rock. A laptop computer. A woman's cardigan over one of the two gray metal folding chairs. The floors were ancient linoleum, dotted with rag rugs that had seen better days. She looked up and saw those old tin ceiling tiles from a hundred years ago, painted white, the finish chipping as everything tended to do in New Mexico heat and, this far south, its inhospitable climate. There were two restrooms, side by side, marked *Men* and *Ladies*. Before this life, the space might've been a mom-and-pop grocery store, or a dress shop, or even a restaurant. Toward the end of the room there was a back door, half screen and half wood.

"Hello?" she called out. "Mrs. Rodriquez? It's Skye Elliot."

She heard a toilet flush, and a heavyset woman dressed in khaki slacks and a flowered top walked out. "Hi there, Mrs. Elliot," she said. "You're early. Did you have a nice drive?"

Did that really matter right now? All she wanted to do was find her daughter. "Good enough," Skye said, forcing herself to be calm.

Mrs. Rodriquez had probably seen it all, Skye thought. What did she see in Skye? Mother material or recovering alcoholic?

"Please have a seat," she said. "Let's chat a little before you see Eleanor."

"Her name is Grace," Skye said. "My mother-in-law wanted her to be called Eleanor, which is her middle name. But her given name is Grace."

"Grace," the woman repeated. "I have a mountain of paperwork for you to fill out. Did you bring your daughter's birth certificate?"

Skye handed it over. Surely she couldn't mean Skye had to fill out the stack of papers on the desk. There must've been a hundred pages. Mrs. Rodriquez handed the stack to her and a pen. "We'll need these filled out. Judge Iglesias was kind enough to fax us the paperwork that will actually short-cut much of the investigation."

"Investigation?" Skye asked.

The woman nodded. "When custody has been awarded to one parent and switches to another, there is always an investigation."

"Investigation into what?" Skye said. "I'm doing my community service, I have sponsors, a car, a place to live, even money. What else do you need to know?"

Mrs. Rodriquez looked down at her own pile of papers. "It looks like a Mr. Wolfgang Schneider has agreed to represent you."

"He has," Skye said. "Is this like going to court or something?"

Mrs. Rodriquez patted her hand. "Not at all. Please don't worry. This is all procedural."

"Oh," Skye said, forcing herself to smile, to be patient, like Duncan had always told her to do.

They sat at the scarred metal desk and filled out papers. Every paper Skye finished Mrs. Rodriquez fed into a scanner, which then appeared on her laptop. The way Skye saw it, they could be here all day, but that was fine with her, so long as it culminated in seeing Gracie.

When they were finally done, Mrs. Rodriquez e-mailed the file to the courthouse, copying Wolfgang and the judge responsible for taking Gracie away in the first place. One click, and it was gone. Her screen saver featured children's faces, one after the other, children needing somewhere to stay, to belong, if only for a short while. Damn you, OxyContin, Skye thought. Double damn you, alcohol. How could I have let pills and booze cost me that amazing little person who brightened my days and drove me crazy with questions?

"Are you ready?" Mrs. Rodriquez said.

"I am *so* ready," Skye answered.

Before they stood up, Mrs. Rodriquez said, "Just a few preparations. You'll probably find that Eleanor—Grace—has grown taller since she last saw you. She's nearly four years old."

"Thank you, ma'am, but I'm aware of my child's birthday."
What else did they get wrong? Skye thought.

"Of course you are. Also, her ability to speak in complete
sentences may surprise you. She can tell time now. Her foster
mother wanted you to know that she has been quite shy since
coming into care."

"My Gracie," Skye said, feeling tearful, "wasn't afraid of anything."

Mrs. Rodriquez said, "I'm sure once she settles in with you,
she'll be just fine. But in case there are a few difficulties, we have
the option for her to spend the night at her foster mother's, if she
wants to."

"I want to take her home," Skye said.

"Of course you do. Let's just see how it goes. There are documents on our website regarding the transitional experience. I also
have the name of a child psychologist. Do you have any questions
before we go see her?"

"No, ma'am. I just want to get my daughter back."

"I understand," she said. "Please keep in mind, we have these
services in place for a reason. Not all reunions go smoothly."

This one will, Skye told herself. Something in my life is going
to go right for a change.

"Okay," Mrs. Rodriquez said, "let's go see her."

Skye felt her stomach flip. "Wait—" She reached out for the
woman's arm. "What if it isn't her?" she asked, her voice catching. "What if I get her hopes up and it turns out not to be Gracie
after all?"

Mrs. Rodriquez patted her hand. "Don't worry. All I've
told her is that she has a visitor," she said, pointing at the back
door.

All this time, Gracie was just out back?

Skye followed Mrs. Rodriquez down the hallway to the screen door. It opened onto a flagstone portal, with a massive elm tree and chamiso bushes along one side. There was a shaded area with children's toys and a faded plastic slide attached to a playhouse with windows and doors to climb in and out of. On its porch, a little girl was reading a book, turning the pages, reading the words out to herself.

"Honey?" Mrs. Rodriquez said. "Your visitor is here."

Gracie's hair had darkened to a strawberry blond, and whoever had hacked it off that short should not have been allowed near scissors. Her two front teeth were missing. The thrift store dress she was wearing looked as if it had come from the bottom of the heap, but however ugly it was, inside it was Gracie.

She looked up from her book, puzzled.

Skye tried to hold herself back, as Mrs. Rodriquez had suggested. *Like a kitten, let her come to you.* It had been nearly a year.

Grace set down her book. She stood up, walked directly to Skye, and said, "Mama, I haven't seen you in so long."

Skye swallowed hard, unsure of what to say. "I know, sweetie. But I'm back for good now. I'm not going anywhere without you. Golly, I missed you so much."

Gracie's little face scrunched up as if she might cry. "Did you go away because I was bad?"

Oh, God, Skye thought, that little voice, tinkling like a bell, carrying almost a year's worth of guilt and confusion no child should ever have to bear. Skye squatted so she was eye level with her daughter. "No way, Little Gee. Mama got sick and had to go to the hospital. I tried my hardest to get well, and the second I was, I came to find you. I'm sorry it took me so long."

It was too much to ask for forgiveness. Gracie was four, not fourteen.

"Gracie?" Mrs. Rodriquez said. "Would you like to spend some time with your mother, or would you rather go back to Mrs. Campbell's house?"

"Home with Mama," Gracie said, and climbed up Skye as if she were a tree. With both hands, she pulled Skye's face close to hers and sniffed.

"What are you doing, honey?" Skye asked.

"Smelling your breaths. You don't smell like medicines anymore."

Skye felt her chin tremble. "That's right. I don't drink anymore," she said.

"Okay, Mama. I'm ready. Let's go home."

DOLORES

TONIGHT I'M ALL atwitter, feeling as if there's some-place I need to be, but I just can't think of where. I made certain Margaret read the letter. If she thinks the first one was a shocker, wait until she reads the rest of them. Her life is going to change in ways she cannot imagine, but she can handle it. She no longer needs me.

Yet I wonder, how will everyone else get along without me? The pregnant woman next door is having twins. Both boys.

I'm watching the dog who is asleep at the foot of Peter's bed. If she could talk, she'd probably tell me that Peter sneaks her people food and she loves it, except for the farting part. I'd tell her my last meal was right over there where the fountain is. My mother was with me. We had a dog, too.

I run the reel of time backward for a while until I recognize my mother. Over lifetimes, the image has blurred. I don't remember her face, but I do remember we had corn for that meal. I don't know if it was good or not. I can't remember how things taste, or how it feels to sleep deeply, and to dream. It has been too long a time since then. I remember that my mother told me to go, to run, but I couldn't leave her. Not even after the white man scalped her, and the blood washed down her face, into her eyes. When he came for me, I sat up and looked into his eyes. I understood that my fate was in his knife, and I did not cry. Instead of following my mother, I remained here, between the worlds. There was a job I had to do, that only I could do. And you know what?

I think I may have done it.

What I was sent here to do.

The space I reside in is filling with light, as warm as molten gold. It bathes me, it cloaks me, and I feel so good, so warm, as if milk and honey are running through me, as if my mother is holding my hand and singing to me. The white hummingbird stirs in her nest. The tiny greyhound lifts his head and yips. If anyone wakes up from a nightmare, the dog will be there to lick the person's face.

I couldn't tell you how I know this, but suddenly I know it's time. For so long I have heard the instructions. But it didn't seem possible until tonight. I do what I have waited so long to do.

I go to the light.

ACKNOWLEDGMENTS

I'M DEEPLY GRATEFUL to so many people for their help and expertise in shaping this book. To my dearest friend and agent, Deborah Schneider, for her terrific feedback and support for so many years. To my wonderful, brilliant, enthusiastic editor, Nancy Miller, and to her equally wonderful, insightful colleague, Lea Beresford, just, wow. Every writer should be so lucky. Not only did they give me great advice, and help to shape what needed to change, they also talked me down from the ledge a couple of times. Lea, you changed the entire course of the book for the best with one small suggestion. Nikki Baldauf, my production editor, certainly earned her wages helping me fix my errors. Thank you. To my publicist, Carrie Majer, who works late and always has time to talk, and everyone else at Bloomsbury Publishing for their support for my books.

For advice in writing about MS, I thank Laurie Lehman, who took pains to educate me on this complex illness and portray the symptoms realistically. Any errors that remain are my fault, entirely.

The poet Alice Anderson generously explained traumatic brain injury, and I have the utmost reverence for the stories she shared. Thank you, Alice, for your friendship and bravery, and for the line from your poem, "The Birds."

My husband, Stewart Allison—who reminds me every time I complain that it's impossible to finish a book, "You said this about the last book and it turned out just fine"—is my rock, my sunlight, and truly my better half. Forty years of marriage next month, and I'm still in love with him. To our son, Jack, who had an especially difficult year, things will get better, I promise. Just take a walk on the beach and think about whales. You can call me anytime.

To my niece Diana, I hope this book brings you peace and happiness. You are so loved.

How my mother, Mary, put up with me remains a great mystery I continually ponder. My siblings, whether they were telling me to lick a frozen pipe (that they promised tasted like cherry), hanging my dolls, or convincing me that tigers resided under my bed, have also been great supporters of my work.

I also send this story into the great beyond, to my mom's best friend, Opal Burgraft, who passed away before I could give her the finished book. Bless your heart, Opal. I'll cherish our chats. Please say hello to my dad for me. Rest in peace.

Without my writer friends, it would take me hundreds of boxes of Kleenex to finish a book. Caroline Leavitt, above all, just knowing you're there on the East Coast is such a comfort. Everything you do for writers I find beyond generous. You're absolutely the hardest-working writer I know. I treasure our discussions and our mutual addiction to Old Gringo cowboy boots, and I consider our friendship a great blessing in my life. Jodi Picoult, ditto the above. Other writers just as important to me include Anne Caston, Rich Chiappone, Nicky Leach, Wolf

Schneider, Sherry Simpson, David Stevenson, Carolyn Turgeon, and Candelora Versace.

To Mary Wolf and Dorothy Massey, owners of Collected Works Bookstore, thank you for recommending my work to customers, for your lovely, kind hearts of steel, and for your perfect bookstore, with its fireplace, comfy couches, and wonderful books.

Finally, to all the readers of *Blue Rodeo*, I hope this story was worth the twenty-year wait. You haven't seen the last of these characters, or of Glory, Joe, and their increasing tribe. They are as dear to me as all of you. And I can't wait to see what they do next.

Thanks to everyone.

A NOTE ON THE AUTHOR

Jo-Ann Mapson is the author of eleven previous novels, including the beloved *Finding Casey*, *Solomon's Oak*, *Hank & Chloe*, *Blue Rodeo* (also a CBS TV movie), and the *Los Angeles Times* bestsellers *The Wilder Sisters* and *Bad Girl Creek*. She lives in Santa Fe, New Mexico, with her husband and their four dogs. Visit her website at www.joannmapson.com.